LONGING FOR LOVE

GANSETT ISLAND SERIES, BOOK 7

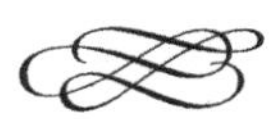

MARIE FORCE

Longing for Love
Gansett Island Series, Book 7
By: Marie Force
Published by HTJB, Inc.

Cover Design by Diane Luger
Print Layout Isabel Sullivan
E-book Formatting Fairies
ISBN: 978-1-942295-22-8

marieforce.com

View the McCarthy Family Tree here. marieforce.com/gansett/familytree/

View the list of Who's Who on Gansett Island here. marieforce.com/whoswhogansett/

View a map of Gansett Island. marieforce.com/mapofgansett/

The Gansett Island Series

Book 1: Maid for Love *(Mac & Maddie)*
Book 2: Fool for Love *(Joe & Janey)*
Book 3: Ready for Love *(Luke & Sydney)*
Book 4: Falling for Love *(Grant & Stephanie)*
Book 5: Hoping for Love *(Evan & Grace)*
Book 6: Season for Love *(Owen & Laura)*
Book 7: Longing for Love *(Blaine & Tiffany)*
Book 8: Waiting for Love *(Adam & Abby)*
Book 9: Time for Love *(David & Daisy)*
Book 10: Meant for Love *(Jenny & Alex)*
Book 10.5: Chance for Love, *A Gansett Island Novella (Jared & Lizzie)*
Book 11: Gansett After Dark *(Owen & Laura)*
Book 12: Kisses After Dark *(Shane & Katie)*
Book 13: Love After Dark *(Paul & Hope)*
Book 14: Celebration After Dark *(Big Mac & Linda)*
Book 15: Desire After Dark *(Slim & Erin)*
Book 16: Light After Dark *(Mallory & Quinn)*
Book 17: Victoria & Shannon (Episode 1)
Book 18: Kevin & Chelsea (Episode 2)
A Gansett Island Christmas Novella
Book 19: Mine After Dark *(Riley & Nikki)*
Book 20: Yours After Dark *(Finn McCarthy)*
Book 21: Trouble After Dark *(Deacon & Julia)*

More new books are alway in the works. For the most up-to-date list of what's available from the Gansett Island Series as well as series extras, go to marieforce.com/gansett.

CHAPTER 1

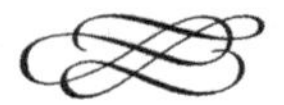

Tiffany Sturgil stood outside her new shop and watched two workmen secure the hand-carved sign over the display window. Drivers on Ocean Road slowed to take a look at what was going on, but there wasn't much to see yet. Tiffany had kept paper over the store's window to maintain the surprise until the last minute. But once the sign was in place, it would be time to unveil her beautiful new shop.

Her heart raced with excitement and anticipation and a tiny bit of dread. What if she failed? What if she'd poured every dime she had—and then some—into the store, only to fall flat on her face?

"I can't let that happen," she muttered, determined to believe in herself, or no one else would. Still, she couldn't help but wonder what her mother and sister would think about the shop, not to mention Jim, her soon-to-be ex-husband, who'd definitely have something to say about it. Not that she cared about his opinion. Not anymore.

"Ready?" one of the men called to her.

"Absolutely!"

At those words, excitement immediately trumped her insecurities. This was it—the moment she'd waited for since that horrible night with Jim, the night she'd landed in jail, and then let the island's ridiculously hot police chief get her off in the kitchen. A tingle of desire heated her core as she remembered that explosive moment.

Tiffany shook off the memory, as she had every day since, to focus on the store.

"Here we go!"

The two men tore the paper cover off her sign and stared at it, dumbfounded.

"Seriously?" one of them said. "On Gansett Island?"

"What?" Tiffany asked.

"*Naughty & Nice?*" the younger of the two men said, snickering.

"It's catchy," she said.

"It's *raunchy,*" the older one replied, to guffaws from the other.

Suddenly, she wanted them gone. No one was going to rain on her parade. Not today, not on the day when all her dreams were about to come true. "How much do I owe you?"

"Fifty bucks."

"I'll get you a check."

She stepped into the space that had occupied most of her waking moments for months. Working long hours seven days a week in between her mothering duties, she'd painted and buffed and polished until the place gleamed. Scented candles burned throughout the store, sending a hint of spicy cinnamon apple into the air. Everywhere she turned there were racks of luscious, frothy lingerie in every style, shape and color, bins of panties, baskets of bras, lotions, potions and candles...

Everything she'd imagined, and then some. Through a beaded curtain, other treasures awaited, designed to bring ultimate pleasure.

"What do you need, boss?" asked Patty, the nervous young woman Tiffany had hired to help her out a few hours a week.

Her mousy brown hair was cut into an unfortunate style that only exacerbated her other unexceptional features. Tiffany had makeover plans for her assistant as soon as things let up a little.

She handed Patty the business card the men had given her. "A check for fifty dollars, please."

"Coming right up."

Patty had been the only one to apply for the job. Tiffany hoped she'd eventually be able to leave the store in the other woman's hands so she could take an occasional break to spend time with her daughter. Her mother and future stepfather Ned had been great about helping out with Ashleigh while Tiffany was getting the store ready to open and were willing to keep her whenever Tiffany needed help.

Once she got the store up and running, she also hoped to jump-start her social life. If the explosive orgasm she'd experienced at the hands of Blaine Taylor had taught her anything, it was that she'd been missing out on far too much during her years with Jim. She was determined to do something about that, as soon as she had some free time.

Tiffany leaned over to sign the check and tore it from the ledger. "Thanks, Patty."

On her way back outside to pay the men, she pulled the brown paper off the inside of the store window and went out to find the two idiots ogling the nearly naked mannequins dressed in racy lingerie. She'd gone with a red theme for her first window—lacy teddies and silk nightgowns, sets of bras and panties, a large bottle of massage oil and lube that heated on contact.

"Holy smokes, lady," the older one sputtered. "I don't know what you think you're doing here, but this ain't that kind of island."

Tiffany forced a smile, when she really wanted to scream. "What kind of island is it?" she asked sweetly. "The kind where no one has sex?"

He stared at her as if he couldn't believe she'd said that. Snatching the check from her hand, he tilted his head to tell his partner to get in the truck.

Tiffany happened to glance down to find the younger man sporting an erection. She smiled when his startled eyes met hers. "Come on back soon," she said in her best baby-doll voice, "and buy something sexy for your lady—and yourself."

Flustered, he bolted to the truck. The men left rubber in their haste to get out of there.

Watching them go, Tiffany experienced a twinge of apprehension.

What if everyone in the conservative island town reacted the same way?

THE NEXT MORNING, she got up early to shower. As she spent extra time on her hair and makeup, her heart pounded with excitement and anticipation. Opening day! She'd planned and prepared for this day for months, and everything was set. From ads in the paper, to balloons out front, to special events to tout her sensual offerings, Tiffany was finally ready to announce her arrival.

"Look out world," she whispered to her reflection.

She'd chosen a sexy red silk blouse over a black pencil skirt with stiletto heels for the opening. Applying lipstick in the same shade of racy red as her top, Tiffany took one last measuring look in the mirror before she grabbed her purse and headed downstairs. Ashleigh had spent the night with Jim, so Tiffany was free and clear to focus on opening day.

Her heels echoed like shotgun blasts inside the empty house. In one of the more acrimonious moves in their divorce proceedings, Jim had shown up one day with a moving truck and taken all the furniture, leaving her and Ashleigh with their beds, and not much else. Until he'd done that, Tiffany had retained some hope that they might patch things up. Now she couldn't wait to finally be free of him. Any day now, her lawyer, Dan Torrington, had assured her. Couldn't happen soon enough for her.

With all her money tied up in the store, it would be some time before she'd be able to replace the furniture. What did it matter? They had what they needed, although she'd been astounded by how fast her savings had dwindled once she'd started buying inventory, shelving units, a computer, a cash register and everything else she needed to open the store.

"It'll all be fine once the money starts rolling in," she reminded herself in a singsong voice.

For the millionth time since their encounter in the kitchen, Tiffany thought of Blaine and how much she wished she could share her excitement with him. Why him, though? Well, why not him? If he could make her come like a cannon with just his fingers, imagine what he could do with his tongue or that impressive shaft he'd pressed against her. Just the thought of it made her tremble with need.

And the way he'd looked at her with such yearning, as if he wanted something he couldn't allow himself to have. Then there had been the time at Luke and Syd's house last fall, when he'd cornered her on a dark deck and told her to call him the second she was free of Jim. For a brief moment, she stopped to wonder if he was still waiting for her to call. Who was she kidding? A guy who looked like him could have his pick of women. He'd probably moved on a long time ago, when he got tired of waiting to hear from her.

She took a deep, shuddering breath and closed the front door. No time for negative thoughts today. Although, spending months surrounded by lacy negligees and thick dildos had left her twitchy with unfulfilled desire. "Someday soon," she said as she approached her little red car with the new NAUGHTY vanity plate. If Blaine wasn't interested in her anymore, she'd find someone else who was. Tiffany was sick and tired of feeling down about herself in the wake of her disastrous marriage. The store was the first step in a whole new life, and she was more than ready to get started.

Tiffany smiled, thrilled with the sun, the cloudless sky, the fragrant, late-spring breeze. She couldn't have handpicked a day better suited to starting her fabulous new life, and she had to curb the urge to wave to everyone she passed on the road.

On the way to the shop (she loved saying that—*the shop*), she thought over her to-do list before the noon opening. She'd chosen to open on a sunny Saturday in early May in the hope that people would be out, about and curious. It was also important to have all the bugs worked out before the Gansett Island Race Week festivities later in the month. The island would be overrun with people in town for the annual sailing regatta.

Driving through town, Tiffany thought about how much she loved Gansett Island and how happy she'd been when she and Jim had returned home to the island after he'd finished law school. That was, until everything went to crap between the two of them for reasons still unknown to Tiffany. Perhaps she'd never know. Over time, she'd begun to make peace with that possibility.

Gansett's waterfront downtown included the requisite New England white-steeple church, a large park next door to the redbrick town hall, and the combined police and fire station. Tiffany's shop was located down the hill from the police station, which she passed daily, hoping to catch a fleeting glimpse of the sexy police chief. But she hadn't laid eyes on him since that night on Luke and Syd's deck. His elusiveness had led her to wonder—more than once—if he was intentionally avoiding her because he'd changed his mind about being interested in her.

She could still remember the gravelly tenor of his voice when he'd grabbed her by the waistband of her jeans and pulled her close to him on the dark deck. A shiver went through her when she thought about what he'd said. *"The minute you're free of him, the very same second it's final, you're going to call me."*

Before that, she never would've thought a dominant man would turn her on. Now, she knew otherwise. But since he'd made himself scarce ever since, she was left to wonder if he still felt the same way.

She pushed that unpleasant thought to the back of her mind, and the last half mile of the ride to work passed in a blur of plans and exhilaration and eagerness. As she pulled into the parking space she'd decided would belong to her as the owner and proprietor of Naughty & Nice, she hoped the women in town would be curious enough to come check out the latest thing.

Rounding the corner to unlock the front door, Tiffany came to a dead stop.

"Oh, my God. *No*."

Multicolored paint, as if shot from a paintball gun, was splattered all over the white brick front wall of her store, on the window and splattering her beautiful new sign—the sign she'd paid a thousand dollars to have hand-carved. Viewing the damage, white-hot rage overwhelmed her. Who could've done such a thing?

A gasp from behind her had Tiffany spinning around to find Patty holding a dozen red balloons and covering her mouth with her hand. "Oh, no. *No, no, no!*" Patty's eyes were shiny with tears. "I'm so sorry, Tiffany."

"So am I."

Tiffany gritted her teeth to keep from shrieking and jammed the key in the lock to open the door. Marching to the storage room in the back of the store, she found an unopened can of white paint and a new roller. She glanced down at her expensive silk blouse and skirt. Since she was unwilling to ruin her gorgeous new outfit, she rummaged around, looking for the gym bag she thought she'd left there the week before.

"Damn it," she muttered when she couldn't find the bag or anything else to change into. Moving to the front of the store, she checked the wall clock. Two hours until opening. Right when she had decided it was worth it to ruin her good clothes to repair the damage, her eyes landed on a saucy French maid costume on one of the racks. Glancing to her scarred window and then back to the outfit, she knew exactly what she had to do.

"They want to screw with me? Well, two can play at that game."

"Boss?" Patty said warily. "Are you all right?"

"I'm just fine." Tiffany grabbed the outfit off the rack and headed for the changing room. "Start getting the wine and cheese ready."

Patty watched her with wide, doe-like eyes caught in headlights. "We're still going to open?"

"You bet your booty we are."

ACROSS THE STREET in the grocery store parking lot, Blaine watched from an unmarked police vehicle.

"What are we doing here, Chief?" Patrolman Trainee Wyatt Abrams asked. "The place was hit by vandals. Shouldn't we take a report?"

"Hang on. I want to see what she does about it."

Blaine tilted a neck gone tight with tension. When he first saw what some idiot had done to Tiffany's store, he'd ached with dismay, and he'd had to resist the urge to fix it before she saw it. That was what the old Blaine would've done. The new-and-improved Blaine kept his distance from "projects" and didn't get involved. From a police standpoint, there wasn't much he could do besides assign additional patrols in the area, which he'd done the minute he first saw the damage.

As he watched Tiffany drive up, seeing the spring in her step and then the devastated curve of her shoulders, Blaine's heart had broken for her. Then he saw her get mad, and he was proud. Now he waited anxiously to see what she planned to do about it. Ten more tense minutes passed before the door swung open. A paint can and roller preceded Tiffany out the door.

"Oh. My. God," Wyatt whispered. "What does she have on?"

Blaine couldn't speak as he stared at Tiffany in a black lace bustier with fishnet stockings, stiletto heels and a bow tie around her neck. Her dark hair had been pulled back into a ponytail, and the lithe dancer's body he remembered in vivid detail after the night he'd seen her naked was on full display. The skimpy outfit reminded him that she was made up of miles of creamy white skin and long, muscular legs.

His erection pressed against his fly, letting him know it approved.

"She's not really going to *paint* in that getup, is she?" Wyatt asked, his tongue practically hanging out of his mouth.

As she bent over to open the paint can, Wyatt got his answer.

Blaine saw red. What the hell was she thinking, parading around like that? This wasn't that kind of town, and he could only imagine what the mayor and town council would have to say about it.

As he was reaching for the door handle to go have a word with her, the squeal of tires and the crunch of metal connecting with metal snapped Blaine out of the stupor he'd slipped into.

"Holy shit!" Wyatt said, his voice high-pitched. "She caused a freaking accident!"

Blaine reached for his jacket in the backseat and threw open the door. "Go take statements at the accident," he said. "Call the paramedics if there're injuries and get some backup over here to handle traffic."

"I could take care of her if you want to handle the accident," Wyatt said with a cheeky grin as they ran from the car to the scene.

Blaine shot the patrolman a glower that succeeded in shutting him up. He noticed Tiffany was watching the two drivers shriek at each other with a horrified expression on her face. She'd been so happy when she first arrived at the store, and now it was all going to crap. Well, project or not, he couldn't let that happen.

He and Wyatt reached the street and went their separate ways. Blaine darted through cars brought to a stop by the accident and approached Tiffany, who seemed frozen with shock. Wrapping his jacket around her shoulders, he tried to ease her toward the shop door.

All at once, she snapped out of it and pushed him away. "What do you think you're doing?"

"Taking you inside."

She shook him off, which caused her barely covered breasts to shake, too.

Blaine peeled his eyes off her jiggling flesh while trying to suppress the memory of how her skin had tasted, and the delicious, raspberry-colored nipples that were threatening to break free at any second. He'd spent a ridiculous amount of time over the last ten months thinking about those nipples.

"I'm not going anywhere. I've got to get this mess cleaned up before I open at noon."

"Wearing *that?*"

Her green eyes shot fire at him, but mixed in with the anger, he saw desire.

Oh yeah, she's thought about me, too.

"It's either this or naked." She tossed his coat back at him. "Take your pick."

Blaine swallowed hard as he remembered the sight of her naked and handcuffed to her scumbag of a husband. "I choose neither," he said through gritted teeth as he realized they were drawing a crowd of spectators who'd figured out that Tiffany's outfit had caused the crash.

The two drivers were arguing with a red-faced and flustered Patrolman Abrams.

"You may not be aware that this town has decency laws," Blaine said.

"All the important stuff is covered," she retorted, bending over to fill the roller pan with paint.

At the sight of her rounded bottom, a surge of lust hit Blaine right in the groin. "It's not covered well enough."

"So write me a ticket and be on your way. I've got work to do and not much time to do it." Running the roller through the glossy white paint, Tiffany began applying it to the splotches of red, green and yellow that marred the front of her store. Up went the roller, down went the front of the black bustier.

Blaine wasn't sure what was going to happen first: either his head was going to explode or her boobs were going to bust free of that thing she called decent. "Tiffany, please. Come on. We'll get someone over here to do the painting."

"Who? Who will *we* get to come help the woman who had the nerve to open a sex-toy shop on this button-downed, sexless, freak-show island?"

He stared at her, his brain attempting to process the words as he began to sweat in earnest. "I thought this was a lingerie shop," he somehow managed to say. "You didn't say anything about, um, toys."

"I said lingerie and *other items*."

"Is that how you managed to get it past the town?" he asked, mesmerized by the sway of her breasts as she worked the roller.

A bead of perspiration traveled from the base of her neck straight down to the valley between her bountiful breasts. Despite his best efforts to keep it under control, his dick surged to full hard-on status. He shifted his coat so it covered the front of him.

"They've been so busy trying to keep Jumbo Mart from invading their pristine island that they barely noticed me."

Blaine glanced at the knot of traffic, the mangled cars, infuriated drivers and his rookie attempting to bring order to the chaos. Relieved to see two more cruisers heading toward the scene, Blaine returned his attention to her. "I think it's safe to say they've noticed you now."

"That's the goal," she said with a saucy grin.

"You caused an accident!"

"Um, no, the person who wasn't watching where he was going caused the accident."

Blaine anchored his free hand to his hair to keep the top of his head from blowing off. "You need to put some clothes on, or I'm going to have to cite you." He couldn't charge her with anything other than creating a public nuisance, but she didn't need to know that. Besides, his threats of law and order had hardly stopped her from finishing the job.

Tiffany covered the last of the red splotches with a wide stroke of the roller. "You know, whoever decided to redecorate my shop has actually done me a favor."

"How do you figure?" Blaine asked, exasperated that she refused to take him seriously.

"Well, I needed to repaint and didn't have anything else to wear. Who knew this little number would get me so much free publicity? Maybe a little 'creative advertising' is just what I need to make a name for my new shop."

Now Blaine was not only sweating but also wondering why the idea of her parading around half dressed in the center of town made him so damned mad. It wasn't like she belonged to him or anything. But if she did—belong to him, that is—you could bet *your* ass that she wouldn't be showing *her* ass to anyone but him. "Sweetheart, it's safe to say you've made a name for yourself that'll be remembered on Gansett Island for years to come."

"Perfect."

"Listen, I'm trying to help you here." Once again, he tried to cover her with his coat, and once again, she pushed it away.

"I appreciate your whole hero-to-the-rescue act, but I'm all set. Go do your job, and I'll do mine. I'm very busy, and you're going to scare all my customers away with that nasty scowl on your face."

Now that just made him mad. "This isn't over." He was dying to ask about the status of her divorce, but this wasn't the time or the place.

Bending to pour the remaining paint from the roller tray back into the can, she gave him another view of her superb backside. When she stood upright again, she turned to him, her face red and flushed from heat and exertion. "*Sweetheart,*" she said in a mocking tone, "it was over before it started."

CHAPTER 2

"You're kidding me, right?" Tiffany's sister Maddie asked as she looked around at the store. "On *Gansett Island*?"

"If one more person says that, I'm going to lose it," Tiffany said, disappointed by her sister's reaction. "Here's a newsflash for you. People—other than me, of course—have sex on Gansett. *You* have sex on Gansett."

Maddie covered her mouth with her hand, as if trying to hide a smile, or worse yet, a laugh.

"Are you laughing at me?"

"No, honey. I'm trying to imagine what Linda McCarthy will have to say about it."

Tiffany told herself she didn't care what people like Linda had to say, but there was a part of her that hoped for the approval of the townspeople. "I suppose I shouldn't show you the rest, then."

"There's *more*?" Maddie asked, wide-eyed.

Tiffany gestured to the beaded curtain that separated the main room from a second, smaller room.

With a look of trepidation for Tiffany, Maddie stepped through the beads. "Oh. My. God!" Parting the beads, she stared at Tiffany, her face scarlet, before turning to take a second, longer look. "Are those... Oh my God."

"Don't knock 'em until you've tried 'em," Tiffany said with a bravado she didn't feel. What if everyone reacted the way Maddie did and no one patronized her store? Her stomach quivered with fear. She'd be ruined. She'd lose her home, and Jim would get custody of Ashleigh. For a second, Tiffany thought she might be sick.

Still red-faced, Maddie stepped back into the main room of the store, fanning herself. "That's some interesting inventory you've got there, Sis."

"I need your support, Maddie. Not your disapproval."

"I don't disapprove at all, but others may."

"I'm prepared for that."

"Are you, honey? Truly?"

"Since when do we care what anyone thinks of us? Are you so far gone being a McCarthy now that you've forgotten where you came from?" The moment the words were out of her mouth, Tiffany regretted them.

Maddie's displeasure showed in the tightening of her lips. "I haven't forgotten anything, and no one wants you to succeed more than I do. You know that."

"Then don't run home and tell Mac I've opened a sex-toy shop so he can go blabbing to his mother."

"With the way the grapevine works around here, I bet she already knows."

"Let her say whatever she wants. I have all the proper paperwork and licenses. There's nothing anyone can do. I'm determined to make a go of this place."

"I wish you nothing but the best of luck." Maddie gave Tiffany a hug. "I've got to get home before my boobs explode. Hailey is due for a feeding. Hope your opening is a smashing success."

"Thanks," Tiffany said, waving her sister off with a sinking sensation in her belly.

When the first hour passed without a single customer, Tiffany didn't think much of it. On a busy spring Saturday, people were at the beach or enjoying other outdoor activities. Maybe this wasn't the best time of year to open a new store after all.

By the time the third hour had come and gone, Tiffany realized she was being snubbed. A sense of panic unlike anything she'd ever experienced seized her. Everything she had was wrapped up in this store. Everything. If no one ever came, she'd be ruined.

"Um, boss," Patty said, flitting nervously about the small store. "Should I put away the cheese?"

Tiffany glanced at the table they'd so lovingly put together with red plates and napkins, crackers, cheese, veggies and dip, and other treats for first-day customers. "Yes," she said. "Please."

While Patty got busy clearing off the table, Tiffany wandered to the front window. Across the street, a Gansett Island Police SUV sat in the grocery store parking lot. Blaine was probably glad her store was a bust. It would mean less trouble for him if people didn't patronize her place and she went quietly out of business. She thought about the stack of bills she'd ignored while pouring every dime she had into her store. Going quietly out of business simply wasn't an option. She had to do something to drum up some business, and she had to do it right now.

Feeling energized, Tiffany turned away from the window and marched over to one of the more scandalous racks of lingerie. She knew exactly what she was looking for and found it toward the back. Holding up the naughty nurse outfit, Tiffany smiled. Desperate times called for desperate measures. She took the outfit into the changing room and put it on, once again carefully hanging up her silk blouse and skirt and then donning her spike heels.

When she saw Tiffany emerge from the fitting room, Patty's mouth fell open. "Um, boss, what're you doing?"

"Just a little advertising," Tiffany said as she adjusted the white bustier over her breasts. "How can they know what we're selling if we don't show them?"

"Well, um, don't you think the name of the store kind of speaks for itself?"

"That's only half the story. I'm going to show them the other half."

"But Tiffany, there were cars crashing earlier. What if that happens again?"

"How is that my fault?"

"Oh, um, well…"

"Wish me luck," Tiffany said on her way out the door.

"Good luck," Patty said warily.

WHEN BLAINE SAW Tiffany emerge from the store, he sat up from the slouch he'd slipped into as he kept an eye on things across the street. "What the hell?" he muttered before he groaned. She was going to be the death of him—the living, breathing *death*. While the horny male part of him took a good long look at the luscious skin and long, firm legs, the cop recognized the potential for further traffic mayhem and reached for the door handle.

But then he stopped himself. What exactly did he plan to say to her? That she couldn't strut around half dressed? Well, *half* might be giving that outfit too much credit. That she couldn't cause a traffic hazard by distracting passing drivers? He'd tried all that before, and she'd brushed him off as skillfully as any woman had ever brushed off a man. He couldn't deny that she'd been right earlier when she'd said it wasn't her fault the men involved with the accident hadn't been paying attention to their driving.

Watching her prance around, waving to and flirting with passersby, trying to entice them into her store, Blaine seethed with jealousy. If he were being truthful, he didn't want anyone else to see her creamy skin and tempting curves. It wasn't like he had any kind of claim on her—yet. But if they were together, she certainly wouldn't be dancing around mostly nude in public. That much was for sure.

She bent in half to wave to a passing driver, and Blaine went hard at the view of barely covered breasts. He'd had more hard-ons today than he normally had in a week! God, she was beautiful. Every guy in town was no doubt talking about her, and Blaine wanted to march over there, cover her and drag her off to bed where he'd quickly uncover her again.

Project alert! *Oh shut up! Shut up, shut up, shut up!* Damned his cursed conscience. His mother's voice was hardwired into his brain, reminding him of how he'd been taken advantage of in the past. That didn't mean it would happen again. He heard his mother reminding him of what he'd gone through with Eden and Kim before that. Tiffany was nothing like them. She was smart and driven and working toward a goal. Eden and Kim had used and abused everyone they encountered, and the only goal either of them ever had was to find someone else to take advantage of. Even though he'd spent less than an hour total alone with Tiffany, he knew she was wasn't like that, which was why his heart broke a little watching her try so hard to entice someone, *anyone*, into her new shop.

For two hours, she worked it hard, pouring on her special brand of Tiffany charm to anyone who ventured a glance her way, but no one stopped. Blaine watched her start to wilt under the hot sun, but her smile and enthusiasm never faded until she had no choice but to concede defeat. As she walked inside, her shoulders dropped with uncharacteristic despair.

Blaine pounded the steering wheel with a tightly rolled fist. The longer he sat there, the more obvious it became to him that he was going to do something stupid. Really, really stupid.

WHILE GRACE WORKED the day shift downstairs at the pharmacy, Evan McCarthy whiled away the Saturday working on his latest song and practicing his guitar. He'd also spent an hour on the phone with the sound engineer he'd worked with on his album, trying to entice him to take a chance on a start-up recording studio on Gansett Island.

The Starlight Records bankruptcy proceedings that had Evan's debut CD tied up in court had also put Josh Harrelson out of work. Evan was working hard to convince Josh to move north and be part of Island Breeze Records. Josh had agreed to think about it, which was all Evan could ask at this point.

He'd been fooling around with a new song that he was calling "Amazing Grace," which he hoped to make the first single released by the Island Breeze label. The equipment they'd ordered was due to arrive any day now, and the old barn on one of Ned's properties they'd be using for the studio was all ready. Evan had spent months reconfiguring, sanding, painting and turning the once-dusty, abandoned space into a recording studio.

Above the studio, his father and Ned had helped him to install four bedrooms as well as a kitchen, bathroom and living room to accommodate visiting musicians. He'd offered Josh a free place to live in exchange for taking a chance on his upstart studio, and Evan was praying he'd take the bait. Without a decent sound engineer, his studio would be sunk before it ever even opened. After a long winter of hard work and planning, everything was coming together, and Evan was itching to get to work.

A knock on the door interrupted the flow of the song, which aggravated him. His family and friends knew to leave him alone during the day when he was often writing and composing. Without bothering to put on a shirt, he pulled open the door, prepared to chew out whichever one of his brothers had once again forgotten his rules about daytime visits. The zinger he had ready died on his lips when he recognized Grace's parents from a photo of her family she kept in the loft. They were both pear-shaped with dark hair and eyes. Right away, Evan could see that Grace looked like her mother, who was staring at him suspiciously.

"We were told downstairs that we'd find Grace here," Mrs. Ryan said.

"She's not at the pharmacy?" Evan asked.

"They said she left a while ago."

He remembered her saying something about seeing his cousin Laura at the Sand & Surf Hotel after work. "She should be home soon if you want to come in and wait for her."

"Who're you?" Mr. Ryan asked, his eyes scanning Evan's bare chest and feet.

"I'm Evan."

They exchanged perplexed glances.

"Her boyfriend?"

"She doesn't have a boyfriend," Mrs. Ryan said.

"Ah, I'm quite certain she does," Evan said, flabbergasted to realize that Grace had never told them about him. He stepped aside to admit them to the loft. "For about eight months now, in fact."

Mrs. Ryan stopped short at the sight of the rumpled bed, the surfboard propped against the wall, the guitars leaning against the sofa and his size-twelve sneakers under the coffee table.

She spun around to face him. "You're *living* here?"

Evan had no idea what to say to that, so he went with the truth. "Have been. For a long time."

"Well, isn't this enlightening, Bill?"

"Yes," Mr. Ryan said, continuing to eye Evan as if he was Jack the Ripper or someone equally unsavory. "Very enlightening."

Evan supposed that finding out your daughter had been sleeping with a guy for close to a year and hadn't bothered to mention it to you might be a little shocking. Hell, it was a little shocking to him that she hadn't told her parents about them—and a little painful, too.

"No wonder why she never has time to come home."

"She's been home," Evan said in Grace's defense.

"Three times in eight months," Mrs. Ryan said, taking a close look at every corner of the loft.

Evan felt slightly violated by her scrutiny and wondered if Grace would be annoyed with him for letting them in. If she was, they'd be even, because he was kind of annoyed with her at the moment.

"And what do you do, young man?" Mr. Ryan asked.

"I'm a musician," he said, gesturing to the guitars. "And a songwriter."

"You make any money doing that?"

"Enough."

"Do you pay rent to live here?" Mrs. Ryan asked.

"I'd say that's between Grace and me."

"Which means you don't," she said, giving him a knowing look.

"It doesn't mean that at all. It means it's none of your business." The instant the words were out of his mouth, he regretted them.

These were Grace's *parents*, he told himself. Tread lightly. "Let me see where she is."

As he picked up his phone from the coffee table, the screen door burst open, and Grace came in, carrying grocery bags. Her cheeks were flushed from the heat, and her silky dark hair curled at the ends, thanks to the humidity. "Hey, babe. I'm home. Sorry I'm late, but Laura wanted to show me the new guest rooms at the hotel—" When she saw her parents standing in the kitchen, the grocery bags slipped from her hands and crashed to the floor.

The distinctive sound of glass breaking had Evan rushing over to her. He took her hand and guided her around the mess on the floor. "I'll clean it up."

She glanced at his bare chest and then at her parents and then back at him. "Did you, have you… You met Evan?"

"Indeed, we did," her mother said. "And now we know why we've seen so little of you since you moved out here."

"She's been working really hard at the pharmacy," Evan said, as he scooped up glass, spaghetti sauce and torn brown bags. A dozen eggs had also been lost in the crash. "She's the only pharmacist on the island, so she works almost every day."

She sent him a grateful smile, but he could see the concern in her eyes. "Why didn't you tell me you were coming?" she asked her parents.

"We wanted to surprise you," her mother said. Glancing at Evan, she added, "But the surprise was on us."

"I was going to tell you…"

"When?" her mother and Evan said at the same time.

When Grace winced, he wished he hadn't piled on. They'd have time later, when they were alone, to discuss why she hadn't bothered to mention him to her parents.

"I'd invite you to stay for dinner," Grace said, glancing at the mess on the floor, "but…"

"We'll go out," Evan said, sweeping the broken glass into a dustpan. "My treat." This was said with a meaningful glance at Mr. Ryan.

"You don't have to do that," Grace said.

"I insist. I'll make reservations. The Lobster House at eight?"

She nodded and added a smile for him, because he'd chosen their favorite restaurant, the place where they'd had their first official date. To her parents, she said, "Where're you staying?"

"At the McCarthy place," her father said with an air of distaste. "No air-conditioning or television! Can you believe it?"

Grace bit her lip as Evan choked back a laugh. His mother was damned proud that her hotel was a throwback to simpler times.

"We'd never stay there again," her mother added. "We tried to move somewhere else, but none of the hotels have TVs or AC. What're we supposed to do when we're in the room?"

Evan raised an eyebrow and made the mistake of glancing at Grace, whose face had turned red from the effort not to laugh. He knew exactly what she was thinking—they'd have no need of a TV or any other form of entertainment in a hotel room. As long as they had each other, they were all set.

"You could try talking to each other," Grace said.

Her parents looked at each other and then at her, as if she'd said something in a foreign language.

"Come on, Bill. I'd like to get changed, and it's a long walk back to the hotel."

"You *walked* here?" Grace asked, seeming surprised.

"We're exercising every day," her mother said in a snippy tone on her way out the door. "There're other ways to lose weight besides going under the knife, you know."

Evan bit back the comment that was burning to get out about how courageous Grace had been to have the lap band surgery that enabled her to lose more than a hundred pounds. But he held his tongue until after her parents had departed. Squirting cleaning solution on the floor, he wiped up the last of the mess and stood to find Grace watching him.

"I know what you're going to say," she said.

He tossed the paper towels in the trash and turned to her, trying to decide whether or not he should make her suffer a bit for keeping him a secret from her parents. "What's that?"

"You don't understand why I didn't tell them about you. And I'm so sorry, Evan. It had nothing to do with you."

As tears filled her eyes, he discovered he loved her too damned much to make her suffer. He went to her and rested his hands on her hips, drawing her in close to him.

She looped her arms around his neck. "I'm so sorry. I could tell you were mad the minute I walked in."

"I'm not going to deny I was a little hurt to realize you hadn't told them about me, but after half an hour in their presence, I get it, baby."

"I wanted to tell them about you. So many times. But I've been so happy, and I didn't want them to ruin it the way they ruin everything for me."

He drew her into a tight hug that she returned in equal measure. "Do you think I'd let anyone ruin what we have?"

"They're so negative and defeatist. So many times I started to tell them about you, but I always stopped myself, knowing they wouldn't approve of us living together. I'm almost thirty! I don't need their permission."

"But you care enough to want their approval."

"And doesn't that make me a fool?"

"No, baby, it makes you a good daughter. You've got nothing to be ashamed of."

"I love you, Evan. You have no idea how much."

Smiling, he tipped his head and kissed her slowly and sweetly. She was like a drug he couldn't get enough of. Every taste made him want another. He was equally addicted to the scent of her silky hair and the softness of her skin.

"I love you just as much," he said as he kissed her collarbone and made her shiver. Glancing at the bedside clock, he let his hands slide down to cup her bottom. "We've got an hour before we have to meet them."

She smiled suggestively. "Maybe we can watch some TV or something."

Evan laughed as he backed her up to the bed and came down on top of her. "Or something."

. . .

TIFFANY DROVE home in a state of shock. The possibility that absolutely *no one* would patronize her store hadn't occurred to her in all the months of planning for the grand opening. Her hands shook with nerves when she thought again about the stack of bills that needed to be paid, not to mention the cavernous house that needed furniture. She swallowed the panic that lodged in her throat.

God, what have I done? I've risked my future and Ashleigh's on this huge gamble, and now...

No.

She forced those thoughts from her mind. Right after she got home and had herself a nice little pity party over what hadn't happened today, she'd pull out one of her favorite self-help books and spend some time rebuilding her faith in herself and her store.

On the way inside, she grabbed the mail and rifled through it to find more bills and something from her lawyer, Dan Torrington, who'd obtained a Rhode Island license to help free her friend Stephanie's stepfather from prison, and then used it to help Tiffany with her divorce. She scanned the letter from Dan that indicated her divorce was now final and referred to the enclosed agreement that gave her joint custody of her daughter, Ashleigh. The settlement check from Jim would go a long way toward relieving some of the debt she'd accumulated in recent months, but it wouldn't solve all her financial problems.

While Tiffany knew she ought to be celebrating the end of a marriage that had died a long, painful death, she hardly felt like celebrating. She wanted her baby girl to snuggle and cuddle up to after the miserable disappointment of her grand opening, but this was Jim's weekend with Ashleigh.

She briefly pondered Blaine's directive that she call him the second her divorce was final so they could pick up where they'd left off last fall. But she was too worn out and defeated after the day she'd had to go another round with him.

Her heels echoed through the empty house, reminding her once again that she would've been better off using her settlement money to buy furniture and pay some bills. "Well, I didn't," she said to the gaping emptiness that was her home. "So stop reminding me of what I *should've* done. What's done is done, and now I have to find a way to make it work."

On the way up the stairs, she unbuttoned her silk blouse and headed to the garden tub in the master bathroom. Pouring in strawberry-scented bubble bath, Tiffany stripped down and watched the bubbles bloom. She grabbed her robe and ran downstairs to pour a big glass of chardonnay and returned to the bathroom as the bubbles reached ideal height. Tiffany went to the stereo Jim had installed years ago and smiled as Andrea Bocelli's distinctive voice filled the room. The only reason the stereo was still there was because he'd hard-wired it into the house. Slipping into the warm suds, Tiffany felt the tension leave her body in one long wave. Nothing fixed what ailed her quite like a bubble bath.

As she floated on a cloud of strawberries and Andrea, she willed away the worries of the day, like she'd done for more than a year, since Jim lost his mind and left his perfectly lovely wife. And she'd been a perfectly lovely wife. That was one thing she knew for certain. She'd cooked and cleaned and worked to support them while he was in college and law school. When they bought this house from his parents, she'd labored nonstop for months to make it a place he'd be proud to bring his friends and business associates. She'd entertained lavishly and often, without much notice, any time he asked. She'd done absolutely nothing to deserve the way he'd treated her. Knowing that gave her some measure of comfort, but it did nothing to warm her bed on cold winter nights.

Tiffany soaked for close to an hour, and only when the water started to cool did she move reluctantly from the tub to the enormous steam shower to rinse off the suds and wash her hair. When she first saw that shower, she'd imagined making slow, steamy love with Jim in there. Never once, in all the time they'd lived there together, had that happened. "What a waste," she whispered, annoyed with herself for still being hung up on the memories of him and what might've been.

All at once, images of the sexy police chief pushed Jim from her thoughts. Blaine had been so hot and so *bothered* earlier as he'd tried to cover her up. Tiffany laughed at how annoyed he'd been. The more he'd tried to cover her, the more fun it had been to torment him. It hadn't been lost on her that once he'd realized she wasn't going to allow him to cover her, he'd kept that heavy jacket of his strategically placed to hide the effect her outfit had on him. Too bad they'd been unable to capitalize on all that chemistry zinging between them.

She towel-dried her hair and brushed it out. Letting it dry on its own would result in wild curls by morning, but she was too tired to bother with the drying and straightening ritual. Wrapped in a pale pink silk robe, Tiffany rinsed out the tub and took her wineglass downstairs for a refill.

The clang of the doorbell echoed through the empty house like the bells at Notre Dame, startling her. She couldn't imagine who'd be calling at this hour. As a woman living alone with a small child, her first thought was always safety. She peered through the peephole and nearly swallowed her tongue when she saw Blaine Taylor's handsome face.

Should she ask him to wait while she dashed upstairs to find more appropriate attire? Why bother when he'd seen her in much less earlier?

She swung open the door. "Have you come to gloat?"

He took a long, slow, perusing look at her, making each of her most important parts stand up to ensure he didn't miss anything. "Of course not."

The bob of his Adam's apple satisfied her. "Then what can I do for you, Chief?"

"I thought we'd progressed to first names."

Standing in the soft spring breeze with only a thin layer of silk covering her, Tiffany was acutely aware of all her pleasure points, because each of them had come to life the moment she opened the door to him.

His deep, gravelly voice, the hint of rough stubble on his well-defined jaw, the honey-colored hair, those liquid brown eyes, the uniform... Tiffany had never understood why women went wild over a man in uniform. Now she got it, and for the first time since Jim left her, she was truly grateful to be single—and now officially divorced.

"What brings you to my doorstep on this fine evening?"

"I wanted to check on you. I thought you'd be more, you know, upset. About today."

Tiffany shrugged. "It's the first day. Things will pick up."

"Are you always so optimistic?"

"What choice do I have?"

"I admire that."

Startled by the unexpected compliment, Tiffany stared at him, taking note of a pulsing twitch in his cheek. All at once, it dawned on her that he wanted her. Fiercely. The realization sent a charge of desire sizzling through her, as if she'd touched a live wire. She felt her nipples get even harder under the soft silk and watched his eyes lower to take in the show. He didn't even try to hide the fact that he was looking, which pleased her. It'd been so long since a man had looked at her with anything other than contempt.

"Would you like to come in?"

"I probably shouldn't."

"Probably not."

He took a step forward to close the distance between them, but still, he didn't touch her. "Are you divorced yet?"

"Funny you should ask. I got the papers today. It's official."

His eyes narrowed a bit at that news. "You were supposed to call me the second it was final. We had a deal."

"I was a little busy today."

"Still, we had a deal."

"I figured maybe you'd forgotten about that."

He shook his head. "I think about you *way* more than I should," he said softly.

His confession warmed her all the way through, the same way a shot of fine whiskey would. "I think about you, too."

"What do you think about?"

As he moved closer to her, his breath whispered against her neck, making her tremble. "What do you think I think about?"

"Probably the same thing I think about."

"Does that mean you want to come in?"

As if he couldn't wait another second to touch her, his hands landed on her hips, sending heat blazing through the silk that covered her. "If I come in, we'll end up in bed."

Tiffany wondered if it was possible for a heart to leap right out of a chest. "You think so?"

"I know so."

"Awfully sure of yourself, aren't you?"

"I'm awfully sure that I want you more than I've ever wanted anyone."

"Well, in that case..." Tiffany somehow managed to saunter away from him on legs that felt like noodles. Casting a glance over her shoulder, she said, "Are you coming?"

"Not yet," he said as he walked in and shut the door behind him. "But I will be soon, and so will you."

CHAPTER 3

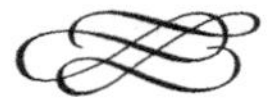

Just as she'd never found uniforms to be particularly sexy, overly confident men had never really done it for her, either.

Until now.

He walked into the house like he owned it and everyone in it. To say he had a predatory look in his eyes would be putting it mildly. Tiffany marveled at how quickly he got her motor running, and he'd barely touched her. He followed her to the kitchen, also known as the scene of their earlier crime, where she planned to buy herself some time by getting a glass of ice water.

But Blaine had other ideas.

He backed her up against the same expanse of countertop that had hosted their previous encounter and pressed his body tight against hers, placing his hands on either side of her on the counter.

Tiffany gasped from the impact of his erection pressing against her belly.

"Where's your daughter?"

"With her father."

His lips hovered over her neck without touching her fevered skin. "I saw you this afternoon."

"I could feel you watching me."

"Was that show for me or everyone else?"

"Mostly you," she somehow managed to say. His nearness, the scent of sandalwood and citrus, the hard press of his muscles against her softness... Tiffany would implode if he didn't do something, *anything*, very soon. She pressed her pelvis against his erection, drawing a low growl from him. Her fingers curled tightly around the edges of the countertop.

"I didn't like it," he said.

Tiffany swallowed hard. "Naughty nurses aren't your thing?"

"I don't like that every guy in this town is thinking about you tonight. Fantasizing about you."

Tiffany glanced up at him. If she were in her right mind, she might've been put off by the almost feral look in his eyes. In her current state, the look sent an urgent surge of liquid heat straight to her core. "You don't?"

He held her gaze as he shook his head.

"Why not?"

Tugging on the sash to her robe, he nudged it open and took a long, measuring look at what he'd uncovered. "I don't want anyone else to see you."

Even though she was wildly aroused, Tiffany couldn't let that statement go unchallenged. "You make it sound like you have some sort of claim on me. One orgasm doesn't give you the right—"

His lips came down hard and fast, his tongue surging into her mouth at the same instant his fingers slipped between her legs and into her slick channel.

Tiffany gasped from the dual assault and gripped his biceps with both hands.

"Do two orgasms give me any rights?" he whispered against her lips as his fingers slid in and out of her in a suggestive rhythm that had her on the brink of climax faster than she'd ever gotten there before.

"I'll let you know after the second one. It might not be as good as I remembered."

His sexy grin lit up his face. "It'll be as good." He shifted his fingers to focus on the spot that burned for him. "It might even be better."

Having no doubt about that, Tiffany let her head fall to his shoulder as he used his feet to slide her legs farther apart. If he hadn't been pressing her so tightly against the counter, her legs would've buckled under her.

"Mmm," he said. "So wet, so hot."

A tremble began in her thighs and worked its way through her entire body.

"I love that you always smell like strawberries." Cupping her breast, he bent his head to suckle on her nipple as he once again drove his fingers deep inside her. "And taste like heaven."

Tiffany cried out when the orgasm slammed into her. Her head fell back, and she was vaguely aware of his teeth closing around her nipple and his hair brushing against her neck. Wave after wave of exquisite pleasure pounded through her. He kept up the movement of his fingers and sucked hard on her nipple, making her come again. *That* had never happened before, and it left Tiffany feeling boneless and sated in a way that was new to her. Before she'd begun to recover her senses, he bent and scooped her into his arms. Her robe fell open as he strode with purpose toward the stairs. She didn't have the energy to care about covering herself.

"Tell me there's at least a bed up there."

"That and not much else."

"That's all we need."

Tiffany directed him to the master bedroom at the end of the hallway.

Blaine kicked the door open and deposited her gently in the middle of the king-size bed.

The silk robe pooled beneath her ultrasensitive skin as his eyes took a leisurely journey from her face to her breasts to her belly and below. Heat rushed through her, stealing her breath as she watched him peel off his uniform shirt, exposing a most excellent chest. He was lean and muscular but not bulky. His chest was covered by the perfect amount of golden hair that made a tantalizing trail into brown uniform pants, where an impressive bulge marked the front. Tiffany stared at that bulge, desperate to see all of him.

"Raise your knees," he said as he reached for his belt buckle.

Tentatively, Tiffany did as he'd asked.

"Now slide your feet apart." He watched her every move while unbuttoning and unzipping his pants. "More."

Tiffany moved her feet until her legs were as far apart as she could get them. Her thighs quivered with anticipation as she waited to see what he'd do next. The breeze from the ceiling fan fluttered against her heated flesh, and she fought for every breath. She felt exposed and vulnerable but completely safe.

Leaving his pants open and hanging from narrow hips, he propped a knee on the bed and bent to press his face to her sex. He took a long sniff and exhaled with what sounded like sheer pleasure.

"Strawberry fields forever," he said as he licked her.

Tiffany fought to stay still as he took another long lick before twirling his talented tongue in circles around her clit. She reached for his hair and buried her fingers in the coarse strands. He had her on the verge of another explosive release with a few more sweeps of his tongue. Her legs closed around his head, and she rode his tongue with total abandon.

He pushed two fingers into her and took her right off the cliff, shrieking like the shameless hussy she became in his presence.

"Mmm," he said, his lips vibrating against her sensitive flesh. "That's four. Do I have any rights yet?"

Even though she was gasping for air, she laughed as she said, "Still haven't decided."

Kissing his way to her breasts, he looked up at her. "Need more convincing?"

Tiffany nodded and curled one of her legs around him. Using her foot, she pushed his pants down and then went back for his boxers.

Blaine rolled off her. "Let me help you with that." He pushed off his shorts to expose his erection.

"Oh." She took a good look at his long, thick penis. It reminded her of some of the larger dildos she'd stocked in the store, and for a brief, paralyzing moment, she wondered if it would fit inside her.

"See something you like?"

"Maybe." When he would've returned to his position on top of her, she stopped him and rose to her knees, shedding the robe as she went. Bending over him, she peppered his chest with kisses. His soft chest hair brushed against her face as she paid homage to both nipples before dragging her tongue over the defined ridges of his belly. She felt his fingers in her hair, and when he tightened his grip, she could tell she was having the same effect on him that he'd had on her.

Her hair slid through his fingers as she traveled down his long body. She dragged the loose strands over his erection, which drew a moan from him. After she'd teased him with her hair for a few minutes, she ran her hands over his legs, pushing them apart as she went. He watched her every move as she learned the muscular contours and planes of his body. When she had him spread open the way she wanted him, she bent to run her tongue over his balls, back and forth several times before traveling up to his weeping cock. She kept her hands on his thighs and felt each reaction as it traveled through him.

"If you keep that up," he said through gritted teeth, "we'll be done before we start."

"I'll take my chances." She looked up at him as she slid her lips over the head and sent her tongue into the salty slit.

"Oh *God*, Tiff," he said, his eyes fluttering closed. "That feels so good."

Emboldened by his surrender and heartened by his use of her nickname, she closed her hand around the base and took him deeper into her mouth, letting her tongue explore as her hand worked him.

His fingers guided her head, and his hips surged, urging her to take him deeper.

Tiffany tried to take as much of him as she could, but he was so big and so thick. Her sex clenched in anticipation.

"*Tiffany*," he said, the warning loud and clear.

Despite frequent pleading, Tiffany had only let Jim come in her mouth once, and she'd hated the taste. So she debated about whether to allow it now. For some reason, she felt freer and more uninhibited with this man she barely knew than she ever had with the man she'd married. So when Blaine uttered one more dire warning, Tiffany went for broke, driving him to an explosive finish that filled her mouth and throat with his essence. She swallowed every drop and then licked him clean as he twitched beneath her. Everything about him was different than what she'd known in the past, even his taste.

Like he'd done to her, she kissed her way up his chest until she was stretched out on top of him. His arms closed around her, and his lips skimmed her forehead. "That was incredible," he said, eyes closed, breathing ragged.

His heart hammered under her ear. "Really?"

"Mmm. The best ever."

Tiffany smiled against his chest. Even if that wasn't true, it felt good to be the best at something.

His hands moved slowly over her back, massaging as they went. He cupped her bottom and squeezed. "Kiss me," he whispered.

Tiffany raised her head to kiss him and laughed when she realized they'd had five orgasms between them but had barely kissed.

"What's so funny?" he asked, his hands kneading her cheeks.

"This turned out to be a pretty good day after all."

He smiled, and Tiffany was struck by how it softened his normally austere expression. "Do you have to work tomorrow?" he asked.

"At noon. You?"

"Three. Your daughter?"

"With her father for the weekend."

The implication lingered in the heavy, humid air. They had hours and hours of sensual pleasure ahead. His reawakened erection made its presence known by pressing against her belly.

"That was fast," Tiffany said.

"All depends on the incentive package."

Tiffany raised an eyebrow. "And I'm a good incentive package?"

"The best."

She nibbled on her bottom lip as she recalled his size. "What if it doesn't fit?"

Under her, Blaine quaked with laughter. "It'll fit."

"Are you always so confident?"

"About some things." He shifted her so she was under him. "About the important things." Kissing her nose and then her lips, he said, "Hold that thought." He got up to find his pants and sat on the edge of the bed to put on a condom. "Come here," he said, crooking his finger.

Every nerve ending in Tiffany's body was on full alert as she crawled across the bed to him. He arranged her so her legs were once again spread far apart, with her feet and bottom at the edge of the mattress. His fingers tested her readiness and found her slippery wet. Blaine brought his moist fingers to his mouth and licked them clean while watching her face to gauge every reaction. Tiffany had never been the focus of such intense concentration, and she quite liked it—until he pressed his hardness against her opening, making her burn as he stretched already-sensitive tissue.

"Relax, honey," he whispered, bending to lick her nipple as he worked his way slowly inside her. "Let me in."

Tiffany broke out in a fine sheen of sweat, struggling to relax and grant him entry.

He pushed again, and she cried out. "Do you want to stop?" he asked, concern etched into his handsome face.

With her hands on his back, she kept him right where he was. "No, don't stop." She gritted her teeth and lifted her hips to encourage him to continue, despite the pinch of pain.

Reaching between them, he ran a finger over her core, which sent a gush of liquid heat to help ease his entry. "That's it," he whispered against her lips. "That's my girl." He kept up a steady rhythm of small movements in and out until she began to yield to him. "So, *so* tight."

"Is that good?" she asked, her voice squeaking.

"It's amazing."

His hands shifted to her bottom, lifting her higher. The new position put him in contact with a spot deep inside her that she'd never known was there.

Tiffany screamed from the sheer pleasure that shot through her entire body, which caused him to freeze. "Don't stop! *Please,* don't stop." She curled her legs around him and began to move her hips, which seemed to spark something in him. He gave up the slow entry and pounded into her.

In the throes of the most incredible passion she'd ever experienced, Tiffany had the presence of mind to realize he was changing her life as he clutched her bottom and pumped relentlessly into her, striking that elusive spot with every stroke. He drove her up, up, *up,* until she broke with a sudden desperate intensity that shattered her into a million pieces that could never, ever be put back together the same way they'd been before.

CHAPTER 4

As a rule, Blaine never spent the night with a woman anymore. Since the catastrophe with Eden, he'd gone to great lengths to avoid getting too involved. The minute he'd walked through Tiffany's front door, however, he'd blown all his own rules to smithereens. Holding her warm, naked body close to him, Blaine couldn't believe he'd thought he'd been having good sex all these years. He'd been having mediocre sex at best. What he'd had with Tiffany could only be called extraordinary. Never before had he felt so connected to a woman during the act, which was exactly why he should get out of her bed right now and go home, while he still could.

Before he could make the move to get up, Tiffany turned over and pressed her lips to his chest, which started the fire burning all over again. Who was he fooling? After months of thinking about her and fantasizing about her, he wasn't going anywhere as long as she wanted to be naked in bed with him.

Blaine rolled to his back and brought her with him, settling her on top of him.

She uttered a sleepy sigh of contentment. Her fragrant hair brushed against his face, and he inhaled the fruity scent that would remind him always of her. How was it possible that he already wanted her again? He reached for the condom he'd put on the bedside table and maneuvered between them to roll it on.

Caressing her back, he worked his way down to firm buttocks while urging her legs apart with his knees.

"Hmm," she muttered. "What're you up to?"

"About nine inches."

Tiffany laughed softly against his chest. "You ought to come with a warning label."

He nudged at her with the tip of his engorged erection. "Is that so?"

She groaned. "I don't know if I can do it again. I'm a little sore. It's been a while for me."

"We'll take it slow," he said, keeping up the persistent thrusting.

"That's what you said last time."

"Then you take charge." He released his hold on her bottom. "You decide how fast or slow we go."

"I *can't*."

His fingers journeyed between them to coax her. "Are you *sure* you can't?"

As much as it cost him, he stayed still, even though he ached with need for her.

Tiffany propped herself up with her hands on his chest.

When Blaine realized she was going to try, he smiled at the determination he saw on her face. He rewarded her by continuing to caress between her legs.

She straddled him and took him in slowly, so slowly that he had to grit his teeth to keep from exploding too soon.

He looked down to where their bodies were connected, and quickly had to look away from the erotic sight of her spread legs, the thatch of dark hair at the juncture of her thighs and the working of her muscles as she eased herself down on him. Blaine moved his hands from her hips to her breasts, rolling her nipples between his fingers.

Tiffany tossed her head back as her tight channel gave way and admitted him. The brush of her private hair against his belly was one of the sexiest things he'd ever experienced. And then she moved her hips and took him straight to heaven.

"That's it, baby." He took hold of her hands. "Ride me."

Her lips parted in an expression of amazement and concentration that tugged at his heart. She moved up and down, her wetness easing the way for both of them. Blaine stayed still and let her set the pace, and oh, what a pace it was! She'd gone from reluctant to enthusiastic in a matter of minutes. He rested his hands on her thighs, reveling in the smoothest skin he'd ever encountered. When he sensed her beginning to tire, he stopped her, sat up against the pile of pillows and raised his knees behind her, urging her to recline against his legs. He smoothed his hands up over her belly to cup her breasts before sending one hand back down to play with the pulsating bundle of nerves between her legs. Using his own legs, he guided her up and down in a more relaxed but no less satisfying movement.

"How do you feel?" he asked.

"Full. Very, *very* full."

"Does it feel good, though?"

"Mmm, so good. I never knew..."

He released her so she came back down on him swiftly. "Knew what?"

Tiffany exhaled sharply from the impact. "That it could be like this."

"I didn't know, either."

Her eyes widened with surprise at his admission.

"I suspected it might be this way with you."

He sat all the way up, arranged her legs around his waist and wrapped his arms around her. The new position put all their most important parts into close contact. Blaine ran his tongue over her lips and once again sent his fingers into the moistness between her legs, hoping to draw one more orgasm from her.

She kissed him deeply, her tongue rubbing against his, her breasts pressed tight to his chest. He felt the now-familiar signs of her impending climax in the quivering of her thighs and the tightening of her inner muscles. She tore her lips free and let go with a cry of completion that tripped his explosive finish.

He was definitely spending the night.

TIFFANY SKIPPED into work the next day with far more energy than she should've had after the all-but-sleepless night with Blaine. They'd hardly said a word to each other, but who needed conversation when the sex was so amazing? For the first time since Jim had left her, she felt hopeful about a future that didn't include him. She was under no illusions it would include Blaine, either. Perhaps theirs would be a summer fling, a pleasurable interlude until they both moved on to more serious relationships.

Tiffany didn't care if he never said more than "spread your legs" to her. The last thing she needed was another big entanglement, after having just gotten free of her ex-husband. Some mindless sex was the perfect way to repair her self-esteem and provide a distraction while she got the business launched.

Whistling as she worked, Tiffany put the OPEN flag outside and waved at a few passing motorists who beeped at her on their way by. Today she wore one of the flirty, romantic, low-cut summer sundresses she carried in the store. Because Blaine had kept her in bed until late morning, she'd had no choice but to leave her hair curly and unruly. He said he liked it that way, and who was she to argue with a hot guy who seemed to like her with wild hair, no makeup, and who left her with a sore but pleasant ache between her legs?

The bells on the front door jingled, and Tiffany looked up to find her assistant Patty reporting for duty. Tiffany sure hoped business picked up soon, so she could keep the earnest young woman on the payroll. As usual, Tiffany itched to get her hands on Patty's stringy hair and dumpy clothes. The girl was a fashion disaster of the highest order, but she was also a hard worker.

"You're awfully cheerful today," Patty said.

"It's a gorgeous day, and I get to come to my gorgeous little shop for work. What could be better than that?"

"Um, maybe a few customers?"

"Now, now, no pessimism allowed in this store. If we keep a positive attitude, good things will come our way."

"Have you been reading self-help books again?"

"Maybe. There's some really good advice in there. You might want to take a look yourself."

"Myself doesn't need any help, thank you very much."

Tiffany tried to decide if she dared. "Your hair could use some help," she blurted before she lost her nerve.

Patty ran a self-conscious hand over her mousy brown hair, and Tiffany immediately felt like a jerk for mentioning it.

"What's wrong with my hair?"

"Nothing. Forget it. I shouldn't have said anything. I'd never want to hurt your feelings."

"You can't take it back now! What were you going to say?"

"It's just that, with a little effort, you could be a knockout."

Patty's blue eyes widened. Tiffany was itching to get some shadow on those lackluster lids. Under her deft hand, those eyes would dazzle.

"You really think so?"

"I *know* so."

"I don't know anything about hair or makeup or clothes. My mother died when I was really young. It was just me and my dad, so I never learned that stuff. My friends were all like me."

Tiffany slipped an arm around the younger woman's slim shoulders. "You wanna be a knockout?"

"Would that get me a boyfriend?" Patty's wistful tone tugged at Tiffany's heart. "I've never had one, and I've always wanted one."

"How about this: If I make you over and you don't get a boyfriend out of it, I'll work weekends for a month."

"And if I do get a boyfriend?"

"You get weekend duty."

Patty thought about that for about ten seconds before she extended her hand to Tiffany. "Deal."

"Step into my office."

. . .

SINCE THEY HAD no customers that morning, Tiffany put her year of cosmetology school to good use in the shop's back room. First, she cut six inches off Patty's hair and then added in layers and bangs that framed her cute face. Keeping Patty's back to the mirror, Tiffany next applied a subtle but effective layer of makeup that totally changed the younger woman's appearance. It made her look older and more sophisticated. No one would ever look at her now and think dumpy or boring. Pleased with her handiwork, Tiffany instructed her assistant to stay put while she rummaged through the racks out front for the dress she wanted to try on Patty.

Taking it to the back room, she directed Patty into the changing room with orders to keep her eyes closed, so she could get the full effect all at once. Tiffany waited anxiously for her to emerge. A minute later, Patty drew the curtain aside and stepped out. Her shoulders were hunched, and her fingers clutched the skirt. Their next lesson would be about body language and projecting confidence.

"Stand up straight," Tiffany said, making a full circle around the other woman. "Well, glory be! You have breasts!"

Patty blushed from her chin to the roots of her hair. "So?"

"That bra is all wrong. I've got just the thing. Wait right there." She returned a minute later with one of the best push-up bras money could buy. "Thirty-four C, right?"

Patty glanced at her, astounded. "How did you know that?"

"Since breasts are gonna be my business, I figured I'd better study up."

"How does one study for such a thing?"

"You'd be surprised," Tiffany said, nudging her back into the changing room. "Don't look in those mirrors."

"I won't." This time when she emerged, Tiffany could see right away that she'd been spot-on with the bra. It made all the difference, and, judging from the cleavage she was now displaying, Patty would have more boyfriends than she could handle.

"Almost perfect," Tiffany said.

"What's wrong? What does it need now?"

Tiffany released the top two buttons on the dress to show off more of Patty's ample breasts. "Now it's perfect."

"Can I look yet?"

"You sure can."

Patty spun around and let out a shriek when she got her first view of Tiffany's handiwork. "Oh! *Oh, my God!* Is that really me?" She ran her hands over her hair and face, as if she were touching a stranger. Then she turned and hurled herself into Tiffany's arms. "I don't know what you did, but you're some kind of magician or something."

Laughing, Tiffany returned her hug. "I took your own natural assets and made the most of them. You have a gorgeous face, gorgeous eyes and gorgeous breasts. Time to show them all off."

Patty released her and spun around for a second look. "No one will believe this is really me."

"It's still you, just a new-and-improved version."

"I'll definitely get a boyfriend now!"

"I have no doubt."

"Thank you, Tiffany." Patty's eyes were shiny with tears. "This is the nicest thing anyone has ever done for me."

"It was my pleasure."

And it had helped to kill a too-quiet morning in the store, Tiffany thought, but didn't say.

The bells on the front door jingled, and the two women exchanged glances. A customer?

Tiffany smoothed her hair and went out front to find Blaine skimming his fingers over one of the lace teddies. Watching his fingers move and remembering what he'd done to her with them made her entire body hot with longing. He looked up, their eyes met, and Tiffany's mouth went dry from the heat that blazed between them.

She cleared her throat. "Patty," she said. "Take a break. Take a nice, long break."

AFTER PATTY SCOOTED out the front door, Tiffany took a calming breath and turned to Blaine. "What brings you in here?"

Silk spilled through his fingers as he examined a floral robe. Why was it that everything this guy did screamed *sex*? Or maybe that was the effect he had on her. She could only hope he didn't have the same overwhelming effect on every woman he encountered.

Since he wasn't working until later, he wore brown leather flip-flops and cargo shorts with a white T-shirt that offset his deep tan. It was official. He was equally sexy out of uniform.

"I was curious." He gave each item of clothing he looked at the same undivided attention he'd given her the night before. "And, if I'm not too late, I'd love to be your first customer."

"Unfortunately, you're not too late."

His eyes took a long perusing journey from her face to her breasts, where his gaze lingered. "Business will pick up."

Her nipples tightened, and she turned away from him. "I hope you're right." She refolded a stack of camisoles, just to have something to do with her hands. "Is there something in particular I can show you?" she asked, glancing at him.

His grin was nothing short of predatory.

"Anything *in the store*, that is."

"I have this friend," he said. "About your height and size. I'd like to get something for her. Something *special*."

Playing along, Tiffany said, "Is she a new friend or an old friend?"

"Newish."

"So you don't want anything too racy."

"On the contrary. The racier the better."

Is it hot in here, or is it me?

Tiffany sifted through the racks until she found the lacy black bustier with matching thong panties that were among her favorite items in the store. Pink satin ribbons ran through the ensemble, which was sheer in all the most important places. "I'm somewhat partial to this myself, but your friend may have different taste."

Blaine took it from her and studied it from every angle, running his fingers over the tiny scrap of fabric that made up the thong. "She'd love it. I'll take it."

"Shall I gift wrap it for you?" she asked, flashing a coy grin over her shoulder as she headed for the register to ring up her first sale.

"That'd be nice. Thank you."

His reply threw her off stride. Tiffany began to wonder if she understood the rules of this game they were playing. Did he have someone else? Would he really come to *her* store to buy something for another woman? When it came right down to it, she knew nothing about him other than what he did for a living, he was a good friend of her brother-in-law's and he was a god in bed. Beyond that, he could be just another sleaze for all she knew.

She tugged a sheet of tissue paper from the shelf behind the register, snipped the price tag from the bustier, wrapped it in the pink paper and sealed the package with a gold N&N sticker before slipping it into one of the red-and-white striped gift bags she'd designed herself.

His warm hands captured hers, startling her and stopping movements that had become jerky as she'd pondered the possibilities.

"There's no one else, Tiff, so stop wondering if I'm screwing with you in more ways than one."

Startled by how accurately he'd zeroed in on her thoughts, she pulled her hands free. "I wondered no such thing."

Laughing in that gravelly, sexy way he did so well, he said, "If you say so." He nodded to the beaded curtain that separated the main area of the store from a smaller second room. "What's in there?"

Tiffany swallowed. "Other stuff."

"Ah, the *good* stuff. Help me out, will you? I may have some questions. In fact, I'm sure I will."

Was he serious? Apparently so, since he stepped through the beads into the more intimate area of the store.

"Well, well, *well*. What have we here?"

Tiffany's entire body felt like it was on fire as she followed him through the curtain. Surely he didn't mean to quiz her on the various items she'd stocked there, did he?

He picked up a multipurpose vibrator and examined it from every angle. Turning to her, he raised an eyebrow. "What's this one's claim to fame?"

Tiffany didn't know what to do with her hands, so she crossed her fingers and squeezed. A riot of emotions and desires cascaded through her, tying her tongue into knots. "Um, the usual stuff. It, ah, vibrates and rotates."

"Rotates, too, huh? That's clever."

She would've killed him for putting her through this torturous exercise except for the pesky fact that he was chief of police.

He pointed to the vibrator's smaller arm. "What's this little doohickey do?"

"That's for the, um, back door."

Blaine's eyes widened with understanding. "You don't say."

To Tiffany's enormous relief, he put the toy down and moved farther into the room to study the wide array of dildos, lubricants, vibrators, handcuffs, massage oils and other sensuous delights.

He zeroed in on the display of butt plugs the vendor had talked her into stocking against her better judgment.

"Speaking of the back door," he muttered. "What's the difference between these two?"

One was shorter and fatter, the other long and thin.

Tiffany wanted to expire on the spot. She'd never been more embarrassed or more aroused. The sound of his voice alone was enough to turn her on, but watching his long fingers touching and caressing the toys on the shelf had her soaked with desire. She had to fight off the urge to drag him to the floor and have her way with him.

Determined to answer at least one of his questions without stammering, Tiffany said, "One is for stretching, the other for stimulating."

He scratched at the stubble on his chin. "Isn't that interesting? I didn't realize there were two different kinds." Turning to her, he studied her with those eyes that seemed to have only one setting: intense. "Which do you recommend? Stretching or stimulating?"

"Oh, well, that's an individual preference."

He curled a lock of her hair around his finger, brought it to his nose and inhaled. "What's *your* individual preference, Tiffany?"

"I, um, well..."

"Have you ever played with any of these toys?"

A flush of heat traveled from her face to her breasts to between her legs. "Of course I have. How else could I sell them?"

He gestured to the shelves of goodies. "Which ones?"

"I don't recall," she said haughtily.

How was it possible that her very first customer was discovering her deepest, darkest secret? After all the hours she'd spent studying the manuals that came with each and every item, that she could be found out so easily was unnerving, to say the least.

Blaine stepped even closer to her, so his face was an inch from hers. He was so close she could smell his cologne and feel the heat of his breath on her face. "Are you a sex toy fraud, Tiff?"

"I have no idea what you're talking about. I answered all your questions."

She turned, intending to return to the main room, but his hand on her arm stopped her.

"Which one do you find most intriguing?"

She couldn't possibly say all of them, could she? Jim would've died before he would've allowed any of the items in this room into their bedroom.

"I can see I've put you on the spot." After pondering the selection for another long moment, during which Tiffany barely drew a breath, he reached for a set of velvet-lined handcuffs, a bottle of lube that heated on contact, massage oil and the first vibrator he'd picked up (with the special back-door attachment). When picked up the shorter and fatter of the two butt plugs, Tiffany put a hand on his arm to stop him.

"I'm not interested in that."

Blaine studied her for a charged moment before he returned the plug to the shelf. "We've got enough to get us started."

She stared at him. "Get *who* started?"

"You, me, *us*. You can't sell this stuff if you've never used it."

"Says who?"

"Says me." He brushed by her on his way back to the main room, stopping to speak close to her ear. "Don't try to tell me you're not curious. I know you are."

"I don't want all that," she said.

"How do you know you don't want it until you've tried it?"

"Besides, that stuff is expensive. Did you even bother to look at the price tags?"

"You can't put a price on pleasure, honey. Whatever it costs, it's worth every penny."

"And does this experimentation you're suggesting work both ways?"

His brows narrowed. "Does what work both ways?"

"If you get to do this stuff to me, I get to do it to you, too."

The very thought of what they were discussing had her teetering on the verge of an explosive release. Every nerve ending in her body was on fire, like it had been the night before, and he'd barely touched her. Words, she realized, could be a powerful aphrodisiac.

"We'll negotiate terms during playtime," he said with a suggestive grin as he dropped the items he'd chosen on the counter.

Three hundred and twenty-five dollars later, Blaine returned his credit card to his wallet.

Tiffany placed the large red-and-white bag on the counter. Not a bad first sale. "Thank you," she said, embarrassed he'd spent so much money.

"My pleasure—and yours. Will your daughter be home tonight?"

Tiffany shook her head. "She's with her father until tomorrow."

He pushed the bag toward her. "I get out of work at eleven. I'll be at your house by eleven thirty. Leave the front door unlocked. Put the black outfit on and lie on the bed at eleven fifteen with your legs as far apart as you can get them. Make sure the ceiling fan is set to high."

A shiver of raw desire traveled through her at the power behind his softly spoken words. It had never occurred to her that being dominated, even lightly, could be such a turn-on.

"Put the other things in the bag on the bedside table so I can reach them. Do you understand?"

Tiffany had lost the ability to breathe, let alone speak, so she nodded.

He leaned over the counter as if he were going to kiss her. "One more thing. You'll need to decide on a safe word."

"Safe word?" she squeaked.

"A word we'll use if either of us wants to stop whatever we're doing."

"Oh, right," she said, swallowing frantically. "A safe word."

"Whatever you want it to be."

This time when he leaned in close, he kissed her long and hard and deep.

Tiffany's legs buckled, and she gripped the counter, something she'd done more often since she met him than she had in her entire life before him.

His fingers sank into her hair, and he tilted his head to get a better angle on the kiss. Sweeping strokes of his tongue had her forgetting where they were and that anyone could walk in and catch them. Oh, who was she kidding? No one was going to walk in, except for maybe Patty.

That thought had Tiffany reluctantly withdrawing from the kiss.

Blaine reached for her hand and came around to her side of the counter. "That wasn't enough, and eleven thirty is a long time from now," he said, his voice husky and deep.

She reached up to comb her fingers through his hair and brought him down for another passionate kiss.

His hands slid down her back to cup her bottom. And then he lifted her and started walking toward the back room. Propping her against the wall, he arranged her legs so they were splayed open, propped on his thighs. Taking the hem of her dress with him, his hands traveled up her legs until her skirt was bunched at her waist.

"What's this?" he asked, running his fingers over her panties. "White cotton? On the town's new lingerie queen?"

"Sometimes white cotton is comfortable," she managed to say.

"It's better to absorb dampness," he said agreeably, "especially a great flood of dampness."

Moaning, Tiffany tilted her hips, begging for more.

Keeping her panties between them, he worked his fingers back and forth, giving fleeting glances to her most sensitive spot. "Do you want to come, Tiff?"

"Yes, *yes*!"

"Are you sore today?" he asked, gentling his touch.

"A little."

"I'm sorry for that," he whispered, his tongue skimming her neck and sending a shiver of goose bumps dancing over her fevered skin. "I never want to hurt you."

She tightened the grip she had on his hair and jerked his mouth to hers for a fierce battle of tongues and teeth and lips.

His finger slipped beneath the elastic and into her slickness. He must've sensed her urgency, because he focused all his attention on the tight nub, circling and pressing until she came with a keening wail that he smothered with another deep kiss.

"I love watching you come," he whispered, capturing her bottom lip between his teeth and rolling it back and forth. "It's the hottest thing I've ever seen."

Mortified to imagine what she must look like at the moment of liftoff, she turned her focus on him. "What about you?" she asked, as he let her slide down the aroused front of him until her feet were on the floor.

She started to press a hand to the bulge in his shorts, but he stopped her.

"Let's save it for later." He kissed her forehead, nose and lips. "You might want to take a little nap when you get home. We'll be up late. Again."

After another passionate kiss, he left her leaning against the wall, trying to recapture her equilibrium. If all her customers were even half as interesting as her first one, owning this shop was going to be one hell of a wild ride.

After the ringing bells on the door announced his departure, Tiffany ran her fingers through her hair, straightened her dress and went into the tiny pink restroom to freshen up. Staring at her reflection in the mirror, she thought about the instructions he'd given her. While part of her couldn't wait to see him again, the other part—the part that still retained a shred of sanity—was filled with trepidation about what he had planned for her.

CHAPTER 5

When Blaine arrived at the police station for his three o'clock shift, Evelyn, the department secretary, handed him a message from the mayor.

"Did he say anything else?" Blaine asked after quickly scanning the summons.

"Just the ASAP thing—a few times."

Blaine tossed the message into the trash and headed for his office.

"Aren't you going to town hall?" Evelyn called after him.

"Eventually."

He could only imagine what urgent matter the mayor wanted to talk to him about. Probably the shop at the bottom of the hill—and its owner—had finally caught the attention of town leaders. Easing into his desk chair, Blaine ached from the sleepless night and the sexual marathon. The last thing he felt like dealing with right now was a verbal spar-a-thon with the pain-in-the-ass mayor.

Evelyn came to the door. "He's on the phone again. He knows you're here."

Blaine groaned and ran his fingers through his unruly hair. At their last meeting, the mayor had made a comment about Blaine's hair that he'd pretended not to hear. He hadn't gotten around to cutting it and didn't want to hear about that, either.

"Fine," he said. "I'm going. Tell him I just left."

As he drove his department-issued SUV up the hill to town hall, he practiced the deep-breathing techniques the counselor had taught him in the aftermath of the Eden debacle. In through the nose. Hold it. Out through the mouth. Repeat. Usually the breathing helped to calm him, but as he parked in front of the redbrick building that housed the town offices, Blaine was still agitated. Not the best frame of mind in which to meet with one's boss, he thought, as he climbed the stairs and headed for the mayor's outer office, waving at the town clerk on the way by.

"Why, hello there, Chief Taylor," said Mona, the mayor's sixty-something executive assistant. She batted her false eyelashes at him as she did every time she saw him. "So nice to see you, as always."

Blaine flashed his most charming smile, having learned long ago that the best way to get in good with the boss was to get in good with his assistant. "You're looking lovely as usual, Miss Mona."

"Oh well," she said, blushing. "I bet you say that to all the girls."

"Are you doing something different with your hair?"

Her plump face lifted into a dazzling smile. "I had foils! They're so expensive. Do you have any idea—"

"Mona!" The mayor's bellow had her smile falling to a frown. "Send him in here right now!"

Blaine winked and shrugged on his way past, earning another furious blush from Mona. Inside the office, he glanced at the bald, red-faced, portly lump named Chet Upton. It was not for nothing that they called him Uppity Upton at the public safety building. His glance at Blaine's hair was followed by a scowl.

"I need you to deal with the situation at the bottom of the hill," the mayor said without preamble. "She's causing a public menace, parading around half naked, not to mention she's making a mockery of our decency laws."

As Upton's face took on an unhealthy purplish tinge, Blaine hoped he wouldn't need his CPR skills before this meeting was over.

"She's already caused an accident down there, and I witnessed her naughty-nurse routine yesterday."

A flash of anger all but blinded Blaine. Even though he knew he had no right to feel possessive, he hated the thought of other men, especially Upton, ogling her luscious curves. He put the anger aside to be dealt with later. "Wearing a costume is against the law? Since when?"

"Calling it a costume is actually generous. It was tiny scraps of fabric that barely covered the good stuff."

Blaine's hand curled into a fist, and it was all he could do to keep from punching the lusty look off the mayor's face. "I'm surprised a happily married man such as yourself would look so closely at another woman's tiny scraps."

Upton sputtered. "Any healthy, red-blooded man would take a gander when a woman who looks like she does is prancing around barely dressed in public! Now, get down there and make it stop."

"No," Blaine said.

"No?"

"She's not doing anything wrong. The council approved her application and gave her the right to open her business. I'm here to uphold the law, not harass hardworking, law-abiding citizens."

His face still a startling shade of magenta, Upton sat back in his big chair and studied Blaine. "Do you know this girl?"

"I've met her."

"And?"

"And what?"

"What's so great about her that you're willing to stand here and *defy your boss* to defend her?"

Careful, Blaine thought. "I'd say the same thing about any other citizen who wasn't doing anything wrong."

After a long, pregnant pause, the mayor said, "Since you refuse to take action, I'll place the matter on the council's docket for the meeting on Monday. Perhaps they should reconsider her application. Until then, you make sure there're no more accidents down there, or else."

"Or else, what?"

"Or else you might be looking for a new job."

Blaine placed both hands flat on the big mahogany desk and leaned forward. "Don't you dare threaten me, Upton. I've worked my ass off for this town for two years. I haven't taken so much as a long weekend off, let alone a vacation. And don't tell me how to do my job. If you don't like how I'm doing it, say the word, and you'll see my tail-lights heading for the ferry."

The mayor's mouth hung open. "Now, wait a minute. I never said—"

"That's exactly what you said."

Blaine spun around and headed for the outer office. As he winked at Mona, the mayor got in one last bellow.

"Get a haircut!"

TIFFANY WAS ALONE in the shop when the bells jangled on the front door. Since she figured it was Patty returning from lunch, she didn't bother to look up from the checkbook register that refused to reconcile.

"Um, excuse me," a small voice said.

Tiffany's head snapped up. A customer! A real, live customer! Blaine didn't count. His visit had been a mission of mercy.

"I'm sorry!" Tiffany rounded the counter to greet the frumpy older woman. "Welcome!"

As the woman took a long look around the store, her rosy cheeks grew rosier. "I think I'm in the wrong place. Someone said this was a gift shop."

"Oh, you're in the right place. We sell all sorts of gifts. What do you have in mind?"

The woman zeroed in on a rack of racy nightgowns and took a step back. "I don't think—"

"Wait." Tiffany tried to keep the desperation out of her voice. "If you tell me something about the person the gift is for, perhaps I have just the thing."

"Well, um..."

"You know," Tiffany said with a warm smile, "I forgot to introduce myself. Where're my manners? I'm Tiffany Sturgil."

The older woman hesitated before she took Tiffany's outstretched hand. "Verna Upton."

Tiffany's mouth fell open. "As in Mrs. Mayor Upton?"

"The one and only."

"Oh, well, why didn't you say so? How lucky am I to have the first lady of Gansett Island in my humble shop?"

Tiffany realized this was the single most important customer she'd ever have. Winning her over would go a long way toward bringing others in.

Verna released a nervous titter of laughter. "You don't have to refer to me as the first lady. Just Verna will be fine."

"All right, Just Verna it is. What can you tell me about this friend of yours?"

"She thinks her husband is having an affair," Verna blurted out in a rush of words, as if she was afraid she'd lose her nerve if she didn't say it fast.

"What makes her think that?"

"She said the spark has gone out of their marriage, and now she's concerned he's found someone else."

Her heart thumping with nervous excitement, Tiffany recalled one of the sayings from her favorite self-help book: nothing ventured, nothing gained. She reached for the other woman's hand and took the plunge. "May I ask you something that's absolutely none of my business, Just Verna?"

Verna smiled at the nickname. "Of course."

"Are we talking about your friend, or are we talking about you?"

Verna's face flushed to scarlet. "Me," she said softly.

"Honey," Tiffany said, slipping an arm around her, "you've come to *exactly* the right place."

ELATED BY THE SUCCESSFUL, productive second day at the shop and tingling with anticipation about the night ahead, Tiffany grabbed the bag Blaine had left with her and was locking the front door when Jim appeared out of the shadows.

"What do you think you're doing?" he asked in a low growl.

Startled, Tiffany dropped the shopping bag, and objects scattered at their feet. Burning with mortification, she squat to quickly refill the bag, but she wasn't quick enough.

He held up the vibrator. "Is this the kind of trash you're selling in your little porn shop?"

Tiffany snatched it out of his hand and put it in the bag. "It's *not* a porn shop, and don't you dare come to *my* place of business and then report that I violated the restraining order you insisted on. Where's my daughter?"

"With my parents. They and everyone else in this town are talking about what a fool you're making of yourself parading around half naked in broad daylight. You're acting like a common tramp, and I won't have it."

As she listened to the vitriol spewing from the face she'd once found so handsome and arresting, Tiffany realized she didn't love him anymore. The discovery made her giddy. He no longer had any power over her. If he hadn't been standing right there, she might've danced a little jig of joy.

She held the shopping bag close to her. While she didn't love him anymore, she certainly didn't want him seeing the other items in Blaine's bag of tricks. "What won't you have?"

"You. This." He gestured angrily toward the store. "I won't have my wife prancing around half naked in the town where I'm trying to build my practice. You're doing this to embarrass me."

"Have you forgotten that you *divorced* me after I worked like a dog to put you through law school? So that, and the papers I finally received yesterday, make me your *ex*-wife, and give you no right to tell me what to do. And P.S., you ought to stop in sometime. I might be able to help with your little *problem*." She glanced down at his crotch. "In the bedroom."

His eyes narrowed, a sign he was about to blow. "What the hell are you talking about?"

"I never had any idea what I was missing. But now that I've got something to compare you to, I gotta say, your technique could use some fine-tuning." She patted his face. "Don't worry, though. It's nothing that can't be fixed."

Batting her hand away, he leaned in close to her. "I'm going to do everything in my power to make sure you're bounced out of here, so don't get too comfortable."

"Give it your best shot," Tiffany said with more bravado than she felt.

"Oh, I plan to, and until then, see if you can keep your clothes on in public."

She forced a careless smile even though her heart pounded. "Now what fun would that be?"

"You won't be so flippant when I shut down your smut shop."

"As interesting as this conversation has been, Jim, I have somewhere far more exciting to be. So if you'd please get out of my way, I'd like to get to my car."

Rather than move, though, Jim dug in.

For the first time since she'd met him in high school, Tiffany was a tiny bit afraid that he might be angry enough to strike her. "I asked you to get out of my way."

He leveled a furious stare at her before he finally stepped aside. "This isn't over, Tiffany."

"Yes, it is. You saw to that. Now go away and leave me alone." She brushed past him and fumbled with her keys but finally managed to get into her car. Her hands shook and her stomach ached, but not because of the ugly exchange with her ex-husband. No, it was the threat to her fledgling business that had rocked her. Jim cared more about what others thought of him than he did about anything else. She didn't doubt he had the wherewithal to put her out of business before she even got started.

She had expected some people in the town to disapprove, but she hadn't expected anyone, least of all her ex-husband, to try to shut her down, especially after the town had approved her business application. Despite her bravado in the face of his threats, he had scared her. Right when all her energy was needed to get her business up and running, now she'd have to face off again with him, too. The idea of it exhausted her. Jim was a lawyer with significant resources at his disposal. What chance did she have against such a formidable foe? Especially one who had a law degree in his arsenal that *she'd* paid for?

By the time she got home, the earlier excitement and anticipation for her night with Blaine had turned to nervous despair. She poured a glass of wine and dropped into the single chair in her spacious living room. Sitting in the dark, she tried to figure out when, exactly, the man she'd once loved with all her heart had come to hate her enough to want to see her and her business ruined. It had happened, she supposed, right around the time he'd finished school and they'd returned to the island. He hadn't needed her anymore and had shoved her aside to focus on his career.

Giving in to exhaustion, Tiffany closed her eyes and rested her head against the back of the chair.

THAT'S where Blaine found her when he arrived after his shift. He was so intent on getting upstairs that he almost missed her sitting in the lonely living room chair. Stopping short, he studied her for a long, indecisive moment. Something must've happened. Otherwise, she'd be exactly where he'd told her to be. Earlier, she'd seemed excited by his directions. Had she suffered a change of heart in the ensuing hours? Or had something else happened?

It occurred to him that he had two choices: wake her up to find out what was wrong or quietly leave with her none the wiser that he'd ever been there. The Blaine who had vowed to avoid projects like the plague should take option B and get the hell out of there. The Blaine who'd been moved by this woman, both in bed and out, squatted, rested his arms on her legs and leaned in to kiss her awake.

She came to with a gasp, her eyes widening at the sight of him.

"Hey," he said softly.

"Oh. Hi." She rubbed her eyes. "What time is it?"

"Eleven thirty."

She moaned. "I can't believe I fell asleep when I knew you were coming, and I was supposed to…"

Blaine smiled at the way she lowered her eyes in embarrassment when she recalled his directions. Could she be any cuter? "What's wrong?"

"Nothing, why?"

"I figured something must be wrong if you're down here rather than in bed waiting for me."

"It's nothing." She started to get up. "Just give me a couple of minutes."

He told himself to let her go. He was here to have sex with her, not start a relationship. What did it matter to him if she was upset about something? Except it did matter. He could tell himself a thousand times not to get involved, not to make her problems his problems. While he'd like to think he'd learned from his mistakes, none of his past disasters had changed who he was deep inside. So rather than let her go, he slid his arms under her, picked her up and turned to sit in the chair with her on his lap.

Right away, the scent of strawberries filled his senses and fired his desires. But he forced his thoughts away from the need that strummed through him whenever she was close to him and focused on finding out what had upset her.

She looked at him with eyes gone wide with surprise at the unexpected move. She'd probably expected him to carry her off to bed. "You don't have to—"

"What happened?"

"It's nothing. Really."

"Tell me anyway."

She sighed and relaxed into his embrace. "Jim."

Every muscle in Blaine's body tensed at the mention of her ex-husband. "What about him?"

"He came by the store."

"And?"

Was she upset about seeing Jim again? Feeling guilty about what they'd done the night before? Did she want to reconcile with that lowlife? Was that what she was going to say? A stab of disappointment caught him off guard. Sure, he didn't want to get mired in another messy relationship, but he didn't want to see her back with a scumbag who didn't deserve her, either.

"He's going to do everything in his power to shut down my 'smut' shop."

Relieved that her dismay had nothing to do with reconciling with Jim, Blaine didn't think this was the best time to tell her the mayor planned to add her and her shop to the town council's upcoming agenda. There'd be time for that later. "There's nothing he can do, Tiffany. You're there legally and have the same right to make a living in this town as he does."

"He's resourceful. If there's a way to put me out of business, he'll find it."

"He's probably annoyed that you're getting on with your life without him and not sitting home feeling sorry for yourself. I'm sure that's what he's most upset about." Blaine had grown up with Jim Sturgil, and in Jim's world, *everything* was about Jim.

"He's mostly mad about my advertising strategies."

"I'm not wild about them myself."

"Because of the accident, I know. But that wasn't my fault."

"Not just because of that."

She glanced at him. "What do you mean?"

His fingers, which had been flirting with the hem of her top, slipped beneath to caress her back. "I hate the idea of anyone else seeing what I get to see."

Her lips pursed into an O that he found adorable. "It's the best way to show people what's for sale in the store."

"I don't like it," he said, his lips teasing the sensitive spot below her ear.

"You don't?"

Was she intentionally squirming on his lap? He wouldn't put it past her.

"Not one bit. In fact, the next time I see you out there 'advertising,' I'll have no choice but to punish you."

His hand moved from her back to her backside, a not-so-subtle warning of what her punishment might include.

A shiver rippled through Tiffany's body. "You wouldn't."

"Oh no?" He spanked her lightly but firmly, drawing a gasp from her. "Want to try me?"

This time when she pressed against his erection, he had no doubt she'd done it on purpose.

"I know you're used to people doing what you tell them to because you carry a gun and wear a badge, but no one tells me what to do. Not anymore."

While he was proud of her for standing up for herself—something he was certain she hadn't done very often during her marriage—he still didn't want her showing off her curves in public. "You've been warned."

"So have you," she retorted.

Blaine smiled at her sauciness and then captured her fresh mouth in a searing kiss designed to show her who was boss. But of course she turned the tables on him by giving as good as she got. By the time he drew back from her, he had to call this round a draw.

"Go upstairs," he said in a firm tone that left no room for argument. "Put on the outfit I bought for you and lie on your bed. Set the ceiling fan to high."

She swallowed hard. "Anything else?"

"You know how I want your legs."

With a dainty move of her tongue, she wet her lips. "Apart?"

Blaine ran his hand up the inside of her leg and pressed his fingers to her heated core, drawing a moan from her. He loved that she was so responsive to his touch. "As far apart as they'll go." Patting her bottom, he urged her up and off his lap. "Hurry."

She grabbed the bag from the shop and sauntered up the stairs, appearing to take her own sweet time. With desire beating through him and heating his blood, Blaine forced himself out of the chair and crossed the room to the small bar set up in the corner. He poured a shot of whiskey, downed it in one swallow and felt it burn its way through him.

For the first time in a long time, he found himself thinking of Eden and the nightmare he'd endured at her hands. He'd discovered far too late that she used people to get what she wanted and then discarded them when she'd sucked them dry in every possible way. He hadn't known Tiffany long, but he already knew she was made of much better stuff than that. She didn't have a user bone in her body. He'd discovered that despite the tough outer shell she showed the world, inside she was made of softer, more compassionate stuff, the kind of stuff a man could fall in love with rather easily if he wasn't careful.

Blaine poured a second shot and took it with him when he returned to the chair. He consumed this one more slowly, reminding himself all the while that he'd embarked on a sexual affair with an attractive woman. That didn't mean he had to solve all her problems or turn into an emotional wreck over her. This was about one thing and one thing only: sex. He glanced at the stairs. Knowing she was up there, spread out and ready for him to feast on, made his dick throb painfully.

As he downed the last of his drink and stood up to go to her, he thought of her earlier distress and chose to ignore the equally painful throb in his chest. Nothing good had ever come of that.

WEARING the black sheer bustier that barely covered the tips of her nipples, Tiffany lay on the bed with her legs spread wide. Her thighs trembled from anticipation and the effect the swirling air from above was having on her exposed flesh. On the verge of her first-ever ceiling-fan-induced orgasm, Tiffany squirmed against the tug of the thong, trying to exert more pressure where she needed it most without involving her hands. She wondered how much longer he planned to make her wait. If his goal was to get her hot and ready for whatever he had in mind, she'd arrived at that destination ten minutes ago. Hell, who was she kidding? She'd been hot and ready from the second she'd woken up to his kiss.

The apple-scented candles she'd lit flickered, and the light breeze filtering in through the open windows only added to her heightened sense of awareness. Her body hummed with tension and desire as she waited for him.

Jim hadn't appreciated sexy underwear. *"It's going to end up on the floor anyway,"* he would say, *"so what's the point?"* The point, she was finding, as the bustier abraded her aroused nipples, was more about the way it made *her* feel: sexy, desirable, wanted. Whatever it did for her partner was secondary.

Blaine appeared at the door and took in the scene before him. At the sight of him in the candlelight, her breath caught in her throat. He was, by far, the sexiest man she'd ever known, and the naked desire on his face, desire for *her*, nearly took her over the precipice she'd been clinging to.

Unbuttoning his uniform shirt, he crossed the room to her.

The trembling in Tiffany's legs intensified as he took his gaze on a lazy journey from the straining nipples he could probably see through the sheer fabric to her quivering belly and smoldering center.

He shrugged the shirt from his shoulders, and she licked her lips at the sight of his muscular chest.

"Are you wet?" he asked gruffly.

"Yes."

"How wet?"

"Very."

He stood by the side of the bed looking down at her, the huge bulge in his pants the only indication that he was equally aroused. "You'd better check, just to be sure."

Mortified by the idea of touching herself while he watched, she hesitated.

"Do it."

Now her hand was trembling, too, as she skimmed her fingertips over her belly and under the waistband of the thong. Her fingers slid through the slippery dampness between her legs.

"Stroke yourself. I want to watch you come."

One part of her was shocked by his frank talk. The other part was hugely turned on. "I *can't*. Not with you watching."

"Yes, you can."

Tiffany closed her eyes and tried to forget he was there, watching her. Under the satiny thong, she moved her fingers back and forth over the tight, tingling bud.

"Push your fingers inside," he said, his breathing sounding choppy.

She bit her lip and did as he requested.

"Farther. Mmm, that's it. Use your other hand on your breast. Roll the nipple between your fingers." He paused, waiting for her to follow his instructions. "Now look at me."

Tiffany did as he directed and imploded, the climax streaking through her like lightning, leaving her quivering with the need for more.

CHAPTER 6

She opened her eyes to find him still standing next to the bed, but he'd removed his pants and was stroking his straining erection. Tiffany held out her arms to him and sighed with satisfaction when his body covered hers. For the longest time, he lay there without moving, holding her close to him, infusing her with his warmth and an odd sense of comfort.

"That was the sexiest thing I've ever seen," he said gruffly.

"Was it?"

"Mmm. Do you like it when I tell you what to do?"

"I shouldn't, but it makes me feel all..."

"What?"

"Hot. Insanely hot."

"You are insanely hot, and there's nothing wrong with enjoying a little domination in bed. It doesn't make you any less of an independent woman in the rest of your life."

"I'm glad to hear you say that." She ran her fingers through his hair. "What do you want me to do next?"

Blaine smiled at the coy look she gave him and reached for the cuffs on the bedside table. Dangling them above her, he said, "Raise your arms over your head."

Before she did what he asked, she ran her hands over his smooth back and down to cup his firm rear end, drawing a gasp from him. Then she slowly raised her arms over her head, which lowered the top of the bustier.

Blaine's eyes were fixed on her breasts, watching intently as they broke free of the tight confines of the garment. Bending his head to ravish each nipple, he seemed to have forgotten the cuffs.

Tiffany floated on a cloud of sensation so intense it took her breath away, her entire focus on the hot mouth tugging and sucking on her breast. Since he had her firmly pinned to the bed, she couldn't move to satisfy the reawakened ache between her legs. The sweet torture seemed to go on forever, until she was certain she'd go mad. She tried to reach for him and found her hands locked to the headboard. When had he managed to do that, and how had she failed to notice?

Tiffany had never been so transported in the midst of lovemaking, and the realization was both unsettling and exciting at the same time. She tested the restraints and experienced a stab of fear at how tight they were.

"Hey," he said, his voice penetrating the fog. "Look at me."

She forced herself to focus on his handsome face.

"Are you okay with this?"

Even though she wasn't quite sure, she nodded.

"Do you trust me?"

She wet her lips. "Yes."

"I'll never hurt you. Not in here or out there." He nodded to the world outside their bedroom hideaway. "Believe me?"

"I want to."

He bent his head to press a sweet, undemanding kiss to her lips. "You can believe me, Tiff."

Her heart ached with longing. She had no illusions that this was anything more than a fling between two consenting adults. But his softly spoken words made her wish for more. So much more.

"Have you decided on a safe word?"

"Will I really need one?"

The idea of it made her legs tremble.

He nodded.

She took a deep breath, knowing it was decision time. Either she put a stop to this now or jumped off the cliff into the unknown. Looking up at him, she found him focused on her, waiting patiently even as his erection pulsated against her belly. As she studied him, she realized that even though she didn't know him very well, she trusted him. Every time they'd been together, he'd put her needs ahead of his own. He'd cared for her in ways she hadn't often experienced.

"Naughty," she said after a long pause.

He smiled. "I like it." Resting his forehead on hers, he said, "I want you to use it. If you feel the slightest bit uncomfortable, say it, okay?"

She nodded. "What's your safe word?"

His brows furrowed. "Will I need one?"

"You never know."

"All right, then," he said. "In that case... Nice."

Tiffany laughed. "Somehow I think your idea of safe and mine are two very different things."

His smile faded a bit. "I doubt that."

"You're safe with me, too, Blaine. I'd never hurt you, either."

"Thank you. You don't know how much that means to me." His lips left a trail of heat and dampness from her neck to her breasts. "Have you ever been cuffed before?"

"Only that one time with Jim, which, as you know, was a complete disaster."

"Mmm." His lips vibrated against her nipple. "How about we create a new memory? A good one this time."

"I'm all for forgetting that incident entirely."

"Let's see what we can do."

As he feasted on her breasts, he unhooked the bustier and tossed it aside, leaving her in just the skimpy thong. He kissed her everywhere, dipping his tongue into her belly button and nibbling on her hipbones. Tiffany was shocked by the sensations zinging through her as he discovered new erogenous zones. Every time she tugged at the cuffs, yearning to touch him, the bindings reminded her she was totally at his mercy.

The pang of fear that accompanied the discovery ratcheted up her desire to levels she'd never before experienced. She'd never truly understood the lure of the cuffs—until now.

Blaine removed her thong and urged her legs farther apart.

Tiffany felt like a total wanton, shackled to the bed and spread open for him.

He reached for the vibrator. Turning it on, he took it on the same sensuous journey his mouth had taken, over her breasts to her belly and below. She lifted her hips, begging him to focus on the place that needed his attention most.

After teasing her with fleeting passes, he pressed the vibrator to her clitoris at the same instant he pushed two fingers into her. The combination overwhelmed her as the climax hovered just out of her reach. And then he brushed the smaller arm over her back entrance, and she came so suddenly that it caught her by surprise, taking her right out of the room to somewhere she'd never been before.

When she returned to herself, her hands had been released and he was hovering over her, dropping soft kisses on her face and lips.

"Okay?" he asked.

When she nodded, he turned her over and ran his tongue along the ridges of her spine. He raised her to her knees, rolled on a condom and pressed his erection into her wetness.

Tiffany gasped from the burn of his large member stretching her.

He gripped her hips and worked his way in a little at a time until he was fully sheathed in her. After giving her a moment to adjust, he began to move.

"Touch yourself," he growled in her ear as he kept up a relentless rhythm.

With all her muscles quivering, she reached down to where they were joined.

Blaine drove into her just as she touched herself, sending them both into an explosive climax that went on for what seemed like forever. Just when Tiffany thought it was over, he pressed into her again and started another wave.

By the time they collapsed into a pile on the bed, she was sweating and tingling from head to toe. Behind her, he released a long deep breath. The air around them was heavy with the scent of apples, his sandalwood cologne and sex. He settled in close to her, slipping his arm around her to draw her tighter against him.

Tiffany sighed with contentment as Blaine's lips moved softly from her shoulder to her neck.

"That was amazing," he whispered, sending goose bumps dancing down her left side.

"Mmm."

"What'd you think of the toy?"

"The screaming orgasm didn't say it all?"

He laughed and cupped her breast, rolling her nipple between his fingers.

"And the cuffs?"

"I liked them, too. In fact, I'm looking forward to returning the favor as soon as I can move again."

"Is that so?"

"Mmm-hmm."

They were quiet for a long time before he said, "I need to tell you something."

Tiffany, who'd been on her way to a nice doze, was suddenly wide awake and on full alert. Did anything good ever come of those words? "What?"

"Turn over."

Filled with apprehension, she turned to face him. "You're not married, are you?"

She couldn't believe she hadn't thought to ask that before now.

Startled, he stared at her. "Of course not."

"Sorry. I didn't mean to insult you. I've gotten used to thinking the worst of people lately."

"With good reason." Blaine ran his fingers through her hair and then down her back. "I had a meeting with the mayor today."

"On a Sunday?"

"With Race Week starting tomorrow, everyone was working today, even the mayor."

"That's funny. His wife came into the shop."

"She did?" He seemed shocked to hear that.

"Uh-huh."

"What was she doing there?"

"I can't talk about it. It's very important that I maintain my customers' privacy. What did the mayor want?"

"He's concerned about the shop and the accident that occurred in front."

A pang of fear settled in her belly. "The town council approved my application."

"He's putting the matter on the council's agenda for Monday."

"What matter?"

"I'm not sure, exactly."

"Why did he tell you this?"

"He wanted me to cite you for indecency."

Tiffany tugged herself free of his embrace and sat up, gripping the sheet under her arms.

Blaine rested his hand on her leg and looked up at her. "I refused to do it."

"You did?"

He nodded. "I told him I won't harass you."

"Didn't that make him mad? With you?"

Blaine shrugged. "A little."

When she realized he'd gone to bat for her, her insides got all soft and squishy. "I don't want you jeopardizing your job for me."

He tugged at the sheet playfully. "So I should've cited you?"

Despite this new worry, Tiffany forced a smile. "Was I breaking the law?"

"Not technically."

"What does that mean? Not technically?"

"Come on, Tiff. You know how the people in this town can be. They're not going to put up with a sexy woman prancing around in her underwear."

"They're not or *you're* not?"

"Don't twist my words. It creates a traffic hazard on the town's main road. I won't be able to ignore that forever."

"How is it my fault that people aren't paying attention to their driving?"

"I believe we've already had this argument," he said yawning.

"And you still haven't answered my question."

"It's a distraction. *You're* a distraction. Any man in his right mind is going to take his eyes off the road to get a better look at you."

"I supposed you expect me to be complimented by that."

"You're beautiful, Tiffany. You have to know that."

Her heart skipped a crazy beat. "You really think so?"

Blaine reached for her and brought her back into his embrace. "Yeah, I really think so. But you might want to cut out the 'advertising' until after the council meeting."

"You're probably right," she said. "But if I don't advertise, how will anyone know what I'm selling in the store?"

"Oh, they'll know, honey," he said, laughing. "Believe me. They'll know."

HIS RINGING CELL phone woke Evan out of a sound sleep the next morning. "What?" he growled.

"Hey, it's Mac."

His older brother sounded chipper and wide awake.

"What the hell time is it?"

"Seven ten."

"You'd better have a very good reason for calling so early."

"I do. I need some help today. Dad and Luke are both off-island, so I'm alone at the marina. Can you give me a few hours?"

Evan bit back a moan. After the awkward dinner with Grace's parents, he'd been awake for hours trying to decide if her not telling her parents about him was a bigger problem than he'd thought.

"Ev? Are you there?"

"I'm here. I'll be there shortly."

"Great, thanks," Mac said.

Grace turned over in bed and curled up to Evan. "Everything okay?"

"Yeah. Mac needs some help at the marina today."

He kissed her forehead and got up to grab a shower and shave. When he emerged from the bathroom a few minutes later, she had a travel mug with coffee waiting for him. He put on shorts and a T-shirt, all the while trying to think of what he should say to her. Everything between them had been so good, and even though he understood why she'd done it, he couldn't help being hurt that she'd kept their relationship a secret from her parents.

"Thank you," he said when she handed him the mug.

"Are you okay?" she asked, perceptive as always.

"I'm fine, why?"

"You've been a little…distant since dinner."

"Because we only had sex once last night, I'm distant now?" The words came out sharper than he'd intended, causing her smile to dim. "Sorry. I didn't mean to say that."

"If something is wrong, I wish you'd talk to me about it."

"Nothing is wrong." He took the mug and kissed her. "See you tonight."

The unusually awkward exchange stayed with him as he walked the short distance to the marina at North Harbor. About halfway there, he realized he'd forgotten to tell her he loved her. Hell, she'd forgotten, too, and they never forgot that.

The morning at the marina passed with a flurry of activity as boats began to arrive for Gansett Island's annual Race Week festivities. It was well after one before Evan and Mac had things under control and headed for the restaurant to grab lunch.

"Thanks for the help this morning," Mac said over bowls of clam chowder and a basket of clam cakes.

"No problem."

"You're quiet today. Everything okay?"

Evan shrugged and focused on his chowder as he debated whether he wanted to air his troubles to his happily married brother.

"How are things at the studio?"

"Coming along. The space is almost ready, and the equipment will be here next week."

"I still can't believe we're going to have a recording studio on the island."

"Neither can I. It's all thanks to Ned's financial support, and I finally heard that my friend Josh is going to take me up on my offer. You can't have a recording studio without a first-rate sound engineer, so all the pieces are falling into place."

"That's awesome. So why do you look so messed up? And don't say it's nothing. I know you better than that."

Evan put down his spoon and wiped his mouth. "Is it weird that Grace and I have been together since last fall and she hadn't said a word about me to her parents?"

"How do you know that?"

"Because I met them yesterday when they came over to surprise her. The surprise was on me—and them."

"What did she say?"

"I guess their relationship is sort of dysfunctional, but I wonder..."

"About?"

"Do you think maybe she's ashamed to be shacked up with a loser who doesn't have a real job?"

"You're not a loser, Evan. You had a tough break with your record company going belly up. You're rebounding with the studio."

"But maybe that's why she didn't tell them, because we have no idea how the studio will do. She probably doesn't want them to know she's living with a guy who's barely employed."

"I'm sure that has nothing to do with it. It's not like you're leaching off her. You're paying your own way."

Evan fiddled with his spoon as he contemplated what Mac had said.

"You need to talk to her. Ask her if that has anything to do with why she didn't tell them."

"Part of me doesn't want to know."

"It probably has nothing to do with you, Ev."

"She said it didn't, but still... I wonder."

"You won't know if you don't ask her."

Stephanie, their brother Grant's fiancée, came rushing into the restaurant looking frazzled. "Oh, hey, guys. How's the chowder?"

She looked so different since she'd decided to grow her red hair longer. Evan was so used to her spikes that he almost didn't recognize her.

"As good as always," Mac said. "What're you doing here?"

"Checking on things and doing the food order for next week."

"How long can you continue to run this place while you're trying to get your own restaurant open?"

"Are you complaining?"

"Not at all," Mac said. "I'm only reminding you that we're more than happy to hire a new manager if need be."

"No need. I've got it covered."

"If you're sure..."

"I'm sure. You'll be at the opening?"

"Wouldn't miss it," Mac said.

Evan nodded in agreement.

"See you then."

As Stephanie walked away, Kara Ballard came in. She was running the new launch service in the Salt Pond, delivering boaters from the anchorage to McCarthy's. Waving to Mac and Evan, she ordered lunch and then came to say hello while she waited for her food.

"How's it going, Kara?" Mac asked.

She wore a Ballard's Boat Builders ball cap with her shoulder-length honey-colored ponytail pulled through the back of the hat. "Great. Business is really picking up with the boats arriving for Race Week."

"The pond will be wall-to-wall by the weekend," Mac said.

Kara started to say something but faltered. "Damn it. What's he doing here *again*?"

Evan turned to look at who she was talking about and saw his brother Grant's friend, Dan Torrington, coming into the restaurant. Tall with dark hair and a dimpled smile, he wore a pink dress shirt rolled up over his forearms, white Bermuda shorts and loafers. You could take the lawyer out of LA, but apparently, you couldn't take the LA out of the lawyer. His idea of casual looked ridiculously out of place at ultracasual McCarthy's Marina, but he didn't seem to care as he zeroed in on Kara.

"I've got to go." Kara grabbed her lunch and headed for the exit.

"Hey, what's your rush?" Dan asked as he followed her.

"What's up with those two?" Evan asked his brother.

"Not sure, but he seems to stop by every day at some point or another."

"She didn't seem too happy to see him."

"Enough about them," Mac said. "What're you going to do about Grace?"

"I have no idea."

"You could start by talking to her."

Evan grimaced. "Do I have to?"

"Evan..."

"I know, I know. We've had it kind of easy up to now. I'm not sure how I'm supposed to deal with this."

"Everyone has bumps," Mac said.

"You and Maddie make it look awfully easy."

"Most of the time it is, but we have our issues, too. We got into it last night because she's thinking about spending time with her dead-beat dad so he'll give her mother the divorce."

"And you're opposed to that?"

"Hell, yes, I'm opposed to it. The guy left them thirty years ago and then he comes back acting like he has rights. Do you know that after he left, she sat in the window of their apartment for weeks and watched all the ferries arrive, hoping he'd change his mind and come back?"

"Jeez."

"She was *five*. Five years old! What right does he have to come back now and get her hopes up?"

"None."

"Exactly. That's my point. Except he won't give her mother a divorce until Maddie spends some time with him."

"So she's doing it for her mom."

"Yes, but at what cost to her, you know?"

"I can see why you're upset about it." Evan thought about it for a minute. "What if you went with her? Then you could make sure he didn't say or do anything to hurt her."

"I offered that, but she wants to do it alone, which is what we argued about." Mac sat back in his seat and crossed his arms. "I hate fighting with her. It screws me all up."

"I'm sure she knows you're worried about her getting hurt and that your intentions are good."

Mac shrugged. "I guess." He gathered up the trash onto their tray and stood. "I'd better get back to work. I can handle things here this afternoon. Thanks for the help this morning."

"Any time."

"Let me know how it goes with Grace."

"Likewise. With Maddie."

As Evan walked up the hill on the way back to the pharmacy, he thought about Grace and the blissful months they'd spent together. Nothing could've prepared him for what it was like to care more about someone else than he did about himself. He'd thought she felt the same way about him, but now he wasn't so sure.

The thought of broaching the subject with her made his stomach knot with anxiety, but he needed to know for sure that the reason she hadn't told her parents about him wasn't because of his employment situation. He only hoped his need to know wouldn't cause trouble between them. He'd do anything to avoid that.

CHAPTER 7

W*hy won't he take the hint and go away,* Kara wondered, as she ate her lunch as fast as she could, wanting to get back on the water and away from the annoyance named Dan Torrington. He'd found an excuse to stop by the marina every day for the two weeks the launch service had been open for business.

"Nice day," he said from the dock.

She was sitting at the helm of the launch. "Uh-huh."

The boat bobbed in the chop from a passing dinghy, making her feel nauseated after shot gunning the lunch she'd planned to enjoy during a leisurely break that he'd ruined with his presence. Most of the time, she ignored him, but today he ventured down the ramp to the floating dock that housed the launch.

"So how does this work?"

"How does what work?"

"The launch service."

Wasn't it rather obvious? "Ah, we give people rides to and from their boats."

"If someone wanted to go along for the ride, how much would that cost?"

"A ride to where?"

"Wherever you're going when you leave here."

"We don't do that. You have to be going somewhere to come for the ride."

He puzzled over that for a minute. "Isn't the goal of this venture to make money?"

Kara hoped her scowl answered for her.

"If I'm willing to pay…say…twenty dollars to ride along, you'd say no to that?"

"If you have money to burn, you should give it to charity."

His lips quirked with amusement, highlighting very appealing dimples. Kara hated herself for finding them appealing. She knew his type. Nothing good came from spending time with guys who thought they were entitled to take anything they wanted. She'd learned that lesson the hard way.

"It's a nice day. I'd like to take a boat ride. You have a boat. Are you sure we can't negotiate a compromise?"

His use of lawyer speak didn't help his case, not that he needed to know that. "Ask Mr. McCarthy if you can borrow his boat." Kara gestured to the pristine Chris-Craft that Luke Harris had lovingly restored.

"Since I don't know the first thing about how to run a powerboat, he'd be crazy to let me borrow his. Besides, I heard he's off-island today. Something about his brother the judge getting an award from the state bar association. Mrs. McCarthy, Shane, Owen, Laura and baby Holden went, too."

He was certainly well informed on island gossip. "Who's minding the store at the Surf?" she asked, and then instantly regretted the question, because her goal was to get rid of him, not to continue the conversation.

"Owen's mom." He squatted to bring himself to her eye level. The scent of his expensive cologne invaded her senses, making her want to lean forward to get a better sniff. "Will you take me for a ride?"

"If I do, will you go away and leave me alone?"

Damn those dimples. "For now."

"Fine. Get in, but don't talk to me when I'm working."

"Yes, ma'am." He scrambled on board and slid precariously when the bottoms of his fancy shoes made contact with the boat's deck. "*Whoa.*"

"Those aren't exactly boat shoes," she said, laughing at the faces he made as he barely saved himself from pitching over the other side and into the water.

He handed her a twenty and took a seat on the bench in the aft portion of the boat.

Kara had expected him to sit near her and was slightly disappointed when he didn't. *Knock it off,* she thought. *What do you care where he sits?*

He rested his arms on the back rail and stretched out his long legs. They were nice legs with dark hair. Not too much dark hair. Just the right amount.

When she realized she was staring at his legs, she forced her gaze off him and out to the busy harbor. Why did she have to react to him the way she had since the night she'd met him at Luke's house last fall? Every time he came around, she felt edgy and off-kilter, the way she had when Matt—

No. Do not go there. Do not think about him. Do not.

As much as she never wanted to think about her ex-boyfriend again, she couldn't help but draw comparisons between two handsome, successful attorneys who walked around like they owned every room they stepped into, as if they were entitled to take whatever they wanted and discard that which they didn't. She'd already been discarded once and had no desire to let that happen again.

"How do you like living on the island?" he asked after a long stretch of silence.

Kara had never wished more for customers to give her something else to do besides talk to Dan Torrington. "What's not to like?"

"I couldn't agree more. I love it here. It's so quiet and peaceful compared to what I'm used to."

"Anything is quiet and peaceful compared to LA."

Damn it, she'd made him smile again. She had to watch out for that. Those damned dimples popped up with no warning and distracted her from her mission to get rid of him.

"Not all of LA is frenetic and crazy. It has its charming areas, too."

"I'll have to take your word for that."

"Ever been there?"

She shook her head.

"You should come out some time. I'll show you the nice parts you don't get to see on TV."

God, he was so much like Matt. He didn't look anything like Matt, but his entire act was right out of Matt's manifesto. Effortless charm and that whole aw-shucks-I-have-no-idea-I'm-ridiculously-hot thing were their trademarks. She'd been sucked in once before by that routine, and it wasn't about to happen again, no matter how appealing she might find Dan.

Kara reached into her bag and pulled out the book she'd started the night before—anything to distract her from giving too much thought to why he'd decided to fixate on her. She thought he'd have something to say about her burying her nose in a book, but he sat quietly, taking in the scenery and adding to his already impressive tan. Not that she was watching him or anything. No, she was reading and enjoying the story. Or she had been, until she realized she'd read the same sentence for the fourth time.

Since she refused to let him know how distracting he was, she continued to pretend to read for at least ten more minutes before a customer finally showed up.

Thank goodness!

"Trouble you for a ride?" the man asked.

He too was young and handsome, but he didn't have dimples, and he didn't make Kara feel anxious or on guard the way Dan did.

"Sure thing. Hop aboard." When he was settled, she said, "Where to?"

He pointed to the northeastern corner of the pond.

Kara tossed off the lines and backed the launch out of the slip, using a combination of throttle and rudder to turn the boat in a tight area. Out of the corner of her eye, she saw Dan watching with interest and what might've been admiration. She told herself she wasn't showing off for him. Of course she wasn't. Why would she show off in front of a man who annoyed her and who she was determined to resist, even if he was often quite irresistible?

On the way through the anchorage, she chatted with the boat owner about the upcoming Gansett Island Race Week activities, the weather, the sailing conditions, her favorite restaurant on the island, and the small New York town where the man lived.

As they got closer to his navy-blue sailboat, Kara made a wide turn and brought the launch right in next to the boat, reaching for a stanchion to hold her boat in close enough for the man to disembark.

"Thanks a lot for the ride."

He's actually quite cute, she thought.

"Hope to see you again before I leave."

"Good luck with the races."

"Thanks."

As they pulled away, she took another call on the shipboard radio and headed to the other side of the pond to make a pickup. About halfway there, an air horn sounded, leading her to another pickup.

By the time they returned to McCarthy's thirty minutes later, Kara had a full boat and people waiting for her on the dock. She loved spending her days on the water and meeting new people, but mostly she loved being anywhere other than Bar Harbor.

Absorbed in collecting money, greeting new customers and helping others off the boat, she almost forgot about Dan.

Almost.

Preparing to leave on another run, she ventured a glance at him. "Are you getting off?"

"I understand each trip is three fifty, so if my math is correct, I've paid for three round trips."

"You've paid for two. Three would cost twenty-*one* dollars."

Very deliberately, he reached for his wallet, pulled out a one-dollar bill and asked the other passengers to hand it to her.

Kara took the dollar bill from the man sitting closest to her, realizing everyone on the boat was intrigued by the exchange.

Great. That only made her dislike him more than she already did.

She made the mistake of looking at him, which was how she caught the smirk he directed her way. Biting back a growl of frustration, she released the lines and backed the launch out of the slip.

GRACE HAD JUST GOTTEN home from the pharmacy when someone knocked on the door. Since she'd seen her parents off on the first ferry that morning, she knew it wasn't them. She swung open the door to find Seamus O'Grady on her deck.

Grace pushed open the screen door to let him in. "Hi, Seamus. This is a nice surprise."

"Hello, Gracie, my love."

His thick Irish brogue always gave her a shiver of delight, not that she'd ever admit that to Evan, who was terribly jealous of the attention Seamus paid her. He gave her a hug and a kiss on the cheek.

"What brings you by?" she asked as she led him into the loft.

"I need a friend," Seamus said with a deep sigh that had Grace spinning around to study his handsome face. The Seamus she knew was never down or dour. He was perpetually cheerful and unfailingly charming. His auburn hair was unusually mussed and his jaw scruffy with whiskers. On closer inspection, she noticed his green eyes were rimmed with red, as if he hadn't been sleeping well.

"What is it?" She took his hand and led him to sit with her on the sofa. "What's wrong?"

"I've done an awful thing."

Grace eyed him warily. "What awful thing have you done?"

"I've fallen in love, Gracie."

She stared at him, astounded. "You've... With *whom*?"

"Someone who doesn't want me."

"Wait a minute... Are you trying to tell me that you've met a woman—a living, breathing, woman—who doesn't *want* you? What the heck is wrong with her?"

That brought a faint smile to his lips. "Ahhh, Gracie. You're good for what ails me, love." He squeezed her hand. "There's nothing wrong with her. That's the problem. Everything about her is right. She's all I think about. Sometimes I wonder if it's possible to expire from the agony of wanting something I can't have."

The despair she heard in his voice touched her deeply. How would it feel, she wondered, to want Evan with every fiber of her being, but not be able to have him? It didn't bear thinking about. "Why can't you have her, Seamus?"

"She's older than me and can't get past that obstacle. Among other things."

"What other things?"

"I work for her son, for one thing."

Grace's eyes bugged out of her head. "*Joe's mother?*"

"Shhh, don't say it out loud. *No one* knows. No one."

"Start at the beginning. Don't leave anything out. I want every detail."

"I probably shouldn't..."

"You'll feel better when you tell someone. Tell me. Maybe I can help."

"You can't tell anyone, Grace. I mean it. Not even Evan."

"I won't breathe a word of it. I promise."

As Seamus haltingly conveyed the story of the unforgettable night he'd spent with Carolina Cantrell, his voice was soft and his eyes full of emotion that made Grace ache for him.

"You haven't seen her since Luke and Syd's wedding?"

He shook his head. "It's killing me, Gracie," he whispered. "I can't sleep or eat. I can't think about anything but how much I want to be with her."

"Have you thought about telling her that?"

"What good would it do? She looks at me and sees a man roughly the same age as her son. I'll always be a couple of years older than him, so that puts me permanently off limits to her."

"That's so ridiculous! If two people love each other and want to be together, what difference does it make if there're a few years between them?"

"If only her thinking was like yours, we wouldn't be needing this conversation. What am I to do? Now that I know she's out there and what it's like to hold her and kiss her and..." He dropped his head into his hands. "I can't bear it. Sometimes I think I'll have to give notice and leave this job I love, because it's too hard to know she's right here on the island but as far away from me as it's possible to get."

Grace put a comforting arm around him, which was how Evan found them a few minutes later when he came in the door, stopping short at the sight of Grace and Seamus sitting close to each other on the sofa.

His smile faded, and his eyes went dark with fury. "What's going on?"

"Seamus is having a rough day and needed a friend," Grace said, shooting her boyfriend a warning look.

"Is that so?"

"I should go," Seamus said, straightening.

"Don't go," she said. "Stay and have dinner. You'll feel better to be around friends."

"You're a love, Gracie, but there's only one thing that'll make me feel better, and it's not to be." He kissed her forehead, squeezed her hand and released it. "Thanks for listening."

"Any time. Will you let me know how you're doing?"

"I will, love." To Evan, he said, "Thank you for letting me borrow your lady for a few minutes. You're a lucky man."

"I know."

This was said in a tone Grace had never heard before from Evan. Her stomach began to hurt.

"You folks have a nice evening," Seamus said on his way out the door.

"Do you want to tell me what that was all about?" Evan said when they were alone.

Clearly, he was spoiling for a fight, and Grace was in no mood. "Not really."

"How would you feel if you came home and found me snuggled up to some woman?"

"We weren't *snuggled up*, and he's not some guy. He's my *friend*."

"A friend who's interested in being much more than friends with you."

"You are such an idiot sometimes, you know that?"

"What the hell is that supposed to mean?"

"He was here talking to me about a woman he's in *love* with, and her name is *not* Grace."

"Oh."

"You can apologize any time now."

"Apologize for what?"

"Implying I was fooling around on you."

"I didn't imply that."

She raised an eyebrow to let him know she wasn't buying his crap. "Oh no? What would you call it then?"

"I don't know." He flopped down on the sofa. "Why are we fighting?"

"Because you acted like a jealous fool when I had a male friend here."

"Sorry," he muttered. "I overreacted, but that guy pushes my buttons with all his Irish blarney."

"I think you mean Irish *charm*," Grace said, sitting next to him and reaching for his hand.

Evan scowled at her.

"Are you still mad at me?"

He shrugged.

She moved so she was straddling him and framed his face with her hands. "Look at me." When she had his full attention, she bent her head to kiss him. "I love *you*, you silly, jealous fool. Only you."

"I know."

"Do you?"

"Of course I do."

"Then why do you still look all funny in the face?"

"I've been thinking..."

"About?"

"I want to understand why you didn't tell your parents about me, and I think I get it, but still..."

"Still what?"

"Is it because my job situation is up in the air right now? Is that why you didn't tell them? Because I'd understand if that was why—"

"No! That has nothing to do with it. I swear to you, I didn't tell them because of stuff between us. Not because of anything to do with you."

"What did they say when I wasn't around?"

Grace diverted her gaze. "Not much."

He cuffed her chin. "Liar."

"It doesn't matter, Evan. They've got nothing to do with us. That's why I didn't tell them."

"They're your parents, honey. You can't disregard them like they mean nothing to you."

"You heard what my mother said the other day about there being other ways to lose weight besides going under the knife?"

"Yes, and I didn't think she needed to say that."

"It's the least of what she's had to say since I decided to have the surgery. Who knows better than she did how I tried every other possible way to lose weight before I opted for surgery? Yet she made me feel like a loser for doing it. She's *still* making me feel like a loser."

"Probably because she doesn't have the courage to do it herself."

"You think so?"

Nodding, he said, "She's probably jealous that it worked so well for you and you've lost so much weight. How long has she been heavy?"

"Always."

"There you have it. You've managed to successfully address a situation she's grappled with her whole life."

"I suppose you're right. Sometimes I wonder why she can't be happy for me, you know?"

"Don't let her—or anyone—take away from your accomplishments, Grace. You have a lot to be proud of."

"Do you know what I'm proudest of?"

"What's that?"

"You and me. We've come a long way in the last eight months. I can't imagine my life without you in it."

"Same here, honey. You're the best thing to ever happen to me, and I'm sorry I overreacted about Seamus being here."

Grace leaned her forehead against his. "And I'm sorry I didn't tell my parents about us."

"It's okay. I have a few thoughts about how you can make it up to me."

"What kind of thoughts?"

As Evan whispered in her ear, Grace felt her face get hot. Would she ever get used to the blunt way he talked about highly personal matters?

"Right now?" she asked.

"Uh-huh." He twirled a strand of her hair around his finger. "Unless, of course, you're not really all that sorry. In that case—"

"Oh, shut up."

"Shut me up."

"Gladly."

As Grace poured all the love she felt for him into a kiss for the ages, she counted herself lucky to have found the one who was meant for her. Seamus's woes made her extra grateful that Evan loved her as much as she loved him.

SINCE HE HAD an hour before he was due to captain the next boat, Seamus took his time walking back to town. He felt bad about the scene at Grace's place. It was no secret that Evan McCarthy didn't like him or the attention he paid to Grace. But they were just friends. Gracie's heart belonged to Evan, and Seamus's heart belonged to a woman who didn't want him. What a fine mess this had turned out to be.

His boss, Joe Cantrell, was due in on the boat coming now from the mainland, and when he had the chance to talk to Joe, Seamus was seriously considering resigning as manager of the Gansett Island Ferry Company. Joe would have the summer to find a replacement before he and his wife returned to Ohio for her third year of veterinary school. Seamus hated to leave Joe in the lurch, especially with Joe's wife Janey due to deliver their first child soon, but it was too hard to be on the island a few miles from the woman he loved but light years from her.

The fact that the woman he loved was Joe's mother only made things more complicated in some ways and simpler in others. He couldn't pine for the mother of his boss, and he couldn't have her because she couldn't handle the age difference between them—or her son's potential disapproval.

If this were happening to someone else, Seamus might've found it comical. But there was nothing funny about this kind of heartache. For the first time in the more than two decades since he'd come to this country as a teenager, he was thinking about going home to Ireland. Nothing here made sense anymore. One night with Carolina Cantrell and his entire life had careened off course like a car that lost a wheel on a curve.

He had a posse of sisters, so he'd certainly witnessed heartbreak before. However, he'd learned it was an entirely different experience when it happened to you. It sucked the life out of a body. It kept you awake at night, thinking about what might've been. It made it nearly impossible to enjoy any of the simple pleasures that used to make life worth living. Food didn't taste the way it used to. Even his favorite Irish whiskey didn't appeal. He was a wreck, and he couldn't continue to function in this condition. Thus his conclusion that the only possible solution was to leave.

Walking with his hands in his pockets and his head down, Seamus approached the ferry landing deep in thought, which was why he didn't see the object of his desire leaning against a piling waiting for the boat that carried her son and daughter-in-law to arrive. He didn't notice her until he was nearly on top of her, until it was far too late to avoid seeing her for the first time since Luke and Syd's Christmas Eve wedding.

When he recovered his senses, he realized she looked even better than she had then. She'd cut her hair, and the shoulder-length style suited her. Ironically, it made her look younger. For some reason, it pleased him that she seemed as stunned to see him as he was to see her.

"I, um..." she said. "Joe and Janey..."

"They're on the boat." He nodded to the ferry approaching the breakwater. "Word tends to get out when the boss makes a car reservation."

"Yes, I suppose it does."

"How've you been, Caro?"

"Oh, well, busy. You know."

"Did you make that?" he asked of the elaborately beaded necklace she wore.

When her fingers covered the beads, he noticed a slight tremble. "This? Yes, a while ago."

"It's quite lovely."

He kept his gaze fixed on her face as he said the words, and watched, mesmerized, as a flush crept into her cheeks.

Realizing he was getting to her, he decided to try one last time. Maybe the passage of months had had the same effect on her. "I've missed you, Caro."

As he watched her process what he'd said, she glanced at the ferry and smiled.

Realizing the moment between them had passed, Seamus followed her gaze and saw Joe at the aft controls, guiding the ferry into port. "Just like riding a bike," he said with feigned lightness.

"He's been a natural from the time he was a young boy. My father went on and on about how he'd had to show him only once, and he got it. He just got it."

Listening to her talk about her son, Seamus finally got it, too. She'd made her choice a long time ago. She'd chosen her son, and nothing he said or did would ever change her mind. It was time to cut his losses and move on.

"Nice to see you, Carolina."

"Nice to see you, too."

"Have a lovely visit with your son and his wife."

Walking away from her, Seamus ached worse than he had before, if that was possible. But at least he had his answer now. He knew what he had to do.

CHAPTER 8

Hoping to run into Tiffany, Blaine accepted Mac's invitation to stop by for dinner. The family was welcoming Joe and Janey home for the summer with a cookout that included all the McCarthys, Ned and Francine, and Joe's mom, Carolina. When he arrived, Blaine couldn't believe how disappointed he was to learn that Tiffany had stayed home because Ashleigh had a stomachache. He'd been so looking forward to seeing her after his shift.

"Are you enjoying the last few weeks of sanity?" Big Mac asked Blaine over burgers on Mac's deck.

Because he was on duty, Blaine was nursing a soda rather than the beer he'd prefer. "It seems to start earlier and earlier every year," he said. "We've already had a couple of kids with alcohol poisoning on the town beach and lots of open container citations. Wyatt, my newest patrolman, stumbled upon a couple of kids getting busy out at the bluffs two nights ago. I think he's scarred for life."

Big Mac roared with laughter. "Poor kid."

"He may as well get used to it. Such is police work on Gansett Island."

Joe came over to shake hands with Blaine. "Good to see you, buddy."

"You, too. Congrats on the impending arrival."

Joe glanced over at his pretty blonde wife, who was hugely pregnant and clearly miserable. "Not sure how we'll survive three more months. Janey's already had enough."

Blaine's radio crackled with a call from dispatch. He winced when he heard the address. "I've got to run," he said to Mac, who was tending the grill. "Thanks for the burger."

"Any time. Come back later if you're free."

"Will do. Thanks, Mac."

"See you later, Blaine."

He bounded down the stairs from the deck to his SUV. When he reached the main road, he flipped on the lights and siren while calling for backup. Daisy Babson's neighbors had called the police. Again. Anxious to get to town before Daisy's abusive boyfriend could hurt her, Blaine pressed the accelerator to the floor.

By the time he pulled up to Daisy's rundown place in town, the neighbors were standing outside, listening to the fight rage on inside.

"Back it up, folks," Blaine said. "Give us some room." The sound of breaking glass had him taking the stairs two at a time. He pounded on the door. "Police. Open up." More crashing of glass and other items, along with thumping and a muffled cry. "Open up, or I'll take the door down."

Wyatt pulled up in his cruiser, and Blaine gestured for him to hurry. When the patrolman was in position on the other side of the door, Blaine drew his weapon and kicked in the door. Daisy was huddled on the floor, surrounded by broken glass, her face and hands bleeding. She looked up at him with big, haunted gray eyes. Her boyfriend, Truck—aptly nicknamed because he was built like one—held a glass vase over his head. His tattooed biceps bulged from the effort to restrain his rage. If he brought that vase down on petite Daisy, he'd kill her.

Blaine had gotten there just in time. "Freeze, Truck. Don't even think about it."

Truck seemed almost surprised to see him, which was no surprise to Blaine. The big man was known for his meth-fueled rages, and Blaine had been trying to get Daisy to leave the abusive relationship for as long as he'd been chief of police.

"Get the fuck outta here." Truck's eyes were red and crazed. "You got no business here."

"When you're beating up your girlfriend and destroying her home, I got business here."

"I ain't beating her up. She's getting mouthy with me—again."

"Put down the vase slowly," Blaine said. "I want your hands on the back of your head. You know the routine." To Wyatt, he said, "Call the paramedics for her."

By the time the ambulance arrived a couple of minutes later, Blaine had Truck cuffed and on his way to the station with Wyatt. After ensuring none of her bones were broken, Blaine lifted Daisy free of the glass. She was so tiny he barely had to strain to pick her up.

"I'm sorry," she said, wiping tears from her cheeks. "I promised you I wouldn't let him in again, but he was so sweet and so sorry. I'm such a fool."

"Don't apologize, Daisy. I know you love the big lug. For some reason."

"Not anymore, I don't. He broke my grandma's china." A new flood of tears wet her bruised and battered face. "That was all I had left of her, and now it's gone."

"We can help you get free of him, Daisy, but you have to want to. The next time he comes around looking to kiss and make up, you have to be strong."

"I know," she said with more conviction than he'd ever heard from her. "No more of this. No more of him."

Blaine carried her out to the paramedics and shielded her face from the gathered crowd of neighbors. He deposited her gently on a gurney.

"Hi, Daisy," Libby, one of the volunteer paramedics, said.

She, too, had been here before.

"Hi, Libby."

"Show me where it hurts," she said as she got busy cleaning the cuts on Daisy's hands and face.

Blaine stepped out of the ambulance and placed a call to David Lawrence. "Sorry to bother you at home, Doc, but I've got Daisy Babson on the way to the clinic."

"Again?" David asked.

"Afraid so. She's going to need some stitches."

"I'll be right there."

"Thanks." Blaine ducked his head inside the ambulance. "Is there anyone you want me to call for you, Daisy?"

She shook her head, as she always did.

"Are you sure?"

"I don't want anyone to know."

"I have to file a report, and I'll need you to appear in court."

She'd done it before, so she knew the drill. "I know."

"I'd hate to see you go through this alone. You have friends."

"Fine. Okay. Call Maddie."

"McCarthy?"

Daisy nodded.

"I'll have her meet you at the clinic."

"Thank you."

Her quiet dignity got to him every time. He'd gleaned a few facts about her past that had led him to believe that she didn't think she could do any better than a violent drug addict named Truck.

"Everything will be okay, Daisy," Blaine said. "We'll take good care of you. Don't worry."

"That's right, Daisy," Libby said as she discreetly produced a tissue Daisy used to dry her tears.

"You all are so nice to me when you must want to shake me for taking him back. Again."

"We don't want to shake you," Blaine said. "We want you to be safe, and we want to help you make that happen."

"Let's get you to the clinic," Libby said.

"I'll follow you." Blaine stepped back from the ambulance and closed the doors, rapping on the side of the vehicle when the doors were secured. "Show's over," he said to the neighbors.

He took a minute to secure Daisy's front door as best he could and placed a call to Mac.

"Hey, didn't I just see you?" Mac said when he answered.

"Yes, you did, but duty called, and I need to borrow your wife."

"What for?"

"A friend of hers had a bit of trouble tonight and could use some support."

"Which friend?"

"Daisy from the hotel."

"Oh jeez. Truck again?"

"Yep."

"Shit."

"Could you ask Maddie to meet us at the clinic? Daisy is pretty busted up, and she's in for a long night."

"She'll be right over."

"Could your folks stay with the kids for a bit?"

"Sure. What else do you need?"

"We broke down Daisy's door to get in there before he killed her."

"Say no more. I'll get it fixed."

"Thanks, Mac. Appreciate the help."

"Happy to do it. Daisy is so sweet. I can't imagine how anyone could raise a hand to her in anger."

"I can't imagine how any guy takes his frustrations out on a woman. Happens far more often than you think, even here in paradise. Thanks again for the help."

"Any time."

Blaine called for a patrol officer to stay at Daisy's house until Mac got there. As soon as the officer arrived, Blaine gave him his instructions and headed for the clinic. On the way, he left a message for Tiffany to let her know he had to cancel their plans for later. This was going to be a long night.

. . .

DAVID ARRIVED at the clinic a few minutes ahead of the ambulance and set up an exam room with bandages and a suture kit. Hearing Daisy had been beat up again had him agitated and furious at her so-called boyfriend. After the last time, he thought he'd been successful in convincing her to leave the abusive relationship.

While he hated to hear that Daisy had been hurt again, he was glad to have something to take his mind off the fact that his ex-fiancée was back on the island with her devoted husband and due to deliver their first child in a couple of months. He'd heard from Victoria, the nurse practitioner/midwife he worked with, that Janey planned to have the baby in Ohio, which was a huge relief.

Ever since he'd saved Mac and Maddie's baby Hailey when she'd arrived blue and not breathing during a tropical storm, the McCarthys had been a lot less chilly to him than they were after Janey had caught him in bed with another woman. But it wasn't like they were all bosom buddies or anything. Luckily, the island was big enough that he didn't cross paths with them very often, and when he did, everyone was cordial enough.

Sometimes he still couldn't believe how stupid he'd been. The Hodgkin's diagnosis had thrown him for a loop and led him to do a few things he regretted—nothing more so than sleeping with one of his chemo nurses. It had taken him a long time to get back on his feet after he lost Janey and to stop thinking about her every minute of every day. Now she was back on the island after another year of vet school, happily married to Joe and about to have the baby that should've been David's. They'd planned to have four of them and had even chosen names—David Jr., Anna, Henry and Ella. He wondered what Janey planned to name her child and then told himself it didn't matter. It had nothing to do with him.

They would've been married nearly a year now. He could've had everything he'd ever wanted, but he'd blown it, and there was nothing he could do but get on with his life and hope that maybe someday he'd again feel for another woman the way he'd once felt for Janey before he'd screwed it all up.

The arrival of the ambulance interrupted his brooding.

"Hi, Daisy," he said when Libby rolled the gurney into the exam room.

Daisy was pale from blood loss and looked a little shocky.

Libby listed her injuries, which included lacerations to her face and hands and a bruised knee. She had applied bandages to the cuts and stanched the bleeding.

"Hi, Doctor David," Daisy said. "Sorry to make you come in after hours."

"It's no problem. I'd hoped we wouldn't see you in here again."

"I know," she said, lowering her gaze. "I made the huge mistake of giving him another chance. I won't do that again."

David had heard it all before, four times since he'd taken over the island's medical practice when Cal Maitland went home to Texas after his mother had a stroke.

"I hope not, Daisy. I worry about him seriously injuring you one of these days. You've been lucky up to now to only have bumps and bruises. This time, you're cut. What's next?"

When she broke down into heartbroken sobs, David wanted to shoot himself for being so blunt. "I'm sorry," he said, wrapping an arm around her fragile shoulders.

She leaned into his embrace, startling him and firing all his protective instincts. He wished he could go teach Truck Howard a lesson or two about what happened to bullies who picked on women. But that wouldn't do anything to help Daisy.

As he ran a comforting hand over her soft, silky hair, he let her cry it out until her sobs became hiccups. "Feel better?"

She shook her head. "I feel so stupid," she whispered.

"Don't. All you can do is learn from it and go on. Blaine will make sure Truck can't come near you again."

"He…he…hurt me."

"I know. We'll get your cuts cleaned up and stitched, and you'll be good as new in no time."

"Not just there."

David pulled back from her so he could see her face. "Where?"

She lowered her gaze, and her face heated with embarrassment.

"Did he rape you, Daisy?"

"He tried. I fought him, but he still hurt me."

"Do you want me to call in Victoria to examine you?"

"No! You. I want you to do it."

"Are you sure you wouldn't rather have a woman?"

"I know you. I trust you."

Her softly spoken words went straight to his heart. "I'll take care of you. Don't worry. Let me have a word with Blaine. I'll be right back, okay?"

She nodded.

"Can you change into a gown for me?"

"Yes."

"Take it nice and slow. You've lost quite a bit of blood, so you're apt to be light-headed."

"I'm okay."

Leaving her to change, David stepped out of the cubicle and went to the waiting room to find Blaine.

"She said he tried to rape her."

Blaine shook his head in disbelief. "Any sign of sexual assault?"

"I haven't examined her yet. She said she thwarted him, but not before he hurt her."

"We can charge him with attempted sexual assault."

David nodded. "Hopefully, he'll get put away for a good, long stretch, and she'll have a chance to move on without him."

"Let's hope so. I've had just about enough of this guy."

"I hear ya."

"I need photos and swabs."

"I'll do a rape kit, but I'm going to call in Victoria to help. She said she wanted me to do the exam, but I need assistance to do the kit. It'll take a couple of hours, if you have other stuff you need to do in the meantime."

"I've got to get to the station to process Truck, get him charged and call in the state police to transport him."

"I'll call you when we're done."

"Thanks, Doc."

As Blaine turned to leave, Maddie McCarthy came rushing into the clinic. "Blaine! How is she? Can I see her?"

"She's all right. I had to talk her into calling someone, just so you know. She's upset it happened again after we talked her into leaving him."

"I understand."

"Right this way," David said, leading Maddie to the exam room where Daisy waited on the table.

The gown was huge on her, making her look even tinier and more fragile.

Maddie put her arms around Daisy and held her close. "Why didn't you tell me you were back with him, honey?"

"I was embarrassed."

"You haven't done anything wrong."

"I loved a man who hurt me."

"It's okay now." Maddie's voice was soothing and comforting. "We won't let him get anywhere near you again. You're safe. I promise."

"Thanks for coming, Maddie."

"I'm so glad you asked Blaine to call me. You shouldn't be alone."

"You all are so nice. Thank you."

While Maddie comforted Daisy, David placed a quick call to Victoria, who promised to be there shortly to help with the rape kit. While he waited for her to arrive, he removed Daisy's bandages to assess the severity of the cuts on her hands and face. Only one of the lacerations on her hand required sutures. As he prepared for the procedure, he felt Daisy's big gray eyes watching his every move.

"Will it hurt?" she asked.

"Only a little when I numb you up, but then you shouldn't feel a thing. When the numbness wears off, it'll be sore for a few days, but I'll give you something for the pain."

"I won't be able to work."

"I'll cover for you," Maddie said.

"You don't want to do that."

"I wouldn't have offered if I didn't want to, so don't give it another thought."

"Ready for a pinch?" David said as he prepared the shot.

Daisy's entire body went tense.

Maddie held her other hand. "Look at me."

Daisy did as Maddie instructed, wincing at the burn of the shot.

"One more," David said, trying not to be moved by the tears rolling down her face as he pushed the needle into the palm of her hand. "There. That's the worst of it."

"Breathe," Maddie said.

Daisy took a series of deep breaths that restored some of the color to her pale cheeks.

"Daisy, may I have your permission to speak about your care in front of Maddie?" David asked as he applied the first suture.

"Yes, of course."

"I called in Victoria, the nurse practitioner, because we need to do what's called a rape kit. Do you know what that is?"

"Not really," she said haltingly.

"It's the collection of evidence that can be used in court. We'll take photos, swabs and collect any hairs or fluids that might tie Truck to the assault."

Daisy stared at him and then swallowed hard. "You have to take pictures *down there*?"

"If there's bruising or abrasions, we need to document that."

Daisy shook her head. "No. I can't. I can't do that."

"Daisy, honey," Maddie said, "if they can't prove he tried to rape you, he'll get away with it."

"Maddie's right," David said. "The assault charges are serious, especially since he's on parole, but the attempted rape charge will ensure he's put away for a long time."

Maddie brushed Daisy's hair off her face and wiped the other woman's tears with a tissue.

"Will you stay with me while they do it?" Daisy asked Maddie.

"I'll be here every minute. For as long as you need me."

Daisy gripped her friend's hand. "I'm scared."

"There's nothing to be scared of," David said. "I promise we'll be very gentle and do all we can to make sure Truck never hurts you again."

Victoria came into the room and stepped up to Daisy's bedside. "That's right." She rested a hand on Daisy's knee. "It won't be all that different from your annual physical."

"Oh," Daisy said. "Really?"

Victoria nodded. To David, she said, "Are we ready?"

"Whenever you are."

"Okay, honey, let's get this over with," Victoria said as she guided Daisy's feet to the stirrups.

Daisy closed her eyes and gripped Maddie's hand a little tighter.

As Victoria raised Daisy's gown and eased her legs apart, David took in the darkening bruises on her genitals and bit back a curse. He'd make sure Truck Howard paid for what he'd done to her, and then David would have to figure out why the idea of her being hurt made him hurt, too.

TIFFANY RAN into her sister the next morning when they were dropping their kids off for a few hours of summer camp.

"Why do you look like something the cat dragged in?" Tiffany asked Maddie.

"Because I've been up all night."

"How come?"

"Have coffee with me, and I'll tell you." Maddie took her by the hand and dragged her to the South Harbor Diner.

"Um, okay," Tiffany said. "I didn't have to go to work or anything."

"Ten extra minutes won't ruin your day."

"How do you know?"

"Sit," Maddie said, full of big-sister authority.

Tiffany decided to humor her. "Fine. I'm sitting. What now?"

"Rebecca, we'll take a couple of coffees and two egg-white omelets with veggies."

"Coming right up, Maddie."

"How do you know I didn't already eat?" Tiffany asked.

As if she hadn't spoken, Maddie said, "So where have you been the last few days? I can't remember the last time I went so long without talking to you."

"I've been *working*. Remember that?"

Maddie frowned. "Don't razz me about not working. I'm still getting used to being retired. I'm not sure I'm going to like it."

"You deserve the chance to be home with your kids, Maddie. Don't feel guilty about taking that time with them."

"Still, it's weird. I've been working since I was fifteen."

"You have a different job now—the most important job."

"That's what Mac says, too."

"So why were you up all night?"

"You know my friend Daisy from the hotel?"

"Uh-huh. What about her?"

"She had some trouble with her boyfriend last night. I'm sure the police report will be public before the day is out, but he's being charged with assault and attempted sexual assault."

"Oh God, poor Daisy. Is she okay?"

"She will be, but she's sore and achy. I only left her when they gave her something to help her sleep. I needed to get home to feed Hailey before my boobs exploded. David and Victoria are keeping an eye on Daisy, but I'm going back over there after this."

"That's really too bad. She's such a sweet person."

"I know. It's awful." Maddie finished her first cup of coffee and signaled Rebecca for a refill. "So what's up with you? How's the shop doing?"

"Okay."

"Just okay?"

"Could be better, could be worse. I'm not panicking. Yet."

"I'm sure it'll pick up when the season really gets started. Until Race Week, things are kind of slow around here."

"I know." Tiffany fiddled with her spoon, wanting to tell her sister the other big news but also wanting to keep it secret for a while longer. "I got my final divorce papers the other day."

"Oh, wow. Are you okay?"

"Sure," Tiffany said. "I knew they were coming any time now."

Maddie reached out to squeeze her sister's hand. "Still, Tiff."

"I'm fine. Don't worry. I've certainly had plenty of time to prepare myself."

"True." Maddie looked down at her coffee and then at her sister. "So, I wanted to tell you… I've decided to see Dad."

"Really?"

Maddie nodded. "Mac is furious with me about it, but I hate that I'm the only thing standing between Mom and a divorce. I want her to be able to marry Ned."

"Are you sure it's a good idea to see him?"

"Hell, no. I'm sure it's a terrible idea, but I can't bear the idea of him denying her a divorce because of me."

"I understand that. What does Mac say about it?"

"He doesn't want me to get hurt again, and I love him for that."

"I don't blame him for worrying."

"I don't either, but he refuses to understand how hard it is for me to be the one thing standing between my mother and what she wants and deserves after all she's been through."

"Mom is perfectly thrilled to be living with Ned. I don't think a piece of paper is going to change anything for them."

"She hasn't said as much to me, but I think she's still old school enough to be uncomfortable about shacking up without the benefit of marriage."

"Probably," Tiffany conceded. "So when are you going to see him?"

"I left him a message. I'm waiting to hear back and tiptoeing around my husband in the meantime."

"Let me know if you hear from him."

"I will."

"I slept with Blaine."

So much for keeping it secret.

Maddie froze, her eyes widened and her mouth fell open. "*And?*"

"It was awesome. Incredible. Amazing. All those things."

"Oh my God! I'm so happy for you! This is the best news I've heard in ages."

"Don't get all crazy. It's not some great love affair, so don't make it into more than it is."

"Oh, I bet it'll turn out to be more than just sex."

"I wouldn't take that bet. We barely talk to each other."

Maddie fanned her face. "That's so *hot*. You have to give me some details."

"No! No way."

"Come on... It's just me. Spill it."

Tiffany's entire body heated when she thought about Blaine and what they'd done together.

"Whoa, it's so hot it makes you blush when you *think* about it?"

"It was pretty hot," Tiffany conceded.

"You gotta give me something. One little tidbit?"

Tiffany got a reprieve when Rebecca delivered their omelets. Maddie dove in like she hadn't eaten in weeks, while Tiffany picked at hers.

"I haven't forgotten," Maddie said between bites.

"You're a pain in the ass."

"I know."

Tiffany rolled her eyes. "I didn't grill you like this when you got together with Mac."

"That's because you were too busy hating him for being a McCarthy." Maddie poked her fork at Tiffany. "I would've been happy to share the dirty details with you."

"Liar. You never talked to me about that stuff."

"That's because before Mac there wasn't much to talk about." Maddie checked her watch. "I need to get back to the clinic to check on Daisy. Are you going to share or not?"

"Not."

"You should know that Blaine was truly amazing with Daisy last night. He's very good at what he does. The island is lucky to have him."

"That's true."

When Tiffany thought of how he'd defied the mayor on her behalf, her stomach turned and she lost interest in her coffee. What if he lost his job because of her? She couldn't let that happen.

Maddie nudged her out of her thoughts. "You have to tell me *something.*"

"Fine! What do you want to know?"

Maddie propped her chin on her upturned hand. "Oh, I don't know. Something...*scandalous.*"

"How do you know there was anything scandalous?"

"Because you two have been having eye sex for months now. I have no doubt it was scandalous."

"What the hell is 'eye sex'?" Tiffany asked with a laugh.

"Tearing each other's clothes off with your eyes."

Tiffany laughed again at that. "This is all I'm saying, you got me?"

Maddie leaned in closer so she wouldn't miss a word. "Got it. I'm ready. Bring it on."

"He made a ceiling fan into a sex toy."

"*What?* How? How did he do that?"

Tiffany flashed her sister a smug smile and slid out of the booth. "That's for me to know and you to find out."

"That's mean!" Maddie called after her. "And so is stiffing me with the check."

"Breakfast was your idea, not mine," Tiffany replied as she waved to Rebecca and headed for the door. "I'll get it next time."

"I'll hold you to that."

CHAPTER 9

Pleased to have gotten the upper hand with her clever sister, Tiffany enjoyed the view of the ferry landing as she made her way to the shop. The light breeze from the harbor was cool but warmer than it had been only a week ago. Summer was right around the corner, and she couldn't wait. She was about fifteen minutes late to open but doubted anyone would notice. As she got closer to the store, though, she noticed someone waiting on the sidewalk outside and moved a little quicker. She stopped short when she realized it was Blaine.

"You're late," he said in a low growl that made the blood zing through her veins.

Instantly aware of him and the gaze that traveled over every inch of her body and lingered on her breasts, Tiffany fumbled for her keys. "I had breakfast with my sister. Have you been here long?"

"About fifteen minutes. I was hoping you'd show up soon."

Tiffany pushed open the door and propped it open with a wooden doorstopper carved in the shape of a woman's bottom. She had dressed it in a pair of the panties she stocked in the store. "How come?"

"I wanted to see you so I could tell you I'm sorry I had to cancel our plans last night."

"My sister told me what happened—and that you were great."

He shrugged off the compliment.

"How's Daisy?"

"She'll be okay. Eventually."

"And how are you?"

He seemed surprised that she'd asked. "Fine. Just doing my job."

"It must be hard to deal with situations like that."

"It can be, but fortunately it doesn't happen very often around here. It was worse in my old job. I saw a lot of crazy crap."

"Like what?"

He shook his head and advanced toward her, every bit the predatory tiger in pounce mode. "I don't want to talk about that stuff. That's not why I wanted to see you."

Once again, he had her backed up to a counter, clutching the edge as she waited to see what he would do. Her heart raced, and her sex clenched in anticipation, even as a niggling voice in the back of her head took note of the fact that he never wanted to talk about himself or his past.

His fingers dug into her hips, and his chest brushed against her nipples, sending a tingle of sensation darting through her.

"We can't," she said haltingly, failing to convince even herself. "Not here."

He grinned at her, and her stomach went into a free fall. "What do you think is about to happen?"

"With you, I'm never quite sure."

"I like keeping you off balance."

"So I've noticed."

"Does it bother you?" he asked as he pressed his erection against her stomach.

"Do I look bothered?"

"Maybe a little *hot* and bothered."

"Maybe a little."

"Could I have a kiss?"

She shook her head. "I have coffee breath."

"I don't care about that."

"I do."

"I'm craving you. Are you really going to deny me?"

Hearing him say he craved her did funny things to her insides. "One small kiss and that's it."

His smile was positively wolfish as he hauled her in even closer to him and brought his lips down on hers for much more than a "small" kiss. By the time he drew back from her five minutes later, her legs trembled, her nipples stood at attention and her sex was tight with need.

"That was *not* a small kiss."

"It wasn't a small craving." He turned his attention to her neck while his hands kneaded her bottom. "Let's go in the back."

"No," she said, pushing at his muscular chest. "I have to behave at work."

"You're no fun."

His boyish pout was too adorable for words.

She flashed him a saucy smile. "You know that's not true."

"I want to see you later."

"I can't. I have Ashleigh tonight."

"Oh. Okay. Another time, then." He held her close to him for another minute before he released her and stepped back, seeming reluctant to let her go. "I'm off until the day after tomorrow." He reached for a pen on the counter and took her hand, writing a phone number on her palm. "Call me if you have any free time."

Pressing a kiss to her palm, he closed her hand around the number.

Ridiculously charmed, she said, "I will."

"Don't wash the number off your hand."

"Go, will you? I have work to do."

"I'm going. Will you be at Stephanie's opening tomorrow night?"

"Wouldn't miss it."

"I'll see you there, if not before."

Her gaze was fixed on his very appealing rear end as he walked away from her. She wanted to call him back. She liked how she felt when he was around—sexy, desired, excited, on edge... However, she was a bit disappointed that he didn't seem to want to spend time with her if Ashleigh was there, too. Of course, it was probably way too soon for her daughter to meet him, especially since theirs was only a fling. The last thing she needed was more trouble with Jim if he caught wind of Ashleigh spending time with Blaine. She'd prefer to keep their relationship private for as long as possible.

Tiffany took advantage of the quiet morning to catch up on a ton of paperwork. She sent off the rent check to the landlord, hoping she'd be able to pay the rent next month, too. It would be close, but if Race Week turned out the business the way it normally did, she should be okay.

The bells on the door jingled, and in walked Verna Upton, wearing a smile that stretched from ear to ear.

"Just Verna!" Tiffany said. "How are you?"

"I am *divine*, my darling. Simply *divine*."

"I take it Mayor Upton approved of your purchases yesterday."

"You could say that. After he peeled his jaw off the floor and got into the spirit of things, he approved wholeheartedly."

"Excellent!" Tiffany clapped her hands while choking back a gag as an image of the rotund mayor in the all-together danced through her mind. She shook her head to clear away the disturbing image. "I'm so happy for you."

"Honey, I'm going to tell you something rather personal."

Oh, I so wish you wouldn't, Tiffany thought while appearing to hang on Verna's every word.

"We haven't had sex like that since our honeymoon. My Chet was positively ravenous. I'm a little...*sore*...today, but it was *so* worth it."

Tiffany winced and hoped Verna took it as empathy rather than revulsion. "That's wonderful." She gave the older woman a hug.

"It's all because of you and your store."

"That's not true! Your husband reacted to your efforts to be sexy. It was because of *you*."

"Well, maybe so, but you certainly helped me. I need something else for tonight." Verna began browsing through the racks, holding up one slinky outfit after another.

"I'll make you a deal, Verna."

"I'm listening."

"The next outfit is on the house if you tell your friends to come into the store."

"Oh, honey, I've already told *all* my friends they need to get down here. I wouldn't dream of taking anything free from you after what you've done for me."

Tiffany considered what she'd said. "Then maybe you could talk to your husband about taking his complaint about my store off the town council's docket for next week's meeting?"

"Are you kidding me?" Verna's outrage was palpable. "I'll have that taken care of. Don't you worry."

"That'd be great, Verna. Thanks so much. Now, let's figure out what you should wear tonight."

"We probably ought to take care of tomorrow night while I'm here, too."

"Absolutely!"

KNOCKING on the door to the office that used to be his was rather strange for Joe. "Hey, you wanted to see me?"

Seamus O'Grady looked up from the paperwork on the desk and greeted him with a smile. "Come in, Joe. Have a seat."

"How's it going?" Joe asked as he handed Seamus the coffee he'd brought for him.

Seamus held up the cup in thanks. "Better now."

"Everything okay?"

Seamus paused for a second, seeming to choose his words carefully. "No, I'm sorry to say it isn't."

Joe sat up straighter, instantly on alert. Seamus had saved his life the last two years by running the ferry company as well as Joe could've done it himself. Janey had two more years of vet school to go, and Joe was counting on Seamus to keep things running smoothly with the company while they were in Ohio. "What's wrong?"

"Nothing to do with the company. I'm afraid 'tis a personal matter that's made it impossible for me to remain on the island."

"Oh." Joe had no idea what to say to that, but rising desperation had him searching for something, anything he could say to convince his right-hand man to stay awhile longer. "We'll switch things around so you don't have to be over here. You can stay in the office in Point Judith."

"We'd have to hire another captain to make that work."

"Then do it. I can't lose you, Seamus. You've done such a terrific job. I was just telling my mom and Janey last night that I'd be lost without you."

"Aw, Joe, you know how to break a fella's heart, but I'm afraid my mind is made up. I'm giving you my notice now so you'll have the summer to find my replacement." He looked down at the desk and then back at Joe. "And I'm awfully sorry to do this to you right before your young one arrives."

"Do you, ah… Do you want to talk about whatever happened?"

"No, but thanks for asking. Just one of those things, you know?"

After spending most of his adult life in love with a woman he couldn't have, Joe certainly understood "one of those things." He slouched in the chair, absorbing the shock of unexpected news.

"Sorry to take you by surprise. You've been a wonderful boss, and I've truly loved the job."

"There isn't anything I can do to convince you to stay?"

Seamus shook his head. "I've done a lot of thinking about it, and I've come to the conclusion this is the only thing I can do."

"I sure am sorry to lose you."

"Thank you. That means a lot to me. I was hoping I could count on you for a reference."

"Of course. Absolutely."

"I'll do everything I can to help you find a replacement."

"I'd appreciate that." Joe stood and reached out a hand.

Seamus stood to shake hands with Joe. "Thank you again for entrusting your business to me. I've tried to take good care of it."

"You've done a brilliant job." If Joe wasn't mistaken, Seamus was on the verge of tears. If that didn't beat all. Now what was he going to do?

KARA WAS ARRIVING at McCarthy's with a boatload of passengers when she saw Dan Torrington waiting on the main pier with a picnic basket sitting next to him. *Oh, for crying out loud! The guy can't take no for an answer!*

She jammed the boat into reverse, jarring her passengers. "Sorry, folks," she said as she looped the spring line onto a cleat, which brought the launch in snug against the floating dock.

Helping two older people off the boat, she exchanged a few words with each of her customers, hoping the personal touch would be good for business.

All the while, she was acutely aware of Dan watching from the pier. He leaned against a piling as if he hadn't a care in the world. A rich guy like him probably didn't. Then she remembered what he'd told her the night they'd met about an engagement that hadn't worked out. She'd witnessed genuine pain in him then, and she'd thought about that for a long time after.

In him, she'd recognized a fellow traveler. Maybe she ought to give him a break. If only he didn't remind her so much of Matt, right down to the profession they had in common. The last thing Kara needed was another money-grubber who didn't care who he stepped on as he climbed the corporate ladder.

Dan strolled down the ramp to the floating dock and handed her two bills—a twenty and a one. "That buys me three trips, right?"

She reluctantly took the money from him. "Uh-huh."

"Great." He climbed on board and took a seat in the back of the empty launch.

Of all the times for there to be no line of people waiting to get to their boats...

"Hungry?"

"No, thank you."

He unwrapped a turkey sandwich and held out half to her. "You sure?"

As she nodded, her stomach let out the loudest growl she'd ever heard, which made him laugh.

"Liar. Take it. I swear—no strings attached."

"Sure there aren't." Because she was, in fact, starving, she took the sandwich from him and didn't protest when he also handed her a diet Mountain Dew. "How did you know I like Mountain Dew?" She sat on one of the bench seats, taking care to keep her distance from him.

"I pay attention."

The comment unsettled her, so Kara got busy checking what was on the sandwich. "Why do you keep coming around?" she asked as she peeled off a slice of tomato.

"I like the view."

She assumed he meant the view of the Salt Pond, but when she ventured a glance at him, he was looking right at her. "I'm not interested."

"In what?"

"You."

"No, *really*? I never would've figured that out from your frosty demeanor or the way you shoot fire out your eyes every time I'm in the vicinity."

"I don't do that!"

His brow arched above the frame of his Ray Bans. "Um, okay. If you say so." He returned his focus to the sandwich, leaving her to puzzle over whether she really shot fire at him every time he came near.

"Are you going to the shindig at Stephanie's restaurant tomorrow?" he asked.

"I was invited, but I haven't decided if I'm going."

"Why not?"

"I don't really know anyone, except for Mac and Luke and Big Mac."

"You know me. I'll be there."

"That's a good reason to stay away. I wouldn't want to burn down Stephanie's new restaurant by shooting fire at you out my eyes."

He threw his head back and laughed—hard.

Watching him, Kara hated herself for being attracted. She absolutely did not want to be. He was exactly like every other smooth-talking guy who'd never heard the word *no* from a woman. She refused to get sucked into his web. Been there, done that, learned from it—or so she'd thought.

"If you want someone to go with, I'd be happy to pick you up."

"That's not necessary. I'm perfectly capable of going to a party by myself."

"Suit yourself."

"Thank you. I will."

He shivered dramatically. "Getting chilly around here."

"You're free to leave at any time."

"Not until I get the three rides I paid for."

"Don't you work?"

"Yep."

"Yet you have all this free time to hang around and bother me?"

"And here I thought I was *charming* you with my wit and turkey sandwiches."

That drew a reluctant grunt of laughter from her.

"Progress," he said smugly.

Kara scowled at him.

"Ohhh, one step forward, two steps back."

"You need to learn to quit while you're ahead."

"If I'm not mistaken, you like talking to me."

"You are quite mistaken. I was hungry. That's it."

"I bet you get hungry around this time every day."

She sent him her most withering look, which worked on most people. Unfortunately, Dan Torrington wasn't most people. He replied with a goofy grin that was positively adorable. Not that she thought *he* was adorable or anything. His grin was. She'd give him that much.

"If you're supposedly working, why aren't you dressed for work?"

He wore a pink Izod polo that would've looked fruity on a lesser man and khaki cargo shorts. Today he was sporting flip-flops rather than the foolish dress shoes he'd worn yesterday.

"What should I be wearing?"

"A tie, for one thing."

He shuddered. "I hate ties. I only wear them in court."

"You're not like any lawyer I've ever met."

"Thank you." He smiled as if she'd paid him the world's biggest compliment. "I hear that a lot."

"What kind of law do you practice?"

"Lately, I seem to be dabbling in all sorts of things, but I specialize in criminal law."

"There can't be much call for your specialty around here."

"Oh, there isn't. I'll let you in on a badly kept secret. I'm writing a book. That's why I'm here."

"What kind of book?"

"You know, the kind with words and pages."

"Very funny." Mad at herself for being intrigued, Kara took a sip of her soda and tried to decide whether she was curious enough to pursue the line of questioning that was running through her mind. The last thing she wanted was to encourage him to keep coming around.

"It's about some of the cases I've worked on," he said, sparing her the need for further questions.

"Do you know how to write a book?"

"Not really, but I'm figuring it out. This is my first."

"Oh." A host of additional questions popped into her head. She wanted to ask about his writing process, specifics about the cases he was writing about, whether he thought the book would sell to a publisher. But she kept those and all her other questions to herself for fear of encouraging his odd pursuit. What did he even want with her? She was boring compared to the women he must know in LA. Growing up with a posse of brothers, she'd never much concerned herself with fashion or makeup or all the other foolishness most women embraced. As a result, she was a twenty-seven-year-old tomboy and way out of her league with a smooth-talking charmer who could have any woman he wanted. She'd learned not to trust the charming men.

"Why me?" The words were out of her mouth before she could stop them, and she was instantly mortified to realize she'd actually *asked* the question.

Naturally, he was nonplussed by her blatant inquiry. "Why not you?"

"I feel like you're playing some sort of game with me, only I don't know the rules."

Much to her dismay, he slid over to sit right next to her. When he took her hand, sensation darted up her arm and zinged through her bloodstream at lightning speed. *This is so not good*. "I'm not playing games," he said in the most earnestly sincere tone she'd heard yet from him. "I promise."

She tried to pull her hand free, but he only held on tighter. "I don't get you."

"What you see is what you get."

"That is *so* not true."

His low laugh stirred something deep inside her. She discovered in that moment that she rather enjoyed making him laugh. "Now what is *that* supposed to mean?"

"Don't act like you're not all complicated and broody and full of yourself."

"I'll give you full of myself—at times. I'm working on trying to be better about that. But complicated and broody? Not so much. I'm an easygoing kind of guy. I work hard and play hard. I like to have fun. Don't you?"

It'd been such a long time since Kara had done anything that could be called fun. Matt had ruined a lot of things for her. "I guess."

"Oh the *enthusiasm*! You bowl me over, Ms. Ballard."

He shifted their joined hands and linked their fingers. Startled to realize she'd allowed him to hold her hand for several minutes, she tried again to pull free of his grasp.

"Stop," he said. "Just relax, will you? I'm not about to cause you harm."

"You may not intend to."

"What happened to you, honey?"

"Don't call me that. I'm not your honey."

"I think I'd like you to be."

"You never did answer my question." The feel of his warm palm pressed against hers was doing odd things to her nervous system.

"Which one was that?"

"Why me?"

"Because the night I met you at Luke's house... Remember that?"

"Yes," she said, exasperated. Of course she remembered! She'd thought about that night so many times during the long, cold winter in Maine, and she'd thought about him, too, not that she'd *ever* admit that.

"I... You..."

"Articulate, Counselor. Seriously. I'm dazzled."

He laughed again and squeezed her hand. "As soon as I met you, I wanted to know you better. I wanted to know who had hurt you, and I wanted to hurt him on your behalf. I wanted to tell you what happened with my fiancée, and I haven't told anyone."

"You haven't?"

He shook his head. "Only she knows the truth. And one other person."

His entire demeanor changed when he spoke of his ex. Kara wondered if he knew that.

"I wanted to talk to you and be with you and maybe kiss you, if you'd let me," he continued.

As if she'd left the door wide open, he was slipping through her defenses. Amazingly, she wasn't nearly as bothered by that as she probably should've been.

"I'm not interested in being part of a harem," she said, hating how prim and proper she sounded.

"Oh, damn! *Really?* There go all my plans to make you one of the sister wives. Shit."

"Stop," she said, laughing as she bumped his shoulder with hers.

"You should laugh more often. It looks good on you."

Kara hadn't laughed in a very long time. It felt good. "My ex dumped me for my sister," she said. Again, the words tumbled out of her mouth before she could take a moment to consider the implications. What was it about him that made her say things she had no intention of saying?

"*Ouch,*" he said with a grimace.

"Yeah. Ouch."

"Are they still together?"

"Married with a baby on the way."

"Oh, man. That's got to be rough."

"I haven't spoken to either of them in two years."

"Can't say I blame you."

"I thought he was going to ask me to marry him. Instead, he took me out for a nice dinner to tell me he'd fallen in love with my sister. I think he did it in public so I wouldn't make a scene."

"I hope you made one anyway."

Kara recalled throwing her glass of merlot in his face in the middle of one of Bar Harbor's nicer restaurants. The town had buzzed over the incident for months afterward. She hadn't touched a drop of merlot since. "Damn right, I did."

"Good for you," he said with another squeeze of her hand. "I caught my fiancée in bed with my best man two days before the wedding."

"Oh my God!" Without releasing his hand, she turned in her seat so she was looking at him. "What did you do?"

"Made a scene, punched my so-called best friend in the face and thought about kicking him in the junk. I should've. When I think back on that day, that's my biggest regret. Funny, huh?"

Kara smiled. "You so should've done it."

"If I ever run into him again, he'd better hope he's wearing a cup."

That drew a genuine laugh from her.

"You are so very pretty, especially when you smile."

Her smile faded.

"You don't think so?"

"My self-esteem isn't quite what it used to be."

"Let me assure you that any man who'd walk away from you is an idiot."

"You're very smooth with the lines."

"Is that right?"

"Like you didn't know that."

"I want you to go with me to Stephanie's party tomorrow night."

"Why?"

"Because I really like talking to you, and I want to talk to you some more. Very soon. Actually, tomorrow night is a long time from now. What're you doing tonight?"

Kara held up her free hand to stop him. "I'll go with you tomorrow night, but I'm busy tonight." She wasn't really, but she felt the need to regain some control over this rapidly evolving situation.

His smile stretched from ear to ear. "Tell me the truth. Was it the Mountain Dew?"

"It didn't hurt," she conceded.

"Where do you live?"

She pointed to a white building that abutted the marina property.

"Ah, well, that's easy."

"Don't make me sorry I told you that."

"You injure me with your lack of faith in me."

"I'm sure you'll recover in due time."

"I'm not so sure."

"Um, excuse me," a male voice behind them said. "Is the launch running?"

Kara had been so caught up in the conversation she hadn't planned to have that she'd completely forgotten where she was and what she was supposed to be doing. She tugged her hand free and jumped up. "Yes, we are. Come aboard."

CHAPTER 10

Tiffany was alone in the store when the bells rang, alerting her to a potential customer. She hustled from the stockroom and stopped short when she saw Linda McCarthy taking a look around.

"Hi, Linda," Tiffany managed to say, even though her mouth had gone totally dry. "Nice to see you."

Linda raised her arms to hug Tiffany. "I wanted to come in and see your store and congratulate you on starting a business. I surely remember what that is like."

"Kind of stressful," Tiffany said, relieved that this would be a friendly visit from her sister's mother-in-law.

"Do you mind if I poke around a bit?"

"Of course not." Knowing Linda's approval and endorsement could be critical to the success—or failure—of her store, butterflies stormed in Tiffany's stomach. "Let me know if I can help with anything."

"I certainly will. Everything is so pretty." Linda held up a floral silk robe and glanced at the price tag.

Tiffany had to hold herself back from recommending items that might interest her. Maybe, if she got very lucky, Linda wouldn't notice the smaller room behind the beaded curtain. The idea of Linda McCarthy in a room full of dildos and vibrators had Tiffany on the verge of a nervous breakdown.

While keeping half an eye on Linda as she perused the racks, Tiffany sorted a stack of invoices and made note of which ones had to be paid sooner rather than later.

"Could I try this on, Tiffany?" Linda asked, holding up a pink floral silk nightgown and robe.

"Of course. Let me get a fitting room ready for you."

"Would also you mind offering an opinion?" Linda asked almost shyly, which was interesting. Tiffany had never known her to be shy.

"I'd love to."

"Great, thanks." Linda stepped into the dressing room. "Okay," she said a few minutes later. "Here goes nothing." She opened the door tentatively. "What do you think?"

"It looks wonderful on you—and I'm not just saying that because I want you to buy it."

"I quite like it myself." Linda took a closer look in the mirror. "I wonder what my husband would think of it?"

"Venturing a guess here, but I'll bet he approves wholeheartedly."

Linda smiled at Tiffany in the mirror. "I bet he will, too. Sold!"

"I'm so glad you found something you love."

"I do love it."

Linda changed and brought her purchases to the register. As Tiffany was ringing up the sale, Linda pointed to the beaded curtain. "What're you hiding back there?"

"Oh, nothing. Just this. And that."

Linda raised an eyebrow. "This and that, huh? Mind if I take a look?"

Tiffany wanted to die on the spot. "Um, well, ah..."

Linda surprised her by giggling. "Must be some pretty good this and that if your face turns bright red."

"It's pretty good, all right."

As she watched Linda walk over to the curtain, Tiffany's heart pounded.

Linda parted the curtain and took a good long look before glancing back at Tiffany with a scandalized expression on her face. "Oh. My."

"I told you—this and that."

"Where does one begin to know where to start with...items...such as this...and that?"

"I recommend starting simply." Tiffany forced her legs to carry her across the room. "May I?"

Linda stepped aside to admit Tiffany into the room. "By all means."

Tiffany reached for an egg-shaped vibrator and handed it to Linda, all the while telling herself to treat her sister's mother-in-law the way she would any other customer who had questions about her inventory. As long as she kept up that pretense, she might get through this without suffering a stroke.

"And what does this little number do?"

"It vibrates."

"*Oh.*"

Watching Linda McCarthy examine the vibrator from every angle made Tiffany want to giggle like a child, but somehow she managed to maintain her professional demeanor.

"I wouldn't know what to do with this."

Images of what Blaine had done to her with theirs flashed through Tiffany's mind like an X-rated movie. "You place it against your, um, pleasure points."

"I don't know if I could do that."

"Well, you don't have to do it. Your, ah...your husband could do it for you."

"*Oh*. Oh." Linda's face turned bright red this time. "I don't know if he could do it, either."

"I bet he'd love to try."

"You think so?"

"I'd almost guarantee it."

"I'm trying to imagine how I'd broach the subject with him..."

"You could say that you stopped into my shop today, and I talked you into trying something new."

"That'd be one way to introduce the idea."

"I'll tell you what," Tiffany said. "Take that one on the house. If you discover you like it, come back and get another one to try."

"I couldn't do that! You're in business to make money. Not to give things away."

"I'm also in business to help people try new things and to spice up their love lives."

"Not that my love life needs much spicing, but I have to admit I'm curious. I'll take it."

Tiffany smiled all the way to the register, where Linda insisted on paying for the vibrator.

"You're very good at this," Linda said as she accepted the red-striped bag from Tiffany. "I predict you'll be a smashing success."

"That'd be very nice."

"Congratulations on your new venture. I'll be sure to tell my friends they need to stop in and check out what you've got."

"That'd be great. Thank you. I, um, I also want to say that I appreciate how good you've been to my sister. She's quite fond of you, and I can see why, after spending some time with you."

"Thank you, honey. I love her very much. She's made my son so happy."

"They are some kind of happy," Tiffany said wistfully.

She was surprised when Linda reached for her hand. "You'll have your turn one of these days. Don't let what happened with Jim make you bitter about love. You can do better."

"That's nice of you to say."

"Well, I must be off. Thanks again."

"Thank *you*. I appreciate the business."

Linda was almost to the door when she stopped and turned back to Tiffany. "You won't tell anyone what I bought, will you?"

"Absolutely not. It's our secret. But I'd love to know what your hubby has to say about it, if you feel like dishing."

Linda flashed a bright smile. "You got it."

As the bells chimed to announce Linda's departure, Tiffany

clapped her hands and did a little jig. The bells chimed again when Patty came into the store.

"Was that Linda *McCarthy*?" Patty asked, wide-eyed.

"The one and only!"

"And she bought something!"

"You bet she did."

"I'm so happy for you, Tiffany."

"Thanks." Tiffany took a closer look at her assistant, noticing she'd made an effort with her hair, makeup and clothes. "You look so nice."

Patty's face flamed with embarrassment. "I'm trying. Still no boyfriend, though."

"These things take time. It's only been a couple of days since you unveiled the new you."

"I suppose you're right."

"I'll give some thought to who might make a good boyfriend for you."

"You will? Really?"

"Sure. It'll be fun to narrow down some candidates."

"We need to get you a boyfriend, too."

"Don't worry about me," Tiffany said, thinking of Blaine, who was hardly her boyfriend. She wasn't sure what he was, exactly. He defied description. "Let's focus on you first."

"I'm fine with that!" Patty said, making Tiffany laugh.

The bells rang on the door again, and a young woman entered, glancing around the store tentatively.

"I've got it," Tiffany said to Patty. Approaching the woman, who wore a polo shirt with shorts and a ball cap, Tiffany said, "Hi there. May I help you find something?"

"I'm looking for a dress, but this seems to be an underwear store."

"Actually, we have some summer dresses in the back. Could I show you?"

"That'd be great, thanks."

"Have we met?" Tiffany asked as she led the woman to the back of the store. "You look familiar to me."

"You were at Luke and Syd's party last fall, right?"

"Yes! That's it. I'm Tiffany Sturgil, Maddie McCarthy's sister."

"Kara Ballard. I run the new launch service in the Salt Pond."

"It's all coming back to me now." Tiffany gestured to the racks of sundresses that lined the back of the store. "What's the occasion?"

"The opening of Stephanie's restaurant."

"I'm so looking forward to that. Should be a great party."

"I have no idea what to wear."

"You've come to the right place." Tiffany looked through the racks for the dress she thought would best complement Kara's coloring and figure. "How about this?" She held up a red halter dress with exotic flowers on the skirt. "Summery but not too flashy. Something tells me you don't do flash."

"Not really my thing," Kara said with a grin. "But I love that. Could I try it on?"

"Absolutely. Patty, would you please open a dressing room for Kara?"

"You got it, boss."

"I've got the perfect strapless bra that'd work perfectly with this dress." Tiffany glanced at Kara's chest, trying to be subtle.
"Thirty-four D?"

Kara stared at her. "How'd you know that?"

"She knows her breasts," Patty said, making Tiffany and Kara laugh.

While Kara tried on the dress and bra, Tiffany rummaged through the bins of panties looking for a particular thong that would work with the dress and match the bra. She found it and turned as Kara emerged from the dressing room, looking stunning in the red dress.

"Fabulous," Tiffany said.

"Definitely," Patty agreed.

Kara stood in front of the three-way mirror and looked at the dress from all angles. "I have to say I agree. Perfect."

"This would make it perfect," Tiffany said, holding up the silky thong.

Kara eyed the thong with trepidation. "Never gone there."

"Oh, honey, you can't have panty lines with that dress," Tiffany said.

"I suppose you're right. I'll take it all."

"Great!" Tiffany started for the register but caught a glimpse of Kara's expression out of the corner of her eye. "What is it?"

"I, um... I have a date. First one since a bad breakup a couple of years ago. You think he'll like this?"

"Any man with a pulse would like that dress and the way it looks on you."

Kara laughed. "You sure know how to fill a girl with confidence."

"That's my job." Instilling confidence in other women was a highly satisfying part of her new job.

Kara went into the dressing room and emerged a few minutes later with the dress on a hanger.

Tiffany rang up the sale. "Going out with anyone I know?"

"Maybe... Dan Torrington?"

"Oh, I love Dan! He did a great job with my divorce, and I have so much admiration for his career."

"What do you mean?"

"You don't know about him?"

"Not too much beyond the fact that he's an LA lawyer with a healthy ego and a handsome face."

"He is rather handsome, isn't he?"

"Rather."

"Girlfriend, you need to spend some time with Google." Tiffany spun her computer monitor around and pushed the keyboard across the counter. "Have a look."

Kara seemed uncertain for a moment, before she took the bait and typed Dan's name into the browser. Watching her reaction as she read through the results that highlighted Dan's successful career in freeing unjustly incarcerated people made Tiffany smile.

"He never said anything," Kara stammered. "He never said."

"Ought to make for one heck of a book, huh?"

"Yes, I'd imagine so. Wow. I thought I had him all figured out, you know?"

"That's a man for you—just when you think you know him," Tiffany said with a grin as she handed Kara the bag containing her purchases. "I'll see you at the opening."

"Thanks so much for your help."

"My pleasure."

"That ought to be an interesting conversation," Tiffany said to Patty after Kara left.

"I can't believe she'd never heard of him," Patty said. "Even I know who he is."

"I'd like to be a fly on the wall for that date."

"No kidding!" Patty smiled wistfully. "She's so pretty and so lucky to have a date with such a hot guy."

"You'll get your turn. I have no doubt."

"I sure hope you're right."

ON THE WAY out of the gym after a rigorous workout, Blaine stopped to talk to the owner, Billy Simpson, for a few minutes.

"Heard you arrested Truck Henry last night," Billy said. "Some people never learn."

Not wanting to say too much, Blaine nodded in agreement. The arrest was public record, so there was no sense denying it. A reporter from the *Gansett Gazette* had stopped into the station with questions first thing that morning. Blaine had managed to keep Daisy's name out of the report, but everyone knew who Truck had been shacked up with for a while now.

"Is Daisy okay?"

"She will be."

"If you see her, tell her I was asking for her. She's a sweet girl who deserves better than the likes of Truck."

"On that we agree."

"I heard he's retained Jim Sturgil to represent him."

Didn't that figure? "Is that so?"

Billy nodded. "People were talking about it earlier. They were saying how Sturgil would represent the guy who beat up his own mother if there was money in it for him."

Blaine choked back a laugh at that accurate assessment. "Probably so. Gotta run. Take it easy, Billy."

"You, too."

Even though he was off duty, Blaine took the long way home, making a check on "his" island. Anything that happened here was his responsibility, and he never forgot that. He'd arranged for the state police to come over to escort Truck to the mainland for arraignment. Assuming the judge denied bail, Truck would be held at the state prison until his trial. At least he'd be off the island for the time being, and Daisy would have a prayer of putting her life back together.

On the way to his house on the island's north end, Blaine noticed a sign for an estate sale at the former home of Mrs. Ridgeway, one of the island's longest standing and wealthiest citizens who had died the year before. Since he'd always wondered what the inside of the place looked like, he decided to check it out.

He took the long, winding driveway that led to the enormous home, which overlooked the ocean. *What a spot,* he thought, as he got out of the SUV and walked toward the house. A man in a suit greeted him in the portico and handed him a brochure outlining the offerings. "Feel free to wander through the house, and let me know if anything strikes your fancy."

"Will do," Blaine said, though he didn't expect anything in the ostentatious house to necessarily "strike his fancy." He ventured into the marble-laid foyer and through one elaborately furnished room after another, each with an exquisite view of the ocean. The place had "rich people" stamped all over it, but it was interesting to see how the other half lived.

Upstairs, Blaine discovered a humbler living area with modest furnishings. This was probably where the family spent most of their time. He turned to find the man in the suit had followed him upstairs. "Is this furniture part of the sale?" he asked, pointing to a tan chenille sofa and love seat in a family room that boasted a television and entertainment center. The comfortable-looking pieces appeared to be in excellent condition.

"Everything is for sale."

"How much for these sofas with the tables and lamps?"

"I could give it all to you for seven hundred."

"That sounds reasonable." Blaine knew he shouldn't do this, and he'd had no intention of doing it until he came into the house and saw exactly what she needed. They didn't have this kind of relationship, and he had no way to gauge how a gift of this kind might be received. But he couldn't bear to think of her and her child rattling around in that unfurnished home if he could do something about it. *Project alert!*

Except, Tiffany wasn't anything like the women who'd used him and taken advantage of his good nature in the past. If anything, she'd be angry with him for doing something like this for her. He figured they could have a nice big fight over it, and then maybe he'd get some awesome make-up sex out of it. The thought made him burn for her.

"I'll take it," Blaine said, forcing images of her naked and willing out of his mind. "The area rug, too."

"Very good," the man said, beaming.

"Any chance you can deliver it to an address on the island?"

"That can certainly be arranged."

"Great. Now, what do you have in the way of kitchen tables?"

"Right this way, sir."

CHAPTER 11

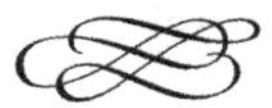

With Patty minding the store for the afternoon, Tiffany picked up Ashleigh and Thomas from camp and took them to the beach for a couple of hours. After the months of endless work to get the store open, it was nice to take a break and spend some time with the kids.

Maddie came to pick up Thomas after dinner.

"He should be good and tired," Tiffany said. "They played hard at the beach." Both toddlers were droopy-eyed after their favorite dinner of spaghetti and meatballs and a bath.

Maddie scooped her son up off the floor. "Hey, buddy." She planted a noisy kiss on his neck that made him giggle. "Did you have fun with Auntie Tiff and Ashleigh?"

"Uh-huh," he said. "We made sandcastles and got ice cream and went swimming."

Maddie let her mouth fall open in playful shock. "You had ice cream *before* dinner?"

"Shhh," he said, putting a finger over her lips. "Don't tell Daddy. It's a *secret*."

Tiffany shared a smile with her sister. She was never happier than when she was with her sister and their kids. Well, lately she'd had some other rather happy times, too, but she couldn't think about that now when she was in mom mode. She was sorry she'd told Blaine she couldn't see him tonight. After the busy day she'd had, Ashleigh would be fast asleep in no time, and the night would stretch out long and lonely.

A knock on the door sent Tiffany scurrying across the empty living room, filled with hope that maybe he'd decided to come over anyway. She instantly hated herself for the thought. Since when did she get so excited to see a man she was only having sex with? That would be something to chew over during that long, lonely night when she could remind herself that theirs was nothing more than a fling. The last thing she needed was more heartbreak, so she'd do well to remember the boundaries of their affair and stay well within them.

She threw open the door to find two burly men outside. "May I help you?"

"Tiffany Sturgil?"

"That's me."

"I have a delivery for you. If you could sign here."

"What kind of delivery?"

"I'm not at liberty to say, ma'am. If you sign here, I can get it for you."

"It's not alive, is it?"

"No, ma'am," he said with a laugh. "Nothing that requires care or feeding."

Filled with trepidation—and curiosity—she signed on the dotted line.

"What's up?" Maddie asked from behind her.

"Not sure."

Ashleigh toddled over to see what all the excitement was about.

Tiffany scooped her up and waited to see what the men had for her. She nearly fell over in shock when they carried in a sofa. "Where... What... Where did that come from?"

"We picked it up from the old Ridgeway place," one of the men said.

Tiffany glanced at Maddie, who watched the proceedings with bug eyes.

"Who sent it?" Tiffany asked.

"Not sure exactly, but we have a note for you in the truck. We'll get it on the next run."

"Wait. There's *more?*"

"Heck, yeah. A lot more."

"Who could've done this?" Tiffany asked her sister after the men went back outside.

"I figured you might know."

"I have no idea."

"It sure is nice," Maddie said, running a hand over the soft fabric.

"Yes." Anything was nicer than nothing, but the sofa was one she would've chosen herself.

Over the next fifteen minutes, the men brought in a gorgeous area rug, end tables, lamps and a kitchen table and chairs that fit perfectly in her empty breakfast nook. By the time they handed over the note that accompanied the gift, Tiffany had tears rolling down her face.

Maddie put down Thomas and took Ashleigh from her, entertaining them while Tiffany wiped away the tears and opened the card.

"Now don't kill me," it said in a masculine scrawl, "but I happened to be going by the Ridgeway place and noticed a sign for the estate sale. I went in to check it out and saw exactly what you needed for dirt cheap. The temptation was too great to pass up. I hope you'll accept this gift in the spirit in which it was given and not kill me or hold it against me or punish me in any way, except for ways that I'll leave to your fertile imagination… I find myself thinking about you pretty much all the time. Blaine."

"Who's it from?" Maddie asked as she stretched out on the sofa.

"Blaine."

"Are you *shitting* me?"

"Shit," Thomas said, making both women laugh.

"Don't say that word, Thomas," Maddie said sternly. "Mommy shouldn't have said it."

Tiffany plopped down next to her. "I can't believe he did this."

"Can I see the note?"

Tiffany handed it to her.

"Oh, wow, Tiff. How sweet is that?"

"It's very sweet." Tiffany contended with a new flood of tears. "I can't believe he did this."

"I hate to be the bearer of bad news, but it's possible your sex-only fling just became a bona fide relationship."

"What does that mean?"

"He really *likes* you, honey."

"I'm not ready for that. I just got divorced."

"Your marriage has been over for a long time. It only *officially* ended. If you like him as much as he seems to like you, why can't you take a chance and see what happens?"

"I'm afraid to," Tiffany said softly. "I'm so afraid of how I already feel about him, and then he goes and does something like this."

Maddie reached for her hand. "Do you remember when you sat in my kitchen and told me you wanted what I have with Mac?"

Tiffany nodded.

"This," Maddie said, gesturing to the furniture, "is right out of Mac McCarthy's playbook. Blaine is a good guy, a *decent* guy. He's nothing like Jim. Not to mention he's hotter than sin."

"Yes, he is," Tiffany said, laughing through her tears. "You don't know the half of it."

"Oh no?" Maddie raised an eyebrow. "Do tell."

"No way."

Thomas crawled into his mother's lap and popped his thumb into his mouth.

"As much as I'd love to stick around for the dirty details, that's my signal to get this tired boy home to bed," Maddie said, lifting her son as she stood. "Think about what I said, okay?"

Tiffany walked them to the door. "How will I think about anything else?"

"I gotta say one more thing."

"You always have to get the last word in."

Maddie laughed. "Mac accuses me of the same thing."

"What's your last word on this matter?"

"Blaine has good taste. Not just in furniture but in women, too." She kissed Tiffany's cheek. "Talk to you in the morning."

After her sister left, Tiffany went through the motions of getting Ashleigh into bed as her head spun over the implications of Blaine's grand gesture. Thankfully, it took only one story, rather than the usual three, to send her baby girl off to sleep. For a long time after Ashleigh fell asleep, Tiffany stayed in bed with her, snuggled up to the child who'd brought her so much joy and comfort during the last three difficult years of her marriage.

Ashleigh smelled of baby shampoo and sweet little girl. Tiffany couldn't wait until she was older and they could go shopping together. She'd be starting ballet class at the studio in the fall, and Tiffany was excited to share her love of dance with her daughter. So much to look forward to all of a sudden, Tiffany thought, at peace, finally, with the changes her life had undergone recently.

Her daughter was healthy and thriving, the store was holding its own, she was free of Jim and the terrible strain of their failing marriage, her mother and sister were happily in love with men who cherished them, and she had a sweet, wonderful new man in her life who couldn't stop thinking of her. It had been a very long time since the inventory of her life had looked as perfect as it did right now.

She was on her way to sleep when the doorbell rang. Shaking off the slumber, she went downstairs, wondering if Maddie had forgotten something that Thomas couldn't live without until the morning. She opened the door, and her mind went blank when she found Blaine looking sinfully sexy in a white button-down shirt and plaid shorts.

He held out a pizza box to her. "A peace offering."

"Why do you need a peace offering?"

"I figured you'd be mad at me for changing the rules on you."

She took his hand and led him inside, placing the pizza box on the coffee table. Turning to him, she put her arms around him and rested her face on his chest. "Thank you."

His arms came around her, holding her snugly and perfectly. "Wow, I got off way easier than expected."

"It's the nicest thing anyone has ever done for me."

"That can't possibly be true."

"It is." She let her hands wander under his shirt and reveled in the tremble that traveled through him when her hands found his back. "I want to pay you back, but I can't right now."

"It was a present, and doing it made me happy, so no more talk of paying me back, okay?"

"Do you really think about me all the time?"

"*All* the time." This was said against her neck, where the brush of soft lips and rough whiskers made her shiver.

As they stood there wrapped up in each other for several minutes, Tiffany realized her sister was right. This was no longer the uncomplicated, sex-only relationship she'd planned to have with him.

"Where's Ashleigh?" he asked.

"Asleep."

"Could I see her?"

"You've seen her before."

"I know, but I bet she's awfully cute when she's asleep."

"She is."

"That's what I want to see."

His words went straight to her heart, making it flip-flop precariously. She took his hand and led him up the stairs. Outside Ashleigh's room, she turned on the hall light and opened the door. Her little girl's dark hair formed a swirl on the white pillowcase, and her lips were pursed into an adorable, kissable bow.

"So pretty," Blaine whispered. "She looks just like her mama."

"I've heard that a time or two." Tiffany rearranged the covers that Ashleigh had already kicked off, kissed her daughter's cheek and followed Blaine from the room.

"Thank you for that," he said.

"You're welcome."

"I'd like to get to know her. If that's okay with you."

"That depends."

"On?"

"What exactly this is that we're doing here."

"What do *you* think we're doing?" As he spoke, he stepped closer to her and kept coming until he had her backed up against the wall. With his body—and his erection—pressed tight against her, he raised his arms over her head.

Tiffany swallowed hard, overwhelmed as always when close to him. "Until today, I thought we were hanging out, having sex, having fun."

"What changed today?"

"I found out you think about me *all* the time."

"You liked that, huh?"

Looking up to find him watching her intently, she nodded.

"So what're we doing now?"

She linked her fingers through the belt loops on his shorts. "The same thing we were doing, only now it seems to mean more than it did before. For some reason."

He bent his head and rested it on her shoulder. "Yes, it does."

Tiffany ran her fingers through his hair.

"Do you think about me once in a while?" he asked in that gruff, sexy voice she was growing to love.

"Pretty much all the time."

He sighed deeply. "I should go."

She hadn't expected him to say that. "Why?"

"Because your daughter is here, and you didn't want me to come over tonight, but I wanted to see you, so I came anyway."

"It wasn't that I didn't want you to come over. I didn't think you'd want to hang out with Ashleigh."

"Now you know better." He raised his head and stared into her eyes for the longest time.

Tiffany was about to grab him and drag his mouth down to hers when he saved her the trouble by tipping his head kissing her so softly and so sweetly she almost forgot to breathe. He kept up the gentle assault, devastating her with his lips alone. When he raised his head, Tiffany moaned.

"Don't stop," she said, desperately. She could only imagine how wanton she sounded to him.

Apparently, he liked how she sounded, because he looked at her with barely restrained lust stamped all over his face. "It doesn't feel right to be doing this when Ashleigh is here."

"She's asleep, and we won't hear from her until bright and early in the morning."

"You're sure?"

She nodded.

With his lips hovering a fraction of an inch from hers, he said, "I want to do something kinky."

Tiffany's belly fluttered, and her pulse beat hard in her throat. "Isn't everything we do kinky?"

The slow, sexy smile that unfolded across his handsome face was positively sinful. "Sweetheart, we've only scratched the surface of how kinky I want to get with you."

She swallowed the lump of fear and emotion and overwhelming anticipation that lodged in her throat. "What do you want to do?"

"Trust me?"

"Yes."

"Are you sure?"

She nodded.

He kissed her again and drew her away from the wall, walking her backward to her bedroom. "Get naked. I'll be right back."

"Where're you going?"

"To get something out of my truck. I'll be quick, so get ready." He took her hand and pressed it against his erection. "I'm more than ready for you, babe."

Tiffany wanted to tell him not to go. She wanted to tell him they already had everything they needed. But she was so painfully curious to know what he had in store for her that she let him go and went into her room. Her hands were shaky as she unbuttoned her blouse and took it off. She had to tug twice on the button to her shorts before it came free.

By the time she removed her clothes and turned down the bed, she was a bundle of nerves with all her pleasure points tingling in anticipation. She lit candles and experimented with several poses on the bed, before she settled on her side with her head propped on her upturned hand.

Blaine returned a minute later and stopped short to take a long, leisurely look at her.

Before him, she'd only been with Jim, so nothing in her experience had prepared her for a man who could turn her on just by looking at her in that particular way.

She wanted to tell him to hurry. She wanted to tell him she needed him. She wanted to beg him to make her feel the way that only he could. But she stayed quiet and waited to see what he would do.

He closed the door and pressed the lock, the sound reverberating through the quiet room and making her shiver again in anticipation. "Will you be able to hear Ashleigh if she wakes up?"

Tiffany pointed to the monitor on the bedside table. "She hardly ever wakes up."

"Good," he said as he approached the bed. "Close your eyes."

Tiffany looked at him for a long, intense moment before she did as he directed. She felt something satiny slide over her eyes and opened them to total darkness. He'd blindfolded her.

"Remember your safe word?"

She nodded.

"Use it at any time. Okay?"

Because she couldn't seem to form words, she nodded again. Her entire body vibrated with tension and desire unlike anything she'd ever experienced before, even with him. To not be able to see what he was doing to her, to be totally and completely at his mercy...

"Tiffany?"

"Hmm?"

"Breathe."

She hadn't realized she wasn't and sucked in a deep breath.

"Okay?"

Nodding, she said, "I'm fine."

He raised her arms over her head and snapped on the handcuffs. "Comfortable?"

Tiffany had to force herself to keep her muscles relaxed when every inch of her was on fire. "Ah, yeah, sure."

Chuckling, he said, "I need a towel."

She cleared her throat. "Bathroom. In the closet."

"Don't go anywhere."

Even though she couldn't leave if she wanted to, Tiffany wanted to laugh at the idea that there was anywhere she'd rather be than right here with him. With her other senses more acutely aware, she heard him go into the bathroom, open and close the cabinet, and return. When he dropped the towel on the bed next to her, the clean scent of fabric softener briefly overtook the vanilla scent of the candles.

She took a series of deep breaths, trying to calm herself.

"Are you still okay?"

"Yes."

"You aren't scared, are you?"

"Scared? No."

His hand landed large and warm on her leg. "What, then?"

"Curious. Nervous. Aroused."

"Anything else?"

She shook her head. "That's about it for now."

He caressed her leg. "Don't be nervous."

"Um, okay. Whatever you say."

His soft laughter made her smile as he used both hands to move her legs apart. "Lift your bum."

Tentatively, Tiffany did as he asked and felt the towel slide beneath her. Listening intently, she heard him undressing. He took his own sweet time about it! Her skin tingled, and her belly quivered with nerves and eagerness to see what he would do. Right when she thought she'd go mad trying to figure out what he had planned, she felt his finger trace a path from her ankle to her knee. Then it was on her thigh, making her muscles tense.

"Have you ever shaved?" he asked as he ran his finger lightly over her sex. "Here?"

Tiffany licked lips gone dry. "Bikini line. Does that count?"

"Ever shaved all of it?"

Her voice sounded squeaky when she said, "No."

"I've heard," he said, running his tongue over a painfully sensitive nipple, "that shaving makes everything feel a thousand times better for women."

"Heard from whom?"

"People."

"Female people?"

He surprised her when he kissed her lips. "You're cute when you're jealous."

"I'm *not* jealous. Don't flatter yourself."

"Whatever you say." His lips moved from her mouth to her neck to her breasts.

Tiffany squirmed, trying to get closer to him.

"Relax, honey. I promise you'll get everything you need. And then some."

"It's that last part I'm worried about."

"Are you? Really?"

She took a second to consider his question. "No. Not really."

"You'd tell me if you were seriously worried or scared?"

"Yes."

"Do you promise?"

"*Yes,*" she said, playfully exasperated, even though she appreciated his concern.

He cupped her sex, his fingers pressing and teasing her. "So, what do you think about shaving?"

"*Now?*"

"Uh-huh." His lips were soft and smooth on her belly.

She tugged on the cuffs, making them jangle. "How do you propose I shave anything when you've got me locked up like a prisoner?"

"I'd do it for you."

"Oh." Her dry throat tightened as images of him shaving her *there* ran through her mind, causing her sex to clench. Thank God she was blindfolded for this.

"Is that a yes?" He pressed harder until he encountered the rush of dampness between her legs. "Ohhh, it seems you approve of this plan."

She laughed nervously and raised her hips, trying to encourage him to focus on where she needed him most.

He withdrew his hand. "Yes or no?"

"*Yes!* Just do it, will you?"

"I thought you'd never ask." With a kiss to her belly, he got up from the bed.

Tiffany blew out a sharp breath and bit back the retort that hovered on the tip of her tongue. She could hear him moving around, making preparations. The water came on in the bathroom and then turned off. She felt the mattress dip when he returned.

"Why are your legs closed?"

She hadn't realized she'd closed them.

With his hands on her legs, he gently pushed them apart, caressing the sensitive skin on her inner thighs. "You can't move, okay?"

"Okay."

He pressed a warm compress to the area he planned to shave. The next thing she heard was shaving cream leaving the can, which she realized he'd brought with him with this in mind. Knowing he'd put so much thought into this gave her racing mind even more to think about as her already sensitized skin reacted immediately to the cool menthol cream.

"Ready?"

"As ready as I'll ever be."

With one hand on her thigh, he held her still as he dragged the razor from bottom to top. The sensation was so titillating and arousing, that she had to force herself to remain still. "Almost done."

"What happens then?"

"I'll show you how amazing it feels."

"How will you do that?"

He wiped the area with the warm cloth.

She felt him shift on the bed.

"I'll start with my tongue."

CHAPTER 12

Tiffany hadn't expected it to feel all that different. However, the second his tongue connected with her freshly shaven skin, she nearly came undone. "Oh, *wow*," she said, gasping from the riot of sensations that erupted from her core. "*God*."

"I take it you approve?"

Moaning, she raised her hips, silently begging for more. When he didn't immediately comply, a tortured-sounding "please" escaped from her lips.

Chuckling softly, he sucked and teased her into a series of orgasms that seemed to go on forever. When she returned from the dazzling journey, he was poised between her legs, his erection nudging at her tingling core.

"I want to see you," she said. Her voice sounded rough and hoarse, as if she'd been screaming. Maybe she had been. She couldn't say for sure. "And touch you."

He removed the blindfold and then the cuffs.

Tiffany stretched her arms and then curled them around him, gazing up at him.

He stared down at her, intensely focused, which only made her want him more. She'd never been the subject of such intense attention from a man, and it was a huge turn-on.

"*Now*, Blaine." With her hands on his back and then his backside, she urged him to take her.

However, he wasn't done torturing her. Rather than take what she offered so blatantly, he bent his head and sucked hard on her nipple. "Not quite yet." He sucked it between his teeth and made her whimper from the arousing combination of pain and pleasure. "Turn over."

"Blaine…"

"Just do it."

She looked up at him. "Will I get a turn to be in charge?"

"Any time you want, baby. Just not tonight."

Reluctantly, she turned onto her belly and waited to see what he would do. She kept her eyes closed and focused on breathing while she could. She'd learned to expect him to steal the breath from her lungs.

When she heard him rustling around with the items on the bedside table, she had to force her eyes to remain closed. His hands were suddenly on her back, gliding and smoothing over her tense muscles as the citrusy aroma of the massage oil he'd bought at the store filled her senses.

"Feel good?" he asked.

"Mmm." All the tension seemed to leave her body as she drifted on a cloud of contentment. "*So* good."

As he worked his way down her back, she felt the hard press of his erection against her bottom.

She raised her hips and pressed against him, hoping he'd take the hint that she was more than ready. Once again, he ignored her signals and continued with his own agenda.

Groaning, she said, "You're out to torture me tonight, aren't you?"

"The way I see it, I'm torturing myself and pleasuring you."

"How's that?"

"You've gotten to come—a couple of times. I haven't."

"Oh," she said, swallowing. "Don't let me stop you."

Laughing softly, he continued to slide his hands over her back, moving lower with every sweep. When he turned his full focus to her bottom, the breath caught in her throat and every nerve ending in her body stood up to take notice. She'd had no idea that was such an erogenous zone.

"Breathe," he said in the sexy voice that was a turn-on all by itself.

Tiffany sucked in a greedy deep breath.

"Keep breathing." His talented fingers kneaded her cheeks, delving into the cleft between them and setting off a whole new riot of reaction throughout her body.

She clutched the pillow so tightly her fingers ached while she focused on drawing air into her starving lungs. She'd had no idea—no idea at all—that sex could be so all-consuming. Nothing in her past with Jim had prepared her for such an inventive, creative, thoughtful, sexy lover.

He leaned away from her, reaching for something on the bedside table.

The next thing she knew, he was urging her onto her knees and arranging her so her bottom was in the air.

Tiffany was both mortified and wildly curious at the same time. Keeping her eyes closed, she heard him rip open a condom and roll it on and was filled with relief to know he was finally getting to the main event. She braced herself for his entry.

"Relax and let me in."

Right, Tiffany thought. *Easy enough.*

He teased and coaxed his way in, and from the tingle and heat his entry generated, she realized he'd used the lube that heated on contact. Later, when she was able to piece together a coherent thought or two, she'd have to think about how the product made the experience even more exciting than it would've been otherwise. Right now, however, she was hardly thinking like a businesswoman.

"Blaine..."

His hands came around to cup her breasts, his fingers rolling and pinching her nipples. "What, baby? Tell me. How does it feel?"

"I need to come. *Please.*"

"You got it." Grasping her hips, he pressed himself against her opening, pushing and retreating, urging her to yield to him.

"Relax, baby. It's okay. Let me in."

Her entire focus was on the burn and stretch of sensitive tissues as he worked his way into her. And then he rolled the tight bundle of nerves at her core between his fingers, and she came in a burst of light and heat so intense she wondered if she would survive the flight. In the throes of the most astonishing orgasm of her life, he hammered into her, taking her higher and higher until there was nowhere left to go. She floated back down to find him still lodged deep within her, pulsing with his own release. His heart beat so hard and so fast, she could feel it against her back as he sucked in one deep breath after another. When he began to withdraw from her, she stopped him.

"Not yet," she said, gripping the hand he'd laid on her belly. "Not yet." As they lay pressed together in a sweaty, pulsating mess, it occurred to Tiffany that she'd had no business opening a sex-toy shop without having the first clue about what toys brought to the act. It would take her days, maybe weeks, to process the impact of this man and the reactions he'd managed to coax from her body.

"What're you thinking?" His lips were soft against her shoulder.

Her overly sensitive skin erupted in goose bumps from that simple caress.

"That I'm glad I let you talk me into trying out some of the stuff from the store."

His chuckle rumbled through him, making his chest hair rub against her back.

Tiffany had never felt more in tune with another human being, except for Ashleigh, but that was different. Very, very different from the overwhelming emotions she'd experienced with him.

"I take it that means you approve."

She nodded. "I read every word that came with each item and felt like I could talk intelligently about them to my customers. But now..."

"Now you can speak from experience."

"Yes." She squeezed his hand. "It's never been like that. Ever."

"For me, too."

"So it was different?" Tiffany cringed to herself, knowing she was fishing, but she couldn't help that she wanted to know more about him. Suddenly, she wanted to know everything.

"Hell, yes, it was different. Right from the beginning, you've been different from anyone I've ever known."

While the slight movement of his hips reminded her he was still lodged deep inside her, his words set off a whole other kind of heat in the vicinity of her badly wounded heart.

"How is it different?"

He was quiet for a long moment. "For one thing, you're not after everything you can get from me, regardless of what it costs me."

Tiffany tried to understand what he meant. "They took money from you?"

"Worse—they went for my soul."

"How so?"

After a long pause, he cupped her breast and tweaked her nipple. "I don't want to talk about that. I'd much rather talk about you and this." He lightly pinched her nipple between his fingers.

While her body reacted instantly to him as it always did, her heart was disappointed that he was unwilling to share more about his past with her.

She ran her hand up his arm and then back down to link her fingers with his. "If I ever ask for more than you've got to give, will you tell me?"

"Baby, you're not made of that kind of stuff. You stand on your own two feet and take care of yourself. It would never occur to you to expect a man to solve all your problems for you."

His gruffly spoken words made her heart contract with a painful rush of emotion. "That might be the nicest thing anyone has ever said to me."

"I mean it," he said, drawing her in tighter against him.

That was when she realized he was once again fully erect and throbbing inside her.

"Hold that thought," he said with a kiss to her cheek. "I need to get another condom."

When he would've withdrawn from her, she stopped him. "I'm on the pill."

He went completely still.

"I've never been with anyone but Jim, and I had a physical recently. I'm healthy."

"I have physicals every year for work."

"In that case..."

"Are you saying what I think you're saying?"

Tiffany laughed softly at the amazement she heard in his tone. "That's what I'm saying."

"I think my heart just stopped." He withdrew from her slowly, and when he was finally free, he kissed her shoulder and then her cheek. "Stay there. I'll be right back."

She delighted in watching the flex of his finely sculpted rear as he strode purposefully into the bathroom to dispose of the condom and clean up. She shifted onto her back and stretched her arms and legs, which set off an explosive reaction that rippled from her bottom to her scalp, toes, fingertips and everywhere in between.

He returned and stood by the side of the bed, staring down at her. His erection was tall and proud, nearly reaching the indented navel on his muscular belly.

Tiffany couldn't believe this strong, sexy, gorgeous man had set his sights on her. She held out a hand to him, but as usual, he had his own ideas about how this would go.

He pointed to the edge of the bed. "Come here."

She moved carefully until she knelt before him at the edge. She reached out to stroke him and enjoyed the sight of his head thrown back, which exposed the strong column of his throat.

And then his hand was over hers, stopping her. "Lie down."

She did as he directed and then watched in amazement as he arranged her legs so they were over his shoulders.

"I've heard dancers are super limber," he said as his hands moved seductively over her thighs. "Is that true?"

"You'll have to find out for yourself."

His eyes blazed with intensity as he slid his arousal through her slickness.

Remembering the difficult entry the last time had her tensing as she waited to see what he would do.

"Don't get tense," he said soothingly. "That only makes it harder."

"Makes what harder?" she asked with a playful grin that masked her inner turmoil.

"Everything." Grasping her bottom, he pushed into her one torturous inch at a time. "Stop thinking so much, and just feel. Just feel." He retreated before surging into her again. "That's it. Take all of me." His lips skimmed her inner thigh as he pressed his thumb against her and made her come suddenly—and almost violently.

With a wild groan, he clutched her hips and went with her. He released her legs, came down on top of her and held her tight against him. Then he raised his head, looked deep into her eyes and kissed her. "I want my pizza now."

Since that was the last thing she'd expected him to say, Tiffany burst into laughter.

DAVID STAYED LATE at the clinic to wade through a mountain of charts that had collected in the last week. They desperately needed some additional administrative help, but the clinic barely had the budget to pay him, Victoria and the receptionist they already had. As it was, he was making far less than he would have in the city, but he had everything he needed. Well, almost everything...

Since he'd lost Janey, he'd walked around with a large, painful hole where his heart had once been. Knowing he had only himself to blame for losing her didn't help much. Pouring himself into his work—that helped. It left him with little time to think about how badly he'd screwed up his entire life. They should've had it all. Instead, he was left to think about how he'd had it all and let it slide through his fingers, like it meant nothing to him.

Forcing himself to focus, he opened a chart and realized it was Daisy's. He made some final notes about her treatment and follow-up care. In a city hospital, he would close the chart and move on to the next. But here on the island, he started to reach for the phone to check on her, but stopped himself, deciding to see her in person on the way home. That was the beauty of small-town medicine. He knew most of his patients personally and went out of his way to spend as much time with each of them as he could.

Every time he tended to an impoverished young family or a lonely shut-in or a battered woman, he liked to think he was paying back the debt he owed for being such a disappointment to the community that once had such faith in him. The people of Gansett had been so proud to send one of their own off to medical school, and then he'd gone and blown it by cheating on Janey McCarthy. He'd found out the hard way that everyone loved Janey and reviled the man who'd hurt her. Saving her baby niece Hailey at birth had gone a long way toward redeeming him with the McCarthy family, but people still treated him differently than they used to.

They also blamed him for derailing Janey's plans to attend veterinary school after college. At the time, he'd thought he was doing the right thing by insisting only one of them attend medical school, reasoning that island practices wouldn't generate enough income to support them and pay off their school loans. Her parents had violently opposed her decision to forgo veterinary school, and his relationship with his future in-laws had never really recovered from that episode. Now that she was free of him, she was attending veterinary school in Ohio, and everyone was happy—everyone but him.

It had probably been a huge mistake to take the job as the island's doctor when Cal Maitland returned to Texas to tend to his ailing mother. But it had been the job he'd always planned to have after medical school, so he'd snapped up the opportunity when it was offered to him. Now he had a two-year contract that he would honor before he considered other options. Maybe by then people would've forgiven his sins.

He let out a harsh laugh. "As if."

His grumbling stomach reminded him that he'd skipped lunch—again—and that it was getting late. He turned off the office light and gathered up some of the remaining paperwork to finish at home. On the way out, he switched the phones over to the answering service on the mainland that covered for them at night. They had his cell number and would call him if anything came up overnight. He locked the clinic's main doors and took a moment to appreciate the soft spring evening on the way to his car.

As he drove into town to Daisy's house, he let himself pretend he was driving home to Janey and that she was waiting for him with dinner they'd enjoy together before spending a long, sensuous night in bed. The memories of making love with her made him hard and horny. Ironically, he hadn't had sex since the day she caught him with the oncology nurse he'd foolishly brought home to his apartment, thinking she could take his mind off the Hodgkin's treatment. In fact, she'd been a momentary distraction that set off a series of events that imploded his life.

Sex had been about the last thing on his mind ever since. Until lately...

Lately, he'd begun to think he might be ready to start over again with someone else, as daunting a proposition as that might be after spending thirteen years—his entire adult life—with the same woman. He couldn't imagine ever being in love again like he'd been with Janey, but it would be nice to have someone to spend time with—other than his mother, who loved to fret about how badly he'd messed up his once-promising life.

He parallel parked in front of Daisy's house and noticed a single light in a room downstairs. Hoping he wasn't disturbing her, he began to regret not calling before he came. With his medical bag in hand, he rapped lightly on the front door and waited several minutes before he heard the shuffle of feet inside.

"Who is it?"

"David Lawrence."

A series of locks disengaged, and the door swung open. Daisy seemed surprised to see him. Her face was bruised and swollen, with one eye completely closed. "What're you doing here?"

"I wanted to check on you."

"Really?"

He smiled. "Yes, really."

"That's so nice of you. Come in." She shuffled back to the sofa and sat slowly and painfully.

"Are you all by yourself?"

"My friends were here earlier, but they left a little while ago."

"Would it be okay if I took a look at your ribs?"

She hesitated for a moment and then nodded.

"Why don't you stretch out on the sofa and try to get comfortable."

Watching her painful effort to move her body into position made him hurt for her. "Let me help you." He gently lifted her legs and helped her recline on the threadbare sofa. By the time he had her settled, she was breathing hard and a light sheen of perspiration had appeared on her forehead. "Is it okay to put on another light?"

"Sure." She closed her one working eye, as if she could no longer make the effort to keep it open.

Moving carefully, David raised her T-shirt to expose the ribs he'd wrapped the night before. In his bag, he found surgical scissors and cut the tape to expose angry-looking bruises. He looked up to check how she was faring and was distressed to see tears rolling down her cheeks. "I'm sorry. Did I hurt you?"

She shook her head.

"Then what is it?"

"It's so embarrassing, you know?" Her luminous gray eye swam with new tears when she opened it to look at him. "That the man I supposedly loved could've done this to me, and I allowed it."

"You didn't allow it, Daisy. This was done *to* you. It's not your fault."

"I keep telling myself that, but still… I let him back in after the other times. That's on me."

"Maybe so, but you can't be faulted for wanting to give someone you love another chance."

"It's nice of you to say that and to come here. You didn't have to."

"I wanted to see how you were doing." His stomach let out an ungodly growl. "Sorry," he said sheepishly.

"Have you had dinner?"

"Not yet, and my stomach is letting me know it's time."

"My friends brought a ton of food, but my mouth is too sore to eat anything. My friend Maude makes the most delicious lasagna. You should have some."

"I couldn't. They made it for you." His stomach protested the words with another growl.

"I'd hate for it to go to waste. You'd be doing me a favor, and it's the least I could do since you were nice enough to check on me."

David wavered. He was starving and still needed to re-tape her ribs.

"Please," she said softly. "After all you've done for me, let me feed you."

"All right," he said, smiling.

"Could I ask you something?"

"Sure."

She hesitated, studying him intently. "Why is it that even when you smile, your eyes are sad?"

Staggered by the question, David stared at her.

"I'm sorry." She looked down at her hands. "I don't mean to pry."

"I've made some mistakes," he said haltingly. The words were out of his mouth before he could think about whether it was wise to share his personal travails with a patient. "You probably know all about them."

"I know you used to be engaged to Janey McCarthy, but I don't know why you broke up."

"You must be the only person on the island who doesn't know why."

"It doesn't matter. You're a good person, right?"

There was something honest and unaffected about her that David found refreshing. When she wasn't bruised and swollen, he realized she'd be very pretty. Why hadn't he noticed that before? "I haven't always been."

"You are now, and that's what matters."

"I'm trying."

"Good," she said as her eye closed. "Go ahead and get something to eat. Bring it in here to keep me company."

Watching her drift off, he noted the aura of serenity that surrounded her despite her injuries and was comforted by it. For the first time in longer than he could remember, he didn't feel lonely or out of sorts. Funny, he thought as he made his way to the kitchen to investigate the lasagna, he'd come to provide care for her, and she'd ended up tending to him. He hoped she'd wake up and talk to him some more. He liked talking to her.

CHAPTER 13

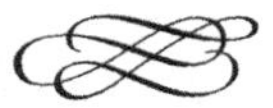

Carolina buzzed around her small kitchen, preparing her son's favorite meal of roasted chicken, mashed potatoes and stuffing. She kept tripping over Janey's menagerie of special needs pets, who were waiting around in the hope of snagging some scraps. Riley, the German shepherd, sat in the corner watching her every move. He made her a little nervous with his intensity, but Janey assured her he was gentle as a lamb.

"You might be gentle as a lamb," Carolina said to the handsome dog, who'd lost his hind legs at some point, "but I bet you'd tear the throat out of anyone who looked at your mama with crossed eyes."

The dog never blinked as he stared at her.

"I take that as a yes."

"Are you talking to the dogs, Mom?" Joe asked as he came into the kitchen and planted a kiss on her cheek.

Carolina's heart soared with love for the son she adored. Despite losing his father at the age of seven, he'd grown into a fine young man who was about to become a father himself. "I was getting to know Riley a little better," Carolina said as she stirred the gravy.

"Don't let him intimidate you. He's a pussycat."

"So your wife tells me."

"It smells amazing, and I'm starving."

"It's about ready. Want to let Janey know?"

"She's taking a nap, but I'll see if I can rouse her."

Watching him go, tall, handsome and broad shouldered, Carolina was reminded of her late husband, Pete. Joe's resemblance to his father used to cause her the occasional pang of sorrow, but now she was grateful for the reminder of the man she'd loved and lost so long ago.

She was thrilled that everything had worked out so well for Joe and Janey. She'd once been in love the way they were and knew how all-consuming it could be. In the thirty years since she'd lost her darling Pete, there'd only been one man who'd ever turned her head.

But she couldn't think about him. She *wouldn't* think about him. That was a brief moment of madness, and it was in the past now. Still, telling herself not to think about him and actually not thinking about him were two very different things, as she'd discovered in the months since the moment of madness. And after seeing him the other day, the memories had been sharper and more painful than ever.

Forcing those thoughts from her mind, she put dinner on the table as Joe led a sleepy-eyed Janey into the kitchen. Carolina was delighted they'd chosen to stay with her—as opposed to the McCarthys' far more spacious home—until Stephanie's restaurant opening. After that, Grant and Stephanie would be moving out of Janey's house and into the home of their own they'd recently bought from Ned Saunders. Having the kids underfoot for a few days would be the highlight of Carolina's year.

"Good nap?" she asked her daughter-in-law.

Janey rested a hand on her protruding belly and let out a huge yawn. "They're all good naps these days."

Joe grinned at his wife. "If you slept any more, I'd never see you."

"I know," she said with a sigh. "I'm such a drag lately."

"No, you're not." He kissed her forehead and settled her into a chair at the table.

Janey's eyes lit up at the sight of chicken and mashed potatoes. "Oh my God, is that *stuffing*?"

"You betcha," Carolina said. "All your husband's favorites."

"Thanks, Mom," Joe said. "It looks so good."

"Seriously awesome," Janey added.

Carolina was pleased by their enthusiasm for the meal. "Dig in."

Over dinner, they talked about island gossip, Janey's studies, the dogs and their plans to be back in Ohio in plenty of time before the baby's birth.

"You'll come out with my parents when the baby is born, won't you?" Janey asked.

"I wouldn't miss it for the world," Carolina assured her.

"Good. I'll need all the help I can get. The timing is awful with the semester starting a month after the birth. Very poor family planning on our part."

"If I recall correctly, nothing about this baby was planned."

"That is *so* true," Janey said with a laugh as she scooped a second helping of mashed potatoes onto her plate.

Carolina noticed that Joe was pushing the food around on his plate and seemed a million miles away. "Everything okay, honey?"

Joe startled when he realized she was talking to him. "Oh, yeah, sorry."

"Where did you go?" Janey asked him.

"Nowhere. Just thinking about some stuff with the business. Nothing to worry about."

"What stuff?" Carolina asked. Even though he did a marvelous job of running the business her parents had left to them both, she liked to keep up with the goings-on.

Joe shook his head but still seemed troubled. "It's nothing, really."

Carolina raised the same brow she'd used to interrogate him as a teenager. "I know you better than that. My son doesn't push chicken and mashed potatoes around on his plate. My son wolfs it down like he's never seen food before."

"That is also *so* true," Janey said.

"Spill it," Carolina said.

Joe put down his fork and sat back in his chair, the slump of his shoulders another sign of trouble. "Seamus gave me his notice today."

An electrical current traveled through Carolina's body at that news. She stared at Joe as if she hadn't heard him correctly.

"*Why?*" Janey asked, giving voice to the question Carolina would have asked if she could've spoken.

"He said it was a personal matter, and he can't remain on the island because of it."

Carolina couldn't seem to breathe. It wasn't because of her. It couldn't be. Their moment of madness had occurred months ago. He wasn't leaving because of her. Was he?

"Mom? What is it? Why are you suddenly pale?"

"I, ah…"

Janey looked on with concern. "Are you okay, Carolina?"

She fought through the shock and dismay, remembering that the primary reason she'd refused to enter into a relationship with Seamus was sitting right in front of her, trying to understand her reaction. "I'm fine. I'm thinking about the business." Somehow, she managed to form the words even as her brain continued to spin. "And the baby. And everything."

"I've been going over it and over it all day," Joe said. "I'll figure something out."

"Isn't there anyone currently working for the company who could do it?" Janey asked, reaching for his hand.

"No one comes to mind, but Seamus said he'd help me find someone."

"I'm so sorry you have to deal with this, babe," Janey said. "Seamus has been such a godsend the last two years."

He squeezed her hand. "Don't worry about it, hon. I'll work it out."

Carolina was stricken by the idea that something she might've done—or not done—had caused such a headache for her son. The irony wasn't lost on her. She'd refused to consider a relationship with Seamus mostly because she feared Joe wouldn't approve of his mother being with a man only two years older than him. And now, if Seamus was leaving because of her, she'd ended up causing an entirely new problem for Joe.

She had to know. As soon as the kids went to bed, she'd go ask him, and if he was leaving because of her, she'd do her best to talk him out of it.

SOMETIMES BLAINE HATED BEING police chief. This was one of those times. His phone was ringing, and he was going to have to disentangle himself from Tiffany to answer it. He answered every call, no matter what time of day. Such was the life of a small-town police chief.

Tiffany didn't stir as he gently shifted her off him so he could get up.

He took the phone into the hallway, shut the bedroom door and answered it without checking the caller ID. "Taylor."

"Blaine."

He held back a groan when he heard his mother's voice. "Mom? Do you know what time it is?"

"What're you doing?"

"Right now?" He honestly didn't think she'd want to know.

"Who are you buying furniture for?"

Cursing the island gossip machine, Blaine leaned against the wall and ran his fingers through his unruly hair. "It's not what you think."

"Isn't it? Is history repeating itself?"

"Absolutely not. This is nothing like that." Tiffany bore no resemblance to the women who'd used him and left him broken.

"Blaine..."

"I'm not having this conversation. I'm a grown man, and I know what I'm doing."

Her sigh spoke for her.

"I've got to go."

"Are you with her now?"

"Mom..."

"I can't bear to watch it happen again."

"I have to go."

"I want to see you tomorrow. I'll be home all day."

"I've got to work."

"Stop by here."

Before he could say another word, the line went dead. "Ugh." He resisted the urge to throw the phone against the wall. Rather, he took a couple of deep breaths to get himself together and returned to the bedroom.

"Everything okay?" Tiffany asked.

"Everything's fine. Sorry if I woke you."

The room was dark, so she couldn't see him reach for his pants on the floor.

"Are you leaving?"

"I thought I might go home."

"Why?"

The single word went straight to his heart. He sat on the edge of the bed and reached for her hand. "I didn't think you'd want me here when Ashleigh wakes up."

She gave his hand a little tug. "That's hours from now."

Even though she couldn't see it, he smiled. She made him happy. She made him feel lighter and less burdened than he'd felt in years. She made him want things he'd long ago convinced himself he'd never have. He slid back into bed and was astounded by the rush of emotion that seized him when she wrapped her warm, supple body around him. The surge of lust he was getting used to, but the emotion... That was new and not entirely unwelcome.

He put his arms around her and kissed her forehead, enjoying the quiet, the peace, the sensation of falling. Not that long ago, the falling sensation would've had him running for his life from the cause. Now he couldn't imagine not wanting to be with her, couldn't imagine not wanting to hold her this way or sleep next to her or make love with her.

"What're you thinking about?" she asked, her hand caressing his chest and belly.

"You."

Her hand stopped moving. "Oh."

"All good stuff." He'd tightened his hold on her, which is how he could feel her relax. The poor thing had become far too accustomed to bad news from the man in her life. She'd stopped hoping for anything good to happen.

He turned on his side to face her. "I want you to meet my mom." The words popped out of his mouth before he took a moment to consider the implications. As he waited breathlessly to hear what she'd have to say, his heart pounded, and it became very, very clear to him that his feelings for her had the potential to change his life.

"You do?" she asked in a squeaky voice that was nothing like her regular, confident tone.

"Yes, I do." He ran his hand from her shoulder to her back and below to cup her bottom and tug her in closer to him.

"What if she doesn't like me?"

"Why wouldn't she like you?"

"I'm a divorced single mom who runs a sex-toy shop. Hardly the 'bring-home-to-Mom' kinda girl."

"You're a big improvement over the other girls I've brought home to meet her. Trust me on that."

"Are you going to tell me what happened with those other women?"

"I'd rather not. It's ancient history and has nothing to do with who I am now. It has nothing to do with us."

His refusal to speak of his past only made her more curious about the women who'd hurt him. The hand that had been moving so softly and sensuously over his chest stopped when it landed on his heart. "Are you over them?"

"*So* over them it's not even funny." He buried his hand in her hair and tugged gently to tilt her face to receive his kiss. "How about you? Over him?"

"Definitely."

"What went wrong between you guys?"

"Damned if I know. One minute, everything was fine, and seemingly the next minute, it wasn't. I never have gotten him to tell me what changed for him."

"That must've been painful for you."

"It was at the time, but not so much anymore. I've accepted it. He stopped loving me. Big whoop. It happens."

"You're awfully matter-of-fact about it."

She shrugged. "I know how guys can be. I learned that lesson early on."

"What do you mean?"

"My dad left when I was three. I didn't see him again until a year or so ago."

"Wow, that must've been weird."

"I guess."

"What did he say? What did *you* say?"

"I don't remember. I was so shocked to realize I was looking at the father I had no memory of, that my mind went totally blank."

"I can't imagine how that must've felt for you. He showed up totally out of the blue?"

She nodded. "My mom had contacted his sister about getting in touch with him."

"How come?"

"Apparently, they never got divorced. Now she wants to marry Ned, so..."

"Are they getting divorced?"

"Not yet. He's being a jerk about it. He wanted to spend time with me and Maddie before he'd agree to a divorce."

"For real? He leaves you, what? Almost thirty years ago? And now he wants a family reunion?"

"Something like that."

"Did you do it? Did you see him?"

"I spent an awkward hour with him for my mom. She deserves a chance to be happy."

"So do you." He punctuated the words with kisses to her face and lips. "You deserve to be happy."

"Ashleigh makes me happy every day, and Thomas, and the rest of my family."

"That's not the kind of happy I mean." As he spoke, he turned them so he was on top of her. He tipped his head and took her mouth in a fiercely possessive kiss.

"What kind of happy do you mean?"

He felt her coy smile against his lips. "This kind of happy." Entering her in one swift flex of his hips, he stopped suddenly when she winced. "Oh God, sorry. Are you sore?"

"A little."

When he would've withdrawn from her, she stopped him. "It's okay. Just give me a minute."

"Take all the time you need. I'm not going anywhere."

She curled her arms around his neck and brought him down to her for more of the amazing kisses he'd come to expect from her. The sense of connection was profound as he moved within her as their tongues tangled in a sweet, sensual dance. Her breasts pressing against his chest and the clutch of her internal muscles made him a little crazy, but he held back, waiting for her.

With a moan, she broke the kiss and squirmed under him. "Blaine…"

"Tell me."

"I need…"

"What do you need?"

She clutched his back. "You. I need you."

When she said those words, his slow fall became a rapid plummet as he gave her what they both wanted. He drove them higher, higher than he'd ever been with anyone, before the dam broke and flooded him with an intense desire to make her happy, to never disappoint her the way she'd been disappointed in the past, to protect her and her daughter, to keep her close. Always.

Jesus, he thought. *Where did all that come from?*

Drifting back down from the incredible high, he realized she was crying. "What, baby? Did I hurt you?"

"No. No." Her hands on his backside kept him firmly embedded within her.

"Then what is it? What's wrong?"

"Nothing. For the first time in longer than I can remember, nothing is wrong."

"Aww, Tiffany. You're so sweet."

"Thank you. Not just for this." She squeezed his ass and got his motor running all over again. "But for making me see that it's possible to be happy again. Even if this doesn't go anywhere, it's made me happy."

"Good," he said with a kiss. "That makes me happy, too."

Her hands moved up his back in a caress that made him shiver. Then her fingers were combing through his hair, and he was overcome with yet another emotion that took him by surprise —contentment.

"You'll be tired tomorrow," she said.

"And you won't?"

"I'm much younger than you are."

Laughing, he took a nibble of her neck to pay her back for the insult. He couldn't believe he was already raring to go again after coming harder than he ever had in his life. Just when he was about to do something with that lovely erection, the baby monitor on the bedside table crackled to life.

They stilled to listen.

"Mommy." The single word was faint but clear.

Blaine withdrew from her, and she scrambled out of bed. He heard her rustling around in the closet, probably grabbing a robe, and then she shot out of the room. He fell back against the pillows, wondering if maybe he should get the heck out of there before her daughter caught him naked in her mother's bed. The internal debate raged on for another minute before he heard the distinctive sound of vomiting.

TIFFANY SAW her daughter through two rounds of vomiting before the little girl fell asleep in her arms. She was burning up with a fever, too. Tiffany sat in the rocking chair in Ashleigh's room, rocking her gently until she was sure Ashleigh was fully asleep. She got up slowly and transferred her to the bed.

"Is she okay?" Blaine whispered from the doorway.

In the glow of the nightlight, she could see that he'd pulled on his pants, but his chest was still bare and his hair adorably mussed.

"She is now, but she's got a fever."

"That came on suddenly."

"Usually does."

"Anything I can do for you?"

Tiffany shook her head. "I think she's okay now." She left the door open so she could hear Ashleigh if she was sick again.

When they were back in Tiffany's room, Blaine put his arms around her. "How about you? Are you okay?"

"Yes." She snuggled into his embrace, comforted by his presence. "Goes with the territory."

"You're a good mom, and she's lucky to have you."

"Thank you," she said, arching into him. Apparently, she couldn't be this close to him and not want him.

His lips were soft against her neck when he said, "Lie on the bed."

Startled by the sudden command, she did as he directed and watched him kneel on the bed between her legs.

"I never get tired of seeing you like this." He bent to run his tongue over the sensitive skin he'd shaved earlier.

Tiffany couldn't believe how easily he took her mind off her sick child.

He continued to lick and tease until she was on the verge of yet another orgasm. When he drew her clitoris between his lips, he made her forget everything but the astonishing pleasure.

"I don't know how you did that," she said, still panting many minutes later.

"Did what?"

"I went from tending a sick child to *that* in less than ten minutes' time."

"My special gift," he said with a sexy grin.

"You just wait. Revenge is a bitch."

"Do your worst."

"Oh, I will. As soon as I can move again."

Hovering over her, he kissed her. "We both need some sleep, so I'm going to go."

She looked up at him, memorizing every detail of his sexy dishevelment. "I wish you didn't have to."

"I wish I didn't, either, but if Ashleigh finds me here in the morning, that could cause you trouble with Jim."

"I don't care about him. It's none of his business who I see. He made sure of that."

"While I agree with you, I still don't want to cause you any hassles." He kissed her once more and got up to finish getting dressed. When he was ready, he leaned over the bed to kiss her again. "I'll check on you in the morning." Glancing at the clock, he added, "Later in the morning, I should say."

"I'm glad you came over."

"So am I. Tonight was...amazing."

"Yes." Tiffany wrapped her arms around his neck and took the lead in another kiss designed to ensure he continued to think about her all the time. When she finally let him go, he groaned, which made her smile with satisfaction.

"Witch," he muttered as he stood to finish buttoning his shirt. "Sleep tight."

"You, too."

She heard him close the door downstairs and fell asleep a short time later with a smile on her face.

CHAPTER 14

Carolina sat in her dark living room for more than an hour after Joe and Janey went to bed. Somehow, she'd managed to keep up the pretense that everything was fine in front of them, even as she continued to absorb the shock about Seamus's decision. Now it was after eleven, and she couldn't wait any longer to find out if she was the reason he planned to leave.

She got up to grab a sweater and her car keys, praying the dogs wouldn't bark and give her away. As she tiptoed to the front door, she almost laughed at the absurdity of sneaking out of her own home in the dark of night. Unfortunately, nothing about this situation was funny.

Riley appeared out of the darkness, dragging himself on his front paws.

Startled, Carolina stopped short. "Don't worry, boy. Everything is fine." She gave him a pat on the head and felt his intense stare on her back as she pulled the door closed behind her. Thank goodness dogs couldn't talk.

As she started the car and backed out of the driveway, she expected Joe to come running out to see where she was going so late. Her heart beat rapidly as she pulled away from the house and released a sigh of relief. She'd gotten out undetected. Hopefully, she'd get back in the same way.

She drove into town and parked across the street from the Beachcomber. Praying she wouldn't see anyone she knew on the way in, she snuck in the side door and bolted up two flights of stairs to the third-floor room that Joe used to use. She'd offered up her home, but he'd preferred the room, as it was across the street from the ferry landing.

At the top of the stairs, she took a moment to gather herself and catch her breath. When she raised her arm to knock on the door, she noticed her hand was trembling. Regardless, she rapped on the door and then waited. And waited some more.

Great, she thought. *He isn't even here.* She wondered if he'd returned to the mainland. Dejected and still in bad need of answers she wouldn't get now, she turned to find him standing in the hallway, staring at her.

He seemed shocked to see her outside his room. "Caro? What're you doing here?"

As always, his lyrical Irish brogue made her a little light-headed. "I need to talk to you. Do you have a minute?"

He made a sound that might've been a laugh or a grunt. "For you, love? I think I can spare some time. Come in."

He undid her every time he called her "love." He made her want things she had no business wanting.

She followed him into the small room that seemed to get smaller after he closed the door, sealing them away from the rest of the world.

When he flipped on a light, she took a closer look at him. His green eyes were weary, and he seemed to have lost his sparkle since she last saw him. Was that her fault, too?

"Why did you quit?" she asked, breaking the charged silence.

Tipping his head, he eyed her with a combination of amusement and trepidation. "You know why."

"You can't do this! You love that job. Isn't that what you said?"

"'Tis indeed what I said. I do love it."

"Then *why?*"

"Caro..." He ran his fingers through wavy auburn hair, over and over until it stood on end. "Do I really have to spell it out for ya?"

Her stomach began to hurt as she took in his tortured expression. "I guess you do."

"I'm *in love* with you. If I can't have you, I can't be here. 'Tis that simple."

She shook her head and held up her hands, as if to protect herself from the surge of longing his words inspired in her. "You... We... We spent *one* night together. How in the world did you turn that into *love?*"

"Damned if I know. Some things just *are*. There's no explaining them."

"Seamus, please. You can't do this to Joe when the baby is due so soon."

His amiable expression hardened. "'Tis all about poor Joe, isn't it? *Poor* Joe will find someone else. No one is irreplaceable. Especially me."

Carolina realized she'd said the worst possible thing by pleading Joe's case. After all, Joe was the primary reason she'd kept her distance from Seamus in the first place.

"I'm sorry," she said. "I know you can't run your life based on what's best for Joe—or me."

"Are you *serious*? I'd rearrange my entire existence for the chance to be with you. I'd do it gladly for you, Caro. Not for Joe, but for *you*."

"I don't want you to go."

"Let me ask you something."

"What?" she asked hesitantly.

"If there was no Joe, would you give me a chance?"

"That's a foolish question. He's my *son*, my heart and soul. No matter what I might want for myself, he'll always come first. Always."

"And what do you want for yourself, love?"

"That doesn't matter. The day his father died, I made a promise to him that I'd always be there for him, no matter what."

"And you have been. You've made him the center of your life for thirty-seven years. Now he has a life of his own, a good life that satisfies him greatly. Do you think he'd want any less for you?"

She shook her head. "He'd never understand this. He'd never understand *us*."

It only took two steps for him to cross the room to her. He framed her face in his hands, compelling her to look at him. "I dream about you. I dream we're together, that I'm holding you and kissing you and sleeping with you and making slow, sweet love to you. And then I wake up alone, and it's like I've lost you all over again. I've gotten so I hate to sleep because it ends the same way every time."

Only when he brushed away her tears with the sweep of his thumbs did Carolina realize she was crying. "I'm sorry," she whispered. "I'm so very sorry. I never meant to hurt you like this—"

He brought his lips down hard on hers, surrounding her with his strong arms and his scent, and the magic he made with the soft press of his lips and the insistent strokes of his tongue. "I've been starving for you," he said gruffly before going back for more.

Carolina clung to him as the understanding that she, too, had been starving settled over her like a blanket, warming her from the inside out.

"Caro, *Caro*," he whispered as he worshiped her neck, "I've tried so hard to stop thinking about you, to stop wanting you, but it only gets worse instead of better. God, I love you so damned much. There's nothing I wouldn't do for you, nothing I wouldn't give to be with you. Nothing."

He took her mouth again, rendering her helpless in the storm of his passion.

Even with Pete, it had never been like this. Nothing had ever been like this. While her rational side urged her to get out of there and go home while she still could, her heart and body cried out for him.

Without breaking the kiss, he lifted her and turned them toward the bed. The next thing she knew she was falling, and he was coming down on top of her.

She turned her head, tearing her lips free of his. "Seamus, we can't do this. We can't."

"Yes, we can. We're both adults. We both want to."

She started to shake her head, but he stopped her with another kiss.

"I'll talk to Joe," he said. "I'll tell him the truth."

"No." She pushed at his chest, seeking space and perspective. "You can't do that."

His frustration was apparent as he rolled off her and lay on his back with his arm shielding his eyes. "Just go, Caro." He sounded so defeated that her heart broke, knowing she'd done that to him. "If there's no changing your mind, please go."

The pain she heard in his voice made her ache. She rested a hand over his hammering heart. "It's not that I don't want you, too."

Raising his arm off his face, he stared at her, incredulous. "Do you think I don't know that? Do you think I don't feel how much you want me in every kiss? That I don't *see* it every time you look at me?"

Astounded by his impassioned words, she had no idea what to say. "I—"

"Please, love, just go. I can't do this anymore. It hurts too much."

"I don't want to go."

He took her hand and brought it to his lips. "But you can't stay, either, can you?"

She shook her head.

"Hell of a dilemma."

"I'm sorry."

"So am I, love. So am I." With another kiss to the palm of her hand, he released her.

Carolina stood on trembling legs. Her lips burned from the force of his kisses. She felt rather than saw him standing behind her. Images of the long, lonely winter she'd passed thinking about him and the night they'd spent together flashed through her mind.

Now was the time to be honest, finally, with herself. Not a day had gone by since they were together that she hadn't yearned to be with him, to talk to him, to hear that lyrical brogue and the outrageous things he said that made her feel so safe and adored.

"I'll talk to Joe." The words were out of her mouth before she took the time to ponder the implications.

"You'll talk to him about what?"

Carolina forced herself to turn and face him. She owed him that much. "I'll talk to him about what I want."

"And what's that?"

"You," she said softly. "I want you."

He rested his hand on his heart. "Don't say that if you don't really mean it, and for the love of all that's holy, don't say it so I'll stay and run the business for your son."

Carolina rested her fingers on his lips. "I never say anything I don't mean, and this has nothing at all to do with the business."

His eyes lit up with delight, and for an instant, he resembled his old self. "You're making me all giddy with foolish hope, love."

For the first time since she'd stepped into the room, she smiled. "You have such a way of saying things."

"I have so many things I'd like to say to you." He put his arms around her and drew her in close to him.

Carolina closed her eyes, wrapped her arms around his waist and breathed in the scent that had haunted her since the last time she'd been close to him.

"I worry I won't live long enough to tell you all the things I want to tell you."

"I'll talk to him."

"I'll be waiting."

THE BABY WOKE Janey from a deep sleep with a sharp kick to the ribs. It was still strange at times to realize a life was growing inside her, letting its mother know that she was in for a wild ride. She rested a hand on her belly, smiling when she felt the ripple of life travel from one side of her belly to another.

"What's wrong?" Joe asked, yawning.

She took his hand and rested it on the baby bump. "Feel this."

"Wow. That's *amazing*." He never failed to stir her with his excitement about the baby they hadn't planned to have quite yet. "Does it feel weird inside?"

"Sort of. He's kicking hard enough to wake me up."

Joe kept his hand next to hers on her belly. "So he's a *he* now?"

They'd decided not to find out what they were having and took turns coming up with nicknames and interchanging pronouns. "For the moment." Seeking a more comfortable position, Janey shifted onto her side to face her husband. "Why are you awake?"

"No reason."

"You're thinking about the business."

"Maybe a little. Nothing to worry about, hon."

"I've been thinking, too."

"About what?"

"Maybe I should take a leave of absence for a year—"

"No. No way. That's not happening."

"Hear me out."

"I don't want to hear you talk about not going back to school. You're so close to being done. You can't quit now."

"I wouldn't quit. I'd just be postponing a bit."

"No."

"Maybe this situation with Seamus is a sign."

"A sign of what?"

"That we should stay here this year, so you can run the business and I can take care of the baby."

"I'll find someone to deal with the business, and I'll take care of the baby so you can finish school. I don't want you to worry about anything."

How could she tell him that the closer she got to delivering the baby, the more conflicted she became about where she belonged? Becoming a veterinarian was a dream come true, but having a baby and being a mother was far more important all of a sudden. After Joe had sacrificed so much to make it possible for her to attend veterinary school in Ohio, how could she tell him that she was no longer certain she wanted to finish? The thought of leaving the baby for hours on end to attend classes and labs and then to come home to all the studying…

What sort of mother would she be if her baby never saw her?

Joe gave her hand a little tug, encouraging her to come closer.

Janey never needed much encouragement to get close to him. She rested her head on his chest and sighed with contentment when his arms encircled her.

He kissed the top of her head. "Go to sleep."

Never one to do as she was told, Janey ran her hand from his chest to his belly. Under the covers, she found him hard and ready. "Want to?"

He snorted out a laugh. "Always. It's more a matter of whether *you* want to."

"I *really* want to, but I'm not sure if the rest of me will cooperate."

"You wanna find out?"

"I'm game if you are."

He hesitated. "I don't know if I can do it in my mother's house."

"Oh, please! You have no trouble doing it in *my* mother's house."

He rolled so he was above her but was careful to keep his weight off her abdomen. "That's different."

"How's it different?"

"It's not *my* mother's house."

Her slug to his shoulder earned her a laugh from her husband, who took her mind off the indignation by kissing her with passionate intent. They'd had to be creative in bed since her burgeoning belly made sex difficult. Ironically, pregnancy had made her ridiculously horny. It was so unfair that she wanted sex constantly but had the ungodly belly standing between her and her husband. She couldn't wait to feel his chest hair against her breasts again. She'd missed that.

Janey ran her fingers up his neck to bury them in his hair, which he'd let grow a bit from the ultra-short style he'd favored until she told him she liked it a little longer.

"Tell me if anything hurts?"

"Mmm," she said against his lips. "Hurry."

"I'll have to keep you constantly pregnant," he said as he pushed up her nightgown and slid into her, nearly making her come from that alone. "I like insatiable Janey."

"*Mmm*, I like her, too." Janey closed her eyes and floated on a cloud of sensation as he gave her exactly what she needed—slowly, gently, reverently.

"Janey..."

She loved the desperate way her name exploded from his lips as his control broke. He threw his head back and came hard but silently, triggering an explosive response from her. Somehow, he managed to stay propped up on his arms until they wouldn't hold him any longer, and then he rolled to his side, reaching for her.

"Quick and dirty," Janey said with a smile he couldn't see.

"Sorry."

"For what?"

"Being too quick."

"You weren't too quick. You were perfect." She kissed his shoulder and breathed in his endlessly appealing scent. "As always."

"You're easy to please."

"I love you love you," she whispered, rubbing his back as she felt him drift off to sleep.

"Hmmm, me, too."

Janey kept up the circular motion on his back until his breathing deepened and she was certain he was asleep. Then she carefully extricated herself from his embrace and got up to use the bathroom. She was on her way back to bed when she heard the dogs stirring in the living room where she'd put their beds. As she moved from the hallway to the living room to check on them, the front door opened, and Carolina came in. The two women startled each other.

"Jeez, you about gave me a heart attack," Janey said.

Carolina had her hand over her heart. "Same here."

"Where've you been? I thought you were asleep."

"I, um, I had something I needed to do."

In the faint light of a single lamp, Janey took a closer look at her mother-in-law. "Have you been crying?"

"No, of course not." But as she said the words, tears rolled down her cheeks. She brushed them away, almost as if she hoped Janey wouldn't notice them.

Janey, who'd never seen Carolina Cantrell rattled, let alone undone, took her by the hand and led her into the kitchen, urging her into a chair at the table. Janey filled the kettle and put it on to boil. While it heated, she rooted around in the cabinet until she found two packets of decaffeinated tea and set them in mugs.

"It's nothing, really," Carolina said. "You need your rest, honey."

"Hush. I get plenty of rest. Clearly, something is wrong, and I'd like to think you feel comfortable enough to talk to me the way you would a girlfriend."

Janey was dismayed to see more tears cascading down Carolina's pretty face. "I do. Of course I do. The day Joe married you, I got the daughter I've always wanted."

"Now you're going to make me cry, too." Janey put the mugs on the table and lowered herself into one of the chairs, which wasn't as easy as it sounded. When she was settled, she leveled a steady gaze at her mother-in-law. "Talk to me. What's going on?"

"I… God, I don't know where to start."

Carolina's distress was truly alarming. "Start at the beginning."

"There's… Ah, well, there's a man."

Janey stared at her, astounded. "*Really?* Who?"

"It's the 'who' that's the problem."

"Is it someone I know?"

Carolina bit her lip and nodded.

All at once, Janey realized that whatever she was about to hear was going to be big—really, *really* big. Her belly took a queasy roll, like it did on the ferry when the seas were particularly choppy. "Who?"

Carolina hesitated for a long, long moment. "Seamus."

Janey gasped. Her eyes went wide, and her mouth fell open. "Holy shit."

"I know what you're thinking." Carolina dropped her head into her hands. "I've thought all the same things myself. That's why I told him it couldn't happen."

Janey's brain literally whirled as she tried to process Carolina's words.

"You're shocked, I know. And probably disgusted. I wouldn't blame you—"

"No, *no.*" Janey snapped out of the stupor and reached for Carolina's hand. "I'm not disgusted. I'm surprised, that's all." And she couldn't help but wonder what Joe would have to say about it. That thought made her stomach ache for real. "Is this why he's leaving?"

Carolina nodded and wiped away more tears. "I told him last fall when, you know, we...got together...that it couldn't happen. And now... Now he's decided he can't stay here if we aren't together."

"Why did you tell him it couldn't happen?"

Carolina stared at her, agog. "Why do you think?"

"Because of Joe."

"Yes, because of Joe and the age difference and because he deserves to have children and a family of his own, not to mention the people who won't get what the heck I'm doing romantically involved with a man only two years older than my son."

"But do you care for him? For Seamus?"

Carolina covered her mouth to muffle a sob as she nodded.

Janey's heart went out to her. "Come here." She reached for Carolina and did her best to hug her with the big belly getting in the way, as usual. "You have to talk to Joe. He loves you so much. He'd want you to be happy."

"He'll never understand this."

"Maybe not at first, but he'll come around."

"I told Seamus I'd talk to him, but..."

"Is that where you were just now?"

"Yes." Carolina straightened and wiped her face on the sleeve of her shirt. "I had to know if he was leaving because of me, so I went to see him. Other than a few minutes when I was waiting to meet your boat the other day, I haven't seen him in months. But I've thought about him. Every day."

"What happened when you saw him?"

"Just like last fall. It was...explosive."

Janey fanned herself. "I wish I was a smoker."

For the first time since the conversation began, a hint of a smile tugged at Carolina's lips.

"If it would help," Janey said, "I'll be there when you talk to Joe."

"Oh, would you, Janey? That would help so much."

"Of course I will. Remember, it wasn't that long ago that I broke up with my fiancé of thirteen years and took up with your son the same night. I know what it's like to worry about what people will say."

"Yes, you do, don't you?"

Janey nodded. "And here's how I think it'll go—people, and Joe in particular—will be wound up about it for a while. And then something else will happen to change the conversation, and they'll forget all about you and your scandal."

Carolina winced at the word *scandal.*

"Sorry. Poor word choice."

"I've never been part of a scandal before."

"Maybe it's time, huh? You've been alone for so long. I know Joe would be thrilled to see you happy again, and so would I. He'd never admit it, especially not to you, but he worries about you."

"I wish he wouldn't."

Janey shrugged. "You know how he is."

"I do, and that's why I'm so afraid to tell him."

"I'll be honest with you, Carolina. I'm not sure, exactly, how he'll take this. He's put a lot of trust in Seamus to run the business in his absence, so he's apt to be quite upset at first. But once he has time to get his head around it, he'll be glad you have someone new in your life, especially someone like Seamus."

"Why do you say that? Especially someone like Seamus?"

"He's *wonderful,*" Janey said. "What's not to love about him and that brogue?" She fanned herself dramatically. "Not to mention he's crazy handsome."

"I've noticed that—and the brogue."

Janey giggled at the besotted expression on her mother-in-law's face. "Joe thinks the world of him."

"As an *employee.* As his mother's boyfriend or whatever he'd be? Will he think the world of him then?"

"There's only one way to find out."

"That's what I'm afraid of."

CHAPTER 15

Watching his son pace back and forth as he engaged in an intense phone conversation on the main pier the next morning, Big Mac McCarthy waited until Mac ended the call before walking out to join him. The pond, placid in the early morning calm before the storm of daily activity, was chockablock full of the sailboats that had gathered for Race Week, and the marina was completely sold out. A bank of fog hung over the pond, an early season staple as the cold New England water did battle with the warming air.

Mario, the pizza-and-bakery man from town, drove his skiff around while singing Italian opera and delivering muffins and baked goods to the boats at anchor. His deep tenor carried across the water as it had every summer since Big Mac had bought the rundown marina almost forty years ago. Another season on Gansett Island was under way, but Big Mac's mind wasn't on business. Not when his firstborn was clearly upset about something.

Mac leaned against a piling, staring out at the pond, lost in thought. *What a handsome man his boy had turned out to be,* Big Mac thought as he approached him. Having Mac working with him every day at the marina was one of the greatest joys in a life filled with great joy.

"Everything okay, son?"

Mac glanced at his father. "No, everything is not okay."

It was so unlike his type-A son to admit anything was bothering him that Big Mac was taken aback for a second. "What's wrong?"

"First of all, Thomas has the stomach bug. Apparently, Ashleigh has it, too."

"Oh, that's too bad. Poor kids."

"And Maddie..."

"What about her?"

Mac shook his head. "She's making me so mad."

Big Mac was truly astonished to hear that. The two of them were so stupid in love they didn't even know they were supposed to fight once in a while. "Over what?"

"Her goddamned deadbeat father wants to see her, and she's actually going to *do* it. And it doesn't even *matter* to her that I don't want her to."

Big Mac leaned an elbow on the next piling. "She's doing it because of Francine."

"Yes," Mac said, sounding weary. "We keep going round and round about it, and I can't make her see reason."

"She's determined to do it."

"That's what she says."

"Then you have to let her do what she needs to do. How'd you like to have it on your mind that you were standing in the way of someone else's happiness?"

"It's not that simple, Dad. She remembers him. She remembers him leaving. She sat in the window for weeks watching the ferries, hoping he'd change his mind and come back." His voice caught on the last words, which tugged at Big Mac's heart. He hated seeing his kids upset about anything. "She was *five*."

"You could go with her."

"She won't let me."

Big Mac held back a smile he knew his son wouldn't appreciate. "How come?"

"She doesn't trust me to behave."

"Can't say I blame her there."

"Thanks, Dad. That helps. Really."

"I'll go with her."

Mac looked up at him. "What?"

"I'll go with her. I knew Bobby Chester a little bit back in the day. I know how he operates. I'll make sure he doesn't say or do anything to cause additional harm."

"You'd do that? Really?"

This time, Big Mac didn't hold back the smile. Was there anything, anything on God's green earth, he wouldn't do for his five kids? Well, seven kids, if you counted Joe and Luke, and they certainly counted as his.

"Of course you'd do that," Mac said, more to himself than his father. "I should've known better than to ask."

"Yes, you should have." Big Mac hoped to draw a small smile from his son and wasn't disappointed. "I'll take good care of her. Leave it to me."

"Excuse me."

They turned to find a man waiting to speak with them—a handsome guy in his mid-thirties, if Big Mac was estimating correctly. "What can we do for you?"

"I'm Steve Jacobson. The woman in the restaurant thought you might be able to help me out."

"Sure," Big Mac said. "What'd you need?"

"I'm here for Race Week, but my crew is down with the stomach flu."

"Seems to be going around," Mac said. "My son and niece have it, too."

Steve winced in sympathy. "Do you know of anyone who might be able to stand in for my crew for the opening race? If I don't sail, I have to forfeit the whole regatta. They think they'll be better for the day after, but tomorrow is the big day."

"You could do it," Big Mac said to his son.

Mac shook his head. "Not with this place so busy and Thomas sick. Maddie's freaked out about the baby getting it, too."

"I understand it's a lot to ask," Steve said.

"Let me ask around," Mac said. "I've got a couple of brothers and some friends who might be into it. How many do you need?"

"Four would be ideal, but I could make do with three if they know what they're doing."

"My kids know how to sail," Big Mac said proudly.

"Required life skill for the children of a marina owner," Mac added, which made Steve laugh. "I'll see what I can do.

"Thanks very much." Steve shook hands with both of them and headed for the parking lot, cell phone pressed to his ear.

"You should take a day off and get away from it all," Big Mac said to his son. "It'd do you some good. I can handle things here, and Mom and Francine can help with the kids."

"I don't know. I'll think about it." Mac glanced at his father. "Thanks. You know, for what you're willing to do for Maddie. I think she'll go for that plan."

Big Mac rested a hand on his son's shoulder. "There's nothing I wouldn't do for you—or for her."

"Have I mentioned lately that I got pretty damned lucky in the dad department?"

The words hit Big Mac right in the solar plexus, but he managed to refrain from overreacting. His kids hated when he overreacted—not that he thought he ever did... "No, I don't think you've mentioned that," he said, going with lighthearted over emotional.

"Well, I did, and so did the others. Seeing what Maddie is going through has brought that home even more than it already was."

"That's nice of you to say, son, but I got lucky in the kid department, too. The lot of ya turned out pretty good despite the mess I tried to make of you."

"That's thanks to Mom," Mac said with a cheeky grin.

Big Mac cuffed his son upside the head and then drew him into a hug. "Don't worry about your lady, son. I'll take good care of her."

"Thank you."

BLAINE KNEW it was absolutely ridiculous to stop by Tiffany's store to see how Ashleigh was feeling and to find out whether Tiffany had gotten any sleep. It was especially ridiculous to go there with Wyatt in tow. He was supposed to be working on some training with the patrolman, but all he could think about was Tiffany. Until he satisfied the need to see her, he wouldn't be able to concentrate on work or anything else. It occurred to him that this thing with her was moving way too fast, but that didn't stop him from pulling the SUV into the grocery store parking lot. "I need to make a quick stop."

"Has there been more trouble with the store?" Wyatt asked.

"Not that I know of."

"Oh."

Blaine was grateful that the chatty patrolman chose to keep whatever comments he might wish to make to himself. He wasn't prepared to explain his relationship with the purveyor of Naughty & Nice, especially to one of his subordinates.

The chime of the bells on the store's door reminded him of the last time he'd visited the store and what had happened then. He quickly forced his thoughts off that topic and focused on a quick visit. However, the scent of the store filled his senses, reminding him of the night before. Honestly, he was like a randy fourteen-year-old boy where she was concerned. With a quick look around, he didn't see her.

Patty emerged from the storeroom, and Blaine did a double take. *Wow*. She looked so different. "Oh, hi, Chief Taylor. How are you today?"

"Doing good, Patty. Did you cut your hair or something?"

Her cheeks turned bright red. "Or something. Tiffany gave me a makeover."

"Well," he said, "you look great."

"Totally great," Wyatt added, his eyes bugging at the sight of Patty's pronounced cleavage.

Before his patrolman could embarrass them both, Blaine asked for Tiffany.

"She's home sick today. Apparently, she caught whatever Ashleigh had."

Blaine hated to think of her being sick. "That's too bad."

"Should I tell her you stopped by?"

"That's okay. I'll give her a call later. Have a good day."

"You, too."

Blaine headed for the door and was halfway across the street when he realized Wyatt wasn't with him. Fuming, he turned to go back after him when the patrolman came bursting out of the store wearing a goofy grin on his face.

"What the hell are you doing?" Blaine asked him as they got back into the SUV.

"Nothing."

Blaine studied the younger man, who looked like the cat who'd swallowed the proverbial canary. "Did you ask her out?"

"Am I required to disclose the details of my personal life to my chief?"

While Wyatt's cheekiness annoyed him, it also amused him, much to his dismay. "At all times."

"In that case, yes, I asked her out—not that it's any of your business."

"If it happens on my watch, it's my business."

"How do you figure?"

"Son, you've got a lot to learn about police work."

"I assume all of this is in the manual?"

The dryly spoken comment earned a genuine laugh from Blaine. "Naturally." He retrieved a binder from the backseat and tossed it to the mouthy patrolman. "Study up. I've got a phone call to make."

"To your *girlfriend?*"

"Shut up and read."

"Yes, sir."

Shaking his head, Blaine got out of the truck and slammed the door. Pain-in-the-ass kid. Was he ever that insubordinate? Thinking back to his early years as a patrolman in a small Massachusetts town, he decided he was probably worse than Wyatt ever thought of being. He found Tiffany's number on his phone and pressed Send.

Her "hello" a minute later sounded tortured.

"I heard you were sick. Are you okay?"

"Dying."

"Where's Ashleigh?"

"Sleeping. We were up all night."

"What can I do for you?"

"Nothing. I'm okay."

"Could I check on you later?"

"I'd permanently scare you away if you saw the way I look right now."

"Nah. I'm not that easily scared."

"I'm also afraid of you getting it. I certainly exposed you to it last night."

"I liked the way you exposed me to your germs. Can we do it again soon?"

"Don't make me laugh," she said with a moan. "Everything hurts."

"Do you think you should call David?"

"Nah, just a flu. Hopefully a quick one. I need to get back to work."

"Patty is holding down the fort at the store. I just saw her."

"Oh, really? Any customers?"

"Not that I saw, but it's early. Get this—my patrolman Wyatt asked her out."

"That's awesome!"

He was surprised by her enthusiasm, especially when she felt so crappy. "You think so? It could turn out to be a pain for both of us."

"She wants a boyfriend so badly. The poor thing has never had one."

"Aww, that's sweet. She was very cute telling me about the makeover you gave her while blushing furiously. That was a nice thing you did for her, Tiff."

"It was fun."

"I'll call you before I come over later to see if you guys need anything."

"Thanks."

Blaine hung up with her and got back in the SUV.

"How's the girlfriend?" Wyatt asked.

"Sick, if you must know."

"I heard there's a stomach flu going around the island. Nasty business."

"She has it and so does her daughter."

"That's too bad. I can cover for you for a while if you need to help her out."

Maybe there was hope for the kid after all. "That's not necessary, but thanks for the offer."

"Where're we heading now?"

"I need to stop by the Sand & Surf for a minute."

"What goes on there?"

"They're getting ready to reopen at the end of the week, and Stephanie's restaurant is opening to friends and family tonight."

"So what do you need to do?"

"Make sure the fire chief got there to inspect the place before it opens, check in with Laura, the hotel manager, to see if there's anything she needs from us for the opening, and I need to speak with Owen Lawry's mother, Sarah, about a personal matter."

"Sounds exciting." Wyatt's tone dripped with sarcasm.

"A lot of what we do as small-town police officers is boring, especially in the off season. But at least once a year, I save a life, usually that of a kid who gets drunk on the beach and doesn't realize he or she has alcohol poisoning. The other night, we saved a woman from her abusive boyfriend, seconds before he would've killed her. It's not like the big city with the nonstop action, but we have our purpose."

As he drove, Blaine glanced at the patrolman. "I'd understand if you decide it's not for you. That's why we insist on a probationary period where either party can terminate the contract. We don't want anyone here who doesn't want to be here."

"I like the job. More than I thought I would. I'm not so sure how I feel about being stuck on the island, though."

"Let me know when you've made up your mind." As much as the kid got on Blaine's nerves at times, he had real potential, and Blaine would hate to lose him.

"I will."

They parked behind the hotel and walked around to the front. The old gray lady gleamed from the facelift she'd been given over the winter. Her shingles had been power-washed, her trim painted, the porch rebuilt and most of the windows replaced. To look at the hotel now, you'd never know it had guarded the northern corner of the harbor town for more than a century or that it had fallen into disrepair after Owen's grandparents retired a few years ago. Pots of flowers sat on the stairs that led to the porch where new white rocking chairs waited for guests to while away a summer day overlooking the waterfront.

"Place looks awesome," Wyatt said.

"I was just thinking the same thing."

Inside, they found Laura McCarthy conferring with the fire chief, Mason Johns. Laura's baby son, Holden, snoozed in a pouch tied around his mother's shoulders.

"Hey, Blaine." Mason extended a hand. "We were just talking about you."

"Is that right?" Blaine shook the other man's hand. At roughly six foot six inches of solid muscle, Mason towered over him and most other men. Someone had told Blaine that Mason had once been a competitive weightlifter before he became a firefighter. Suffice to say, Blaine wouldn't want to screw with the guy.

Wyatt stared at the fire chief with blatant admiration and a healthy dose of intimidation.

"Laura was saying she's talked to you about parking and crowd control for the open house tonight," Mason said.

"That's right. I've got two patrol officers assigned to keep an eye on things here and to handle any traffic issues."

"Sounds good," Mason said. "I've signed off on my inspection, so you're approved to open, Laura."

"That's the best news I've had in weeks," Laura said. "I was so afraid Stephanie's opening would get messed up by something I missed in the hotel."

"Not to worry." Mason handed her a certificate. "You covered all the bases. Wish you a lot of luck with the place."

"Thank you. We need all the luck we can get."

Blaine looked around at the cozy lobby that boasted freshly painted white wainscoting, sage walls and furniture he'd heard called "shabby chic." Taken as a whole, it worked magnificently. "It looks so good, Laura. It's great to have the Surf reopened. The town wasn't the same without her."

"I agree. Fingers crossed for a smooth opening." As she said the words, Blaine watched her wobble and reached out a hand to steady her. He noticed a fine sheen of perspiration on her forehead.

"Are you okay?"

"I can't believe it, but I think I'm getting sick. I feel awful."

"It's going around the island," Blaine said.

"I've heard the clinic is overrun today," Mason added.

"Great," Laura said with a moan. "This is *so* not what I need right now."

Laura's fiancé, Owen Lawry, came bounding down the stairs, wearing a red bandanna pirate-style over his unruly blond hair. "Hey, Blaine, Mason." He shook hands with both men. "How goes it?"

"We're good," Blaine said, "but poor Laura is not so good."

Owen's attention immediately shifted to his fiancée. "What is it? What's wrong?"

"I'm not feeling so great, but don't worry. I'll soldier through." She barely got the words out before she turned a disturbing shade of green.

"Owen," Blaine said, worried that she might pass out with the baby attached to her.

"I've got her." Owen deftly transferred the baby pouch to his own shoulders and put an arm around Laura.

She leaned into him. "I can't puke in front of you again. I just can't."

"Morning sickness," Owen said for Blaine and Mason's benefit. "It was brutal." To Laura, he said, "Let's get you upstairs, honey."

"I have so much to do!"

"My mom and I have got you covered. Don't worry."

"Speaking of your mom," Blaine said. "Is she around?"

"Second floor, far left," Owen said. "I just left her giving the bathrooms up there a final cleaning."

"I'll find her."

"Everything okay?" Owen asked, seeming anxious.

Blaine knew he was thinking of the night last fall when his mother arrived on the island beaten and broken after the final showdown with her abusive ex-husband. Owen's father, a retired air force general, was due to stand trial on domestic assault charges later in the year. "Everything is fine. I could use her help with something. That's all."

"I'm sure she'd be glad to do anything she could for you after all you've done for us."

During the short exchange, Laura's eyes had closed, and she was leaning against Owen.

"You'd better get her to bed."

When Owen tried to rouse her, she didn't budge. "Asleep on her feet."

"Let me take the baby," Blaine said, "and you can take her."

"Thanks, man." Owen dipped his head so Blaine could work the baby free of the pouch.

"Stay put," Blaine said to Wyatt. "I'll be right back."

"You got it."

Holden molded himself to Blaine's shoulder without waking. As the sweet scent of baby shampoo and powder filled his senses, Blaine was filled with a new kind of longing. What would it be like, he wondered, to have a baby son of his own? What would it be like to have a baby who had Tiffany's and Ashleigh's dark hair and green eyes? As he carried Holden upstairs, it dawned on him that the idea of being a husband and father didn't terrify him the way it would have even a few weeks ago.

She'd changed something in him, something he wasn't sorry to see changed. She'd smoothed out his bitter edges and given him reason to hope again. Halfway up the stairs, he stopped short, astounded to realize he was falling in love with her. He, the guy who'd sworn he was done with love, was suddenly on his way to being flat on his face in love again. This time was different, though. This time he was falling for someone real and genuine and sexy as all get-out.

"Blaine?" With Laura in his arms, Owen looked down from the third-floor landing. "Everything okay?"

"Yep. I'm coming." He delivered Holden to the apartment Owen and Laura shared on the third floor. Owen was pulling the covers over Laura's shoulders when Blaine entered through the door Owen had left open for him.

"Let me know if you guys need anything," Blaine said as he handed over the baby to his stepfather.

"Thanks for your help." Owen kissed the baby's forehead. "Heck of a time for Laura to get sick with the hotel opening this week. She'll be in a panic about work."

"It'll all be fine. This is Gansett. People expect things to be laid-back."

"That's true. I'll remind her of that when she wakes up having a panic attack."

"Good luck," Blaine said as he left Owen to take care of his family. Descending the stairs to the second floor, he looked for Sarah Lawry in each of the three bathrooms and found her in the last one he checked. "Sarah?"

The woman nearly jumped out of her skin, and Blaine berated himself for sneaking up on her. "Sorry to startle you."

"Oh, hi, Chief Taylor. No apology needed. I'm jumpy by nature."

Blaine was certain that years of abuse at the hands of her ex-husband had contributed to her jumpy nature. "Please, call me Blaine. How're you doing?" He took in the faded blonde hair that she wore in a stylish bob and the gray eyes that were so much like her son's.

"Very well. Busy getting the hotel ready to open. It's so exciting to see it back in business. Mother and Dad have been so sad that it was closed since they retired a few years back. Thank goodness for Laura."

Her chattiness astounded Blaine, who'd become accustomed to one-word answers and downcast eyes whenever he spoke to her. To see her emerging from her shell was nothing short of miraculous. "I was just with Laura, and it seems she's come down with the flu that's making its way around the island."

"Oh no! Poor thing! It's the worst possible time."

"She said the same thing. Owen is with her and taking care of her and the baby."

Sarah's smile lit up her face, and Blaine caught a glimpse of the pretty young woman she'd been before her husband broke her spirit. "He's so crazy about both of them. Never thought I'd see that happen."

"Happens to the best of us eventually, I suppose."

Sarah tilted her head to take a measuring look at him as only a mother could do. "Is that so?"

Blaine smiled and shrugged, unwilling to disclose his newfound feelings to anyone until he shared them with Tiffany. "I was wondering if I could ask a favor."

"For you? Anything."

"That's very kind of you. There's a woman in town who I think might benefit from your wisdom."

"What wisdom do I have to share with anyone?"

"You left an abusive relationship."

"Oh. That kind."

"She's recently come to the understanding that she can no longer be with the man who hurt her, but I worry about her wavering and going back to him. Next time, I fear he might kill her."

"And you think I can help her?"

Blaine feared he might've made a misstep by bringing up this subject with her when she seemed to be doing so much better. "I do. You can tell her that it doesn't get better. It only gets worse."

A long moment passed while she considered what he'd said. "I'd be happy to talk to her if you think it would help."

"I'd appreciate that."

"When would you like to do it?"

"How about tomorrow?"

"That'd be fine, as long as the kids don't need me to help with the baby."

"I'll call you, and we'll set something up. Thanks again. I'll let you get back to work."

"Blaine?"

He turned back to her.

"You're good at what you do."

"Thank you," he said, ridiculously pleased by her praise.

"Sarah!" A male voice boomed from the stairway to the third floor.

Sarah stood up a little taller and looked over Blaine's shoulder, her face turning an intriguing shade of pink.

Blaine turned to find Stephanie's stepfather Charlie Grandchamp in the hallway.

"Sorry," Charlie said in the gruff, clipped tone he favored. "Didn't realize you were busy."

"It's fine, Charlie. You know Chief Taylor?"

"Can't say I've had the pleasure."

"Good to meet you." Blaine shook Charlie's hand. "Heard a lot about you."

"Bet you have."

Blaine wasn't surprised by the terse response to a police officer. "I've heard only good stuff," Blaine said. "Stephanie and Grant speak highly of you."

Charlie eyed him with skepticism that Blaine suspected was ingrained after his years in prison. "Nice to hear."

"I won't keep you folks," Blaine said. "I know you've got work to do. I'll be in touch, Sarah."

"Thanks, Blaine."

CHAPTER 16

"What was that all about?" Charlie asked after Blaine walked away.

As always, when he turned his pent-up intensity in her direction, Sarah's heart pounded and her palms went damp. "He asked for a favor."

"What kind of favor?"

In all the months Charlie had worked at the hotel and chipped away at her defenses, she'd never mentioned her husband or what had happened between them—and she didn't plan to. "The kind of favor a friend asks another friend to do for them."

"Hmm."

Sarah was well used to Charlie's one-word answers, along with his grunts, his scowls and his overall surliness. None of that had kept her from developing a world-class crush on the ex-con. Imagining what her parents would have to say about it almost made her giggle. Imagining what her soon-to-be ex-husband would have to say made her feel euphoric. Thinking about what her seven children would have to say, however, filled her with nervous energy.

Although, she thought, Owen liked Charlie, but liking him and approving of his mother desiring him was another thing altogether.

Her eyes settled on Charlie's bulging biceps and the intricate tattoo that circled his arm. She'd love to ask him about it and what it meant, but she wouldn't dare. Instead, she took every opportunity to admire the muscles on top of muscles that were always on full display thanks to the tank-top shirts he wore to work. Even though he was only in his early fifties, his hair was completely gray, but he wore it in a severe-looking buzz cut that made Sarah wonder what it might look like if allowed to grow longer. She'd love to find out.

As compelling as she found the rest of him, his steely blue eyes and sensual lips really did her in. Sometimes, when she allowed herself to think about what it might be like—

"What're you staring at?" Charlie asked, interrupting Sarah's musings.

Horrified to realize she'd been staring at him, Sarah cleared her throat and tried to find something to do with her restless hands. "Nothing."

"Looked to me like you were staring at me."

"I was *not* staring at you."

"Must've been that other guy standing behind me, then."

Sarah's mouth fell open. "Did you just make a joke?"

"So what?"

She loved that she'd managed to fluster him. "So you never make jokes. You never smile or laugh or say more than you absolutely have to."

His face twisted into a smug grin. "Been paying pretty close attention, huh?"

Damn it. She'd given far too much away with that statement.

He took a step closer, and Sarah wasn't sure what she wanted more—to rush toward him or run for her life. Because she couldn't decide, she remained absolutely still and waited to see what he would do.

"I've been paying attention, too." This was said in a low, sexy tone that made goose bumps pop up on her arms.

"Oh." Her throat felt tight all of a sudden. So did her skin, as if it was too small for her body. "You have?"

He nodded. "You don't like eye contact. You don't care for being startled or surprised. When someone moves too quickly near you, you shy away as if you're expecting to get knocked around or something."

Too close. He was getting far too close with both his words and his presence.

Sarah took a step back.

"Don't do that."

"Don't do what?"

"Don't be afraid of me."

"I'm not," she said, even though he terrified her for entirely different reasons than her ex-husband had.

Eyeing her skeptically, he tipped his head to one side. "No?"

Determined to be brave, she shook her head.

"You're going to the restaurant opening tonight?"

Sarah nodded. "Of course."

"You want to go with me?"

Her mind went blank again and then came raging back to life when it dawned on her that he was *asking her out*. Charlie Grandchamp, the object of the first crush she'd had in forty years, was *asking her out*.

"Often when a man extends himself to a lady, he expects her to answer with a yes or a no. Either answer will do, but it would be nice to hear one of them."

And he was funny, too. Who'd have guessed it? "Um…"

"That wasn't one of the options."

Sarah couldn't help but smile at the startling discovery that underneath all the gruffness and bluster was a rather charming man. Who cared what her parents, children or godforsaken ex-husband would have to say? She liked Charlie. She had enjoyed working with him at the hotel. She was curious about him, about his life, about how he'd ended up in prison for something he didn't do. And most interestingly of all, she was attracted to him.

Apparently, the attraction worked both ways, and wasn't that lovely?

"Yes."

He released a deep breath she hadn't realized he was holding. "You know how to make a guy suffer."

"It wasn't intentional."

"I know that. A classy dame like you going out with a guy like me..." He shrugged. "I don't blame you for being reluctant."

"I'm not reluctant. Not one bit reluctant."

"Is that right?"

"Uh-huh." *God, this is fun,* she thought, as blood zinged through her veins. It had been a very long time since anything had interested or excited her the way Charlie Grandchamp did.

"Well, good. I'll pick you up at your room around seven. Don't go downstairs without me."

"Wouldn't dream of it."

He nodded, turned to leave and ran smack into Owen. Judging by the astonished expression on his face, her son had overheard the last part of their conversation.

"See you folks tonight," Charlie said as he passed Owen.

"Ah, yeah, see you," Owen said.

When they were alone, Owen stared at his mother for a long time, so long she had time to wonder if he was merely surprised by what he'd heard or angry. "Did he... Are you..."

"Yes and yes."

"Oh. Okay."

"Is it?"

"Is it what?"

"Okay with you?"

"Jeez, you certainly don't need my permission to go out with a guy."

"I don't?"

"Mom, come on..."

"You know he was in prison, right?"

"Everyone knows that."

"And it doesn't matter?"

Owen looked past her at something on the wall, obviously thinking about what he wanted to say. When he finally brought his gaze back to meet hers, Sarah ached at the pain she saw in his eyes. "For so long you were married to a man the whole world thought was a hero, when he's the one who should've been in prison. It doesn't matter to me what baggage Charlie might be dragging around behind him. We've all got our share. All that matters to me is that he treats you with the respect you deserve."

"Owen..."

He stepped forward to put his arms around her.

Sarah rested her face against his chest and held on tight. "I don't know how you did it growing up the way you did, but you're a man any mother would be proud to claim as her son."

"You had an awful lot to do with that."

Shaking her head, she pulled back from him. "I failed you so profoundly. All of you."

"Don't say that. You did the best you could in an unimaginable situation. None of us blame you for what he did."

"You should blame me for not getting you out of there, for not protecting you the way a mother should, for putting up with his abuse when I should've left him years ago. There's a lot you should blame me for."

"We choose not to, so maybe it's time you gave yourself a break, too."

Sarah thought about that and how happy she'd been living at the hotel she'd called home as a girl, this time with Owen and Laura and baby Holden. She thought about getting to know Charlie and other people on the island that had begun to feel like home again, and she thought about how her children had supported and propped her up during the divorce and legal proceedings as her case against their father wound its way through court.

"Perhaps you're right. It might be time to give myself a break."

Owen's smile reminded her, achingly, of his father, not that she would ever tell him that. "Good." He kissed her forehead. "I came down to tell you about Laura being sick. I need to get back upstairs to check on her and Holden."

"Let me know what I can do to help."

"Laura would want me to tell you what she said the other night—that without you, we never would've been ready in time."

"That's nice of her to say."

"She's not saying it to be nice. It's true. You've made a huge contribution here. You should be proud of that."

"Gran and Grandpa sure would be pleased with the way the place looks."

"I can't wait to see them at the wedding."

Sarah couldn't wait to see her beloved son married to the lovely Laura McCarthy. "Me, too."

"See you later, Mom."

As Owen went to go check on his family, she couldn't help but smile. For the first time in longer than she could remember, she was happy. She'd be happier when she was officially divorced and no longer had to worry about testifying against her violent ex-husband, but for right now, today, she was content, and that was more than enough.

TIFFANY WONDERED if it was possible to die from the stomach flu. She couldn't remember ever being this sick. After the last round of vomiting, she'd crawled back to bed. And now someone was pounding on her door. Hoping Ashleigh would sleep for a while longer, Tiffany dragged herself out of bed and put on a robe. Halfway down the stairs, she had to pause when her swimming head had her wondering if she might pass out.

"You can't do that," she said out loud, as if that might keep it from happening. "You have to take care of Ashleigh." She shook off the dizziness and continued down the stairs as the pounding on the door continued unabated. Who the heck needed her so badly? She sure hoped it wasn't Blaine. He'd probably die of fright if he saw her right then. With that possibility in mind, she smoothed her hands over her rat's nest hair and pulled open the door.

The young man standing on her doorstep cringed at the sight of her.

She must look even worse than she'd thought. "Yes?"

"Tiffany Sturgil?"

"That's me."

He thrust a clipboard at her. "Sign here."

Because she desperately needed to sit down, she signed where directed and took the envelope from him. She shut the door and made it to the sofa before her legs gave out under her. She must've dozed off, because when she came to a few minutes later, Ashleigh was standing in front of her.

Tiffany reached for her daughter. "Hi, baby. How do you feel?"

"My belly hurts."

"I know. Mine does, too."

Ashleigh ran her hands over Tiffany's face, checking for fever the way Tiffany did to her. The gesture drew her first smile of the day. "Mama sick, too?"

"Yep."

Ashleigh leaned forward to rest her head on Tiffany's shoulder. "I take care of you."

"That's very sweet of you."

Behind the little girl's back, Tiffany tore open the envelope and had to blink when the words swam before her eyes. The letterhead was from Jim's law firm, and Tiffany had to read the letter twice before the words permeated the fog in her brain. Her store was being evicted. Her landlord asserted that her rent check had bounced, and he'd hired her ex-husband to have her removed. She had fifteen days to vacate the premises.

"Mama needs to get up, honey."

"I watch Dora," Ashleigh said.

"Sure. Go ahead." Tiffany handed her daughter the remote control and bolted for the kitchen, where she was violently ill in the sink. Her hands were shaking and her legs were weak by the time it was over. She reached for the phone and managed to drop it. By the time she bent over and picked it up, she was already feeling sick again. She punched in the phone number to the store and waited for Patty to answer.

"Naughty & Nice," her assistant said, sounding far too chipper to Tiffany's sick ears.

"It's Tiffany."

"How're you feeling?"

"Like death."

"That hunky cop of yours was in here to see you, and you'll never guess what!"

Tiffany wanted to tell Patty that Blaine wasn't *her* hunky cop, but she lacked the energy to debate the point. "Wyatt asked you out. I heard."

"I'm so excited! I can't believe—"

"Patty."

"Oh, sorry. What's up?"

"Remember when you took the deposit to the bank for me?"

"Yep."

"What account did you put it in?"

"The savings account, like you told me to."

Tiffany held back a moan. She'd specifically told her assistant to put it in the checking account.

"Did I do something wrong?"

"No, everything's fine. Any customers today?"

"Quite a few, actually. Mrs. Upton was in with a couple of her friends, and Mrs. McCarthy stopped by, hoping to see you."

"Did she say what she wanted?"

"Just to tell you that her husband loved the items she brought home the other day."

Under normal circumstances, that would've been the best news Tiffany had had all year. "Good. I'm glad to hear that."

"Did the messenger guy find you at home?"

"Unfortunately, yes."

"Oh, sorry to disturb you. He said it was urgent."

"It's okay. I'll see you tomorrow."

"If you don't feel good, I don't mind covering for you."

"Thank you." If only Tiffany could afford to pay her for that many hours. "I'll call you in the morning if I need you."

"Talk to you then."

Tiffany ended the call and dialed her mother. "Mom," she said when Francine answered. "I need you."

"I heard you two are sick."

"I hate to expose you guys, but Ashleigh is feeling better, and I think I might be dying." Tears leaked from her eyes as it registered with her that her ex-husband had meant what he said when he told her there was nothing he wouldn't do to see her driven out of business.

"We'll be over to pick her up in a few minutes. Hang in there, honey."

"Thank you," Tiffany said, weak with relief. When she put down the phone, she ducked her head into the living room. "Ash, do you think you could eat something?"

Without taking her eyes off the television, her little girl nodded.

Tiffany filled a sippy cup with apple juice and put some crackers in a bowl. "Here you go. Take it slow at first. Mama needs to make a phone call, okay?"

"Okay."

Mesmerized by Dora, Ashleigh ate and drank while Tiffany dialed Dan Torrington's phone number and left a message on his voice mail, hoping she'd hear back from him soon.

While she waited for her mom and Ned, she dozed on the sofa. All the while, her mind raced with worry about the business. Surely her landlord couldn't evict her over one bounced check, could he? Trying to remember what the lease agreement had stipulated had Tiffany feeling sick again, so she forced her mind off those thoughts and focused on not throwing up. There couldn't be anything left in her stomach.

The next time she stirred, her mother and Ned were standing over her. She glanced at the clock and saw it was after five o'clock. How in the world had the day gone by without her knowing it? "Ashleigh?"

"Is fine," her mother said.

Thank goodness for *Dora the Explorer*, Tiffany thought for the thousandth time since Ashleigh became hooked on the cartoon a year ago.

"Where did the furniture come from?" Francine asked.

"Estate sale at Mrs. Ridgeway's house." Tiffany couldn't muster the wherewithal to relay the full story, nor was she ready to tell her mother and Ned about Blaine. They'd find out soon enough.

"She don't look too good," Ned said of Tiffany.

Francine rested her hand on her daughter's forehead, and Tiffany wanted to weep from the sweet relief of her mother's cool hand on her overheated skin. "You're burning up, honey. Did you take something for the fever?"

"Couldn't keep it down."

"Poor thing."

"Ya need to keep hydrated," Ned said. "Don't want ta see ya end up in the clinic."

"We brought you some ginger ale and chicken soup," Francine added.

"Thanks," Tiffany said, gagging to herself at the thought of either.

"I'll get you a glass of the ginger ale and put the soup on to warm."

"No soup, Mom. I can't do it. Not yet."

"Okay, I'll leave it here for when you feel up to it."

Ned scooped up Ashleigh and planted noisy kisses on her cheeks, making her laugh. "Ya feeling better, baby girl?"

"Uh-huh, but Mama is sick now."

"We're going to let her sleep while we take you to our house for a sleepover. How's that?"

"Good!"

Ned put her down and took her hand. "How bout we go pack yer bag?"

Ashleigh tugged him up the stairs to her room.

"He's so good with her," Tiffany said. "You'd never know he didn't raise a bunch of his own kids."

"I wish he'd been your father."

"That would've been nice. I could've picked a better father for my child, too." Tiffany gestured to the letter on the table.

Francine picked it up, read it and began to fume. "Is he *for real?*"

"Apparently so."

"Oh my God, what'll you do?"

"Fight him tooth and nail. What else can I do?" The thought of yet another legal battle with Jim, not to mention the expense of hiring Dan, had Tiffany fighting another round of nausea and more tears.

"I'm so sorry." Francine shook her head with dismay. "That boy needs to be horsewhipped. After all you did for him, that he would treat you this way—it's unconscionable."

"I agree."

The door opened, and Blaine walked in, stopping short when he saw Tiffany's mother sitting with her on the sofa. "Oh. Sorry. Didn't mean to interrupt."

Francine looked from Tiffany to him and back to her again, raising an eyebrow in inquiry that reminded Tiffany of Maddie, who did the same thing. "Something you want to tell me?"

"Um, no. Not really."

Rather than dig for more information, Francine only smiled. She leaned in and pressed a kiss to Tiffany's forehead. "Good for you," she whispered before she got up. "Chief Taylor, nice to see you."

"Um, you, too. Ma'am. Please, call me Blaine."

"I'd be happy to, *Blaine*. I'm Francine."

"I didn't mean to interrupt," he said. "I can come back later."

"Don't leave on our account," Francine said. "Ned is helping Ashleigh pack up to spend the night with us so Tiffany can get some rest."

Tiffany felt like an observer at a tennis match as her mother and her…lover, or whatever he was…conversed like old friends. *Lover…* She hated that word. It was so corny and over-the-top romantic. Sex buddy. She liked that a lot better, only it didn't go far enough to describe the way her heart raced at the sight of him or her palms got damp—and not because of the fever. No, it was him and the way he sucked all the oxygen out of the room just by stepping through the door.

"How's the patient?" he asked her mom.

"Burning up with fever and not interested in food."

"I'll be around tonight if she needs anything."

"It makes me feel a lot better to know she won't be alone."

Tiffany rolled her eyes at her mother.

Ned came down the stairs with Ashleigh, who made a big production out of hugging and kissing Tiffany.

Her daughter stopped short at the sight of the policeman standing in her living room.

"Hi, Ashleigh." Blaine squatted and extended a hand to the child. "Remember me? I'm Blaine, Uncle Mac's friend."

While Tiffany held her breath, Ashleigh nodded and shook his hand. "Are you my mama's friend, too?"

"I sure am. While you have a sleepover with your grandparents, I'll keep an eye on her for you. Would that be okay?"

"Uh-huh." To Ned, she said, "Can we have ice cream tonight?"

Realizing they'd gotten through the introduction of Blaine into Ashleigh's life with nary a speed bump, Tiffany released the deep breath she'd been holding. She watched as Blaine's chest expanded, indicating his relief, too. The realization that he'd been nervous made her all swoony inside for reasons other than the stomach bug.

"Absolutely," Ned said in response to Ashleigh's question. "Let's get going, ladies. We've got a lot to do tonight."

"Thanks, Ned, and you too, Mom."

"Happy to help," Ned said as he ushered his ladies out the door.

"We'll check on you later," Francine said, squeezing Blaine's arm on the way by.

After he closed the door behind them, Blaine came over to see her. "Jeez, talk about walking into a snake pit—your parents *and* your daughter, in one fell swoop."

"Trial by fire," Tiffany said with a weak smile. She loved that he referred to her mom and Ned as her "parents." Over the last year, Ned had become the dad she'd never had, and she loved him more every day. She probably ought to tell the old guy that at some point.

Blaine brushed the hair back from her face and kissed her forehead. It was entirely different, she decided, when he kissed her forehead than when her mother did it. For one thing, his kiss set off a series of goose bumps over her fevered skin.

"How you feeling?"

"I've been better."

"What can I do for you?"

She took his hand and wrapped her fingers around his. "This is nice."

"I have a proposition for you."

"Oh my goodness, no *way*. Not tonight—"

Laughing, he said, "Hush up, you silly girl. Not *that* kind of proposition."

"Thank God."

"It's good to know your mind is always in the gutter, even when you have the flu. I like that in a woman."

"I'm sure you do," Tiffany said, amused by him. "So what's your big proposition?"

"I'm on call tonight, so I need to be at home by a landline."

"They don't have your cell number?"

"They do, but I insist on everyone having landlines, since cell service can be spotty out here. Long story short, I have to be home by eight."

"That's okay. I can take care of myself."

He scowled playfully. "You haven't heard my proposition yet."

"I apologize. Please proceed with propositioning the sick girl."

His scowl turned to a smile. "You're not so sick that your sarcasm is affected. How about I take you to my place so I can take care of you and be on call at the same time?"

She groaned. "I can't move. I don't know if I could do it."

"I'll do everything. I'll pack you a bag and carry you to my car and then carry you into my house. You won't have to do a thing."

"When you put it that way, I might be game. Are you sure you want to further expose yourself to this? It's no fun."

"I hardly ever get sick, and if I wasn't sure, I wouldn't be here." He kissed her forehead and her cheek before he got up. "I'll go pack some clothes for you."

"The PJs are in the third drawer."

"Got it. Be right back."

Even though she felt worse than she had in years, she wasn't dead yet, so she watched his sexy ass go bounding up her stairs and shivered with delight that he was here, that he hadn't run screaming for his life when he saw the scary sight of her, and that he cared enough about her not to want to leave her alone when she was sick.

It would be so damned easy to fall madly in love with a man like that, a man who put her needs before his own, who was thoughtful and caring and considerate. Jim had never been any of those things. Everything in their lives had been about him. Nothing had ever been about her. With Blaine, she felt like everything was about her all the time. And wasn't that a refreshing change of pace?

However, Tiffany was wise enough now to know that a one-sided relationship would never work. So as soon as she felt better, she'd show him what it was like to be the center of *her* attention for a change. With that thought in mind, she drifted on a cloud of contentment until he lifted her off the sofa, and she woke with a start.

"Easy, baby. I've got you."

CHAPTER 17

His gruff, sexy voice was extremely comforting as she nuzzled her nose into the curve of his neck and inhaled the sandalwood scent that was becoming so familiar to her. She relaxed into his embrace and let him do all the work as he settled her into the front seat of the SUV and buckled her in.

"Be right back," he said. "I'm going to lock up the house."

As he walked away, her cell phone rang, and she took the call from Dan Torrington. "Thanks so much for returning my call."

"Not a problem. So our friend Jim is acting up again, huh?"

"And probably taking great pleasure from my troubles. Can they really have me evicted for one bounced check? It was a banking error. I have the money." *Just barely,* she thought, but she did have it.

"Write a new check in the morning and get it to the landlord. I'll have a conversation with your ex-husband and see what I can do."

"Oh, thank you so much. I won't be able to pay you for a while—"

"Don't worry about it. This one's on the house. That guy gets on my nerves."

"Mine, too."

"Try not to worry," Dan said as Blaine got into the truck. "We'll get this taken care of."

"Thank you so much, Dan. I really appreciate your help."

"Not a problem. I'll be in touch."

Tiffany ended the call to find Blaine studying her intently. "What was that all about?"

She told him about the rent check, the landlord and Jim.

"Really?" he asked, incredulous. "What the hell is wrong with him? You're the mother of his child, for Christ's sake."

His outrage on her behalf only made her like him more than she already did—if that was possible.

"That guy needs to be taught a lesson."

"Not by you," Tiffany said.

"I'd never hit him—even though I'd love to—but I could make his life a little difficult around here."

"How?"

"I have my ways," he said as he backed the truck out of the driveway. "All of them legal. Don't worry."

Tiffany was finally able to release the tension that had been building since she received Jim's letter earlier. She had friends who'd go to bat for her, she realized, a thought that pleased and comforted her. They'd help her figure this out, she thought as she closed her eyes and gave in to the exhaustion.

The next time Tiffany woke up, Blaine was carrying her again, this time into his house. She wanted to stop him so she could take a better look at his place, but she couldn't keep her eyes open long enough to look at anything. Tomorrow, she decided. She could look to her heart's content tomorrow.

THE RED DRESS LOOKED AMAZING, Kara decided as she twirled before the full-length mirror one last time. She'd taken the time to actually blow-dry her hair, something she did twice a year, usually for weddings or funerals. Which was this, she wondered? Though she felt lighter and more frivolous than she had since the "Great Betrayal," as she referred to her boyfriend falling for and marrying her sister, she wasn't sure she was ready to risk her heart again.

Going out with a new man meant the end of her self-inflicted mourning period over her relationship with Matt. To portray him as only a villain didn't do justice to the two years they'd spent together. She'd been happy for most of that time and thought he was, too. Only when he confessed to having feelings for her sister did she discover he wasn't happy at all. He'd been miserable, she later learned, trying to figure out a way to tell her his feelings had changed.

In some ways, that was the worst part of the whole thing. She'd had two long years since it all blew up to consider the various injustices that'd been inflicted upon her. Time after time, she came back to the same thing—*how* had she not known? Had there been signs she'd missed? There must've been, but she'd gone over and over the last few months they'd spent together and couldn't recall anything that would've indicated what was going on behind her back. She'd spent time with her sister during those months, too, and again, nothing had stood out.

After it all came out, Kara had been left with her self-confidence in shambles, along with her judgment. If two of the people closest to her could betray her so completely, how was she to trust anyone ever again? That thought filled her with unwelcome sorrow and grated on her nerves as she grabbed a sweater to take with her. She was determined to go out with Dan tonight and have a good time without making it into a big, bloody deal. He was just another guy who wanted the same thing every guy wanted from a woman, though she had no interest in that with him or anyone else.

She was still mid-pep talk when he arrived with a light knock on her door.

"Here goes nothing," she whispered as she went to answer the door. She pulled it open and had to bite back the gasp of amazement that nearly slipped from between her lips. He was *gorgeous*. Dressed in a navy sports coat with a light-blue dress shirt and khakis, he'd combed his dark hair into submission and looked positively dashing.

He held out a festive-looking bouquet of red, yellow and orange gerbera daisies. "For you."

Rattled by his appearance and the unexpected flowers, she stepped back from the door. "Come in."

He stepped into the big open room that housed her living area and kitchen and took a look around. "What a great space."

"I like it." She took the flowers from him and went to rummage around in the cabinets for something she could use as a vase. "Mr. McCarthy owns it and rented it to me for practically nothing. He and his family are really nice people." *Stop yammering*, she thought.

"I like them, too. I've been friends with Grant for years, but I'd never met the rest of his family until recently." He picked up a picture of Kara with her parents, studied it and returned it to the table. "They make you feel like you've known them forever."

"Yes, they do." She finished arranging the pretty blooms in a beer glass. "Thank you for the flowers. They're my favorite."

"Are they really?" He seemed pleased to hear that he'd gotten something right. "I took a guess that you'd prefer them over the more obvious choice of roses."

Kara recalled that Matt used to bring her roses, even after she'd told him she was one of five women alive who didn't like the smell of them. How was it possible that this man she'd only just met already understood her better than Matt had after two years together?

"Did I say the wrong thing again?" Dan asked, seeming genuinely concerned.

"No."

"Right when I think I've seen all your expressions, you surprise me with a new one."

Kara had no idea how to respond to that. She'd never had anyone pay that kind of attention to her before.

"By the way," he said, "you look amazing. When you answered the door, I was rendered speechless for a second there. You probably know me well enough by now to suspect that doesn't happen very often."

Kara couldn't help but laugh at the self-deprecating face he made.

"I like when you laugh," he said, watching her intently.

"It's been a while since anything made me laugh."

"That's too bad." He extended a hand to her. "What'd you say we go have some more laughs?"

Kara stared at his outstretched hand for a breathless moment before she took what he offered.

THE KITCHEN of Stephanie's restaurant was a beehive of activity as she and her staff put the finishing touches on a wide array of appetizers and entreés for the guests who were expected any minute now. She'd planned to go home for an hour to shower and change, but she'd had to call Grant to bring her dress to the restaurant inside the Sand & Surf when she ran out of time.

Three of her servers had gone down with the flu that afternoon, which had required her to recruit Grace, Jenny and Sydney to help out with the serving.

"Here we are," Grace said when she breezed into the kitchen looking fresh and pretty in a floral dress. "Reporting for duty."

"You guys are saving my life," Stephanie said.

"We're happy to do it," Jenny said. The lighthouse keeper's blonde hair was twisted into an elegant knot, and her black cocktail dress was both sexy and elegant. "Everything smells so good!"

"I'm *starving*," Sydney added.

"I set you up with a little bit of everything." Stephanie gestured to a butcher-block table, where a platter of appetizers and a steaming bowl of pasta awaited her friends, along with a bottle of pinot grigio she'd chilled with them in mind.

"This is the best job *ever*," Jenny said, eyeing the offerings.

"Dig in," Stephanie said. "You'll be running your butts off for a couple of hours, so fuel up."

"You don't have to tell me twice," Sydney said, making a beeline for the asparagus and lobster dip Stephanie had made from a recipe of her own creation.

Judging from the moan Sydney emitted, the dip was a surefire hit.

"Astonishing," Sydney said, dipping a second cracker.

"How did your trip to the mainland go, Syd?" Grace asked.

"It was good." Sydney filled four wineglasses and handed one to each of the others. "The doctor says I'm a good candidate." For Jenny's benefit, she added, "Tubal ligation reversal."

"Oh, wow," Jenny said. "I didn't know you were considering that."

"That's great news," Stephanie said as she took a moment she didn't have to enjoy a glass of wine with her friends.

"Are you going to do it, honey?" Grace asked, her expression full of compassion for the woman who'd lost two children in a tragic accident.

"We're talking about it."

"What does Luke say?" Stephanie asked.

"That it's totally up to me. He never thought he'd get married or have a family, so according to him, being married is way more than he ever expected. He says he'd be perfectly content if it was just us."

"I bet he'd be a wonderful father, though," Jenny said thoughtfully.

"I know he would," Syd said. "I've been thinking a lot about that and about whether I could bring another child into this world without worrying all the time about something happening to him or her."

"I can understand why you'd be worried about that," Grace said. "After what you've been through, it's a natural concern."

"The last thing I want is to make a nervous wreck out of a poor kid who was unlucky enough to be born to a freak-show, overprotective mother."

"Luke wouldn't let that happen," Jenny said. "He'd balance you out."

"That's true," Sydney said. "He's the calm one."

"You don't have to decide right away, do you?" Stephanie asked.

"We're not getting any younger, and kids are *so* exhausting. Especially when they're little."

"We're here for you." Grace squeezed Sydney's arm as Jenny and Stephanie nodded in agreement. "If you want to talk about it, we're happy to listen."

"Thank you, guys. Maddie said the same thing when I talked to her about it. I'm lucky to be surrounded by such awesome friends."

Grant rushed into the kitchen looking sinfully handsome in a dark suit and a blue dress shirt that made his eyes an even crazier shade of blue than usual. "Sorry I took so long. The phone was ringing off the hook at the house and... And you don't care because you're too busy to care. I've got your dress." Reaching into his suit coat pocket, he produced her engagement ring. "And your ring, as requested."

The other women laughed at how flustered the usually unflappable Grant McCarthy was on his fiancée's big night.

Stephanie held out her left hand to allow him to do the honors. As he slid the ring on her finger, she looked up to find him watching her with fire in his eyes. She wondered if he, too, was remembering the day he'd proposed last fall. Thus far, they hadn't discussed a wedding, and she hoped it was only because they'd both been so busy—her with getting the restaurant ready while still managing the marina restaurant and him with the screenplay about how she spent years trying to free her stepfather from prison. After they got the restaurant opened, she hoped he might be ready to talk about setting a date.

"Could I borrow you for one minute?" Grant asked when her ring was firmly in place.

Stephanie closed her fingers around his. "That's about all I have."

Grant led her around the corner, out of the hubbub.

"Everything okay?" she asked.

"Everything is great." He drew her in close to him and planted a lingering kiss on her lips. "I wanted to wish you luck and tell you how very proud I am of you. Look at this place." He pointed to the dining room, which shimmered in the light of a hundred candles. "You did it, babe."

Overwhelmed by emotion, she leaned her forehead on his chest. "I couldn't have done it without your love and your support, not to mention your money."

"That's *your* money, earned fair and square."

Grant had paid her and Charlie a boatload for the rights to their story, and sometimes Stephanie had to remind herself that the days of counting every penny to pay lawyers to plead her stepfather's case were over now. Charlie was free and living nearby on the island, working at the hotel and contributing—sparingly but regularly—to

Grant's story. At times, Stephanie wanted to pinch herself to believe the changes to her life that had occurred in the last year had actually happened and weren't part of a lovely dream.

She owed most of her recent happiness to the man in her arms, who'd hired his friend Dan to help free Charlie and had welcomed her into his family and his home. Most important, Grant had given her unconditional love, something she'd never had from anyone other than her beloved stepfather.

"Thank you," she said, looking up at Grant.

He seemed genuinely perplexed. "For what?"

"My whole life changed the day I met you. I had no idea it was possible to be this happy."

His sexy smile lit up his face. He took her hands and brought them to his lips. "Your happiness makes me happy. Now, my love, you need to go get ready to knock 'em dead tonight. If there's anything I can do to help, you know where I'll be."

"Don't worry about helping after you greet the guests with Shane. You've already done enough. Have a good time."

"Speaking of good times, Mac asked me about joining him on one of the boats that's racing tomorrow. Apparently, the captain's crew is down with the flu, and he needs some stand-ins so he doesn't have to forfeit the whole regatta. Do you care if I go?"

"I don't mind at all. I plan to sleep in and take one last full day off before we open to the public."

"Great, thanks." He gave her another kiss. "We'll have our own private celebration later."

"You're on."

"I love you," he said, giving her a tight hug.

"Love you, too. Thanks for propping me up during all of this."

"Propping you up is one of my favorite things to do."

He left her with one of his hundred-watt smiles and went to help his cousin Shane welcome their guests.

Since she never tired of the elegant way he moved, she watched him walk away and then went to get changed.

. . .

WHAT HAD SEEMED like such a good idea earlier in the day became more and more preposterous as the clock edged closer to seven. Sarah's hands shook as she attempted to apply mascara, something she hadn't done in years. She'd bought a few cosmetics at Ryan's pharmacy so she wouldn't look like an old hag when Charlie came to pick her up. But if her hands didn't quit shaking, she'd have the mascara everywhere but on her eyelashes.

The frustration built to overwhelming levels, until she finally threw the wand into the sink. "This is ridiculous," she said to her reflection. "*You* are ridiculous. What business do you have going out with a man when you're not even divorced yet from the monster you married?"

Except the part of her that hadn't forgotten the giddy sensations that came with new love refused to be silenced. She couldn't help but be curious about Charlie, especially after seeing a hint of the man who might be lurking under his gruff exterior. After nearly forty years married to the wrong man, was it too late to start over with someone else?

She smoothed a trembling hand over the one good dress she'd brought with her to the island and hoped the dark pink silk wasn't too fancy for opening night at the restaurant. Taking another critical look at her reflection, Sarah decided she didn't look too bad for an old gal. She cleaned up the mess the mascara wand had made in the sink and sprayed on a spritz of her favorite perfume.

Now, if only she could make her hands stop shaking before Charlie showed up.

Because she didn't know what else to do with herself, she sat gingerly on the edge of the bed. After years of social events tied to her husband's illustrious career, Sarah knew how to perch just so to keep from wrinkling her dress. It was one of the few useful skills she'd taken away from her life as a general's wife. Most of the other lessons she'd happily forget if only she could.

At times, she wondered if he missed her or if he merely missed having someone to knock around when the rages overtook him. Knowing him, he'd probably found someone new to victimize. No way would he have gone this long without sex, so it was likely some poor other woman was learning the hard way that Mark Lawry was hardly the charming retired air force officer he wanted the rest of the world to think he was. She and her children knew much better.

A pervasive sense of sadness tried to settle over her, but a gentle knock on the door pushed those thoughts away. Tonight wasn't a time for sadness. It was a time for new beginnings and new friends and a whole new life. Dwelling on her painful past was pointless and counterproductive.

Sarah stood and willed her trembling legs to cross the room. She almost didn't recognize the clean-shaven, well-dressed man outside her door. He looked so different she actually had to blink to be sure she wasn't imagining him. "You clean up nicely."

"Same to you," he said, his eyes taking a slow and appreciative journey from her face to her knees and back up again to meet her gaze. "Very nice indeed."

His praise and the not-so-subtle interest behind his words sent a flash of heat through her that settled between her legs, reminding her that while her marriage might be dead, she was still very much alive and still very much a woman.

Charlie extended an arm to her. "Shall we?"

Sarah didn't hesitate when she curled her hand into the crook of his elbow. "By all means."

BLAINE SETTLED Tiffany in his bed, and pulled a light blanket over her. Her dark hair fanned out on his pillow as her sweet lips moved adorably in her sleep the way Ashleigh's did. She'd thought he'd be disgusted by how she looked, but to him, she was beautiful all the time, even when sick.

Keeping the bedside light on so she'd be able to find the bathroom if she got up, he went to the kitchen and located an old plastic bowl that he put on the bed next to her, in case she needed it.

Over the next couple of hours, he made a sandwich and drank a couple of beers, watched a few innings of the Red Sox game and reviewed some reports he'd brought home from the office. By nine o'clock, he could no longer take knowing she was asleep in his bed while he was in the next room acting like it didn't matter that she was asleep in his bed.

He took a long, cold shower to remind himself that this night was about comfort and not about sex before he slid in next to her and wrapped an arm around her. Damn, she was still blazing hot with fever.

While he knew he should try to get her to take something for the fever, he was afraid her ravaged stomach wouldn't be able to handle it.

She turned over and curled up to him, her face pressed against his chest.

The implied trust she conveyed by reaching for him in her sleep set off a chain reaction of emotion in him. She was so damned sweet, even if she wanted the rest of the world to see her bitter, edgy side. He'd seen the sweetness, but he adored snarky, sarcastic Tiffany, too. Blaine smoothed a hand over her hair, hoping she'd sleep off the worst of the bug overnight.

He must've dozed off, waking when she moaned in her sleep.

"Tiffany," he whispered.

Her eyes opened, and she blinked him into focus.

"Are you okay?"

She nodded.

"Need anything?"

"Maybe some water. I'm so thirsty."

"Coming right up." He released her to get up and retrieve ice water from the kitchen. When he returned to the bedroom, he helped her sit up and held the glass for her.

She took a couple of greedy sips. "That's good."

"Take it slow. You don't want to get your stomach going again."

As if it had heard him, her stomach let out a huge growl that made them laugh.

"That's attractive," Tiffany said. "In fact, I must be knocking your socks off with how attractive I am right now."

Blaine leaned in and kissed her square on the lips. "You're gorgeous, even when you're sick."

"Sure I am."

"Would I lie to you?"

"I don't know. Would you?"

Even though they'd been joking around, he sensed that she expected a serious answer. "Never."

"That's good to know," she said with a small smile that told him how much his one-word answer had meant to her.

"How about some crackers to see if your stomach can handle a little food?"

"Earlier, I thought I'd never eat again, but now crackers sound good. I feel a hundred times better than I did before."

"That's good. Be right back." He returned a minute later with a box of oyster crackers and a couple of painkillers to combat the fever, which she took with another big swallow of water. "This was the best I could do."

"I love them."

Propped on pillows, he sat next to her and held the box while she munched on a handful of the small crackers.

"This makes me want clam chowder," she said.

"A sure sign that you're on the road to recovery."

"No kidding. A few hours ago the words clam chowder would've made me puke."

"If it makes you feel any better, the flu is taking the island by storm. I've heard of at least two dozen cases."

"Lucky me."

He took her hand and linked their fingers. "Lucky *me*. I get to take care of you."

"It's all part of your devious plot to make yourself essential to me."

"How am I doing so far?"

"Pretty good."

"Only *pretty* good? That's disappointing."

He loved listening to her laugh, loved the way her eyes danced with mischief and her lips pursed in thought. There were a lot of things he loved about her, he realized in a moment of clarity.

"Why did you suddenly get all serious?" she asked, mimicking his expression.

"Did I?"

She nodded. "What're you thinking about?"

Blaine chose his words carefully so as not to drive her away by getting too serious too fast. "I was thinking that I like being with you like this."

"When there's not a snowball's chance in hell of sex?"

That made him laugh. "Even then."

CHAPTER 18

Owen gently shook Laura awake. She'd been asleep for hours, and he could no longer pacify Holden, who needed to be fed.

"Laura," he whispered.

Holden's hungry cries escalated to piercing shrieks that roused his mother from a deep sleep.

"Is he okay?" she asked, her voice rough and sleepy sounding.

"He's hungry. Should I make him a bottle?"

"No, I can feed him." She pushed herself into an upright position. "I hope I won't be getting him sick if I do, though."

"Wouldn't he already be exposed?"

"I suppose I've exposed you both."

"And wasn't that fun?" Owen said with a grin.

Laura smiled as she unbuttoned the front of her nightgown, and the baby latched on as if he hadn't eaten in a week rather than a few hours. The sight of her breastfeeding the baby never failed to stir Owen's most protective instincts. "Thanks for taking care of him."

"It's my pleasure to take care of him. We played with some blocks and had a workout on the baby gym. Pumped some iron. Guy stuff. You wouldn't get it."

"Glad you got in some male bonding time. How are things downstairs?"

"Seems to be going well. Stephanie got a great crowd."

"Are people checking out the guest rooms we opened?"

"We've had a steady stream of visitors on the second floor. Holden and I went down to take a look a little while ago and answered a few questions."

Laura frowned and ran a hand over the baby's head. "I should be down there."

"My mom and Charlie and Shane are leading people through the rooms. Don't worry."

"It should be me."

"You're sick, honey. Half the island has the same bug, so don't feel bad. In fact, Stephanie had to recruit Grace, Jenny and Sydney to fill in for three of the servers who have it."

"Everyone is having fun while I'm stuck in bed. It's not fair."

Owen leaned in to kiss the pout off her lips.

"Don't kiss me! I don't want you to get it!"

"Far too late to worry about that. Besides, I never get sick." He patted his belly. "Iron gut."

"You can join the party if you want. He'll be down for the night after he eats, and I'm fine."

Owen stretched out next to her on the bed. "I'm right where I want to be."

Over the nursing baby's head, her gaze met his. "If that's the case, then why do you look so pensive?"

"Do I?"

She nodded.

"Hmm, I didn't think it showed."

"Maybe not to anyone else, but I know you, and I can tell by now when something is troubling you."

It was, Owen mused, at times astonishing and confounding to be so in tune with another person. Since he'd never had that kind of connection before, he was still getting used to it. "My mom."

"What about her?"

"She's on a date with Charlie."

Laura gasped and startled the baby. She took advantage of the opportunity to switch sides. When she had the baby settled again, she placed her free hand on Owen's chest. "How do you feel about that?"

"I'm happy for her, but I'm worried, too."

"About what?"

"That she's not ready to start something new. It hasn't been that long since everything happened with my dad, and I'm so afraid of her getting hurt again."

"I don't know Charlie all that well, but he seems like a very nice man. He's a hard worker, and Stephanie thinks the world of him. That should count for something."

"It does. It counts for a lot. Still..."

"She's your mom, she's been through an awful ordeal and you're allowed to worry about her. But you have to let her spread her wings. She's got a lot of time to make up for, and so does Charlie. In some ways, she was just as imprisoned as he was."

"That's very true."

"Does his past bother you?"

"Not so much. I'll tell you what I told her—she was married to a guy who everyone thought was a hero but should've been in prison. And then there's Charlie, who, to hear Stephanie tell it, saved her life only to learn that no good deed goes unpunished. Which one would I rather see her with? Charlie. No question about that."

"I like that, and it's so true. We might be getting ahead of ourselves anyway. It's one night."

"Have you noticed the way he looks at her?"

Laura glanced over at him, hesitantly. "Maybe."

"I suspect it's going to be more than one date."

"I suspect you might be right."

Play it cool. That was Dan's strategy for the evening with Kara. Don't act too interested or too charming or too anything. It had taken weeks of effort to get her into his car, and he was petrified he'd say or do something to ruin his chances before he could get to know her better. And he desperately wanted to know her better.

The car itself might've been his first misstep of the evening. Unlike the women he dated in LA, she hadn't seemed impressed by the convertible Porsche he'd spent an ungodly amount of money to have shipped to the island. Some things a guy shouldn't have to live without, and his car was definitely one of them.

In hindsight, he realized the car contributed to her already formed impression of him as a pretentious climber who cared more about things than he did about people. He'd considered telling her the truth about his work, but he decided to save that ace for when—not if—he needed some points.

The car had a story all its own behind it that he'd like to share with her at some point, if the opportunity presented itself.

"Nice car," she said after a protracted period of silence that did nothing to settle his nerves. He'd been reeling from the second she opened the door and he caught sight of her in the incredible red dress. And her hair... It was so smooth and shiny, falling in soft waves around her face. As he'd suspected, underneath her tomboy exterior lurked a very sexy woman.

"Thanks." *Why not tell her,* he thought. He wanted her to know him —really know him. "It was my brother's." Even all these years later, the pain still took him by surprise. "He was an army ranger, killed in Afghanistan in 2005."

She rested her hand on his arm. "I'm so sorry, Dan."

"Thanks. It was a long time ago."

"I... I thought..."

"What?"

"My first thought was that the car is pretentious, and now I feel terrible for thinking that."

Dan laughed. "It's pretentious as all hell, and Dylan *loved* it. Having the car he loved makes me feel closer to him, if that makes sense."

"It does. It makes perfect sense. Do you have other siblings?"

"Two sisters, both older."

"It must've been so hard to lose your only brother."

"Worst thing I've ever been through. Wouldn't wish it on anyone."

Kara seemed to be chewing over what she wanted to say next, so Dan forced himself to stay quiet and let her ask whatever she wanted to. "The other day when we talked about your work, why didn't you tell me what you really do?"

Dan grimaced. "Heard about that, huh?"

"Yes."

He couldn't tell if she was annoyed or merely curious. "Are you mad I didn't tell you?"

"I'm more surprised, I guess. It's been my experience that people like to talk about themselves, especially when they're trying to impress someone."

Her blunt approach to life was so damned refreshing. "Is that what I've been doing? Trying to impress you?" He was mindful to interject a suitable amount of humor into the question, lest she think he was making fun of her. Had he ever tiptoed so carefully around another woman? Not that he could recall.

He could feel rather than see the roll of her eyes. "What would you call it?"

"Well, I, ah…"

"Are you this articulate in court when you're pontificating on behalf of your clients?"

"Okay, first, I don't *pontificate,* and second, I'm known for my articulate elocution."

Her lusty laugh did strange things to his insides. He suddenly felt warm all over, so he opened a window.

She gathered up her hair and kept a firm grip on it.

"What's the matter?"

"The fog will make my hair *huge* in like five seconds."

"Sorry," he muttered, rolling up the window, resigned to his fate of being far too warm in her presence.

"So why didn't you tell me about your work?"

"I don't know." He tugged at his shirt collar. "It wasn't because I don't want you to know about it. I didn't want to sound, you know…arrogant."

"*Far* too late for that," she said, laughing some more.

While his arrogant self might be annoyed that she found it so easy to poke fun at him, the part of him that ached for what she'd been through loved that he could make her laugh. For that reason, he was happy to be her patsy. "You're being kind of mean to me to say it's our first date. I'd think you'd want to impress *me*."

"Is that so? I thought I'd already impressed you just by having freckles. Are you saying I need to do more?"

"If you want to keep my attention." He'd meant the comment as a joke but immediately regretted it. "I didn't mean that the way it sounded, Kara. You have my undivided attention, as you well know."

The animation had left her voice when she said, "I knew what you meant."

Dan took a huge gamble and reached for her hand. At first, she resisted, but then she relaxed and seemed to accept the intrusion. "He was crazy to let you go."

"When you get to know me better, you might not think so. For all you know, I'm a controlling shrew who likes to be in charge all the time."

His heart did a happy dance at the idea of getting to know her better. "Why, Ms. Ballard, are you talking *dirty* to me?" he asked with a dramatic shiver.

"Shut *up*," she said, laughing again.

He really loved it when she laughed.

A STEADY POUNDING on his front door woke Blaine from a sound sleep. He glanced at the bedside clock and saw that it was only ten thirty. When was the last time he'd gone to bed so early? With a mighty yawn, he eased himself out of bed, hoping Tiffany would stay asleep. He pulled on jeans, zipped them and closed the bedroom door behind him when he stepped into the living room of his small cottage.

Since he was always wary of people he'd arrested showing up uninvited at his front door, he looked through the peephole he'd installed to see who was there. When he saw his mother's frowning face, he groaned and threw open the door.

"I believe I told you I wanted to see you today," she said without preamble as she marched by him into the house. She was petite with dark hair gone gray and brown eyes. He loved her dearly, honestly he did, but sometimes she drove him crazy. Clearly, this was going to be one of those times.

"I believe I told you I was busy. You know, *working*."

"Don't give me that, Blaine Michael Taylor. I know darned well that as the chief of police, you can go anywhere you wish to on this island at any time you wish to."

She usually saved his full name for only the most heated of exchanges, and the idea of a big fight with her exhausted him. "What's got you so wound up?"

"You know exactly what's got me 'wound up,' as you put it. Once again, you've taken up with a needy woman who already has you buying her things like furniture. What kind of self-respecting woman lets her new boyfriend—or whatever you are—buy her *furniture*?"

"That's not how it happened, Mom. She didn't *let* me do anything. I did that completely on my own."

"What happened to her furniture?"

"Her scumbag ex-husband took it all with him when he moved out, not that it's any of your business."

She threw up her hands. "How is it any of *your* business?"

He absolutely refused to squirm, the way he would've back in high school when she looked at him that way. "I made it my business. I like her. She needed it. I saw it. There's nothing more to it than that."

"If you want to tell yourself that—"

"Mom! Stop it. I've heard enough. I don't have to explain myself to you. I'm a grown man."

"Who's made some very, very bad decisions where women are concerned in the past. Do you even know what she's selling in that little store of hers? Why, the whole town is talking about it! Just tonight at bridge club, Myrna Applegate said the word *dildo*. I almost had a heart attack right there on the spot."

"Mom—"

"And to think my own son is *dating*—or Lord knows what the two of you are doing—the town *dildo* queen! Well, my God, Blaine, I can't bear it. Loretta called her store the 'The House of Dildos,' and the whole group had a big laugh over it. All the while, I was *dying* inside knowing you're all wrapped up in her. What will they say when they find out my son is…" She waved her hand around as she searched for the word. "*Dating* her?"

"Stop. You don't know anything about her. You have no idea—"

"Is she or is she not selling dildos on Gansett Island?"

He shifted from one foot to the other, his face heating at that word coming from his mother's lips. "Maybe."

"There you have it. What else do you need to know about her?"

"How about the fact that she's sweet and loyal and genuine and funny and a wonderful mother and sexy as hell? Do any of those things matter, or are you so hung up on what she's selling in her store that it'll never matter to you that she's a good person?"

"A good person doesn't bring that kind of filth into a town like this."

He snorted as he pictured the apoplexy she'd have if she knew that he'd tried out—and greatly enjoyed—some of Tiffany's so-called filth. "Come on, Mom, it's the twenty-first century, for crying out loud. You sound positively puritanical."

"I don't care how I sound, and I can't help how I feel. I don't approve, Blaine, and there're plenty of other people on this island who agree with me. Need I remind you that you *lost your last job* because of a woman? Are you really going to let that happen again? Mayor Upton won't be happy to hear you're seeing her, especially with all the traffic trouble her smut shop is causing in town. I'd think you'd be concerned about your job, taking up with a woman like that."

Hearing his mother call Tiffany "a woman like that" made him as mad as he could ever recall being. "Listen and listen good."

Startled by his tone, she took a step back from him.

"I *like* her. She's *nothing* like Kim or Eden, and I don't give a rat's ass what you or your bridge club or the mayor or anyone else thinks of her or her business. You got me?"

She shook her head in dismay. "You're making another huge mistake with this girl."

"It's my mistake to make."

"Don't expect me to pick up the pieces when it blows up in your face and you get fired—again."

"I wouldn't dream of it."

"Blaine, please..."

"I was going to bring her to meet you, but I guess there's no point in that now."

She set her lips in the stubborn expression he knew far too well.

"Maybe you ought to go."

"You think about what I said."

He opened the door and held it for her. "You do the same."

As she moved past him, she stopped and looked up at him with sad eyes. "I love you. I don't want to see you hurt again."

"I know that. Trust me when I tell you I'm fine. She's good for me."

Her cluck of disapproval wasn't lost on him. He closed the door, turned the lock and rested his head against it. While he understood her concern, how could he make her see that everything about this relationship was different?

It was his own fault for leaning on her and his family after the earlier disasters. With hindsight, he should've kept the details to himself. But he'd been so blindsided and devastated both times that his parents and siblings had come to him out of concern and helped him get his life back on track. He'd given his mother—hell, his entire family—reason enough to worry about him. He couldn't deny that, but this time, he was older and wiser and had chosen a far more worthy woman to spend time with.

He turned and was shocked to find her standing in the doorway to the bedroom. *Shit. How much of that did she hear?* Judging by her stricken expression, she'd heard enough.

"I'd... I'd like to go home, please."

The quiet dignity in her voice broke his heart. He crossed the room to her in two strides. "Tiffany—"

When she looked away from him, something in him tore and began to bleed.

"Please," she said softly.

If he let her go now, he'd never get her back. That much he knew for sure. "Didn't you hear my half of the conversation?"

"I heard it."

"And it means nothing to you that I told her I *choose* you?" He rested his hands on her shoulders and felt her warmth through the thin robe. "I choose you, Tiffany. I want you. I need you. I..."

"Don't. Please don't say what you think I need to hear."

"That's not my style, and you know it." Slipping his arms around her, he drew her in close to him, rubbing his hands up and down her back until she acquiesced and returned his embrace. "I'm sorry you had to hear that."

"I've been deluding myself, thinking I got off easy because the islanders didn't kick up much of a fuss about the store. Naturally, they're talking about me and my store, but they're doing it behind my back."

"So what? Let them talk. Today's gossips are tomorrow's customers."

"It's not that simple, and you know it. What she said about your job—she's right. You should be worried."

"I'm not. This town needs me far more than I need them, especially going into the season. Don't add me or my job to your list of worries. I can take care of myself." He kept his arms around her as he walked her backward to the bed.

"I should go."

"No, you shouldn't. You've been sick, and I don't want you to be alone."

"But—"

He kissed the words off her lips. "No buts." When she was settled in bed, he dropped his jeans and crawled in next to her. "Come here."

She turned into his outstretched arms, resting her head on his chest.

"I don't care what anyone says," he whispered. "Being with you feels right, and that's all that matters."

She didn't say anything, which worried him. The Tiffany he'd come to know always had something to say. Blaine fell asleep with the uneasy feeling that he might've dodged a bullet he'd have to deal with tomorrow.

STEPHANIE'S grand opening wound down to include only her closest friends and Grant's family gathered on the porch in Adirondack chairs they'd pulled into a circle around the outdoor fireplace.

When she walked out to join them, the group erupted into applause.

"There she is," Grant said as he stood to welcome her with an outstretched hand. "My superstar fiancée. Everything was awesome, babe. Congratulations."

Glowing from the compliment and the warmth in his eyes, Stephanie took his hand. "Thank you, and thank you everyone for coming and for liking the food."

"It was amazing," Jenny said. "All of it."

"Totally awesome," Grace added.

Stephanie raised her wineglass. "To my dear friends Grace, Jenny and Sydney, who absolutely saved my hide tonight by filling in for sick servers. To Laura and Owen and Sarah, who put up with me and my restaurant during the final hotel renovations and never once threatened to have me killed. To my amazing dad, Charlie, who was my jack-of-all-trades over the last few months and never said no to any challenge I tossed his way. I can't possibly tell you how much it means to me to get to see you every day, to work side by side with you, to..." Her throat closed, taking the rest of what she wanted to say with it.

Charlie stood to hug and kiss her. "So proud of you, kiddo," he said gruffly.

"Thank you," Stephanie said, returning his hug. "To my future in-laws, who kept me on as the marina restaurant manager even while I was working over here, too."

"Couldn't do it without you, honey," Linda said, raising her glass.

"Hear, hear," Big Mac added.

Stephanie's heart slowed to a steady thump when she turned to Grant. "And last but not least, thank you thank you *thank you* to my wonderful fiancé, who has supported me every step of the way. I love you so much."

A collective "Awwwwwww" followed her toast as Grant gave her a kiss and then a hug.

"Have a seat and take a load off," Grant said, tugging her down onto his lap.

Stephanie had never been so happy to sit in her life. In fact, she decided as Grant's arms came around her, she'd never been so happy, period. Here were most of the people she loved best in the world, less those who were home sick and those who were tending to them.

Evan, who'd provided the evening's entertainment, strummed his guitar and had them all laughing when he turned "Hotel California" into "Hotel Sand & Surf."

Sarah came outside carrying a plastic shopping bag.

"What've you got there, Sarah?" Stephanie asked.

"A little treat for the late-night crowd." She handed the bag to Stephanie, who laughed when she looked inside and found the makings for s'mores. "To break in the new fireplace."

It had been Stephanie's idea to offer s'more makings to guests enjoying the fireplace on the porch. Laura and Sarah had been all for it.

"I forgot to bring the sticks for toasting the marshmallows," Sarah said. "Be right back."

Stephanie watched as Charlie followed her into the hotel. "Something's up," she whispered to Grant.

"With Charlie?"

"And Sarah."

"Really? Wow, that'd be cool, right?"

"I adore her, but I worry about him."

"Old habits are hard to break, but he doesn't need you to worry about him anymore. He wants nothing more than for you to be happy and worry free. That's what I want, too."

The spring breeze off the water was chilly, so she snuggled in closer to him. "I'm happier than I ever hoped to be."

"Good," he said, kissing her forehead and then her lips.

"So, hey," Mac said, "who's in for sailing tomorrow? I've gotten a definite from Grant. Anyone else? Going once..."

"I'll go," Evan said. "I'm at a standstill until my equipment gets here. May as well play while I can."

"I could use one more able body," Mac said.

"What for?" Dan asked.

Mac explained about the crew that'd been sidelined by the flu.

"I'll do it," Dan said.

"Do you even know how to sail, Torrington?" Grant asked with a laugh.

"I'll have you know I was on the sailing team at Yale," Dan retorted.

"Oh, pardon us and your Grey Poupon," Grant said in a snobby tone, making the others roar with laughter. "You might be too good for this crew."

"I can probably teach you a few things," Dan said with a good-natured grin.

"You're in," Mac said. "I'll text the captain and let him know we're good to go. Zero seven hundred, boys," he added to groans from the other guys.

"Better call it a night, then," Evan said.

"Oh, poor baby needs his beauty sleep," Grant said, rubbing his eyes and making baby-crying noises.

Evan threw an empty beer can at his brother. "Shut up."

"Children," Linda said from her perch on her husband's lap. "Try to behave in public."

"It's him, Mom," Evan said with a pout. "He's bothering me."

"Grace, would you please deal with him?" Linda asked.

"Happily," Grace said, looping her arms around Evan's neck and kissing the pout off his lips.

Evan slid his arms under her and stood so quickly that Grace might've toppled off his lap if he hadn't been holding her so tightly. She let out a squeak of surprise. "If she's going to *deal* with me, it's not going to be in front of you jokers," Evan said to groans from his brothers and parents as he carried his girlfriend toward the steps. "Great time, Steph. Best of luck with the restaurant."

"Thanks for coming, and Grace, thanks again for the help."

"My pleasure," Grace called over Evan's shoulder.

He made a comment about her pleasure that earned him a slap on the back from Grace. "Not in front of your parents," she said loud enough that everyone on the porch heard her and laughed.

"Thank goodness we have her to manage him now," Grant said.

"And thank goodness we have Stephanie to manage you and Maddie to manage him," Linda said, gesturing to her firstborn.

"*Hey,*" the brothers said in stereo.

"Hay is for horses," their mother said. "If only we could find a nice girl to manage Adam, I'd have nothing left to worry about."

"Good luck with that project," Mac said.

To her husband, Linda said, "Take me home, my love."

"With pleasure, babe." Big Mac followed his son's lead by picking up his wife and heading for the stairs.

"Check it out," Grant said, grinning. "The old man's still got game."

"You know it," Linda said suggestively to gagging noises from her sons.

"Disgusting," Mac said.

"Totally revolting," Grant added. "Good thing Janey and Joe already left, or she'd be barfing all over the place hearing that."

"We're out, too," Luke said, standing with Sydney in his arms.

"Another man refuses to be outdone by Evan McCarthy," Grant said as they bade good night to Luke and Syd.

"Are you going to be outdone by Evan McCarthy?" Stephanie asked, raising a brow in inquiry.

He patted her bottom. "You'll have to wait and see."

Stephanie loved when he looked at her in that particular way, letting her know she was the most important person in his life. She wasn't sure, exactly, how he managed to convey so much emotion in a look, but she'd learned not to question their amazing connection.

"Jenny," Mac said as he stood to leave, "I'd love to give you a lift off the porch, but I'm afraid my wife, who's stuck at home with a sick kid, wouldn't approve."

"That's all right," Jenny said with a laugh. "I completely understand. If you wouldn't mind walking me to my car, we'll call it even."

"You got it." He mussed Grant's hair on the way by. "See you in the AM, bro."

"Thanks again for the help, Jenny," Stephanie said.

"It was so much fun. Thanks for asking me."

After they left, Shane got up, said good night and went inside.

"He's so quiet," Stephanie said. "You'd never know he was here until he says good night."

"He never used to be," Grant said. "But he's been through some rough shit."

"Haven't we all?" Dan said with a small smile for Kara.

"I worry about him," Grant said of his cousin. "I'd hoped he'd be bouncing back by now, but he just gets more withdrawn all the time. I know Laura worries about him, too."

"Give it some time," Kara said, surprising them all with the comment. "Not everyone bounces back on the same schedule."

"That's very true." Dan gazed out at the darkened sea with a brooding expression on his face that he quickly shook off. "We ought to call it a night, too."

"Don't even think about trying to outdo Evan," Kara said in a warning tone that made Grant and Stephanie laugh.

Grinning, Dan said, "Wouldn't dream of it." Instead, he stood and bowed before her, holding out his hand to help her up.

"Jeez," she said, rolling her eyes as she took his hand.

"I like to think I've got my own moves, thank you very much," Dan said.

"Don't injure yourself showing them off."

Grant howled with laughter. "Oh, I like her. I like her very, *very* much."

"So do I." Dan shocked Kara when he brought her hand to his lips and pressed a kiss to her knuckles. "I like her a whole lot."

"Best of luck to you, Kara," Grant said gravely. "You're going to need it."

"I can handle him," she said. "He's mostly all talk."

Dan's mouth fell open in surprise, and then his eyes darkened with what might've been desire. "Not *all* talk."

"I like her, too," Stephanie said, intrigued by the sparks flying between them.

Kara smiled at her. "Thanks for inviting me, and best of luck with the restaurant."

"I appreciate that. I need all the luck I can get."

"If tonight was any indication, you're going to be a huge hit," Dan said, bending to kiss Stephanie's forehead on the way by.

In the months since he'd helped to free Charlie from prison, Dan had become a dear friend to her, too, and she'd love to see him happy with a nice girl like Kara. With all he did for others, he deserved nothing less.

"See you in the morning," Dan said to Grant as he kept a firm hold on Kara's hand and led her to the stairs.

"That's seven a.m. *East Coast* time," Grant called after him. "Not seven a.m. LaLa time."

"Yeah, yeah, I got it."

When they were alone, Stephanie rested her head on Grant's shoulder and snuggled in closer to him.

"Cold?"

"A little."

"Ready to go home?"

"In a minute."

He kissed her forehead and tightened his arms around her. "What're you thinking about?"

"I was wondering if you ever miss LA."

"Not at all."

"Never?"

"Why in the world would I miss that rat race when I'm here with you and my family, and now one of my best friends has found his way here?"

"I don't know. I wondered. That's all."

"Are you afraid I'll wake up one day and have a sudden longing for my old life?"

His question struck right at the heart of one of her deepest fears. "Maybe."

"Let me put your mind at ease, then." With his finger on her chin, he turned her face, forcing her to meet his intense gaze. "I'm exactly where I want to be with exactly who I want to be with, and I've got no plans to be anywhere else. Ever." He punctuated his sweet words with an even sweeter kiss. "I love you so much, and I'm so happy to see you finally getting everything you've always wanted. I'd never do anything to mess with that."

Closing her eyes, she leaned her forehead against his. "I love you, too." Listening to the ocean pound against the breakwater that formed South Harbor, Stephanie experienced a moment of profound peace unlike anything she'd ever known. Her entire life up to now had been a chaotic disaster. To finally be free of the chains of the past, to be wildly in love with the most amazing man, to have some of the best friends she'd ever had, to be part of a big, funny, wonderful family, to have her own business and to know her stepfather was finally free... She, who'd never allowed herself to want anything, now had everything. Sometimes she feared her heart would simply explode from the overload of emotion.

"Ready to go home for part two of our celebration?" Grant asked suggestively after an extended period of silence.

"I suppose," she said with feigned boredom.

Not to be outdone by his brother or father, Grant scooped her up.

As Stephanie smiled at him, another thought occurred to her. "My dad and Sarah never came back!"

CHAPTER 19

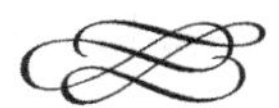

"Walk with me," Charlie said.

Sarah spun around to discover he'd followed her into the kitchen. "But the kids are waiting—"

He took her hand. "Walk with me."

Sarah reacted instantly to the feel of his work-roughened hand wrapped around hers. It'd been such a long, lonely time since anyone had touched her so tenderly. "The kids will—"

"Be just fine without us." Giving her hand a gentle tug, he led her from the kitchen to the hotel's back door.

"Where're we going?" Her heart raced with a mixture of fear and curiosity, but Sarah refused to let the fear get the better of her, so she focused on the curiosity instead.

"Does it matter?"

Sarah thought about that for a second. "I guess not."

"Relax. I promise you'll be perfectly safe with me."

"Somehow, I find that hard to believe," she said drolly, and then she was instantly concerned that she might've offended him. But before she could apologize, he laughed.

"Am I that scary?"

"It's not you."

"Well, it can't be *you*."

"Why do you say that?" Sarah tried to forget that he was still holding her hand as he walked them toward the breakwater. Thankfully, the full moon and the streetlights made it possible to follow the path that wound behind the hotel to the beach.

"Because you're one of the nicest people I've ever met. You're gentle and sweet and accommodating."

Sarah heard the words but couldn't bring herself to believe he was talking about her.

"I wish you could see how you light up when you're holding baby Holden. It's a sight to behold."

She never would've thought gruff, intense Charlie capable of waxing so poetic. "You certainly pay attention."

"I had nothing better to do for fourteen years than to observe the people around me. Fascinating, to say the least."

"Was it awful all the time?"

"Pretty much."

"I don't know how anyone can stand prison, but it has to be especially difficult for those who are innocent."

"I wouldn't change anything," he said in a gruff tone that was more in keeping with what she expected from him than his gentle-poet side. "I don't like to think about what might've become of Stephanie if I hadn't gotten between her and her mother."

"You must love her very much."

"I have from the first day I met her. She was a special kid then, and she's a special kid now. All the years I was inside, she never forgot about me or stopped fighting to get me out. She's my family. She's all I've got."

"And her mother? Do you hear from her at all?"

"She died a couple of months after the incident that landed me in jail. I don't think much about her anymore. I had to let go of the bitterness or let it eat me alive."

Sarah thought about that as she stepped onto the first of the huge flat-faced stones that made up the breakwater. "Is it safe to be out here at night?"

"As long as we watch where we step."

"Stephanie's mother," Sarah said, picking up the conversation after they settled into an easy pace on the rocks, "what was she like?"

"Very sweet and lovely, when she wasn't an abusive addict."

Sarah had wondered about him for such a long time that it was hard not to pepper him with questions now that he seemed willing to talk.

"What else do you want to know?"

She caught a hint of a grin in the pale moonlight. "I'm sorry. I don't mean to pry."

He stopped so suddenly that she might've run into him if he hadn't anticipated that possibility and held out his other hand to steady her. "Will you do something for me?" he asked, sounding serious and intent.

"If I can."

"Will you never apologize to me again? Will you never be sorry for asking an honest question or expressing an honest feeling? Will you never worry that I'm suddenly going to become angry with you or become someone different because I don't like what you said? Can you do that for me?"

Since he'd rendered her speechless as well as breathless, Sarah only stared at him for the longest time. "I…I don't know if I can do that. I… I don't know what it's like not to be afraid of those things."

"Sweet, sweet Sarah," he whispered as he put his arms lightly around her, asking her without words to let him hold her.

He didn't make her feel pressured or overwhelmed or afraid. Rather, he surrounded her with his quiet strength, the scent of his aftershave and the promises he'd made to be nothing like the man who'd harmed her so profoundly.

She swayed toward him and was proud of herself when she didn't flinch as his muscles tightened around her.

"Hold on to me, sweet Sarah."

Her hands found his hips in the dark.

"That's the way." They stood there for the longest time as the cool breeze whipped at her hair and flattened her skirt against her legs.

They stood there as the foghorn blared and a group of young women laughed their way through town. "Now what else do you want to know about me?"

Even though the air was chilly, Sarah felt warm from the inside out as his much bigger body formed a shelter from the breeze. "Did you love your wife?"

"Very much so, until I found out who she really was. Stephanie blames herself for not telling me her mother was an addict. She doesn't think I know that, but how could I not know she was so afraid I'd leave them that she hid the truth from me?"

"The poor kid was hanging on to the one person she could count on."

He nodded in agreement. "I was happy to be that person for her. When they accused me of abusing her..."

Sarah felt the shudder travel through his muscular body.

"That was the worst day of my life."

"I'm so sorry for all you went through."

"Thank you." His lips brushed against her forehead, setting off a reaction that traveled to all her most important places.

It'd been so long since Sarah had experienced desire that she was surprised she still recognized it.

"Are you going to tell me what happened to you?"

"Maybe someday, but not tonight."

"That's okay. You don't have to ever tell me if you don't want to."

Knowing he didn't expect her to spill her secrets was somehow freeing. "Thank you. I've had a lovely time."

"Me, too. Next time, it'll be just you and me."

As Sarah rested her face against his chest, she decided she couldn't wait for next time.

TIFFANY WAITED until she was certain Blaine was asleep before she slipped out of bed and went into the bathroom. With the door closed, she slid down to sit on the floor to process everything she'd overheard.

He'd lost his last job because of a woman. She desperately wanted to know what had happened, but another part of her didn't want to know. The idea that she could cause him the same kind of trouble made her feel sick all over again, but this time, she was heartsick. She couldn't let him risk his career and livelihood, and she certainly didn't want to wait around for him to figure out that she was more trouble than she was worth.

Her father had left her. Her husband had left her. Why would Blaine be any different? Sure, he'd said all the right things, but he wasn't the kind of man who'd discount his mother's concerns. Eventually, she'd wear him down, and he'd leave, too.

A sharp pain under her ribs took her breath away. She understood in that moment that losing Blaine would be far more painful than any of the other losses. In the short time they'd spent together, he'd worked his way past her defenses and had given her a glimpse of what might've been if things had been different. She hadn't planned to fall in love with him, she thought as she wiped away tears.

With hindsight, she should've known she would. From that first explosive moment in her kitchen through every other meeting, the signs had been there. At times she felt like she barely knew him. At other times, she felt like she'd never known anyone better.

It was her own fault, she concluded as the pain in her chest intensified and a sob escaped from her lips. She'd failed to remember that theirs was only a fling and had made the huge mistake of allowing her heart to become involved. Her course of action became crystal clear: She had to leave him before he left her. That was her only choice. As painful as it might be at first, it would be far better to have it happen now, before she fell any deeper in love with him. She'd convinced herself, but how would she convince him that their relationship had been doomed before it ever began?

Right as she had that thought, she heard the heavy thud of footsteps approaching the bathroom door. She couldn't let him find her crying, so she scrambled for the toilet.

He knocked softly on the door. "Tiffany? Are you okay?"

She wiped her face frantically. "Come in."

He opened the door and stopped short when he saw her leaning over the toilet. “Were you sick again?”

“False alarm.” She ventured a glance at him over her shoulder and noticed he’d pulled on a pair of gym shorts. The concern she saw on his face made the ache in her chest worsen.

Behind her, she heard water running. He handed her a cold washcloth that felt heavenly against her fevered skin. “Thank you.”

“Can I get you anything?” he asked, studying her intently. No doubt he could tell she’d been crying.

She shook her head.

“I know what you need.”

She watched as he went over to the tub and turned on the water and then came back for her, reaching out to help her up off the floor. He squeezed toothpaste on her brush and kept an arm around her as she brushed her teeth.

“I don’t have any of that strawberry stuff you love so much, but the hot water will feel good.”

A bath, she realized, was exactly what she needed. How had he figured that out before she knew it herself? “Thank you.” She waited for him to ask why she’d been crying, but he didn’t.

When the water was ready, he helped her out of her robe and nightgown and held her hand as she stepped into the steaming bath. He surprised her when he knelt next to the tub and reached for a bottle of shampoo.

“Get your hair wet.”

She dipped her hair into the water and waited to see what he would do.

He massaged the shampoo into her hair and scalp, making her sigh with pleasure. Had anything ever felt so good?

She kept her eyes closed as he soaped every inch of her skin, except for the area that burned for him. He saved that for last, running soapy fingers over her smooth folds, arousing her with only a few strokes.

“Blaine…”

“Sorry. I forgot you’re sick.”

When he would've withdrawn his hand, she grabbed his wrist and kept him there. So much for her resolve to put a halt to things with him. It had taken him five minutes of tender care to show her how lacking in willpower she was where he was concerned.

"Is my girl not as sick as she pretends to be?" he asked with amusement in his voice.

Her heart beat faster when he called her his girl. "I'm never too sick for this."

He pressed his fingers deeper into her, surprising her when he used his free hand to tweak her nipple.

She shuddered and came the second his fingers made contact with the heart of her desire.

"So, so beautiful," he whispered as he continued to stroke her sensitive flesh.

"Blaine..."

"What, honey?"

"I want you to..." Tiffany stopped herself, unaccustomed to asking for what she wanted from a man. His sweetness had left her feeling raw and exposed to feelings she'd only recently tried to deny. How foolish that seemed only a few minutes later, after he'd proven her powerless to resist him.

"What, baby? Anything you want."

"Will you hold me?"

"God, yes. There's nothing I'd rather do. Let's get you out of there."

He helped her to stand and ran a towel over her reverently, leaving no part of her untouched, and even towel-dried and brushed her hair. Watching him tend to her made her heart melt and her sex ache with the need for more. Even though she still felt lousy, she wanted to be close to him. She *needed* to be close to him. When had he become her anchor? When had he become so *necessary*?

"Steady," he said when her legs wavered under her. His hands on her shoulders kept her on her feet until he scooped her up and carried her into the bedroom, depositing her gently on the bed. When she began to shiver, he pulled the covers up and over her, surrounding her with his appealing scent. She watched him drop his shorts and held out her arms to welcome him into bed.

"Oh, you're so warm!" she said as he wrapped himself around her.

"Snuggle closer to get the full impact."

The "full impact," she discovered, was indeed quite full and pressed insistently against her belly. She couldn't resist reaching down to stroke his heated skin and reveled in the groan that seemed to come from deep inside his chest.

"That feels so good."

"I want you." Why be coy? Why pretend otherwise? Why pretend that hadn't been the case from the first time she ever laid eyes on him?

"You've been so sick, honey."

"I'm okay. I need you."

He cupped her bottom, holding her even tighter against him as he pushed rhythmically into her hand. "You have me," he said gruffly. "I'm right here, and I'm not going anywhere."

"There's nothing you could say that would mean more to me than that."

He captured her lips in a breathtakingly intense kiss that had her straining against him, begging for more. "How could he ever let you go?"

"I wasn't like this with him." She squeezed him to make her point. "I was always afraid to take what I wanted."

"Don't ever be afraid with me. I'd give you anything. All you have to do is ask."

Encouraged by his sweet words and the even sweeter sincerity behind them, she wiggled down to kiss his chest, giving special attention to his nipple, which made him gasp and expand in her hand. She moved farther down, running her tongue over muscles in his belly that quivered in response. When she took his straining erection into her mouth, she kept up the steady strokes of her hand at the base.

Her free hand traveled around to his rear, squeezing and running her nails over his cheeks. That seemed to make him a little crazy, so she let her middle finger delve into the crease, which was all it took to make him come—hard. She licked up every drop of his intense release before she let him slide from between her lips.

"Wow," he said. His eyes were closed, and his chest heaved.

Tiffany loved that she'd done that to him. Maybe it would never work between them in the long run. Maybe it would blow up in her face the way her relationship with Jim had. Maybe, maybe... She couldn't remember being so content or happy. Even the threat of eviction hanging over the store couldn't dampen the sweet feelings Blaine inspired.

"Come here," he whispered.

"Where?"

"Up here."

She worked her way closer to his face. "I'm here."

"As beautiful as this face is," he said, cupping her cheek for effect, "it's not the part of you I want."

Tiffany's eyes widened with surprise—and a tiny bit of alarm. "What part do you want?"

His hand coasted over her back to cup her bottom. "This part. If you feel up to playing some more, that is."

At some point in the last half hour, she'd forgotten all about being sick—and that she'd planned to leave him. "Ah... What do you want with that part of me?"

"Come find out." His tone was heavy with desire and challenge.

Never one to back down, Tiffany was at once curious and anxious. He seemed to possess endless ways to arouse and stir her. Filled with trepidation—and excitement—she knelt and turned her back to him. "Like this?"

His hand traveled from her shoulder to her bottom in a light caress that made her insides flutter and her sex ache with anticipation. "It's a good start." He gripped her hips and encouraged her to keep her back to his face when she straddled him. When he had her arranged the way he wanted her, his hand on her back encouraged her to bend over him. She felt horribly exposed and terribly aroused by a position that was all new to her. Waiting to see what he would do made her skin tingle.

"Mmm," he said as his lips coasted over her inner thigh. "What a lovely, *lovely* sight."

She was glad he thought so, because she was about to die of embarrassment. Tiffany had no idea what she was supposed to do with her hands, so she rested them on his thighs and felt his muscles jump in reaction, letting her know he wasn't unaffected by this new game.

And then his tongue was outlining her sex, laying a tantalizing path of sensation over her bare skin that turned her muscles to water.

"Don't move," he ordered.

"I'm trying not to." She sounded breathless and positively wanton as she tried to wriggle closer to his questing tongue.

"Try harder." His hand came down on her right buttock in a light smack that made her moan. Before she had a chance to recover from the spank, his tongue was delving inside her and she was on the verge of an explosive release.

"Don't come yet."

"But I—"

This time his hand landed on her left cheek, leaving a fiery sting in its wake.

Tiffany gasped and panted, pushing her sex against his face. She started to imagine how she must look, naked and spread out on top of him, and then realized she didn't care how she looked. He liked what he was seeing, and that was all that mattered.

His finger at the base of her spine roused her out of her musings to pay close attention as it traveled down, down, down. He paused only to press against her back entrance before continuing on to slide into her slick heat.

"Don't come," he said again, more harshly this time as his tongue teased her and his fingers slid into her, pressing against that spot deep inside for a brief instant before retreating once again.

She noticed he was hard again and decided to even the score by using her tongue on him, teasing the tip with the same darting strokes he was giving her.

His growl was the only sign he gave that she was getting to him, so she kept it up, cupping his balls for added effect.

"Do *not* come," he said, sounding less fierce this time as he raised his hips. "Suck me." He punctuated his harsh command with another stab of his tongue.

She wrapped her lips around the head of his penis and sucked as hard as she dared.

Growling, he returned the favor by tightening his lips around her and sucking just as hard as he pressed his fingers into her.

A sharp cry escaped from her lips the second before she exploded, shattering into a million pieces in an orgasm that went on for what felt like forever. Every time she thought it was over, he proved her wrong, taking her up and over again and again until he finally joined her, filling her mouth and throat with his essence.

She came down from the incredible high to the feel of his tongue soothing her sensitive skin and his fingers still embedded deep within her.

He wiggled them just to make sure she knew he was there, and Tiffany nearly came again from that alone. Finally, he withdrew from her and encouraged her to turn toward him.

"Ride me."

She looked down, shocked to realize he was already hard again. The man was positively insatiable!

"*Please.*" He sounded so desperate that Tiffany moved faster than she thought she could to give him what he needed. Even though she was more primed than she'd ever been in her life, it still took a few torturous minutes to take him in. The whole time, his lips were parted, his eyes were closed, and his hands gripped her hips so tightly she had no doubt there'd be bruises.

"*Yes,*" he whispered when she sank down on the final inch. Keeping his hands on her hips, he set the pace. "Tiffany, God, *Tiffany*..." He cupped her breasts, tweaking her nipples as he seemed to get harder and bigger inside her. His eyes opened slowly, and he looked up at her. What she saw in his eyes told her everything about how he was feeling, and she couldn't look away.

He thrust up and into her, stealing every thought from her mind that wasn't about ultimate pleasure. After the last orgasmic frenzy, she would've bet her life she couldn't do it again. She would've been dead wrong because once again she was climbing as he kept up the steady and relentless pace. She was supposed to be riding him, but he'd taken control of her mind, her body and her heart. To deny that would be foolish. She loved him. How could she not? But she couldn't tell him. Not yet. Not until she was absolutely certain he wouldn't leave.

He stole the last remaining thoughts from her mind with a mighty thrust that sent them both into release. For the longest time, she lay on top of him, pulsating with aftershocks. With his strong arms tight around her, she felt safe and adored. And loved.

CHAPTER 20

"Are you going to tell me why you were crying before?"

As Tiffany shook her head, a tear escaped from the corner of her eye.

Blaine used the tip of his index finger to brush it away. "What's wrong?"

"Nothing."

"Tiffany..."

After the intense way he'd loved her, she couldn't possibly tell him she'd been planning to leave him.

"Are you still upset about what my mother said? I told you, it doesn't matter. I don't care what anyone thinks."

"I'm afraid that eventually people like your mother will convince you I'm not worth the aggravation—"

"Stop. Please don't do this. Don't be driven by fear or worries about what other people might say. I'm not Jim. I'm not your dad. It's not fair to expect me to do the same thing they did."

How did he do that? How did he zero in on her deepest fears and allay them so effortlessly?

"Do you think I don't understand?" He tucked a lock of hair

behind her ear. "Your father left you, your husband left you, so naturally, if you let yourself have feelings for me, I will, too, right?"

Tiffany's throat tightened with emotion. "Maybe."

"Please don't worry about that. I'm right where I want to be. I waited so damned long to be able to hold you and kiss you and make love with you. I thought I'd go crazy waiting for you."

"Really?"

"Really."

"I don't want you to lose your job because of me."

"If I lose my job, it'll be because of me, not you. I've been pushing the mayor's buttons since the day I got here. He's up my ass all the time about everything, including the length of my hair."

"I like the length of your hair," she said, running her fingers through it.

"All the more reason not to cut it," he said, holding her still for his kiss. "Why are your brows still furrowed?"

Once again, she was unsettled by the intense way he paid attention to her. "Are they?"

He ran a finger from one eyebrow to the other. "Uh-huh."

"What your mother said—"

"I told you not to pay any attention to her."

"I was wondering how you lost your last job."

After a long pause, he said, "I don't like to talk about that."

"You don't like to talk about anything."

The fingers that had been combing through her hair stilled. "That's not true."

"I don't know anything about you, other than what you do for work, and who some of your friends are."

"What do you want to know?"

Tiffany tried to think of some innocuous questions she could ask to work up to what she really wanted to know. "Do you have siblings?"

"Two brothers, two sisters."

"Where are they?"

"My younger brother is in college, but the others are scattered around New England."

"Are you close to them?"

"I talk to them all just about every week. Does that count as close?"

Tiffany, who used to yearn for a big family, would've loved to have four siblings she talked to every week. She'd often been envious of the closeness she'd witnessed among Mac and his siblings. "Yes, that counts. Are you the oldest?"

"Second oldest. What else do you want to know?"

"I want to know everything. I've told you about my bad stuff. Are you going to tell me about yours?"

"I hate to think about it, let alone talk about it. It's all in the past. I'd like to leave it there."

Tiffany started to protest but thought better of it. Despite his tender care and intense lovemaking, she felt stung by his unwillingness to share his past with her.

He kissed the top of her head and squeezed her tightly. "Do you remember the first time we met?"

The abrupt shift in conversation caught her off guard.

"In Maddie's hospital room after the accident at the marina," he said. "Remember?"

"Yes," she said with a secretive smile.

"What?"

"I thought you were hot and said as much to Maddie."

"Funny, I thought the same about you—that day and every time I ran into you afterward. When I saw Mac, the first thing I asked was if you were single. I thought I'd *die* when he said you were married."

"Is that so?"

Nodding, he traced the outline of her lips with the tip of his index finger. "But then he said your marriage was on the rocks, and I was filled with foolish hope. The night you handcuffed yourself to Jim, and he called the police... Seeing you...naked..." His finger moved in a tantalizing path over her chin to her chest, between her breasts and back up to circle her nipple. "It was all I could do to function professionally when the only thing I wanted to do was unlock those cuffs and drag you away from him. I wanted you all to myself, which is why I acted so unprofessionally when I took you home that night."

"Is that what you call it? Unprofessional?" she asked with a laugh, remembering the earth-shattering minutes in her kitchen.

"What would you call it?"

"Incredible. Amazing. Life changing."

He brought her hand to his lips, and she suddenly realized she was no longer thinking about how to leave him. Rather, she was thinking about how she might try to keep him forever. "It was all those things for me and so much more. I thought about you all the time. I had no idea divorces could take so long."

Tiffany's mind raced as she tried to process what he'd said. He'd thought about her all the time. Her heart stood up to do a happy little dance at that news.

For a long time, he was silent, and then he curled a lock of her hair around his finger. "I know I'm not the easiest guy in the world to be with, but I hope you'll be patient with me and give me a chance. I waited so long for you."

While he hadn't given her what she'd wanted, he had given her something else she hadn't known she needed—hope.

"I'M NOT ready to go home yet," Dan said as he drove Kara back to North Harbor.

"What do you want to do?"

"What is there to do around here?"

"Not much." Kara was quiet for a minute before she said, "I know something we can do."

"Sounds promising," he said in his best suggestive tone. Dan knew it wasn't wise to needle her, but he couldn't seem to help it.

"Not *that*."

"Oh, damn. Can't blame a guy for being hopeful. What, then?"

"How about a ride on the Salt Pond?"

"In the dark?"

"You're not afraid, are you?"

"Of course not, but how will you be able to see where we're going?"

"I have exceptional night vision."

"This I have to see." A few minutes later, Dan parked in the lot at McCarthy's and followed Kara to the floating dock where he got on first and held out a hand to help her aboard.

"I'm only allowing you to help me because I'm wearing a dress."

"I'm only helping you because you're wearing a dress."

She tried to hold back a smile and failed, shaking her head at him.

Under the bright lights from the main pier, he watched her unlock the console and start the boat. After letting it warm up, she cast off the bowline and gestured for him to get the stern. The night was clear and very dark. Dan gazed up at a star-filled sky that got more spectacular the farther they got from the lighted docks.

"It's quite something, huh?" she said from her post at the helm.

"Indeed. Something tells me this isn't the first time you've been out here late at night."

She shrugged. "I don't sleep very well, so it's something to do."

Without thinking through the implications, he came up behind her and sat on the seat, urging her to lean back against him.

She immediately went rigid. "Um…"

"Relax," he said. "I only want to keep you warm."

"I'm not cold."

Behind her, he smiled. He expected nothing less from her. "This way, you won't get cold."

She remained stiff and unyielding for several minutes before she gave in and leaned back against him.

Dan celebrated the victory silently as her hair whipped around his face. He gathered it into a ponytail and held back the urge to kiss the sweet curve of her neck, where the straps of her dress came together in a single button that would be so easy to release.

"You're getting awfully familiar," she said.

The scent of her hair was driving him crazy. "Am I?"

"You know you are."

"Is that so bad?"

"I haven't decided yet."

"Let me know when you make up your mind."

"Dan—"

"Shhh. I'm trying to enjoy the ride."

Even though he knew she had plenty to say, she stayed quiet as she navigated the boat to the far side of the vast pond. He was intrigued to realize it was rather easy to see once his eyes became accustomed to the dark. It took about twenty minutes to travel around the anchorage.

"Isn't that your friend what's-his-name's boat?" Dan asked.

"Do you mean *Robert?*"

He couldn't believe how furious that made him. "So now you actually know his name?"

"Of course I know his name. He asked me out."

"You… He… He did?"

Kara laughed softly, and he tugged on her hair.

"Don't laugh at me."

"Why not? You're funny."

"So…what did you say?"

"To what?"

Dan wanted to growl with exasperation, but then he realized she was enjoying playing with him. He liked her playfulness, even if it was at his expense. "When he asked you out."

"I told him I'd let him know."

"What does that mean?"

"I wanted to see how tonight went before I gave him an answer."

Dan reached around her and turned off the engine.

"Hey!" She turned to him, as he'd hoped she would. "You can't do that!"

Remaining seated, Dan released her hair and reached up to put both hands on her face. When she tried to turn away from him, he resisted. "Don't."

For a charged moment, they stared at each other in the darkness, and then he drew her down to him, slowly but purposefully.

"Dan—"

"Shhh. I had no idea there was so much riding on this date. I have to make sure you don't want to go out with anyone else."

Their lips met softly, tentatively. He was careful to go slow when every cell in his body was urging haste. This, he reminded himself in a final moment of clarity, was her first kiss in years. He couldn't screw it up by demanding too much too soon. For the longest time, he thought she wouldn't respond, and then her lips moved against his. When it dawned on him that she was kissing him back, he slid one hand around to the back of her neck to keep her anchored as he tipped his head to the right to better align their lips.

She was so sweet, so careful and so wounded. He couldn't forget that last part as he stood and drew her in closer to him. And then her arms came up to encircle his neck, and he wanted to whoop with joy. Rather than do that, he painted her bottom lip with gentle brushes of his tongue, hoping she'd take the hint and let him in.

As the water lapped against the hull of the boat, he teased and cajoled until her mouth opened and her tongue pressed against his. He wasn't proud of the growl that escaped from him as he took her up on the invitation for more. As the kiss deepened, she pressed herself against him, making the small space between the seat and the console too tight to hide his growing arousal. Without breaking the kiss, he eased her out of the confined area and backed her up to the center seating area that also served as a cover for the boat's life jackets.

She shocked the shit out of him when she tugged him down on top of her. Who was this girl and what had she done with shy, reserved Kara? Not that he was complaining, but he couldn't help but wonder what had gotten into her.

With their bodies now tightly aligned, Dan could no longer hide the proof of what her sweet kisses were doing to him. He pressed against her and waited for her to push him away. Instead, her arms tightened around his neck and her lips became greedier.

He couldn't remember the last time he'd wanted anything the way he wanted her, and the thought of her going out with someone else was completely unbearable.

She arched her back, released her tight hold on his neck and shoved her hands inside his sport coat to tug his shirt free of his pants. The feel of her soft hands on his back had him gasping.

"Oh, sorry," she whispered as she began to withdraw from him.

"No, *no*, don't be sorry. Don't stop. Touch me."

Her hands slid from his waist and up his back to pull him back down for more kisses.

"I want to touch you, too," he said. "Is that okay?" He waited, breathless, until he saw her small nod. Then he reached for the button that held up her dress and released it, peeling back the dress before she could change her mind. With a single flex of two fingers, he released the front clasp of her strapless bra.

Her rapid breathing was all he could hear over the roar in his own head as he exposed her breasts and watched her nipples pebble in the cool night air. "So pretty," he whispered as he bent his head and took a stiffly beaded tip into his mouth.

She cried out and gripped his hair, holding him tight against her chest as he sucked and licked and tugged, all the while grinding his erection into the welcoming V of her legs. "God, Kara. I want you." This was whispered against her neck in the second before he bit down on her earlobe.

Her hands were clumsy and fumbling when she reached for his belt and tugged it open.

There was something he meant to say just then, but the words died on his lips when she unzipped his pants and shoved her hand inside. On the verge of immediate release, he returned his attention to her other breast and tried to buy some time by distracting her. He couldn't believe this was happening. Where was shy, reluctant Kara? And how far was she planning to take this? He hoped it was pretty damned far, because he wasn't going to last much longer with her sweet breast in his mouth and her soft hand caressing his shaft.

Dan reached down to her leg, pushing it up and over to open her. Waiting for her to call a halt to this whole thing, he focused his attention on her inner thigh for the moment, all the while continuing to suckle her breasts. Determined to distract her, he drew her nipple between his teeth, biting down only hard enough to ensure he had her full attention. He took advantage of her distraction to move his hand higher and encountered a small strip of satin covering her mound. *Holy Jesus*, he thought as he moved the scrap of material over the dampness between her legs.

She wanted him as much as he wanted her.

Somehow, he managed to gather his wits. "Kara—"

"Don't stop. Please don't stop."

"Are you sure?" The last thing he wanted was to deal with her regret in the morning and have to start again to win her over.

She nodded and stroked him again, harder than before, and all Dan could think about was sinking into her heat. With that in mind, he disentangled from her and quickly shucked his jacket, shirt and pants. Pushing her dress up to her waist, he tugged the thong from between her sweet cheeks and brought it to his face to take a deep sniff of the crotch. "Mmm." He wished he could've seen her face right then. He'd bet everything he had that it would be bright red. In his wallet, he found a condom he hoped wasn't too old and rolled it on before lowering himself to her embrace. "You're still sure?"

"Yes."

"Do you promise you won't hate me tomorrow?"

"The only way I'm going to hate you is if you don't hurry up."

He didn't need to be told twice. With her arms around him and her body arching into his, she was sending every signal that she wanted this as much as he did. He could only hope that was true. His fingers found her slick and ready, and when he focused his attention on the tight bundle of nerves at her core, she gasped in reaction. As his control snapped, he pushed into her while continuing the insistent movement of his fingers.

And then he was kissing her again with far less panache than he normally displayed. All that mattered was getting as close to her as he could while taking as much as she was willing to give. He hammered into her, knowing he'd regret being rough but unable to stop himself.

Like a wave determined to reach the shore, the intensity built and built until it broke in a simultaneous release that had them both crying out into the dark night around them.

Her fingers dug into his shoulders, holding on for dear life as she rode the waves of her own climax, clutching him with tight internal muscles that had his eyes rolling back in his head from the sheer, unbelievable pleasure of it. Nothing had ever been like this, he realized as he floated back to earth to find her shivering beneath him.

"Cold?"

"Sort of."

Reluctantly, Dan withdrew from her, reached for his coat on the floor and wrapped it around her. "Better?"

"Yes, thanks. There's a beach towel under the pilot seat if you want to grab that, too."

Dan retrieved the towel and stretched out next to her, covering them both with it. "Come here," he said gruffly, needing her close to him after what they'd shared.

She turned toward him, her eyes wider than usual and her hair tangled.

He put an arm around her and smoothed her hair back from her face. "You promised you wouldn't hate me."

"I don't."

"Or yourself."

"I never promised that."

"Kara—"

"It's okay," she said with a small laugh. "I'm remarkably okay."

He buried his face in her hair and breathed in her sweet scent. "I have another condom."

"Is that right?"

"Mmm." This was said against her neck and punctuated with a stroke of his tongue that made her tremble. "Should I get it?"

"How about we continue this back at my place, where it's quite a bit warmer and the bed is significantly softer?"

Dan couldn't believe she was inviting him into her bed. After months of mad, crazy crush, he wanted to pinch himself. "You won't change your mind between here and there?"

She brushed a lock of his hair off his forehead, a gesture that made his heart stagger. "I won't change my mind."

"And you won't go out with Robert?"

She stared at him, and then she laughed—a deep husky laugh that fired him up all over again. "I won't go out with Robert."

Relief flooded through him. "Then I'll share my other condom with you."

"You're just *too* good to me."

"I completely agree."

JOE WOKE to his favorite sight—his gorgeous wife looking at him with those big blue eyes that usually gave away her every thought. Today, however, her eyes were closed off and shuttered. A ripple of anxiety traveled down his backbone. "What're you thinking about over there?" He rested a hand on her belly and was greeted with a thump from within that made him smile.

"You."

"What about me?"

She bit her bottom lip, a sure sign that something was on her mind. "Your mom has something she needs to talk to you about."

Joe immediately went cold with fear. "Is she sick?"

"No, baby." She caressed his cheek. "Nothing like that. I didn't mean to scare you."

He released a deep breath. "What is it? Do you know?"

"Yes, she talked to me about it, but it's something you should hear from her."

"You're freaking me out, Janey."

"I know. I don't mean to. I wanted you to be prepared, but I'm messing it all up."

"Prepared for what?"

"Your mom… She loves you so much."

"I know that. I've always known that. Sometimes I've worried that she loves me too much."

"What do you mean?"

"She sacrificed her own life to make sure I had everything I needed."

Janey reached for his hand and held on tightly. "I want you to remember you said that. When she tells you what she needs you to know, remember that."

"As long as she isn't sick or worse, I can handle whatever she throws at me."

"Remember that, too."

He wished she'd just tell him, but he understood that she was unwilling to betray a confidence. Since the love his mother and wife had for each other made him happy, he wouldn't expect Janey to tell him something that clearly needed to come from his mother.

Joe gave Janey's hand a final squeeze and got up to shower. As he ran a razor over his face, he reviewed the last few days, wondering if he'd missed something. All he could recall was her unusual reaction to hearing that Seamus had given his notice.

Was she concerned about the business? Did she know something about it that he didn't know? He went out of his way to make sure she was never burdened by the business they co-owned, but he'd been away from the island a long time. Maybe something had happened and she'd waited until he was home to clue him in.

When he emerged from the shower, Janey was standing in front of the bedroom mirror, securing her hair into a ponytail. She looked so fresh and pretty—and round—that Joe took a moment to hug her from behind. He pressed a kiss to her neck and made her shiver. Here in his arms was everything he'd ever wanted but never dreamed he'd have.

She turned and slid her arms around his waist, above the towel he'd knotted at his hips. Her lips were soft on his chest as she laid a trail of kisses that ended at his lips. "I love you love you," she whispered.

"Me too. So much."

"Please listen to your mom with an open mind and an open heart."

"I will. Of course I will." He didn't want to be annoyed that she thought he'd approach his mother any other way, but it did bother him that she was so concerned about him being unreasonable.

"Joe—"

"Let's get this over with. You've got my stomach in knots." He pulled on shorts and a T-shirt, sliding his feet into flip-flops. As he left the bedroom and headed for the kitchen, he was aware of Janey following him.

CHAPTER 21

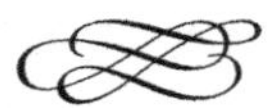

Carolina sat at the table with a mug of coffee cradled between her hands as she stared out the window, lost in thought. The early morning light cast a glow upon her, and Joe realized she was still very pretty. Her eyes, however, were tired and troubled.

"Mom."

Jolted out of her thoughts, Carolina glanced up at him, her gaze filled with unusual trepidation that did nothing for his already out-of-control nerves.

"You're up early," Carolina said.

"Janey told me there's something you need to talk to me about." He watched her glance at Janey and then back at him. "Sit, honey. Can I get you some coffee?"

"No, I don't want any damned coffee. I want someone to tell me what the hell is going on."

Unaccustomed to such an outburst from him, both women seemed surprised.

Joe immediately regretted the harsh words but not enough to apologize. He sat next to his mother, took the mug and covered her hands with his. "Tell me. Whatever it is, we'll figure it out together the way we always have."

"Oh, honey. I so hope you mean that."

"I do mean it. Why wouldn't I?"

Janey sat at the table and folded her hands in front of her.

Filled with trepidation, Joe looked from his mother to his wife and back at his mother, waiting…

"I…um, remember when Seamus told you he was resigning and—"

"Is that what you're worried about? I told you I'd take care of it, and I will."

"No, Joseph. Listen. Just listen. Please."

She only called him Joseph at the most important moments. Releasing her hands, he sat back against his chair, vibrating with tension.

Carolina cleared her throat. "He… He told you he was leaving for personal reasons."

"Yeah, so?"

She looked him right in the eye. "I'm the personal reason."

Joe had no idea what she was talking about. "What do you mean?" He shot a glance at Janey, who was intently studying her hands on the table.

"Seamus and I…"

All at once, Joe got exactly what she meant. He stood up so quickly his chair toppled backward, making both women gasp. "What the hell are you saying?" he asked as he picked up the chair.

"Joe." The single word from Janey and the way she said his name brought him back to earlier when he'd promised to remember what his mother had given up for him.

"What're you saying?" he asked again, more rationally this time, though he felt anything but rational.

"Seamus and I… We have feelings for each other."

Joe saw red as he thought of the trust he'd put in Seamus, and to think, while his back had been turned—

"Whatever you're thinking," Carolina said in her stern mother voice, "it's probably unkind toward Seamus, and I won't stand for that. He hasn't betrayed your trust or acted less than honorably or any of the things you're no doubt thinking. If anything, I'm the one who's been guilty of all that."

Janey gasped with surprise. "I don't believe that, Carolina."

"Well, it's true. He was never anything other than kind and wonderful to me, and in return, I treated him as if he'd done something shameful by caring about me. That was wrong of me."

Joe gripped the back of the chair so tightly his knuckles turned white.

After a long, uncomfortable silence, Carolina looked up at her son. "Would you please say something?"

"When did this happen?"

"Last fall. When I planned to come out here, but the boats were canceled—"

"It happened at *my* house?"

She never wavered when she said, "Yes, but I want you to know I didn't see him again afterward, except for once at a party at Luke and Syd's. I told him it couldn't happen, because..."

"Because why?"

Her mouth twisted into an ironic little smile. "Because of you, Joe, among other things."

"Me? What did I have to do with it?"

"Joseph... You... God, you're everything. I knew it would upset you —the age difference, the fact that he's your employee, the trust you'd placed in him, your ideas about me, and how I should behave."

"I don't have ideas about you. What does that even mean?"

"I knew you wouldn't approve," she said quietly.

"I..." His chest felt tight, and suddenly he had to get out of there or risk saying something he wouldn't be able to take back. "I have to go."

"Where?" Janey asked, alarmed.

"Somewhere. Anywhere. I have to go."

Carolina stood. "Joe, wait."

"No, I have to go." He rushed through the house and out the door, taking deep breaths of the cool morning air as he climbed into his truck. The tires made spinning noises as he pulled out of the driveway and headed for town.

. . .

"We need to go after him," Carolina said to Janey as the truck peeled out of the driveway.

"No," Janey said, somehow remaining calm despite the storm of emotion. "We need to let him work this out in his own way."

"Even if that means he's looking for blood from Seamus?"

"I don't think he'll do that."

Carolina raised a brow. "Did you think he'd break David's nose?"

"No, but—"

"We need to go after him." Carolina grabbed her keys off the counter. "Are you with me?"

Janey sighed, recognizing defeat when she saw it. "I'm with you."

Navigating the first boat from the mainland through the morning fog, Seamus guzzled coffee and tried to stay focused on the task of staring into the murkiness while keeping a careful eye on all his navigational aids. He'd passed another sleepless night fretting over Carolina telling Joe about them and wondering if they were making a huge mistake by telling him, or if they might be paving the way for a possible future together.

Stop. Don't even go there until you know for sure. The idea of a future with her was so tantalizing, so delightfully overwhelming that it literally hurt to think about it, especially when it remained possible that her son's disapproval would derail the whole thing.

He'd never been more relieved to see the breakwater to South Harbor as it emerged from the fog. Before he left the island on the two o'clock boat, he'd check in with Carolina to see what was going on. Otherwise, the waiting would certainly kill him. He walked to the aft controls located in the stern, backed the ferry smoothly into port and waited until the cars began driving off the boat before he locked up the control box and returned to the wheelhouse to gather his belongings and fill in the ship's log.

After a stop in the main office to check in with the employees there, he headed across the parking lot to his office, determined to wade through the work he'd been putting off for a week now—anything to take his mind off his worries.

He was so preoccupied with his own thoughts that he was through the office door before he noticed Joe sitting behind the desk with a stormy expression on his face. Seamus stopped short, uncertain of whether he should proceed into the office or turn and run for his life. As appealing as the latter option was, he forced himself to stay put and face the music head-on.

"Joe."

"Seamus."

"What brings you into town so early?"

"What do you think?"

Filled with nervous energy, Seamus removed his Gansett Island Ferry Company ball cap and ran a hand through his hair. "I imagine you've had a talk with your mum."

"Indeed I have."

Since this was Joe's show, Seamus withheld comment and waited on him.

"What I'd like to know is where you get off thinking it's all right to take up with my mother."

Seamus knew it wasn't wise to laugh right then, but damned if he could help the chuckle that escaped from his lips.

Joe's expression grew even stormier, if that was possible. "I fail to see what's funny about this situation."

"No, I bet you don't. There's nothing funny about it, trust me. What's amusing is that you think I somehow had control over it."

"Of course you had control over it! You're a grown man, for Christ's sake."

"'Tis true, I am, which is why for a whole year I hid the instant attraction I felt for your mum from everyone—even her. The day I met her..." Seamus shook his head in amazement. He'd never forget the moment her eyes met his for the first time and the absolute *certainty* he'd experienced that she would somehow change his life. "It was quite something," was all he said to Joe.

"I don't understand—"

Seamus tilted his head and smiled. "Don't you?"

Joe snorted with disgust. "Don't even try to compare this to me and Janey."

"Why not? Didn't you too yearn for a woman you couldn't have?"

"Yes, but—"

"Love is love, Joe. I love your mom. I want to be with her. I want to make her happy and take care of her. How is that any different from what you feel for Janey?"

"She's a lot older than you, for one thing."

"Is she?" Seamus asked, feigning shock. "I had no idea!"

"Stop trying to be funny. This isn't funny."

"Stop acting like a little boy who's miffed because his mum got a boyfriend behind his back."

Joe stood and seemed to be fighting the urge to charge at Seamus. "I'm not doing that!"

"Don't you want your mum to be happy?"

"Of course I do! But what happens a few years down the road when you decide being with an older woman isn't working for you anymore? Or you want kids of your own? What happens then?"

"What happens a few years down the road when you decide being with Janey isn't as great as you thought it would be?"

"That'll never happen! I love her with everything I am. What does that have to do with what we're talking about?"

Seamus only smiled and watched as the realization settled into Joe's expression and his demeanor.

"You love her that much?" Joe asked in a whisper.

"I love her that much."

They stood for a long time, hands on hips, neither of them blinking, until Joe finally looked away, eyes cast downward. "I don't know how I'm supposed to feel about this."

Seamus was trying to think of what he should say to that when Carolina rushed into the office.

"Oh thank God," she said, breathing as if she'd been running. "You didn't hit him." This was directed at Joe, who scowled at his mother.

"No, I didn't hit him." Glancing at Seamus, he added, "But I wanted to."

Janey waddled in, red-faced and panting. "Did he hit him?"

"Not you, too," Joe said.

"Sorry." Janey went to her husband and put her arm around him. "You do have a bit of a history."

"One broken nose doesn't make for a *history*, and PS, that guy deserved it."

"And I don't?" Seamus edged closer to Carolina. No time like the present for her son to get used to seeing them together. Since Joe hadn't, in fact, murdered him, Seamus was filled with irrational hope.

"I never said that," Joe said. "I *chose* not to hit you."

"And I thank you for that," Seamus said gravely, which earned him yet another scowl from Joe.

When Seamus tried to take Caro's hand, she shook him off.

Baby steps.

Carolina focused on her son. "Are you going to be able to live with this?"

"You haven't given me much choice."

"Actually," Seamus said, "that's not true. You know as well as I do that if you disapprove or express your disappointment or in any way seem put out by it, she'll throw me over like yesterday's news. So it does matter. If you're going to do any of those things, I, for one, would appreciate you doing them now before this goes any further."

Carolina started to say something in protest, but the challenging look Seamus tossed her way had her closing her mouth.

Everyone looked to Joe, waiting breathlessly to see what he would say or do.

After a long moment, Joe said, "I'm not going to do any of those things."

"Are you sure?" Seamus asked. "You don't get to change your mind in a week or a month or a year."

"Neither do you," Joe said pointedly.

Seamus, who understood what Joe was saying, nodded in agreement. "Neither do I."

"It might take me a while to get my head around it, but I won't stand in the way." To his mother, he said, "I'd never want to be the cause of your unhappiness. I hate that you thought I would."

Tears filled Carolina's eyes as she went to her son and hugged him. "Thank you."

Out of the corner of his eye, Seamus caught Janey wiping away a tear. "Caro?"

She pulled back from her son and turned to Seamus. "Come here."

The glance she directed at her son was filled with trepidation.

Joe nodded and squeezed her shoulder.

Carolina took a couple of halting steps toward Seamus.

He held out his arms to her. "Come to me."

She seemed hesitant to get close to him with her son and daughter-in-law watching, but Seamus knew it was vital that she take this first most important step in front of them.

"It's okay, love," he whispered. "Everything's going to be okay now."

A sob escaped her as she moved into his embrace and buried her face in his shirt.

As his heart pounded erratically, Seamus closed his eyes, said a silent prayer of thanks to the Lord above and closed his arms around her. "Shhh, don't cry, my love," he said, running a hand over her back. "Please don't cry."

He opened his eyes to find Janey leading her husband from the room. Joe met his gaze, and the message was clear—*hurt her, and you'll answer to me*. Seamus gave a small nod to show he understood and then refocused his attention on Carolina. "There, love, it's all good. Joe knows about us, and nothing bad happened."

She rested her hands on his hips, her fingertips pressing into his back as her sobs became hiccups. "Nothing bad happened."

Seamus smiled and tightened his hold on her. "Do you know what that means?"

She shook her head.

"It means," he said, tipping her face up so he could see her eyes, "there's nothing standing between you, me and this." He kissed her softly when he would've preferred to kiss her much more intently. But now they had a lovely future stretching before them, and he could afford to be patient.

Carolina, however, wasn't in the mood to be patient and surprised him with her passionate response. Her fingers clutched his hair—almost painfully—as her tongue tangled with his.

Seamus was on the verge of doing the unthinkable at work when he came to his senses and broke the kiss. "Not here."

"Where, then?"

Startled by the urgency he heard in her voice, he took her hand. "Come with me."

"Don't you have to work?"

"I've got three hours until my next run." All thoughts of the paperwork he'd plan to do had been abandoned.

"That won't be enough time."

"We've got all the time in the world, love. All the time in the world."

WHEN KARA'S alarm went off at six, Dan wanted to weep. He'd only been asleep a short time and was sincerely sorry he'd ever agreed to sail this morning. But Mac and the others were counting on him, so he wouldn't renege. However, he wanted to. All he wanted was more of what he'd had during the night—the best sex of his life.

He glanced over at Kara, asleep next to him with her hair spread out on the pillow and her lips pursed in her sleep. She was so damned gorgeous, and he felt like the luckiest bastard on the face of the earth to have spent the night with her.

Where they'd go from here was the big question. Would this be one magical night, or was it the start of something more? He wanted very badly to know the answer to that question but wouldn't wake her to ask. Instead, he slid out of bed and got busy gathering his clothes, which were flung about the room.

She hadn't changed her mind about inviting him home. If anything, she'd been even more enthusiastic when they got to her place. The missing buttons on his dress shirt were an indication of just how enthusiastic she'd been. To Dan, the gaps in his shirt were like hard-won trophies. Now he had to ensure that he didn't mess up what had been a promising start.

"Are you leaving?"

Dan turned, surprised that she was awake. "I've got to be at the dock in an hour." He sat on the edge of the bed and kissed her exposed shoulder.

She shrank away from him.

"What?"

"Nothing."

"You promised you wouldn't hate me."

"I don't."

"But?"

"Nothing," she said again.

"Why do you keep saying that?" he asked as anxiety worked its way down his backbone.

"Because that's what I want—nothing. Last night was fun. I enjoyed it very much. But it doesn't mean we're a *thing* now."

"So you were just using me to get laid?"

"I didn't say that!"

"How would you put it, then?" Needing to channel the hurt and anger, Dan stood and grabbed his belt off the floor, jamming it through the loops with unsteady hands.

"I don't want to be involved with anyone," Kara said, looking remote and closed off, the way she had for weeks, before he finally got through to her. "I told you that from the beginning."

"I knew we shouldn't have had sex. I suspected I'd regret it when it was happening, and now I know it for sure."

"I'm sorry you regret it."

"The only thing I regret is that we're back to square one." He snapped his watch on his arm and grabbed his coat off the chair in the corner of her bedroom. "And I regret that I don't have time now to discuss it further because I have somewhere to be."

"That's fine. There's nothing left to discuss."

He stared at her, incredulous. "I'm disappointed in you, Kara. I thought you had more guts than that. I guess I was wrong." He made the mistake of taking one last look at her face, which was how he discovered she was stunned and hurt. Though he regretted hurting her, he didn't regret saying it, because she'd hurt him, too.

In the car, he pounded on the steering wheel until his hand was sore. "Goddamn it!"

CHAPTER 22

"You never went back to work," Carolina said when she opened her eyes from the deepest sleep in recent memory to find Seamus watching her.

"You noticed that, huh?"

"Uh-huh." In the span of a few seconds, images from their interlude flashed through her mind, indelibly imprinted upon her memory —Seamus all but dragging her across the street to the small room on the third floor of the Beachcomber, the thud of the door as it closed behind them, the abandon with which they'd torn at each other's clothes, coming together frantically at first and then slowly and reverently a second and third time.

His hand landed on her shoulder and moved slowly down her arm to link their fingers. "I called the office to tell them I had a personal situation, and they brought in one of our backup captains to cover for me for the rest of the day."

She felt her face heat as she continued to relive the erotic hours they'd spent together. And now they had a whole day together. For that matter, they had the rest of their lives.

"What're you thinking, love?"

"I can't believe this has happened. That we get to be together. I never thought..."

"I always hoped, but I didn't think it'd happen, either. And now that it has..." He dipped his head to kiss her. "I may not let you out of my sight for at least a year, if not longer."

"Stop," she said with a hand to his chest. "Don't be ridiculous."

"If you marry me, I won't have to worry about you slipping through my fingers or meeting someone you like better while I'm over on the mainland."

Her eyes widened as his words registered. "*Marry* you? I just agreed to *date* you!"

He cupped her breast and squeezed her nipple, making her want him all over again, as if she hadn't already had him three times. "Is that what we're doing here, love? *Dating?*"

"You know what I mean."

"Aye, I know what you mean, and I also know you're not a hundred percent sold on the idea."

"What does that mean? I'm here, aren't I?"

"You're here this way," he said, squeezing her breast for emphasis, before releasing her to tap a finger against her forehead, "but up here, you're still worried what everyone will think of Carolina Cantrell taking up with a much younger man."

Perturbed by his analysis, she said, "You don't know that."

"Am I wrong?"

Cornered and uncertain of what she should say, Carolina shifted her focus to the wall over his shoulder.

"We could always go away from here to a place where no one knows either of us," he said.

"This is my home. I don't want to be anywhere else."

"Are you prepared to deal with the people who won't understand this? Who won't understand us?"

"Yes," she said haltingly. "Of course I am."

"If we got married, everyone would know we're serious."

"That's no reason to get married."

"The fact that we love each other is a pretty good reason, too."

Carolina thought about that.

"You do love me, don't you?" he asked.

Her gaze shot up to meet his, looking down at her with a wary, expectant expression on his handsome face. "You know I do."

"Do I? You've never said it."

"I... I meant to."

His face lifted into an adorable half smile. "I'm listening."

"Are you always this pushy?"

"Only when it really, *really* matters."

Listening to him talk was almost as sexy as making love with him. "I love you, Seamus O'Grady, giant pain in my ass."

Laughing, he pushed his imposing penis against her hip. "I'd happily be a giant pain in your ass, if you'd like."

Shocked to the core by the implication, she stared at him.

"I want to do everything with you." He moved over her and brushed the hair back from her face as he stared down at her. "*Everything*. Most of all, I want to marry you and have a life with you."

As if she'd always loved him, Carolina's legs parted to admit him. She was sore and achy and still tired, but she'd wanted him so badly for so long, she couldn't imagine denying him.

"Ah, Christ," he muttered as he sank into her. "There's nothing in the whole world better than this."

Carolina could hardly disagree as he filled her and stirred her and surrounded her with his love.

"Marry me," he whispered in her ear as he thrust into her. "Marry me, marry me, marry me."

She kept her face buried in the curve of his shoulder. "I can hardly think when you're doing that."

"What's there to think about?" Without losing their connection, he turned them so she was on top looking down at him, unable to hide from him any longer. His green eyes were sharp and intense and filled with love and longing and so many other things she couldn't begin to process it all. "I love you, Carolina. I'll always love you."

"I love you, too."

His fingers dug into her hips to keep her from moving. "But?"

"I need to think about it."

The disappointment registered in his expression for an instant before he rallied and surged into her, stealing the breath from her lungs. "You do all the thinking you need to do. In the meantime, I'll keep you entertained until you decide."

With him moving inside her, it was hard to think about anything other than how badly she wanted to feel this way every day for the rest of her life.

THIS, Tiffany decided as she dragged herself to the store, must be what it was like to get hit by a truck. The worst of the flu symptoms were gone, but her body ached from being sick and from having sex with Blaine for half the night. What did it say about her that even when stricken with the flu, she couldn't keep her hands off that man?

She hung out the Open flag and pulled out a mannequin dressed in a see-through teddy with matching black panties to the sidewalk. As she went about her opening routine, her mind wandered to Blaine and the evening they'd spent together. When she thought about the things they'd done... Even the owner of a shop like hers could still be embarrassed, remembering being face down on top of him with her bottom and other important parts right in his face. And the stuff *he'd* done!

A flash of heat tingled between her legs, making her shudder from the impact. She couldn't wait to do it all again.

Her cell phone rang, and she took the call from Dan. "Please tell me you have good news."

"I have good news."

The din of voices in the background made it hard to hear him. "What's all that racket?"

"Oh, sorry, I'm sailing today with a bunch of *very loud* guys who've been razzing me about working when I'm supposed to be helping them. I wanted to let you know I called your landlord this morning, and he's willing to accept a new check, provided this doesn't happen again."

"It won't," Tiffany said. "I promise."

"That's what I told him."

"I can't thank you enough for this."

"The landlord told me it was Jim's idea to begin eviction proceedings."

Nothing he did should've shocked her anymore, and yet...

"Tiffany?"

"I'm here."

"I took it upon myself to give Jim a call to let him know how much I'm enjoying life on Gansett and how I'm thinking about permanently relocating, since there seems to be a pressing need for a second attorney on the island."

Tiffany snorted with laughter. "Oh, that's fabulous! He must've been totally freaked out."

"To say the least," Dan said with a chuckle. "I told him how after seeing him in action a few times, how happy I'd be to run him right off the island by hanging out my own shingle."

Tiffany laughed again. "There's nothing you could've said that would frighten him more than threatening his monopoly on the island's legal work."

"That's what I figured. I gotta say, it was fun to give him a taste of his own medicine. I told him to leave you alone or we'd file defamation charges, which would really do wonders for his practice. I don't think you'll be hearing from him again, except where it concerns Ashleigh."

"Thank you so much."

"It was completely my pleasure."

"Send me a bill for your time."

"No way. I haven't had that much fun in years. It's on the house."

"Well, if you're ever in need of a gift for a special lady, come by the store, and I'll hook you up."

"You got a deal. Talk to you soon."

"You really didn't have to do this," Maddie said to her father-in-law as he waited with her for her father to arrive. She'd invited Bobby to come to her home and had a pitcher of lemonade waiting on the table on the deck so he wouldn't have to come inside. Mac was off sailing for the day, Thomas had felt well enough to return to camp, and Hailey was down for her morning nap.

"I promised my son I'd take care of you," Big Mac said, "and I never break a promise."

"You're a good dad—to all of us."

He seemed taken aback by the unexpected compliment. "That's awfully sweet of you, honey."

"It's true. I had no idea how fathers were supposed to behave until I met Mac and got to know you. After seeing the way you are with your kids, I know why Mac is so amazing with ours."

"You couldn't pay me a finer compliment."

Maddie looked out over the meadow where she and Mac had been married almost two years ago. The encroaching fog made it impossible to see the normally spectacular view of the water. "It's getting kind of foggy out there. Will they be okay?"

"Of course they will. They're my kids."

Maddie stared into the fog for a long moment. "It's embarrassing, you know?"

"What is?"

"This whole thing. I'm a full-grown adult, but the idea of seeing my dad again reduces me to a quivering five-year-old."

"Which is exactly why Mac didn't want you to see him alone."

"I'm glad you're the one he recruited to babysit me."

Big Mac smiled. "I volunteered. I've got a few things I wouldn't mind saying to Bobby Chester if the opportunity should arise."

Maddie laughed at the calculating expression on his face, but her laughter faded at the sound of tires crunching over the gravel driveway. "Here he comes."

"Don't let him intimidate you, sweetheart. You're strong and brave and resilient—and you're all of those things no thanks to him. Don't you forget that."

She squeezed his hand, fortified by his support. "I won't." Despite his assurances, her stomach was a mess as she waited for her father to come up the stairs to the deck. And then there he was—tall, stocky, gray-haired, slightly bloated. Nothing at all like the pictures of the handsome, smiling young man her mother had kept around the house long after he left them.

"Nice place you have here," Bobby said, casting a tentative glance at Big Mac, who remained seated and stone-faced.

"Thank you. We're happy with it. I believe you know my father-in-law."

Bobby nodded. "Mac. Good to see you again."

Big Mac replied with a steely stare that was so far out of character for him that Maddie nearly laughed.

Realizing he wouldn't get anywhere with Big Mac, Bobby returned his attention to Maddie. "I, um, thank you for seeing me. I know you didn't want to."

Since Maddie couldn't deny that, she withheld comment. "Would you like something to drink?"

"That'd be nice."

Maddie hated the slight tremble in her hands as she poured the three glasses. "Have a seat."

The three of them sat at the table in uneasy and awkward silence for a long time. Maddie knew she could make this easier on her father, but why should she? This was his show, so she waited. And waited.

"Are your children here?"

"One of them. She's sleeping."

"Oh. I would've liked to have met them."

Maddie would've like to have told him that he lost the right to know his grandchildren the day he left his family, but that wouldn't do much to accomplish her goal of getting this meeting over with as quickly as possible.

"I understand you don't like me very much."

"I don't know you. You're no one to me."

Bobby winced. "Ouch."

"What did you expect me to say? Or I should ask, how did you expect me to feel?"

"I suppose I hoped you'd be a little more forgiving. I don't deny I made some rather significant mistakes—"

"Is that how you see it? A *mistake*? You left your family and never looked back. In this day and age, you could be put in jail for abandoning your children with no means of support."

"You remind me of your mother," he said disdainfully.

"Be careful. If you say one word to disparage my mother, this meeting is over."

"I only wanted the opportunity to talk to you, to tell you I'm sorry for what I did, that I regret it. I wish I could have my life to do over again. I would've done things differently."

"That's good to know."

"Do you have anything you want to ask me?"

"I'd like to know why you left."

Bobby looked away from her. "I wish I could give you an explanation that you'd find satisfying, but the truth of the matter is I never should've gotten married. I wasn't cut out for family life, even though I loved your mom and you girls."

Maddie raised an eyebrow in disbelief.

"I don't blame you for not believing me, but it's true. I did love you —very much. I always have. I just couldn't live on this island, and your mother didn't want to live anywhere else."

"Don't you dare blame her."

"I'm not blaming her. The blame is all mine. Some men aren't cut out to be family men. I was one of them."

"Too bad you didn't realize that before you brought two kids into the world," Big Mac said, breaking his silence.

"I was hoping I'd feel differently once I had kids."

"I think I've heard enough." Maddie stood to let her father know she was done. "I've given you what you wanted. Now please give my mother what she deserves—the chance to finally be happy."

"Is that the only reason you saw me? So I'd give your mother the divorce?"

"Yes."

He didn't seem pleased to hear that but nodded and got up to leave. "Thank you for seeing me. I'm sorry I let you down."

"You let yourself down, too, Chester," Big Mac said. "You'll never know the two amazing women you fathered or their beautiful children. You missed the only thing that really matters in this life by being selfish. I feel sorry for you."

"Stuff your pity. I don't want it. I'm sure you consider yourself father of the year—"

"I wouldn't go that far," Big Mac said, "but I've been there for my kids every day of their lives, and I'm proud to say I've never missed anything important with any of them—or the extra ones I picked up along the way."

"It's time for you to go now," Maddie said to her father, gesturing to the stairs.

Bobby started to say something else but thought better of it and headed down the stairs. They heard him drive off a minute later.

"You all right?" Big Mac asked.

"Surprisingly, yes. I didn't expect to gain closure from seeing him again, but that's what I got."

"Let's hope he holds up his end of the bargain," Big Mac said as he stood to hug her. "Your mom and Ned have waited long enough."

"I agree." Maddie returned his embrace. "Thank you so much for being here and for what you said about Tiffany and me."

"I only spoke the truth." He kissed her on the forehead and released her. "There's nothing I wouldn't do for you after you've made my boy so happy."

Maddie smiled. "He'll be very happy to hear I got through that unscathed."

"Yes, he will. I'd better get back to the marina to give Luke a hand."

"Thanks again for coming."

"Any time."

CHAPTER 23

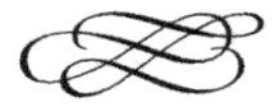

Blaine picked up Sarah at the hotel and drove her to Daisy's place. He could tell she was nervous by the way her hands twisted repeatedly in her lap.

"Wow, look at the fog!" Sarah said as they drove past the ferry landing. The entire harbor was shrouded in a thick, soupy cloud that chilled the air.

"I heard they called off the morning races shortly after they began," Blaine said. "An auspicious start to Race Week."

Sarah was quiet for a long time before she said, "Are you sure it's a good idea for me to talk to her?"

"I'm not sure of anything. But I can't help but think it would do her some good to hear how many times you took back your husband before you realized he was never going to change. Might save her some time and heartache, not to mention it could save her life."

"When you put it like that, it seems like a worthwhile effort."

"That was my thinking."

"Why is it that you don't seem yourself this morning?"

He looked over at her, surprised by the question. "I don't?"

She shook her head. "Not at all. I could tell from the minute you came into the hotel that something was off. Call it mother's intuition."

Blaine rubbed a hand over the stubble on his jaw and imagined what the mayor would say about the scruffy beard that matched his scruffy hair.

"Girl trouble?"

He thought of Tiffany and the erotically charged night they'd spent together and felt guilty—for about the hundredth time—for going at her like a madman when she'd been so sick.

"Has to be girl trouble," Sarah said. "I see all the signs. Hangdog expression, sleep-deprived eyes..."

"It's not trouble, per se," Blaine said, giving in to her.

"Then what?"

"My mom doesn't approve, for one thing."

"Because of the store."

Blaine knew he shouldn't be surprised that people in town knew he and Tiffany were seeing each other, but it was surprising to hear it was common knowledge. "Partially. She's worried I'll end up endangering my job by helping Tiffany."

"And would you? Endanger your job to help her out?"

"Probably."

"You must care about her an awful lot."

"I do."

"Then do what you have to do to protect her."

"Think maybe you could have a chat with my mom?"

Sarah laughed. "You're on your own with her, pal."

"Jeez... Thanks a lot."

"She must have a good a reason for being worried about you."

"I've given her ample reason over the years."

"Then don't judge her too harshly for not wanting to see you hurt."

"I'll try not to."

"Motherhood is the best and worst job in the world. No matter how great a job you might do, you always feel like there's more you could've and should've done. That's certainly true for me. Sometimes we overcompensate for the past by hovering a little too closely over our adult children."

"She doesn't have anything to compensate for. She was a great mom."

"Yet still you suffered and stumbled. Any mother worth her salt would do what she could to keep that from happening again."

What Sarah said made a lot of sense. "And you think you have no wisdom to impart to Daisy." He parked in front of Daisy's house and cut the engine. "Thank you for doing this."

"I only hope it helps."

"It can't hurt, that's for sure." He went around the truck and held the door for her while she got out.

"Your mother might be giving you fits, but she raised you right."

"I'll let her know you said so," Blaine said, amused by her.

Daisy met them at the door and let them in. "Hi, Blaine."

"Daisy, this is my friend, Sarah. I wanted you to meet her."

Daisy's hand went up to the fading bruises on her face. "I'm not really prepared for guests."

Sarah stepped forward and put an arm around Daisy, leading her to a sofa. "Don't you worry about that, honey. I've been right where you are, and I know all about bruises you did nothing to deserve."

"You do?"

"I sure do. Let me tell you all about the elegant, charming, young air force officer who turned out to be a monster."

Watching Daisy hang on Sarah's every word, Blaine felt comfortable enough to take a phone call from Linc Mercier, the coast guard captain who ran the island's search and rescue outpost. Stepping onto the front porch, he said, "What's up, Linc?"

"Hey, Blaine. I'm glad I caught you. We've just had a report that one of the boats heading out for Race Week collided with a freighter in the fog, with at least one confirmed fatality. Word is there were some islanders on the boat. I thought you might be able to figure out how many people were on the boat and who they were."

"We'll do our best. What was the name of the boat?"

"*Shadow Dancer*. Navy blue hull, about thirty-eight feet. Don't have the make or model. We've got three of our boats heading to the scene now. I should have more info soon."

"Got it," Blaine said. "I'll get back to you." He went inside to find Sarah hugging Daisy. "I have to go," he said. "Can you get home?"

Sarah nodded and used her free hand to gesture for him to go. "I'll call Owen."

"Thanks, Sarah. Bye, Daisy."

Blaine jumped in the truck and headed for North Harbor, stopping first at McCarthy's. Mac and his dad knew everything that went on in the harbor and would be the best possible resources. He made a rare exception to his no-lights-unless-absolutely-necessary rule and skidded to a stop at McCarthy's a few minutes later. The fog was so thick, he couldn't see five feet in front of him. Taking off at a run, he found Mr. McCarthy on the far end of the main pier, bullshitting with a bunch of guys.

Business as usual, even in the fog.

"Blaine?" he asked. "What's got you in such an all-fired rush?"

"Do you know of a boat named *Shadow Dancer* that was heading out to the races?"

Big Mac went entirely still—so still that Blaine got a very bad feeling. "What about it?"

Blaine looked the older man in the eye when he said, "There's been an accident. The boat collided with a freighter—" For the rest of his life, Blaine would never forget the sound that came from Mr. McCarthy. It was a cross between a roar and a scream, and it chilled Blaine all the way to his bones.

"My boys," Big Mac said haltingly as several of his friends surrounded him. "My boys are on that boat."

Blaine forced himself past his own shock and dismay to ask, "Which ones?"

"All three of 'em."

Since Adam was in New York, that meant Mac, Grant and Evan. *Jesus.* Blaine swallowed his own panic to ask, "Was there anyone else?"

"The skipper... I can't recall..."

"Steve Jacobson," Luke Harris said, looking stricken by the news.

"And Torrington." Big Mac ran a trembling hand through his wiry gray hair. "Dan Torrington, Grant's friend." His eyes filled with tears that nearly undid Blaine. Big Mac McCarthy had been his Boy Scout leader, and there were few men Blaine respected more. "Tell me what you know."

Blaine shook his head.

"Tell me."

"I—"

Big Mac placed one of his huge hands on Blaine's shoulder. "Tell me, son. Please tell me what you know."

"There's one confirmed fatality."

"Oh God," one of the other men uttered.

Big Mac's face drained of all remaining color and animation.

Luke put an arm around Big Mac. "Let's go sit down and figure out what we can do to help find them."

"Yes," Big Mac said, snapping out of his stupor. "We have to help. We have to go out there and find them."

"The fog is too thick," Luke said. "You can't endanger yourself—"

"I don't care about myself! I need to find my boys!"

"The coast guard is searching with high-tech equipment," Blaine said. "They'll find them."

"I *need* to be out there," Big Mac said to Luke, who held him back.

Blaine took his other arm and helped Luke escort the older man up the dock to the restaurant.

"My wife," Big Mac said. "She went into town to get her hair done and something…else."

"Can we call her?" Luke asked.

Stephanie, who was working behind the counter, looked up when they came in.

"We can't do that to her over the phone," Big Mac said.

Stephanie took one look at Big Mac's ashen face and came around the counter to him. "What?" she asked. "What's wrong?"

Luke settled Big Mac in a chair and turned to Stephanie. "There's been an accident. The boat Grant and the others were on was hit by a freighter."

"*Nooooooooo.*"

Her primal scream brought everyone in the room to tears.

"We don't know anything yet." Luke refrained from sharing the one thing they did know. He gave her a tight hug. "You have to stay strong until we know more."

"Grant," she said with a whimper. "Please, no. Please."

"Sit." Luke held a chair for her. "I'll get you something to drink."

Big Mac held out his arms to Stephanie, and she launched into his embrace.

"This can't be happening," she said between sobs.

Big Mac held on tight to her while she cried her heart out.

"What's going on?" another woman asked.

Blaine recognized her as the one who was running the launch service. Kara…that was her name.

In a halting voice, Stephanie filled her in.

"Oh my God," Kara said, sinking into a chair. "I was just with Dan. I saw him this morning. He was fine. He has to be fine, right?"

Stephanie reached out for Kara's hand and squeezed.

"I've got to call Linc back with the names, and then I'll go find Mrs. McCarthy in town," Blaine said to Luke.

"I'll be here with them," Luke said.

"No matter what, don't let him go out on the water," Blaine said, glancing at Mr. McCarthy, who stared blankly over Stephanie's shoulder.

"I won't."

"Blaine."

The single word from Stephanie stopped him. "Someone needs to tell Grace and Maddie."

"I'll take care of it."

"Thank you."

With a heavy heart, he walked out of the restaurant and headed for town.

TIFFANY WAS STILL CELEBRATING the excellent news from Dan when the bells on the door jingled, and Laura McCarthy came in, looking pale and wan.

"Laura! I heard the flu hit you, too."

"It was awful, but I feel almost fine today. Almost, but not quite."

"Me, too. I didn't think I'd see you out and about today with the hotel opening tomorrow."

"It's Owen's mom's birthday, so I need to get her something while she's out with Blaine."

At the mention of his name, Tiffany was instantly curious. "Where did she go with Blaine?"

"Did you hear about what happened to Daisy?"

"Yes," Tiffany said, shaking her head. "It's so awful. Daisy is such a sweet girl."

"Blaine thought Sarah might be able to help her, so he asked her to talk to Daisy."

"Oh." Tiffany had heard about Sarah's dramatic exit from her violent marriage last fall. "What a great idea."

"He's always thinking, that one." Laura held up a slinky nightgown and turned toward the mirror.

"I thought you were shopping for Sarah," Tiffany teased.

"Well, I do have a wedding and honeymoon to prepare for."

"You've come to the right place for that." As she said the words, it occurred to her that it might be fun—and good for business—to host a lingerie shower for Laura. She made a note to discuss it with Maddie, who was one of Laura's bridesmaids.

"I have *no* idea what to get Sarah." Laura replaced the nightgown on the rack. "You have gorgeous things, but she might not be ready for sexy yet. She only just started seeing Charlie."

"Stephanie's stepfather?"

"Yep. He asked her to go to the opening of the restaurant with him, and I heard they snuck off afterward without a word to anyone."

"Good for them. Can you think of two people who deserve to be happy more than they do?"

"Not really. Well, except for my poor brother. He deserves to be happy after what his ex-wife put him through." Laura turned a calculating eye Tiffany's way. "You just got divorced, too, right?"

"Um, yeah," Tiffany said warily, sensing where this might be going.

"Are you seeing anyone?"

She still wasn't sure how she was supposed to answer that question. Was she *seeing* Blaine? Mostly she was having incredible sex with him. "Sort of."

Laura leaned in closer. "Do tell."

"Ah, well, um... Blaine."

Laura laughed and clapped her hands. "Oh, I love it! I can totally see you two together!"

"Is that right?"

"Definitely. He's some kind of good looking."

"You'd better not let your fiancé hear you talking like that."

"Owen has no doubt that I am hopelessly in love with him, but that doesn't mean I fail to notice a guy like Blaine." She leaned in even closer, as if someone might hear them. "He's got that whole strong, silent thing going on, doesn't he?"

"He's a little *too* silent sometimes."

"What do you mean?"

"His idea of talking is 'spread your legs.'"

Laura dissolved into laughter. "What's wrong with that?"

"Nothing. I guess."

"It makes it difficult to get to know him."

"Right."

"Well, if it's any consolation, a man who would think to pair up two abused women because they might be able to help each other clearly has a heart of gold."

"That's true." Tiffany thought of the furniture and the bath and the night he'd comforted her after the confrontation with Jim. It occurred to her that with Blaine it was more about *actions* than words, and his actions said a lot about how much he cared for her.

"*What* do I get Sarah?" Laura asked, looking around the store with dismay.

"How about some scented bubble bath and candles?"

"Now that's an idea. She works far too hard and needs to relax more."

"Let me show you what I have."

As Laura was leaving with her purchases, Francine came in, took a hesitant look around and then sought out Tiffany. "It looks wonderful, honey!"

Delighted her mother had finally come to see the store, Tiffany said, "Thank you." She stepped forward to welcome her with a hug. "It's nice to see you here."

"I've been meaning to come in for days now. I don't know where the time goes."

"It's okay. You've been helping out with Ashleigh."

Francine laid a hand on Tiffany's forehead. "Fever's gone. Are you feeling better? You look better. Still a bit pale but better."

"I feel a lot better—even better since Dan told off Jim and made the eviction thing go away."

"Oh, thank heavens! That's excellent news. No one deserves a comeuppance more than Jim Sturgil."

"No kidding. Anyway, thanks for taking Ashleigh last night."

"We had so much fun with her. She was raring to get back to camp this morning, so we dropped her off on our way into town."

"I don't know what I'd do without you—and Ned."

"We're happy to help you. We love spending time with Ashleigh. She's such a cute little girl and so polite."

"That's good to hear."

"Are you going to show me around the store?"

"Do I have to?"

Francine laughed and gestured for Tiffany to lead the way. Tiffany had thought having Linda McCarthy in the store was nerve racking. That was nothing compared to leading her mother through the beads into the back room.

"Are those..." Francine leaned in for a closer look. "*Oh*. So *that's* what has everyone in town all abuzz—no pun intended."

Hearing that, Tiffany's recently ravaged stomach started to hurt again. "What've you heard?"

"They were talking in the diner this morning about the town council meeting. Apparently, Royal Atkinson, one of the councilmen, is determined to shut you down."

Tiffany was filled with nerves at that news. She'd thought Verna Upton had taken care of that for her. "I've heard that, but I have all the proper permits. The town clerk signed off on them."

"Then you should be fine. Don't let the haters get you down. My daughters aren't quitters."

"We learned that from you," Tiffany said as she led her mother back to the store's main room.

"Thank you, honey."

Despite her new worries, Tiffany reached across the counter for her mother's hand. "It's so good to see you happy again, Mom."

"I could say the same for you. That handsome policeman seems awfully taken with you."

"He's very…nice." When she thought of him, as she did so many times each day, her heart fluttered.

"He seems like a lovely young man."

"He is." Tiffany flipped a pen back and forth between her fingers.

"What's the matter? Don't you feel the same way he does?"

"I do, but… I just got divorced, and after everything with Jim—"

"Jim is a self-centered asshole. I've thought so since the first time you brought him home back in high school."

Tiffany's mouth hung open in shock. "Why didn't you ever say so?"

"Would you have wanted to hear it?"

"Probably not."

"You had stars in your eyes for that boy from the very beginning, but I never thought he was good enough for you."

"Good enough for *me*?"

"You heard me right. Just because he went and got himself a fancy law degree—that you paid for, I might add—doesn't make him smarter than you. It only makes him better educated, and don't you forget that. If you let him ruin this second chance for you, then he *wins*, Tiffany. Do *not* let him win."

Fascinated by this new insightful side of her mother, Tiffany pondered what she'd said. "You've changed."

"Lord, I hope so," Francine said with a laugh. "I had three long months in jail to think about my life and the changes I wanted to make when I came home."

Seeing her mother locked up for passing bad checks on the island had been a low point in her life—and her sister's.

"And then I saw Ned..." Francine's entire demeanor softened when she spoke of her fiancé.

"I love how you found each other again all these years later."

"He's the best thing to happen to me in a very long time. Don't be a fool with Blaine, Tiffany. He's a good man, the kind of man you and Ashleigh deserve. Don't be so jaded by what happened with Jim that you let fear drive you away from him. Do you hear me?"

"Yes, ma'am," she said reflexively, the way she had as a child.

The bells on the door jingled, and Tiffany looked up to make eye contact with her father as he came into the store. "Um, Mom..."

Francine turned and recoiled at the sight of her ex-husband. "What're you doing here?"

Bobby Chester scowled. "I came to see my daughter, not that it's any of your business."

"It's absolutely my business. I don't know what you're hoping to prove by forcing these girls to see you—"

"I'm not hoping to prove anything. I only want to know them. That's it."

"You had ample time to know them when they were children." Francine stepped forward and smacked Bobby right across the face.

Before Tiffany could say a word, Bobby had her by the arm to keep her from hitting him again.

The bells jingled again as Ned walked in. "Ready to go, doll? I've got just enough time to run ya home before the next boat." He stopped short when he saw Bobby gripping her arm. "Ya got one second to let her go, or I'll drop ya on yer fat ass."

Tiffany wasn't sure what was more shocking, that her mother had actually hit her father or that Ned had threatened him.

Bobby released her and stepped back. "She hit me."

"Good for her," Ned said. "Someone shoulda smacked ya years ago, leaving yer wife and kids the way ya did. Now listen here. By now ya've seen Maddie, over the express wishes of all of us who love her. So yer gonna end this foolishness and give yer wife a divorce. Ya got me?"

"Who're you to tell me what I'm gonna do?"

"I'm the man who loves Francine and her girls as if they's my own, and I've had just about enough of yer happy horseshit."

Listening to Ned tell off her father, Tiffany realized two very important things: She loved the man who loved her mother, and she loved Blaine—with her whole heart. As soon as she got the chance, she was going to tell him so. Her mother was right—if she let fear drive her away from Blaine, Jim would win. She couldn't let that happen.

Bobby grunted at all of them and then turned and hightailed it out of the store.

Francine threw herself into Ned's arms. "You were positively magnificent! Wasn't he magnificent, Tiffany?"

"Positively," she said, smiling at her mom. She couldn't wait to tell her sister about this. "And in case you were wondering, Ned, we love you, too."

His eyes got all misty looking. "Aww, shucks, gal, now don't go doin' that."

Tiffany stepped around the counter to hug him. "I've never had a father," she said. "Better late than never."

"Cut that right out," he said, sniffling as he returned her embrace. He stiffened in her arms and pulled back from her. "What's in there?" he asked, pointing to the beads.

Francine took him by the hand. "Mind if I show him?" she asked Tiffany.

"Um, please… By all means. As long as I don't have to do it."

Laughing, the happy couple went into the back room as the bells jangled yet again to admit Patty.

"Hey, boss."

"Hi, there. What're you doing here? You're off today."

"I know, but I was thinking with the first day of Race Week fogged out, we might want to 'work the street,' as you would say."

Intrigued, Tiffany leaned forward on the counter. "What've you got in mind?"

A soft giggle came from the back room.

Patty glanced at the beaded curtain. "Who's in there?"

"My parents."

Patty's eyes got very wide. "Yikes. Kinda embarrassing, huh?"

"Just a tad." Tiffany prayed they didn't buy anything. "So, what about this idea of yours?"

"Oh, right." Patty clapped her hands and went to the racks, holding up two racy sailor outfits. "What do you think?"

"You're brilliant, but I can't afford to pay you for today."

"That's okay. I wasn't doing anything, and this'll be fun." She held out one of the outfits to Tiffany. "Shall we?"

Tiffany thought for a minute about how Blaine had promised to "punish" her if she strutted her sexy wares in public again, but with all the racers heading back into port due to the fog, she'd be crazy not to try to drum up some business. She also considered what Royal Atkinson and the rest of the town council, as well as her landlord and vindictive ex-husband, might have to say about it and decided she didn't care. She had the same right as everyone else to earn a living in this town, and their threats weren't going to stop her.

"I'm in."

BLAINE PULLED into the pharmacy parking lot and took a moment to gather himself before he walked into the store. He hated having to do this kind of thing. Thankfully, it didn't happen very often on the island—nowhere near as often as it had in his past job, when he'd often had to tell people their loved ones had been hurt or worse. That Mac and his brothers were his good friends made today even more difficult.

He found Grace in the back of the store at the pharmacy counter.

She smiled when she saw him coming. "Morning, Blaine. How are you?"

"I'm… Ah, could I speak with you for a minute? In private?"

She tuned right into his distress, and her smile faded as she came down the steps to meet him. "What's wrong?"

He took her aside, away from customers. "The boat Evan is on."

"What about it?" she asked, taking a step back from him as if to escape from whatever he was about to say.

"There was an accident. The boat was hit by a freighter... Grace. *Grace!*" He reached out and caught her as she fainted. "Someone call 911."

By the time the ambulance arrived a few minutes later, Grace was awake and crying hysterically.

"What happened?" a female voice asked Blaine as the paramedics talked to Grace. "I'm Jenny Wilks, a friend of Grace's."

Blaine told her about the accident and that Grace had fainted.

"I'll stay with her," Jenny said.

Relieved to have help, Blaine said, "Everyone is gathering at McCarthy's Marina."

"I'll get her there as soon as she's able."

"Thank you very much. Tell her to stay strong, and I'll see her later."

Blaine left the pharmacy, dreading that he had to go through this twice more. On the way to the hair salon, where he hoped to find Mrs. McCarthy, he tried to call Tiffany's cell phone and the store line to let her know her sister needed her. When she didn't answer either time, he wondered if she'd changed her mind about going to work and decided to run by the store after he located Mrs. McCarthy.

At the Curl Up and Dye salon on Ocean Road, he found Linda mid-dye, having an animated conversation with the owner, Chloe Dennis, who also cut his hair twice a year, if that.

"Hey, Blaine," Chloe said when he walked in. "Did Mayor Upton finally wear you down and talk you into a haircut?" She was tall and curvy, and her hair color changed with her moods. Today she was a redhead.

"Not yet," he said, glancing at Mrs. McCarthy.

"Everything all right?" Linda asked.

"I'm sorry to say it isn't."

"Not my husband," she said with a hand over her heart.

"No, it's the boys."

To her credit, Linda maintained her composure. "What about them?"

Blaine told her about the accident.

Chloe gasped and put a comforting hand on Linda's shoulder.

"I need to be with my husband." Linda started yanking foils out of her hair. When she was done, she stood and pulled off the black cape. To Blaine, she said, "Can you take me to him?"

"I will," Chloe said. "I'll take you wherever you need to go, Linda."

"He's at the marina," Blaine said. "I need to see Maddie, and then I'll be there."

"Thank you for letting me know," Linda said.

Concerned about her eerie calm, Blaine exchanged glances with Chloe.

"I'll take care of her," Chloe whispered.

"Thanks." Since the salon was only two blocks from Tiffany's store, Blaine left the truck and walked, staring out at the fog as he went, imagining his friends fighting for their lives in the midst of it. Were they injured or worse? Were they conscious? He doubted any of them had been wearing lifejackets, as they were all experienced yachtsmen. At times like this, Blaine wished he were more religious, because it would take an act of God to bring them all back safely. What if the McCarthys lost three of their sons? That thought didn't bear entertaining, so Blaine refused to go there.

He was half a block from Tiffany's store when he stopped abruptly on the sidewalk, shocked to see her prancing around outside the store with Patty. And what the hell were they wearing? Sailor suits? If you could call them "suits." Tiny scraps of fabric held together with a square knot placed strategically between two sets of full breasts. His cock stood up for a better look at Tiffany, but he willed it into submission by allowing in the anger. He'd told her he didn't want her doing that! A crowd of men had gathered to watch the two women as they teased and flirted and tried to entice customers into the store.

The squeal of car tires tore his attention off her as two cars narrowly avoided colliding in front of the store.

All the stress and emotion of the last hour bubbled to the surface, filling him with fury as he covered the remaining distance, laser focused on Tiffany. As if he was outside himself watching someone else, he grabbed her arm and marched her into the store, slamming the door in Patty's face as she scrambled after them.

"What do you think you're doing?" Tiffany asked, outraged as she pulled her arm free.

Blaine hadn't been this angry since he'd heard about what Eden had been up to while he worked nights. "What did I tell you about that?"

"In case you haven't noticed, I'm a grown woman who can do whatever she wants, and the last thing I need is another man in my life thinking he can call all the shots while I watch passively from the sidelines."

He took her hand and pulled her over to the window. "See those guys over there?" Pointing to the crowd of randy, leering young bucks who'd gathered on the sidewalk, Blaine said, "They're all picturing you naked right now."

"So what? They're never going to *see* me naked."

"You're goddamned right they're not."

"Neither will you if you don't get out of here right now."

He pulled his citation book from his back pocket. "Not until I cite you for public indecency."

"You've got to be kidding me."

Blaine knew he'd probably regret throwing his official weight around, but at the moment, he was too damned mad to care about repercussions. "Don't act like I didn't warn you. The mayor has been all over me about your 'advertising' strategies, and you've given me no choice."

"You absolutely have a choice."

He pulled two pages from his book. "A citation for you and a warning for Patty. Now put on some clothes and quit creating a nuisance."

Right before his eyes, Tiffany tore the citations into tiny pieces and sprinkled them like confetti at his feet.

"You're just begging me to arrest you."

She held out her hands. "Go for it."

"If I didn't have much bigger problems at the moment, I would, so count yourself lucky."

When she stuck her tongue out at him, it was all he could do not to take her up on the blatant invitation.

"You need to put on some clothes."

"I have clothes on." Tiffany put her hands on her barely covered hips and met his mulish stare with an even more mulish stare of her own.

"*That,*" he said, gesturing to the suggestive outfit, "does not count as clothes."

"Everything is covered."

"Not covered enough."

"I asked you to leave."

"Not until you change."

"I'm not changing, and you're leaving."

"Mac and his brothers are missing." The moment the words left his mouth, Blaine felt like a total ass for telling her that way. "That's what I was coming to tell you."

Her lips parted, and her eyes filled with tears. "What do you mean missing?"

Blaine told her about the crash with the freighter. "There's one confirmed fatality, but we're keeping that info close until we know more."

She bolted for the changing room. "Oh God, I've got to get to Maddie. Does she know?"

"Not unless one of the others called her."

Tiffany emerged from the dressing room wearing jeans and a formfitting T-shirt that Blaine didn't like much better than the skimpy sailor suit. The woman was too sexy for her own good—and his. When she reached for her purse and keys on the counter, her hands were shaking so badly she dropped the keys.

"I'll drive you," he said.

"I can drive myself."

"Tiffany, you're upset. Let me take you."

"Not if you're going to lecture me about how I choose to run my business."

"I won't say another word about it—for now. We'll talk about it later."

"Fine. I'll let you take me to my sister." She pulled her cell phone out of her purse and hit a number on speed dial. "Mom, I need you to get Ashleigh and Thomas from camp and meet me at Maddie's." Tiffany told her mother what'd happened as she followed Blaine from the store. On the sidewalk, she stopped to tell Patty she was in charge at the store for the rest of the day.

"You got it, boss."

On the way to Maddie's house, the unusual silence between them grated on Blaine's already frayed nerves. "Tell me what you're thinking?"

"I can't even imagine what'll become of my sister if he's dead."

"He can't be dead. He's too vital and too stubborn to die."

"Do you really think so?" she asked, turning to him.

Out of the corner of his eye, he saw tears rolling down her cheeks and pulled the car over to the side of the road. "Come here." He held out his arms to her and was relieved when she allowed him to comfort her. "Try not to think the worst until we know more."

"It doesn't sound good, though, does it?"

"No, it doesn't." He rubbed his hand over her back. "Try to get yourself together. She's going to need you."

"Yes, you're right." She wiped away the tears. "She's always there for me, so I need to be there for her."

"That's the way. Ready?"

"As ready as I'll ever be."

CHAPTER 24

Three hours later, a subdued group waited for news at McCarthy's Marina. The unusual quiet in the normally boisterous group told the story of how concerned everyone was.

Big Mac paced relentlessly from one end of the restaurant to the other while Luke kept a watchful eye on him, as if he was waiting for the older man to make a break for his boat to go aid in the search.

In between bouts of weeping, Stephanie cooked for everyone, saying it helped her to stay busy. Grace, Jenny, Laura and Sydney helped her while Joe stood behind Janey, massaging her shoulders and trying to keep her calm.

Seamus O'Grady and Carolina Cantrell came rushing into the restaurant.

"We just heard," Carolina said as she embraced Linda and then Big Mac. "What can we do?"

"All we're allowed to do is *wait*," Big Mac said, sounding angrier than he had all day. "I'm supposed to sit here and *wait* and do *nothing* while my boys are out there possibly fighting for their lives!"

Kara, who was sitting next to Linda, began to cry softly.

Linda slipped an arm around Kara and patted her shoulder.

"There has to be *something* we can do," Owen said. He'd done almost as much pacing as Big Mac.

"The fog is as bad as it was earlier," Seamus said. "Anyone heading out in it would only be adding to the coast guard's burden."

"He's right," Joe said. "As hard as it is, we have to wait. They're doing everything they can."

"They're going to be fine," Linda said, and all heads turned to her.

"How do you know that?" her husband asked.

"If they were gone, I'd know," she said with her hand resting on her heart. "I'd *know*." She went over to her husband and took his hand. "Come sit by me while I call Adam. We need to let him know what's going on."

Big Mac let his wife lead him to a table away from the others to make the call to their son in New York.

By the time another hour came and went, most of the townspeople had gathered at McCarthy's to wait for news.

Blaine took advantage of the opportunity for a moment alone with Royal Atkinson. The rotund town councilman gave Blaine an earful about how he could be doing more to keep the "damned kids" from drinking on the town beach.

"You're absolutely right, Royal. I'll put some more people on that problem as soon as I figure out what to do about the drunks pouring out of the bars and the moped accidents, not to mention the regular occurrences of domestic violence, the break-ins at the empty summer homes—"

"All right, boy," Royal grunted. "No need to get cheeky. I get your point."

"We've got a lot of issues on this island—important issues that require the cooperation of all the town's leaders."

"I don't disagree."

"Then why are you wasting the council's time trying to run off an honest, tax-paying businesswoman?"

"You talking about that smut shop in town?"

Blaine made an effort to keep his cool. "It's not a smut shop. Have you been there?"

"I have not," he said indignantly.

"Maybe you ought to at least stop by and see what it's about before you decide she's got no right to be there."

Royal thought about that for a moment. "I suppose I could do that."

"Think of it this way—if she's a big success, the town benefits from the tax revenue. Couldn't we use some additional revenue?"

"We're always in need of more money," he conceded.

"Don't be too quick to run her off. I think she's sitting on a gold mine over there."

Royal's eyes lit up at the words "gold mine." "Is that right?"

"Uh-huh."

"Well, maybe I've been a bit...hasty in my judgments."

"I'm glad to hear you say that. Shall I tell Ms. Sturgil she won't have to worry about facing the council on Monday?"

"Even though Mayor Upton tried to remove it from the agenda because of something to do with his wife, it's too late to take it off now. We've already publicized the agenda."

"I was afraid you'd say that." Blaine's mind immediately began to race as he thought about how Tiffany might approach the council meeting. As much as she angered him with her advertising, he didn't want to see her lose the store she'd worked so hard on.

"Don't get me wrong, I like a pretty young thing as much as the next guy—"

Blaine's hand rolled into a fist. "I get it, Royal. Enough said."

"Tell me the truth, Chief. You got a shine for that pretty gal?"

Blaine continued to hold back the urge to punch the lusty look Royal directed at Tiffany off his face. "You could say that."

"You're a lucky man."

When something tugged on his pants leg, Blaine looked down to find Ashleigh staring up at him with Tiffany's big eyes. Ned and Francine had dropped her off at the marina after she had cried for her mother earlier.

She raised her arms to him. "Up."

Charmed, Blaine reached down and lifted her. The smile she gave him, full of satisfaction after having gotten what she wanted, made him grin for the first time in hours. She would cause her mother a lot of trouble in a few years.

"Excuse me, Royal. This pretty girl requires my attention, and I never say no to pretty girls."

Ashleigh giggled at him.

"By all means, Chief," Royal said. "Don't let me keep you."

"How are you today, Ms. Ashleigh?" Blaine asked as he moved away from the nosy councilman. He felt the eyes of everyone else on him as he held Tiffany's daughter. After this, everyone would probably know they were together, which was fine with him—as long as he could convince her to cut out the sex-kitten act in town. Otherwise, they had a possibly insurmountable problem. He'd be goddamned if he would allow his woman to behave that way in public.

His woman... When had he begun to think of her that way? If he were being truthful, probably the first time he ever laid eyes on her.

"I'm sad," Ashleigh said, drawing him out of his ponderings. "I miss Uncle Mac."

"I'm sure he'll be back soon."

As she popped her thumb in her mouth and rested her head on his shoulder, Blaine breathed in the sweet strawberry scent of her shampoo. Like mother, like daughter. Across the room, Blaine caught Tiffany watching them. She'd been by her sister's side every minute since they broke the news about the accident to Maddie. Like her mother-in-law, Maddie had been rock-solid in her conviction that if Mac were dead, she'd know it. Her cool calm in the face of crisis had been admirable.

Blaine watched as Maddie got up abruptly and rushed outside.

Tiffany followed her, glancing at Blaine to make sure he still had Ashleigh. He waved at her to go ahead and found a seat.

"Are you sad, too?" Ashleigh asked with her thumb still in her mouth.

"I'm more worried than sad."

"Do you like my mommy?"

Amused by the shift in topic, Blaine said, "I like your mommy very much."

"She's a nice mommy."

"Yes, she is."

"And a pretty mommy."

"Very pretty."

"You're nice, too."

"Thank you," Blaine said with a smile. Could she be any more adorable?

"I'm sleepy."

"Use my shoulder as a pillow."

"Okay." She snuggled into him and let out a deep sigh.

Suddenly exhausted himself, Blaine closed his eyes and rubbed her back. He could get used to this, he decided. He could definitely get used to this, but first he needed to do something about the very pretty mommy strutting around town half naked.

TIFFANY CHASED her sister down the main pier. "Maddie, wait!"

"I need to move. If I don't move, I'm going to lose my mind."

When they reached the end of the pier, Maddie stopped and stared into the murkiness. "I can't bear that he's out there somewhere, lost in the fog, cold and scared and worried about me worrying about him."

"They'll find him. He won't give up—not when he knows you're here waiting for him."

"It's been a long time, and the water is still really cold." Maddie hugged herself and shivered. "It's really cold."

Tiffany couldn't think of anything comforting to say to that and was saved by the ringing of Maddie's cell phone.

"I don't recognize the number," she said. "Hello?" She closed her eyes and tears leaked from the corners. "Oh, thank God it's you. Are you okay?" She paused to listen. "I knew you were fine. I knew it. What about the others?"

Overwhelmed with relief when she realized Mac was on the phone, Tiffany waited breathlessly to hear the report.

"I'll be here," Maddie said. "I love you so much. So much." She ended the call and fell into her sister's arms, sobbing. "I was s-so scared."

"You sure didn't show it," Tiffany said, clinging to her as tears rolled down her face, too.

"He said they've got Evan. The captain was killed on impact, and they're still looking for Grant and Dan."

Tiffany said a prayer for them. "Dan has been such a good friend to me. I only talked to him this morning. He told off Jim."

"Then that makes him my friend, too." Maddie gave Tiffany a final squeeze before she let go. "Don't give up hope."

"We need to tell the others that Mac called."

"Yes," Maddie said, wiping her face. "Thank you for propping me up today."

"That's what we do for each other."

Arm in arm, the sisters returned to the restaurant to share the news about Mac's call. Their announcement was met with mixed emotions. While everyone was elated to hear that Mac and Evan were safe, they wouldn't be able to celebrate until they heard that Grant and Dan had been found, too.

Stephanie, who'd been a whirling dervish all day, seemed to wilt after hearing there was no word about Grant. Her stepfather, Charlie, put his arm around her and led her away from the group. Tiffany's heart ached for the pain she saw on Stephanie's face and was thankful to Charlie for taking care of her friend.

Janey and Joe were talking to Kara, who was crying again after hearing there was no news about Dan.

Tiffany went over to them.

"Hi, Tiffany," Kara said, brushing away her tears.

To Joe and Janey, Tiffany said, "Could I talk to Kara for a minute?"

"Of course," Janey said, giving Tiffany a hug. "Thanks for all the support today."

Startled by Janey's spontaneous show of affection, Tiffany returned the hug. "I know it's been an awful day for you."

Janey's eyes watered as she nodded. "They're my stupid brothers, and I love every one of them. The minute I see them, I plan to smack the crap out of them for putting me through this."

Behind her, Joe smiled. "I'll help you."

They wandered off to talk to her parents, and Tiffany sat next to Kara. "How're you holding up?"

Kara shrugged. "All I can think about is what an awful bitch I was to him this morning."

"This morning, huh? Does that mean the date went well?"

"You could say that. He loved the dress." Kara wiped away more tears that seemed to keep coming almost against her will. "Now all I can think about is what if I never see him again and the last thing I said to him was that I didn't want to see him anymore when that isn't even true? I certainly got my wish." She dropped her head to her folded arms, her shoulders shaking with sobs.

Tiffany ran her hand over Kara's back, trying to think of something she could say.

"He's so annoyingly persistent, you know?"

"He must really like you."

"I think he does, and I was so mean to him because he freaks me out with how into me he is. What if he's... God, I can't even say it."

"As hard as it is, try not to think the worst until we know more."

"I'm trying, but I'm not succeeding."

Tiffany drew Kara into a hug.

"Thank you," Kara said when she drew back. "You're a good friend."

Warmed by the compliment, Tiffany said, "Will you let me know if there's anything I can do for you?"

Kara nodded and used her sleeve to wipe her face. "I was so mean to him."

"He's a big boy, and he doesn't give up easily."

"No, he certainly doesn't," Kara said with a small laugh.

A quick glance around the room indicated the tension was wearing on everyone, and since Maddie had received good news, Tiffany decided it was time to take Ashleigh home.

. . .

WITH ASHLEIGH SLEEPING in his arms, Blaine watched Tiffany come toward them.

"Is she asleep?"

"Has been for a while."

"I should take her home."

"I'll drive you."

"That's okay. I can get a ride."

Blaine wanted to scream. "I said I'd drive you."

"And I said I don't want you to. I wouldn't want you to find some other reason to cite me. Maybe my trash cans are too close to the neighbor's house or something."

God, she could be infuriating. "You didn't give me any choice."

"We all have choices."

He glowered at her, holding back a retort that would only make things worse.

"Thank you for watching Ashleigh." She held out her arms. "Could I please have my daughter?"

"Not unless I can drive you both home."

"Fine, but you're not coming in."

"Who said I wanted to?" Keeping a tight grip on Ashleigh, he stood and gestured for Tiffany to lead the way. She let Maddie know they were going, and as they went through the door, Tiffany stopped short. "What're you doing here?"

Blaine glanced around her to see Jim staring daggers at him.

"I came to get my daughter," he said.

"Why?" Tiffany asked. "It's my night with her."

"I figured you might be preoccupied with your precious sister and her latest crisis."

"Watch your mouth, Sturgil," Blaine said.

"What's it to you, *Chief*?"

Before Blaine could fire off a reply, Tiffany said, "Ashleigh is fine. We're taking her home to bed now."

"*We're* taking her home? What's that supposed to mean?"

"Exactly what I said. Blaine and I are taking Ashleigh home."

Jim looked from Tiffany to Blaine and then back to her, his expression stormy. "You two are *together*?"

"What's it to you?" Blaine asked, throwing Jim's words back at him.

"That didn't take long," Jim said.

"We'd been waiting," Tiffany said.

Blaine bit back a laugh and wanted to give her a high five for her audaciousness. She was truly magnificent.

"Waiting for what?" Jim asked.

"Waiting for our divorce—one of the best things to ever happen to me, by the way. I can't tell you how much I appreciate you leaving me and giving me the chance to discover what a *real* relationship ought to be like."

Blaine felt like he'd been electrocuted. He wished he knew if she was just saying that to piss off Jim or because it was true.

"Not to mention," Tiffany added, lowering her voice, "discovering what I was missing in the bedroom."

Jim's eyes bugged, and his face turned a worrisome shade of red. For a brief second, Blaine feared he might strike his ex-wife. Time to get her out of there.

"Come on, Tiff," Blaine said. "Let's get Ashleigh home to bed."

Jim grabbed Blaine's arm. "Wait just a minute!"

Blaine looked down at Jim's hand on his arm and then at Jim's face, using his most intimidating cop glare. "You have one second to get your hand off me."

Jim wisely pulled back his hand. "You can't leave with *my* family—"

"Tiffany's not your family anymore," Blaine said. "You saw to that. You got exactly what you wanted, and now I've got exactly what *I* want. I'd encourage you to keep your distance from her unless you want to deal with me."

"That's my daughter you've got in your arms."

"And tonight is her mother's night with her, which means you've got no business here."

Jim glared at Tiffany for a charged moment before he turned and stormed off.

"Thank you," she said softly.

Blaine's heart ached at the defeat he heard in her tone. Only because Ashleigh had slept through the ugly encounter, Blaine said, "I don't know what you ever saw in that guy."

"I don't know anymore, either."

"Everything all right, you guys?" Maddie asked.

"It is now," Tiffany said, smiling up at Blaine. "We'll see you tomorrow. Give Mac and the others our love."

"I will."

Keeping one arm around Ashleigh, Blaine put a hand on Tiffany's back and guided her to his truck. "Shit," he said.

"What?"

"I don't have a car seat." He'd have to rectify that soon. He wanted to be able to drive Tiffany and her daughter anywhere they needed to go.

"I'll borrow Maddie's. Be right back."

Blaine leaned against the truck and stared into the relentless fog until Tiffany returned with the seat.

On the way to her house, Blaine took a call from Linc. "What've you got, Cap?"

"We found the other two—hypothermic but alive. Torrington broke his arm and a couple of ribs. Apparently, Grant McCarthy saved his life by keeping him conscious and alert all day while they clung to seat cushions from the boat."

"Wow, that's incredible," Blaine said. He held the phone to the side and filled in Tiffany.

"Oh, thank God," she said.

"Can you help me round up some EMS support to meet us at the town pier?" Linc asked. "We're on our way in. Mac and Evan seem fine, but Grant and Dan were in the water a lot longer and need a doctor."

"Will do. See you shortly." Blaine hung up, pulled over and placed a call to the marina to share the news with the euphoric McCarthys and then called dispatch to request ambulances. When he was done with the calls, he pulled the truck back on to the road and continued to Tiffany's house.

Once they arrived, she removed Ashleigh from the seat and carried her into the dark house.

Blaine retrieved the seat, took it inside and waited for her to get Ashleigh settled.

A few minutes later, Tiffany came downstairs and seemed surprised to find him still there. "I thought you had to leave."

"I do."

"Do you want to come back later?"

Yes, he wanted to come back. He wanted to come back and never leave, but they had to get some things straight first and now wasn't the time. "Not tonight."

"Oh. Okay."

"I need some time to think."

Her expression was achingly vulnerable as she looked up at him. "About what?"

"About things."

"About me."

"Partially."

"If you've changed your mind about wanting to be with me, I wish you'd say so."

Blaine couldn't resist the powerful need to touch her, cupping her face in a gentle caress. "I haven't changed my mind about wanting to be with you. If anything, I want you too much."

"I don't know what that means."

"It means I need to think." He kissed her forehead and then her lips. "I'll call you."

"Okay."

"By the way, I talked to Royal about the council meeting and got him to see that the town stands to gain some good tax revenue if the store is a success. He seemed swayed by that, but it's too late to take it off the agenda for Monday's meeting. He did mention that you have to stop prancing about in the all-together if you want his support on Monday."

Her brows narrowed, and her hands landed on her hips. “He said that or you did?”

“He did!”

“Sure.”

“Tiffany, I swear—”

She held up a hand to stop him. “It’s good to know how far you’ll go to get what you want.”

His ringing cell phone interrupted what would’ve been a world-class comeback. Blaine took the call from Mason, the fire chief, who had a question about the estimated time of arrival for the coast guard boat. While he handled the call, he watched Tiffany go into the kitchen to pour herself a glass of wine.

He jammed his cell phone into his pocket. “I’ve got to go. We’ll talk about this later.”

“Fine. Whatever.”

“Tiffany—”

“Just go. Please.”

Blaine had never been more torn between what he wanted to do and what he needed to do. Reluctantly, he headed for the door. Right now, he had to take care of his job. He’d take care of her later.

THE NIGHT PASSED in a whirl of tearful reunions between loved ones, paperwork, reports and other details. Blaine assisted the coast guard in taking statements from each of the injured men and helping to track down the friends and family of the man who’d been killed. By the time they finished, the sun was rising on a new day.

David Lawrence caught Blaine as he was leaving. “Do you know a Kara Ballard?” David asked.

“Yes, what about her?”

“Dan Torrington is asking for her. Could you find her and bring her in for me?”

Since Blaine was already running on fumes, what was another hour? “Sure. No problem.”

“Thanks.”

"How's everyone doing?"

"Mac and Evan are fine—bitching to go home. We're still working on getting Grant and Dan warmed up, and Dan broke an arm and two ribs. Apparently, Grant is the only reason he's still alive."

"They're all lucky to be alive."

"And they know it. Sobering, to say the least. I'd better get back to them."

"I'll go get Kara." On an earlier routine patrol, he'd noticed the Ballard Boat Builders truck outside the house that abutted the marina. A few minutes later, he pulled up to her house and left his truck running when he went to knock on the door. When she answered, her red eyes and nose told the story of a very long day and a night without sleep.

"Chief Taylor? Is everything okay? Is Dan—"

"He's fine and asking for you. Dr. Lawrence asked me to bring you in to see him, if you're willing."

"He's asking for *me*?" Her ravaged eyes filled. "Really?"

"Really," Blaine said with a smile.

"Let me get my bag."

They drove to the clinic in silence. Her tension was palpable as she sat rigidly straight in the passenger seat, staring out the window. "Is he… Is he okay?" she asked, breaking the silence as Blaine pulled into the clinic parking lot.

"He broke his arm and a couple of ribs," Blaine said. "He also has hypothermia from being in the water so long."

"Oh. Okay."

He brought the truck to a stop outside the clinic's main door. "Do you want me to stick around to take you home?"

She shook her head. "I'll probably be here awhile, and I can walk home later."

Blaine reached for one of the business cards he kept in the ashtray and wrote his cell number on the back. "Call me if you need a ride. Don't walk after the upsetting day and night you had."

Kara took the card from him. "Thank you. You've been very nice."

"Happy to help."

She hesitated for a second and then was out the door like a shot, rushing into the clinic.

Smiling, Blaine shifted the truck into drive and headed home. He was more than ready for some sleep, and he needed to figure out what he was going to do about Tiffany.

CHAPTER 25

Kara's heart beat so hard she worried she'd end up a patient at the clinic before she got to see Dan. No one was around in the reception area, so she headed for the treatment rooms, passing Mac asleep with Maddie next to him, Evan curled up to Grace, and Stephanie standing beside Grant's bed, staring down at him. The men were attached to IVs and other machines that beeped and blinked.

Stephanie looked up when she saw Kara.

"Is he okay?" Kara whispered.

Stephanie nodded.

"Are you?"

Stephanie shook her head and began to cry.

Kara went into the room to hug her. They'd all bonded during the long, difficult day, and each of the women already felt like a close friend to Kara. "It's okay now. Everything is okay."

"I keep telling myself that, but I'm having a hard time believing it."

Grant stirred and let out a moan. "Steph."

She pulled back from Kara and wiped her face. "I'm here, babe. I'm right here."

"Closer. I'm cold. So cold."

As Stephanie slid into bed with her fiancé, Kara backed out of the room and found Dan sleeping next door. Dr. Lawrence was standing watch over him, writing something on a chart.

"Are you Kara?" he asked when she appeared in the doorway.

She nodded, unable to take her eyes off Dan. He was pale, and his face was battered with bruises. His hair was standing on end, and his lips were dry and cracked, but he was alive. Thank God he was alive, and she had another chance to tell him...

She wasn't sure what she'd tell him, but the word "nothing" wouldn't be mentioned ever again.

She glanced at David. "Can I..."

"Come in but try not to jostle him. He's in a lot of pain from the broken ribs."

Kara stepped cautiously into the room. "Okay."

Dan's eyes opened and found her. When he tried to smile, his lips fought back, making him grimace.

"Is there something I could put on his lips?" Kara asked.

"Let me get some ointment," David said.

"You came," Dan said, his voice little more than a croak.

"Of course I came."

"I wasn't sure you would."

"You scared me." Kara dropped into the chair next to the bed and gripped his left hand. His right arm was bandaged and resting on his belly.

He turned his hand so their palms were aligned. "I scared myself."

"It must've been terrifying."

"Luckily, I don't remember much past the moment of impact. I was pretty out of it. Grant saved my life about fifty times yesterday. He was amazing."

"I'll have to remember to thank him."

"How come?"

"Because now I've got the chance to apologize."

"For what?"

"For acting so badly yesterday morning, for letting you leave thinking I didn't like you or enjoy being with you or—"

He squeezed her hand. "Stop. I know all that. It was your first time after a bad breakup, and you had a little freak-out. I get it."

"You do?"

"Sure." He tried to move and groaned from the pain. "I didn't like leaving things that way, either. Thinking about you…about our night together…it got me through yesterday, so thanks for that."

"Glad I could help," she said, smiling for the first time since she heard he was missing.

"You did help."

"I'll be there for you while you recover. I promise."

"You don't have to do that."

"Hush. After you ingratiated your way into my life, it's the least I can do for you."

"I like to think I *charmed* my way in."

Bantering with him the way they always did made her heart feel lighter and less burdened. Finally, she could breathe again. "*Ingratiated.*"

David returned with the ointment.

"Thank you," Kara said as she took it from him and applied it gently to Dan's tortured lips.

"No kissing for a while," he said mournfully when she was done.

Always happy for an excuse to argue with him, she bent over the bed to kiss his cheek, the tip of his nose and each lid as he sighed and closed his eyes. "Sleep. I'll be here when you wake up."

His eyes remained closed when he gave her hand another squeeze.

THE NEXT FEW days were frantically busy for Tiffany. When she wasn't working at the store, she was taking care of Ashleigh and Thomas and helping out with Hailey as much as she could so Maddie could tend to her cantankerous husband, who was already sick of everyone fussing over him.

After David released Mac with orders to stay quiet for a few days, Maddie flatly refused to allow him to leave the house until he'd had forty-eight hours of total rest.

Tiffany wondered if they'd all be driven mad before the time was up.

The activity helped to keep her mind off the fact that she hadn't heard a word from Blaine in two days. Not that she thought she'd hear from him after their argument, but still... She missed him. Terribly. And she couldn't help but wonder what he was thinking about and why it was taking so long.

Maddie came to take Hailey from her. "Feeding time," she said. "Would you mind keeping an eye on *him* while I take care of her?"

Tiffany eyed her brother-in-law, who was fuming on the sofa as he had for almost two days now. "Do I have to?"

Laughing, Maddie said, "Yes, you have to. It's in the sisterly handbook."

"I must've missed that. What page is it on?"

"*Please*, I beg of you. If I wasn't so grateful he survived the accident, I might be tempted to kill him."

Tiffany let out a dramatic sigh. "I suppose if it means keeping you from committing murder, I could take a turn. But just remember, I don't love him the way you do, so I might not be so merciful."

"I can hear you two," Mac growled.

"Hi, honey," Maddie said in the endlessly cheerful voice that hid her true aggravation with her husband—and her true feelings about the close call that had nearly taken him from her. "Can I get you anything?"

"Yeah, the keys to my truck."

"No can do, but Tiffany is going to keep you company while I feed Hailey and get her down for her nap." Maddie went over to the sofa and bent to kiss his forehead. "If you give her a hard time, I'll withhold sex for a month. You got me?"

He glowered at her. "You're a terrible nurse."

"You're a horrible patient, but I love you anyway."

"Yeah, yeah. If you really loved me, you'd give me my goddamned keys."

"You're not getting your goddamned keys until you sit your

goddamned ass on that sofa for forty-eight goddamned hours the way David told you to."

"You're my wife, not my mother."

Maddie raised that famous eyebrow. "Want me to get your mother back over here?"

"Good God, no."

Tiffany held back a laugh that she knew Mac wouldn't appreciate. Watching Maddie manage her husband was about as entertaining as it got. Since the accident, Linda had been hovering over her sons and generally driving them all to drink.

"Then behave, or I'll call her and tell her you need her," Maddie said as she headed for the stairs with Hailey. "Tiffany, he's all yours."

"Oh, joy." In truth, she was filled with joy to see Mac alive and well and full of beans. At some point, she'd come to love the pain in the ass.

She flopped down in the chair next to the sofa and stared at him.

"What're you looking at?"

"It's funny."

"What is?"

Had she ever seen him quite so grumpy? Not that she could recall. Usually his boundless cheerfulness and optimism got on her nerves. "It's hard to believe Thomas isn't your biological son. You've got the same pout."

"I am *not* pouting."

"What would you call it?"

"Don't you have your own house and your own people to bother?"

The reminder that she hadn't seen Blaine in a couple of days stole the smile from her face.

"Sorry," he grumbled. "That was kinda mean, since you just got divorced."

"I'm not thinking about him. He's ancient history."

"Then who are you thinking about?"

Tiffany bit her lip, debating whether or not she should tell the ultimate busybody that she'd been seeing his good friend on the sly. "Someone else."

"Anyone I know?"

"Maybe."

"Come on, Tiffany. We're both grown-ups here."

"Well, I am. The jury's still out on you."

"Very funny. You're supposed to be entertaining me." He folded his hands behind his head and settled in. "So entertain me."

"Blaine."

Mac's mouth fell open. "So you two *finally* got together? It's about damned time. He drove me crazy asking when your divorce would be final."

Tiffany was speechless. "He *did*?"

Mac nodded. "Every time I saw him, for months all he wanted to talk about was you."

"Why didn't you tell me?"

"Because he told me not to. He said he didn't want you to know how much he was suffering, waiting for you to be free of what's his name."

"How come he can tell you that, but he can't tell me?"

"Guys are weird that way."

"No kidding. He doesn't tell me much of anything about himself."

"He's had a tough go of it with women."

"So I've heard—from everyone but him."

Mac seemed to be debating whether or not he should say more.

"Will you please just tell me what you know? I can tell you're dying to."

"You should probably hear it from him."

"Probably, but I've given him so many chances to tell me. He clams up every time."

Mac scrubbed at the stubble on his chin. "The first one he was in love with cheated on him."

"Oh jeez."

"Took him totally by surprise. He found out after she cleared out his bank account and left town with the other guy."

Tiffany ached for Blaine. No wonder he didn't want to talk about it.

"Have you heard about Eden?"

"He's mentioned her name, and I heard his mother ranting about how she caused him to lose his last job, but he won't tell me how."

"Probably because he's still embarrassed about what happened."

Tiffany was literally on the edge of her seat as she waited for Mac to proceed.

"He was a cop in a small Massachusetts town. He'd done quite well and had just been promoted to sergeant when Eden was busted for dealing drugs while he was working nights."

Tiffany gasped. Even her vivid imagination couldn't have come up with that scenario.

"No one believed he didn't know about it, so they put him on administrative leave and set out to prove he'd been complicit. The local paper had a field day with the biggest story to hit the town in years. Basically, by the time he was able to prove he'd had nothing to do with it, his reputation was in tatters, and he had no choice but to resign."

"God, what a nightmare."

"Seriously. He lost the girlfriend he'd loved and trusted, and the job he'd loved, too. It was a tough time for him. We all worried about him for a long time, but then he seemed to land on his feet when he got this job."

"Does the mayor and the council know about his past?"

Mac nodded. "That's why they made him serve a probation period before they gave him a long-term contract."

A lot of things suddenly made sense. This was why he was so angry about what she'd been doing at the store. He'd already had one girlfriend derail his career. He could hardly afford another similar incident. And she could see now why his mother was so upset. The realizations, one on top of the other, had her reeling. She'd never forgive herself if she caused him to lose his hard-won second chance.

"Tiffany? What's wrong?"

"I..."

A knock on the sliding door that led to the deck drew her attention as Blaine came in. Her heart leapt at the sight of him, and she noticed right away that he looked tired and stressed and surprised to see her—and maybe a tad bit happy? It took all the fortitude she could muster not to go to him and throw herself into his arms. In that moment, she knew with absolute certainty that she would never love another man the way she loved him. And after what Mac had told her, she also knew with the same certainty that she should probably stay away from him.

"I'll leave you two alone," she said, brushing past Blaine on her way upstairs to find her sister.

Maddie was in the bedroom, nursing Hailey.

Tiffany's composure broke the minute she made eye contact with her sister.

Maddie held out a hand to her. "Oh, honey, what is it?"

Tiffany crawled into bed next to her sister and covered her face with her hands. "I love him."

"Of course you do."

Tiffany raised her hands and looked at Maddie. "Why do you say it like that? Like you've known all along?"

"Because you've been in love with him for more than a year. You've only recently gotten the chance to act on it."

"That's not true!"

"Tiffany," Maddie said in her best chastising mother voice, "it's absolutely true." Maddie ran her free hand over Tiffany's hair. "If you love him—and he clearly loves you—why are you so miserable?"

"He doesn't love me. He likes having sex with me."

Maddie laughed hard enough to dislodge Hailey from her nipple. She switched the baby to the other side and got her settled.

"Why're you laughing at me?" Tiffany asked.

"Because you're so silly. Of course he loves you. Anyone can see that. Did you see him with Ashleigh the other night? He loves her, too."

"He's mad at me—and I'm mad at him. He actually wrote me a *ticket* for wearing a sexy sailor suit on the sidewalk."

Maddie's mouth fell open, and her eyes danced with mirth. "Did he really? How funny is that?"

"It's not funny! I don't want him thinking he can tell me what to do or throwing his badge around whenever I refuse to obey him."

"I want you to know that I'm absolutely on your side—always—but if I pranced around town in my underwear, Mac would lose his freaking mind and do a lot worse than write me a ticket. He'd lock me to the bed and keep me there until I agreed to never do it again."

"That's sort of what Blaine threatened to do, too," Tiffany grumbled.

"Because he loves you, and he doesn't want you showing off your body to other men."

"Why does it sound so ridiculously rational when you say it, but when he says it, I want to clobber him?"

"I have a feeling he's a little less diplomatic about it than I am. The ticket would be Exhibit A."

Tiffany thought about what Maddie had said. "The whole time I was married to Jim, I let him call the shots. I let him be in charge and never thought to speak up for myself until it was too late. I don't want to make that mistake again."

"Then find a way to compromise. Maybe you can give him what he wants without feeling like you've rolled over and played dead, you know?"

"I'll think about it as soon as I get past the town council meeting on Monday."

"What town council meeting?"

"The one where they're going to make me fight for my business."

"Oh, honey," Maddie said with genuine dismay that quickly morphed into anger. "If they want a fight, we'll give them a fight."

"What do you mean?" Tiffany asked, alarmed by the calculating look in her sister's honey-colored eyes.

"You just wait and see."

"SHE'S DRIVING ME CRAZY." Blaine paced from one end of Mac's living room to the other. "Every time I think I've finally gotten through to her, I find her dressed in something even more scandalous, and it's all

I can do not to take her over my knee right there in public and spank the living shit out of her."

Mac busted up laughing, which only made Blaine madder. "What the heck are you laughing at?"

"You. You're hilarious."

"It's not funny! How would you feel if Maddie was walking around town in her underwear?"

Mac's smile became a frown. "A. That would never happen. B. If it *did* happen, I'd feel the same way you do—and I'd have no hesitation whatsoever about spanking her ass until it was bright red."

"Then maybe you can tell me what the *hell* is so funny?"

"Can't talk right now. I'm still thinking about spanking my wife."

"Mac!"

"Sorry," he said, not seeming the slightest bit sorry. "I'm wondering if it's occurred to you yet why her sex-kitten act makes you so bloody mad."

"I don't follow."

"Blaine..."

"I'm not in love with her, if that's what you're getting at."

"No?"

"No! Half the time I want to strangle her!"

"And the other half?"

"I want to do stuff to her that I'm not about to tell you."

Mac laughed—hard. "No need. I get the picture."

Hands on his hips, anger coursing through his veins, frustration gripping his chest like a vise, Blaine stared at Mac as the truth hit him like a punch to the gut. "Oh Jesus," he whispered. "You're right. You're so right." Blaine felt foolish for needing to be led to the obvious conclusion. After all, he'd been in love before. He remembered what it felt like to have absolutely no control over his emotions.

"I usually am," Mac said smugly.

"Shut up." Blaine glanced up the stairs, debating whether he should go after her. He dismissed that thought the same second he had it, knowing that in his current state of mind, he'd only make things worse—if that were possible. "I cited her for public indecency the other day."

"Always a surefire way to win a woman's heart."

Blaine glowered at him. "Are you this much of an asshole all the time or only after near-death experiences?"

"According to my siblings, I'm an asshole most of the time."

"They're absolutely right."

Mac seemed to take that as a compliment. "So what're you going to do?"

Blaine thought about that for a long, *long* moment. And then he knew exactly what he needed to do. He made for the door.

"Is that why you came over? So I could point out that you're in love with my sister-in-law?"

Blaine stopped and turned back to his friend. "Are you feeling better?"

"I'm feeling fine and very thankful to be alive."

"Good. I gotta go."

"Thanks for the visit!" Mac's laughter followed him all the way down the stairs.

CHAPTER 26

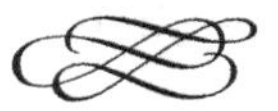

Tiffany wore the most demure, sexless dress she owned—one her former mother-in-law had given her—to the town council meeting. Every square inch of controversial skin was covered. Her hair was contained in a simple ponytail, and she'd gone with only a hint of mascara and a touch of lipstick. She'd been a nervous wreck all day as the hours ticked down to the seven p.m. meeting at town hall.

Arriving at six-thirty, she took a seat in the front row of chairs and wondered if Blaine would be there. As the days had gone by without a word from him, she'd gone over and over the last time she'd been with him. He'd been so mad with her, and even though Patty reported record sales from the day of the sailor-suit incident, Tiffany had already made up her mind that she was done with the provocative advertising campaign.

It wasn't her goal to make everyone, including Blaine, mad. Her goal was to make sales inside the store, and from now on, that was where all her energy would be focused. If only they allowed her to remain open. All day, she'd tried not to think too much about what she'd do if they shut her down. She and Ashleigh would have to move to the mainland so she could get a job that paid well enough to dig her out of the enormous debt she'd incurred to open the store.

The thought of leaving their home and their family and friends nearly brought her to tears, so Tiffany pushed it to the back of her mind as people began to file in for the meeting. She turned to see if anyone she knew was there and almost fell over in shock as Mac and Maddie came in with their entire cadre of friends and family in tow. Francine and Ned, Big Mac and Linda, Evan and Grace, Grant and Stephanie, Jenny, Sydney, Luke, Owen, Laura, Sarah, Charlie, Shane, Janey, Joe, Seamus, Carolina... They kept coming and coming, filing into the rows of chairs behind Tiffany. Even the women Maddie used to work with at the hotel and the old men who hung around at the marina were there. Patty came in with Wyatt and flashed her boss a big smile and a thumbs-up.

When Maddie reached forward to squeeze Tiffany's shoulder, the dam nearly broke. "Don't cry," she whispered. "And don't worry. We won't let them hurt you."

"Thank you so much," Tiffany said, reaching back to clutch her sister's hand.

"We got your back," Mac said.

Tiffany smiled at him, thankful for his support.

Kara and Dan came in next. His arm was in a sling, and he moved slowly and carefully until he reached the seat next to her.

"I thought you might need your lawyer."

"You shouldn't even be out of bed!" Tiffany cried.

"Thank you," Kara said. "I couldn't agree more."

"Ladies," Dan said, dismissing their concerns with the sweep of his hand. "I wouldn't have missed this for the world."

Over his shoulder, Tiffany saw Jim glaring at her as if he couldn't wait to savor her defeat. That alone would've been enough for her to fight like a tomcat but having all her friends and family behind her made her realize she didn't need Jim or the anger or the bitterness he caused anymore. He no longer had the power to hurt her. She and her daughter were well loved, and that was all she needed.

As she had that thought, Blaine came in, looking ridiculously sexy in his uniform. As he shook hands and joked around with Mac and the other McCarthys, Tiffany was filled with yearning. She'd missed him more than she'd realized and wondered if he'd missed her at all. That he never glanced her way as he took a seat in the front row on the other side told her he was probably relieved to be rid of her and the threat she posed to his career.

The other side of the aisle filled with a variety of stern-looking older people who probably couldn't wait to air their disapproval of her store. Tiffany wondered if Blaine's mother was among them. Then Verna Upton came in with several of her friends in tow and buoyed Tiffany's spirits with a friendly wave as the mayor gaveled the meeting to order.

While the council moved swiftly through the first part of their agenda, Tiffany battled out-of-control nerves. Her entire life hinged on the outcome of this meeting, and despite the show of support behind her, the council might not be swayed. If that happened—

"Royal, you added the matter of the Naughty & Nice shop to the agenda," Mayor Upton said.

Royal cleared his throat and directed his attention to Tiffany. "Mrs. Sturgil."

"Objection." Jim jumped to his feet. "She's no longer *Mrs.* Sturgil."

"Sit down, Mr. Sturgil," the mayor said disdainfully. "This isn't a courtroom, and you're out of line."

"Douchebag," Mac muttered, nearly making Tiffany giggle.

Apparently, Maddie wasn't as strong and tittered with laughter.

"*Ms.* Sturgil, please move to the microphone," Royal said.

With every eye in the crowded room on her, Tiffany got up and walked to the microphone located in the center aisle.

"You're the owner and proprietor of the boutique, Naughty & Nice, on Ocean Road?" Royal asked.

"I am."

"And what do you sell in this boutique?"

With her hands tightly clasped at her waist, Tiffany cleared her throat and fought to keep the nerves out of her voice. "Gifts, candles, lotions, underwear, lingerie and other novelty items."

"Would you please describe these novelty items?"

A male voice rang out from the back of the room. "Dildos and vibrators!"

Nervous laughter rippled through the crowd.

Tiffany felt her face get very warm and probably very red.

"Please contain your outbursts, or I'll clear the room," Mayor Upton said sternly.

"Ms. Sturgil?" Royal said.

"I sell a number of products designed to enhance sexual pleasure." She'd spent all day working out that rather innocuous way to say "sex toys" without using the words *sex toys*.

"And why was it that you felt Gansett Island needed a store such as yours?"

Relieved that he hadn't asked her to elaborate on her products, Tiffany was pleased he'd posed that particular question. "Because I believe we had more than enough T-shirt and souvenir shops, and my research showed that stores such as mine were very successful in other tourist towns. I can provide the council with sales data from similar stores in Newport, Nantucket and Mystic, if you are interested."

"I'd be very interested," Royal said. The other council members nodded in agreement.

Tiffany returned to her seat and retrieved the copies she'd made earlier in the day that showed significant revenues from the other stores and distributed them to each member. Returning to the microphone, she said, "I realize this is something very different in our town, but judging by our early data, I expect the store will do quite well in its current location. Our business has more than doubled during Race Week, and we hope that will continue throughout the season."

"About your advertising strategies—"

Tiffany held up a hand to stop him. "I've reconsidered my strategies and will be going in a different direction in the future."

A buzz of chatter cut through the audience.

"And that direction won't include public indecency?" Royal asked.

"Your definition of indecency and mine differ, but it will not include women in skimpy outfits outside the store."

"Very good. Now I'll open the floor to anyone who wishes to speak on this matter."

She walked away feeling like she'd done a good job defending her store, but by the time Tiffany returned to her seat, a long line had formed behind the microphone.

BLAINE BIDED his time as one detractor after another questioned the town council's judgment, morals, ethics and values by allowing a store like Tiffany's in their town. Unfortunately, only the mayor and Royal seemed to be supportive of Tiffany. The other five members were nodding in approval of the comments from Tiffany's foes.

When Linda McCarthy approached the microphone, Blaine held his breath. He wasn't sure if she'd be for or against the shop.

"I have patronized Ms. Sturgil's store," Linda said to startled gasps from her children and others in the audience. "The merchandise is sexy but tasteful and the more adult items are kept in a separate area. There's absolutely nothing indecent about the store, and with all the legitimate problems this town has, I can't believe the council is wasting its time on this."

The crowd behind Tiffany cheered long and hard after Linda sat down.

Blaine wanted to cheer, too, until Jim Sturgil had his turn.

"I wanted to raise my daughter here because of the values this town has always had," Jim said. "Lately, however, I have to question whether this is the best place for her to live." He glared at Tiffany. "She's just doing this to spite me for leaving her—"

That's it, Blaine decided. *I've heard more than enough.* He stood and went over to pluck the microphone from its stand.

"What do you think you're doing?" Jim asked indignantly. "It's my turn."

Into the microphone, Blaine said, "It was your turn. Now it's mine. You want to talk about values, Sturgil? What kind of man lets his wife work two jobs to put him through law school and then leaves her when the money starts rolling in?"

Jim's eyes bugged out of his head, and for a moment, Blaine thought Jim might be stupid enough to hit him. He really, *really* wished he would.

"What kind of man asks his very nice wife for a divorce, moves out of the house and takes all the furniture, leaving the wife who put him through law school *and* his young child in an empty house?"

Jim's fist rolled into a ball, and Blaine gave him a challenging look that dared him to go for it. Assaulting a police officer could get him disbarred, which Jim well knew.

"Sit down, Sturgil," the mayor ordered.

"You heard the mayor," Blaine said. "And we've *all* heard enough out of you."

Everyone sitting behind Tiffany whooped and clapped. Blaine didn't dare look at her, or he might lose his nerve. To the council, he said, "This whole thing is ridiculous. For better or worse, the town approved Ms. Sturgil's application, and now you've got to live with it. She has the same right to make a living here that all of you do. She's an accomplished businesswoman who has run two successful businesses on this island for years. She pays her taxes just like everyone else. This is a witch hunt because you're all afraid of something different. To you, this is about sex toys and sexy nighties. To her, it's about food on the table and a roof over her child's head."

"She's caused at least one accident on Ocean Road," one of the councilmen reminded him.

"How was that her fault? Was she driving the car? Did she take her eyes off the road and run into another car? We cited the driver who caused the accident, not her."

"She caused a distraction."

"And she's said she won't do that anymore."

"I'm ready for a vote," the mayor said.

Blaine glanced to the back of the room, pleased to see that everyone was in place. "Before the council votes, I'd like to remind you that you represent the citizens of this town. It might be helpful get a sense of where the citizens stand on this matter. With the election coming up in November, I'd think you'd want to be sure you're following their wishes."

After some whispered discussion among the council members, the mayor said, "I'll allow that. With a show of hands, how many are opposed to the Naughty & Nice shop remaining open?"

Quite a few hands were raised, including Jim's and Blaine's mother's in the back of the room.

"And how many are in favor of the shop remaining open?"

All the hands on the side of the room where Tiffany sat went up, along with the hand of every police officer, firefighter, first responder, paramedic, ambulance driver and the guys Blaine worked out with at the gym. He'd even gotten Linc and some of the officers from the coast guard station to come into town for the meeting.

Blaine finally allowed himself to look over at Tiffany and caught the exact moment when she realized what he'd done. Her eyes got very big when she saw the men and women in uniform lining the back wall casting their votes for her.

With their help, she had more than enough votes to sway the council.

"Motion to table the matter of the Naughty & Nice store indefinitely," Royal said.

"Second," one of the others said.

"All those in favor?" the mayor asked.

All seven members voted "aye."

Pandemonium broke out as Tiffany's family and friends surrounded her to celebrate the victory. The enormous smile on her face pleased him tremendously.

"That was rather ballsy of you, Chief Taylor," Mayor Upton said over the din of celebration. "Taking on the council that you report to."

"Some things are more important than jobs."

"I hope you'll invite me to the wedding."

Blaine's eyes bugged out of his head as he stared at the mayor. "*Wedding?* What wedding?"

Upton smiled knowingly and started to walk away, shooting over his shoulder, "Get a goddamned haircut, will you?"

Mona, the mayor's assistant, gave Blaine a hug. "If she won't marry you, I will."

Laughing, Blaine hugged her back and saw his mother waiting for a word with him. "You're on, Mona."

"I see some things never change," his mother said, arms crossed and mouth set with displeasure.

"That's right, Mom. Apparently, I don't know any other way to fall in love than to go all the way."

"I honestly hope it works out better this time than it has in the past."

"It already has. No matter what happens, I've already had more with her than I've ever had with anyone else."

"Is that so?" Tiffany asked.

He hadn't noticed her approach them. Nodding, he looked down at her, greedily taking in every detail of her gorgeous face after several torturous days without her. Sliding his arm around her shoulders and bringing her in close to him, he said, "Mom, this is Tiffany."

"Nice to meet you, Mrs. Taylor."

Because she was too polite not to, his mother shook Tiffany's outstretched hand. "Likewise. I hope you and your daughter will come to dinner soon so we can get to know each other."

"We'd love that."

"Thanks, Mom," he said, relieved to realize she was going to give Tiffany a chance.

"I'll see you soon, son," Mrs. Taylor said, going up on tiptoes to kiss his cheek.

"Yes, you will."

After his mother walked away, Blaine glanced at his watch. "I need to get back to work."

"What time are you done?" Tiffany asked.

"Midnight."

She waggled her finger to bring him down to her and whispered in his ear, "Leave your door unlocked. I want you completely naked in bed. Any questions?"

Just one, Blaine thought. How was he supposed to walk out of town hall sporting an erection? "Um, no. No questions."

"Good. See you later."

Tiffany sauntered off to rejoin her sister and the rest of her family, putting some extra wiggle in her walk for his benefit.

It was official—she'd be the absolute living, breathing *death* of him, and he absolutely couldn't wait.

EPILOGUE

At one thirty the next morning, Tiffany tiptoed into Blaine's house and closed the door softly behind her. The last time she attempted this mission, she'd had no idea how she would be received. This time, she had no doubt at all about the reception she could expect, and her entire body zinged with anticipation. After what he'd done for her, she couldn't wait to worship every inch of him. If she could only give him a fraction of what he'd given her, she'd leave happy.

She moved stealthily into the bedroom, pleased that he'd left the light on in the bathroom. He appeared to be asleep, but she wasn't entirely sure. Since she wouldn't put it past him to fake sleep, she moved quickly to retrieve the items she'd brought with her from the bag she carried.

Beginning with the handcuffs, she slid one cuff on his wrist and lifted his arm to bring it closer to the headboard. If he was faking sleep, he was doing a hell of a job. His arm weighed a ton! By the time she got the cuffs looped around one of the rails on his headboard and secured his second hand, she'd worked up a sweat. He let out a soft snore that startled her. He really was asleep!

She bounded off the bed to remove her clothes, slid the blindfold into place and then drew the sheet down over his hips, exposing his raging erection. "You *are* faking!"

Laughing, he said, "You really think I'd be asleep when you ordered me to be naked in bed when you got here?"

Wanting to see his gorgeous, devious eyes, she pushed up the blindfold. "Why didn't you say something?"

"Because that was one hell of a show. I liked the striptease the best. Can we do that again sometime? Soon?"

"I ought to leave you like this and let them find your carcass sometime next week."

"You wouldn't do that to me."

Leaning over him, she kissed him, softly and slowly. "No, I wouldn't, especially not after what you did for me."

"You liked that, huh?"

"I *loved* it. I'm not sure which part I loved best—it's a toss-up between you publicly humiliating Jim and getting all your friends to vote for me."

"Humiliating Jim wasn't part of the plan, but I have to say it was the highlight of the evening for me, too."

"Thank you," she whispered. "Thank you so much for risking your job and your career and your reputation and your mother's wrath to stand up for me. No one has ever done anything like that for me before."

"No one has ever loved you as much as I do."

She hadn't seen that coming and stared at him, almost waiting for him to take it back. "You do?"

Nodding, he said, "For a very long time now, I suspect."

"I love you, too. For probably just as long."

"Now that you have me," he said, smiling suggestively and tugging on the cuffs, "whatever will you do with me?"

"I have a few ideas." She slid the blindfold back over his eyes and began with kisses all over his face and neck and then tortured him with suggestive strokes of her breasts and hair over his chest and belly.

"Do you promise you'll never leave me, no matter how mad you get with me?"

"God, yes. I promise." His groan and the arch of his hips made her smile with satisfaction. "Why would I leave the best thing to ever happen to me?"

Pleased with his answer, she touched him everywhere but where he wanted her most, starting at his feet and working her way slowly up his legs, only to deny him time and again, making him thrash and pull against the cuffs.

"Do you promise to never again use your badge to bully me?"

His erection lay heavy against his belly, weeping and straining for the contact she refused to give.

"Right about now I'd let you use my badge to bully *me*."

Laughing, she said, "I'm afraid I need a promise." From the bedside table, she retrieved the vibrator and turned it on, making him tug even harder against the tight hold of the cuffs.

His Adam's apple bobbed in his throat. "I promise."

"Remember what you said after our first 'encounter,' when you were leaving my house?"

"I barely remember my own name right now," he said through gritted teeth.

Hoping to arouse him even more, she turned the vibrator up to high. "Allow me to refresh your memory. You said if I snuck into your bedroom and handcuffed you, you wouldn't call the cops. You'd cry for mercy. Remember?"

"Yes," he growled.

She brought the vibrator down on his nipple, and he cried out from the surprise and shock of it. Then she did it to the other side, garnering the same reaction. Trailing the buzzing toy over the rippled muscles on his abdomen made his erection grow impossibly larger, and still she hadn't touched him there. She used the vibrator on his inner thighs, coming perilously close to his balls before backing off again.

"*Christ*," he muttered. "*Mercy*."

Filled with her own power and loving every minute of it, Tiffany held back a laugh.

"If this is how you reward a guy, remind me not to do you any more favors."

He sounded so tortured that Tiffany withdrew the toy. "You don't like it?"

"If you stop now, I'll spank your ass until it's so red you can't sit down for a week."

"Tell me how you really feel."

"Watch that saucy mouth, or I might spank you just for the fun of it."

"You're talking far too much," Tiffany said, dragging the vibrator up the inside of his right leg, bringing it to a stop under his balls.

With a sharp cry, his hips surged off the bed.

Tiffany was ready for him, taking his straining erection into her mouth and sucking on the tip. She positioned the vibrator so the smaller arm made contact with his back door. The combination made him come explosively.

"Holy shit," he whispered many minutes later. He tugged hard on the cuffs. "Take them off."

"Do you promise not to spank me?"

"No promises."

Despite her trepidations, she released the cuffs.

The first thing he did was tear off the blindfold, and then he was reaching for her. Before she knew what hit her, she was under him with her knees raised and her arms around his neck. "I know about what happened to you. With Eden."

That stopped him short. "Oh. Mac?"

Tiffany nodded. "But only after significant cajoling. I'm sorry you had to go through that."

"I'm sorry I didn't tell you myself. I should have."

"I understand that some things are too painful to talk about."

"We've both had enough pain," he said, kissing her sweetly. "I don't know about you, but I'm more than ready to be happy."

She brushed a strand of hair off his forehead. "Maddie asked me how I knew I was in love with you, and I told her being with you makes me happier than I've ever been. And when I thought I'd lost you—"

He pressed a finger to her lips. "You never lost me. Not for one minute. You've had me from the very beginning." Punctuating his words with soft kisses, he added, "You may not realize this, but before you, before us, I never would've been able to give up control the way I just did. Being in control of everything—all the time—has kept me sane the last few years, but it gets exhausting after a while."

She curled her arms around his neck and brought him down for a kiss. "I'll shoulder some of the load for you."

"I love you," he whispered as he surged into her. "I want everything with you. Tell me you want the same thing."

He moved rapidly, slamming into her so fast and so furious he stole the breath from her lungs. "Tell me," he said again, more urgently this time.

"Yes, yes, *yes*," she cried, as he drove them both to a shattering climax that left her shuddering and quivering and on fire for more of him.

"What were you saying yes to?" he asked with a smile after he gave her a few minutes to recover while he continued to pulse inside her.

She looked up at him, taking in every detail of the face that had become so precious to her. "Everything."

He kissed her gently and reverently and then rested his forehead on hers to gaze into her eyes. "Good answer."

Thanks so much for reading *Longing for Love*! I hope you enjoyed it.

Check out *Waiting for Love*, Adam and Abby's story, available now. Turn the page to read Chapter 1!

WAITING FOR LOVE

CHAPTER ONE

"I'm absolutely, positively, totally and *completely* done with men," the woman sitting behind Adam McCarthy announced—loudly—to everyone on the noon ferry to Gansett Island. "Done, done, *done*."

The voice was familiar, so Adam sat up taller, hoping to overhear enough to figure out who she was without having to get involved.

"I've followed two men to the ends of the earth and regretted it both times. From now on, I'm off men. You heard it here first."

A slight slur to her words had him wondering if she'd been drinking. *Who cares? What business is it of yours? Ignore her.*

"Did I mention I'm *done* with men?"

Adam had no idea who she was talking to, and figuring that out would require him to turn around. And there was no way he was turning around. He had his own problems and no desire to take on someone else's, even if it was possible that he knew her. He knew a lot of people. That didn't mean he had to jump to their rescue when they were on the verge of making fools of themselves.

With the day stormy and the seas rough, the woman played to a captive audience inside the crowded cabin. Adam was used to rough rides. He'd been taking the ferry all his life. Others weren't so fortunate, and the distinctive sound of barfing soon filled the airless cabin.

Rough seas and rocking boats had never made him sick. The smell of vomit, however... No one was immune to that. He got up and told himself to get out of there. Walk to the door and the fresh air... But curiosity got the better of him, and he made the huge mistake of turning around.

His mouth fell open when he saw his brother Grant's ex-girlfriend Abby Callahan scrambling for the garbage can.

While she was violently ill, Adam stood paralyzed with indecision. She hadn't seen him, so he could still get out of there unscathed. And then, as if Adam had conjured him from a dream, Big Mac McCarthy's voice sounded in his conscience, warning of dire consequences if Adam walked away from a family friend in her time of need.

Not for the first time in his adult life, Adam cursed the values his father had hammered into him and his brothers from the time they were young boys.

He took a deep breath he instantly regretted due to the pervasive smell of vomit filling the cabin, choked back a wave of nausea, walked toward her, took her by the arm and escorted her outside.

Naturally, she fought him off. "What do you think you're doing?" Her words were garbled and slurred, and she smelled as if she'd spilled an entire bottle of eighty-proof something or other on her clothes.

"Did you sleep in a bar last night?" he asked when they were outside and both taking deep, gulping breaths of cold, damp, fresh air.

"Adam," she gasped when she realized who he was. "No, I did *not* sleep in a bar. I had two drinks on the plane this morning, and the man in the next seat spilled his tequila all over me."

Adam cringed at the thought of tequila for breakfast. Those days were a distant memory. "As I recall, you don't drink."

She wobbled when the boat pitched violently to the side, and he steadied her with a hand to her arm. "I had an occasional glass of wine," she said as she pushed him away. "I'm all done being a nice girl who does what everyone expects of her. I'm going to drink and party and curse like a sailor and have sex with strangers and..." Her chin began to quiver.

"Don't you dare cry."

"I'll cry if I want to. I'll do any damned thing I want."

"Since you're new to swearing, you might consider adding a 'god' in there." She seemed to have no idea what he meant, so he elaborated. "*God*damned is a lot more hard-core than plain old damned."

Her eyes were big and brown and shiny with unshed tears. "Are you making fun of me?" she asked, incredulous. "Feel free. My day can't get any worse. My *life* can't get any worse, so do *your* worst."

"What're you even doing here? Don't you live in Texas now?"

"Not anymore." Her chin trembled violently, and tears spilled from her eyes as if someone had turned on a faucet.

Adam was instantly sorry he'd asked. Mascara ran down her blotchy face as she sniffed and sobbed. Because he was too much of a gentleman not to, he patted her shoulder and muttered a soothing word or two, all the while wishing the deck would open up and swallow him.

He'd had a hellish few days of his own and didn't need to take on anyone else's problems. In the midst of a professional implosion the likes of which he'd never imagined possible, he'd received word from home that his brothers were missing in a boating accident. Thankfully, they'd all been found safe, but Adam wouldn't be completely at ease until he saw them with his own eyes.

As for Abby, the last he'd heard, she was engaged to the island's former doctor, Cal Maitland, and living with him in his home state of Texas. Adam took a surreptitious glance at her left hand and didn't see a ring. Uh-oh. Even as he wondered what'd happened between her and her fiancé, he didn't dare risk more tears by asking.

"I'm homeless at the moment," she said after a long period of silence as the boat bobbed and weaved through the surf.

Retching noises from the deck above had Adam pulling Abby back from the rail, just in time to avoid a direct hit.

The momentum propelled her into his arms. She pressed her face into his shirt and broke down into sobs.

Oh, for God's sake! Why had he turned around back in the cabin? Why had he allowed himself to get sucked into this situation? None of that mattered now that he was firmly *in* the situation. Because he'd known her all his life, because she'd very nearly married his brother, he put his arms around her and patted her back. "It'll be okay."

"No, it won't." She sniffed and seemed to be using his shirt as a tissue. Lovely. "It's never going to be okay again."

"That's not true," Adam said, though he tended to agree with her. He'd had the same feeling repeatedly in the forty-eight hours since his world blew up in his face.

"It is true. All I ever wanted was to fall in love with a wonderful man, get married, have a family and maybe a career that satisfied me. Now I have nothing. I gave up my business for him! Do you *know* how successful Abby's Attic was?"

"I heard it was very popular."

"I made a quarter of a million bucks there last year, and I walked away from it like it meant nothing to me. All for a man who wasn't worth my time."

While Adam knew he should at least attempt to defend mankind, he was stuck on the money. "You made a *quarter million* dollars selling T-shirts?"

"And toys. There's big money in toys, especially when you're the only toy store on the island," she said, hiccupping loudly. Her hand covered her mouth. "Oh my. Excuse me." This was followed by another hiccup, louder than the first, and more tears. "My life is a mess."

He shouldn't ask. It was none of his business. And yet… "What happened with Cal?"

She used her own sleeve—thankfully—to wipe her nose and eyes, which smeared the mascara into dark smudges under her eyes. "His ex-girlfriend happened. Apparently, he's not completely over her, or some such baloney."

"You mean bullshit."

"What?"

"If you're going to swear now, you want to say bullshit rather than baloney."

"Oh, right. Yes, it's a big pile of bullshit."

"Much better."

That drew a tentative smile from her.

"So what's the deal with the ex?"

"She comes sashaying up to him every time she sees him and makes sure to flip her fake blonde hair and bat her fake eyelashes and rest her fake boobs on his arm, and he acts like it's no big deal that she's *totally* flirting with him. This goes on for weeks. She's over at the house every day, supposedly to check on his sick mother because they're *so very close,* you see, but really it's all about more chances to hang all over Cal. I finally got sick of it and confronted him about it. That's when..." Her chin quivered anew, but she managed to blink back the tears this time. "That's when he admitted he still thinks about her. *Candy*. Her name is *Candy*! Can you stand that? She makes me sick. It's all so...so..."

Nearly breathless with anticipation, Adam raised his brows.

"Screwed up," she said.

He shook his head. "You can do better."

"I can't."

"Yes, you can. You're a whole new woman now, remember?"

Her face turned bright red, and in that moment, he discovered she was rather adorable, raccoon eyes and all. "Fucked up," she whispered, turning a deeper shade of scarlet as the curse passed her lips.

Adam rewarded her with a big smile. "Now we're getting somewhere." The ferry passed the buoy that marked the island's northern coast, but the mist was so thick he could barely make out the bluffs. "So you really think you can have sex with strangers?"

The question clearly caught her off guard. "Of course I can."

"I don't think you can. You're not that kind of girl."

"How do you know what kind of girl I am?" she asked, indignant.

"Um, you dated my brother for ten years. I think I have a slight idea."

"You don't know me at all. He never knew me either. No one does."

"Abby... Come on, that's not true. You and Grant were the real deal for a long time."

She shook her head. "No, we weren't. I thought we were—I thought Cal and I were, too, but I've never had the real deal." Turning her big eyes up at him, she said, "Have you?"

The question hit him like an arrow to the heart. "I thought so until recently, but no, I haven't either."

"What happened to you?"

Adam smiled and shook his head. "Not worth talking about."

"I told you all my bad stuff," she said between persistent hiccups. "It seems only fair that you tell me yours."

Adam hadn't intended to tell anyone at home about what'd happened in New York. He'd planned to see his brothers, make sure they were okay, check on his parents and get back to the city to resurrect his career before the damage became irreparable. But here was Abby looking up at him with her liquid brown eyes, and suddenly the whole sordid tale was pouring out of him. When he was done, she stared at him, openmouthed, until a hiccup lurched her out of the trance.

"That's... It's... It's *horrible*."

He tilted his head, urging her silently to try again.

"Seriously fucked up." This was said with no hint of whisper or blush, which made Adam want to cheer. "How long had you been seeing her outside of work?"

"Seeing her for three years, living with her for two of them."

"And no one at work knew?"

"Nope. My own company policy of no fraternizing at work had come back to bite me in the ass, so we went way out of our way to keep it quiet. From what I can gather, one of the employees saw us somewhere, and we were...we were kissing...and reported us to the board. The funniest part, if you can consider any of this funny, is that it all came down to a dentist appointment."

"How do you mean?"

"The chairman of the board called both of us. I was at the dentist. She was at the office and took the call. Before I was out of the chair, she'd accepted a deal to force me out of the company I founded. I'd lost my company and my girlfriend in the time it took to get my teeth cleaned. Hilarious, huh?"

"No," she said, her tone hushed and the hiccups gone. "It's not funny at all."

"It's kinda funny." He hated to think what he might do if he didn't laugh.

"I'm sorry that happened to you, Adam." Her hand on his arm was strangely comforting. He'd felt very alone during the last few unbelievable days. "You've worked so hard to build that company."

"Fourteen years, and the only mistake I made was taking on a partner four years ago." He leaned against the rail as the breakwater for South Harbor came into view. "You know what the best part is?"

"What's that?"

"I'm the only one with the first clue about the actual work we do. She runs the business side. I oversee the technical end. She and the board have no idea what they're in for without me there to take care of the technical stuff. I'd love to be a fly on the wall."

"They'll be begging you to come back in no time at all."

"Probably."

"Will you go?"

He shook his head. "I gave that company everything I had, and this is the thanks I get? They can kiss my ass."

"I don't blame you for being bitter. You got royally screwed—in more ways than one."

"Yep."

"So what'll you do now?"

"I'm not sure exactly. After the accident, I wanted to come home and see my brothers—"

Her eyes went wide. "What accident?"

"You didn't hear about the sailboat in Race Week that got hit by the freighter? All three of my brothers and Grant's friend Dan were on the boat."

"Oh my God! Are they all right?"

"They will be. Grant and Dan got the worst of it, but Mac and Evan were fine."

Abby looked like she might be sick again, so he nudged her closer to the rail. "Take some deep breaths."

She did as he directed while blinking rapidly. "It's been over between Grant and me for a while now, but to hear he could've died..." The hand she rested over her heart said it all.

"Believe me, I've had some rough moments of my own since I got that news from my parents. It was a very close call. All three of my brothers." He shuddered just thinking about what could've happened.

The next thing he knew, she was hugging him, tightly, and it felt really good to have the arms of an old friend around him. And then he felt her breasts pressed against his chest, and his mind went blank. She was no longer an old friend—or his brother's ex-girlfriend—offering comfort. Rather, she was a sexy, curvy woman who fit perfectly in his arms and had awfully nice breasts, too. Had he ever noticed that before? Not that he could recall. She'd always been Grant's girl, so he hadn't looked too closely.

Adam released her and stepped back, noticing how shiny her dark hair was. He wondered if it was as soft and silky as it looked.

Surprised by his abrupt retreat, Abby stumbled, forcing him to reach out and steady her. With his hands on her shoulders and her gaze once again focused on him, Adam had to remind himself that this was *Abby*. She'd nearly been his brother's *wife*. He withdrew his hands from her shoulders and was thankful when the ferry passed through the breakwater into South Harbor.

They stood side by side at the rail as the ferry backed up to the pier and the cars began to drive onto the island.

"You won't tell anyone, will you?" she asked in a small voice after a long period of awkward silence.

"Of course not. You won't either, right?"

She shook her head. "If you need to talk to someone who knows what's going on, I'll be at the Beachcomber."

"Not at your folks' place?"

"No way. My mother told me I was a fool to give up a successful business to chase after yet another man. The last thing I need right now is her reminding me every day that I can't trust my own judgment when it comes to men."

"Well, I'll be at my parents' place for a day or two while I figure out what's next if you need someone to talk to."

"That's nice of you. Thanks, Adam. Thanks for everything. You've been really...nice."

"I know everything seems awful right now—for both of us—but this has got to be the worst of it, right?"

"If you say so," she said with a weary sigh as they took the stairs single file to the lower deck.

Since he had only a backpack, he helped her with two of her three suitcases, dragging them up the hill from the ferry landing and across the street to the Beachcomber Hotel. A bellman came down the stairs to assist with her luggage.

"You'll be okay?" Adam asked.

"Sure. I'm a survivor. It's how I roll."

If only she didn't look so devastated, he might've bought that line. He cuffed her chin playfully. "Hang in there."

"You, too."

Adam walked away, heading in the direction of his parents' North Harbor home. At the corner, he glanced back to find Abby exactly where he'd left her, looking up the steep staircase to the Beachcomber, as if seeking the fortitude to move forward.

Waiting for Love is available in print from *Amazon.com* and other online retailers, or you can purchase a signed copy from Marie's store at *shop.marieforce.com*.

OTHER BOOKS BY MARIE FORCE

Contemporary Romances

The Gansett Island Series

Book 1: Maid for Love *(Mac & Maddie)*

Book 2: Fool for Love *(Joe & Janey)*

Book 3: Ready for Love *(Luke & Sydney)*

Book 4: Falling for Love *(Grant & Stephanie)*

Book 5: Hoping for Love *(Evan & Grace)*

Book 6: Season for Love *(Owen & Laura)*

Book 7: Longing for Love *(Blaine & Tiffany)*

Book 8: Waiting for Love *(Adam & Abby)*

Book 9: Time for Love *(David & Daisy)*

Book 10: Meant for Love *(Jenny & Alex)*

Book 10.5: Chance for Love, *A Gansett Island Novella (Jared & Lizzie)*

Book 11: Gansett After Dark *(Owen & Laura)*

Book 12: Kisses After Dark *(Shane & Katie)*

Book 13: Love After Dark *(Paul & Hope)*

Book 14: Celebration After Dark *(Big Mac & Linda)*

Book 15: Desire After Dark *(Slim & Erin)*

Book 16: Light After Dark *(Mallory & Quinn)*

Book 17: Victoria & Shannon (Episode 1)

Book 18: Kevin & Chelsea (Episode 2)

A Gansett Island Christmas Novella

Book 19: Mine After Dark *(Riley & Nikki)*

Book 20: Yours After Dark *(Finn & Chloe)*

Book 21: Trouble After Dark *(Deacon & Julia)*

The Green Mountain Series

Book 1: All You Need Is Love *(Will & Cameron)*

Book 2: I Want to Hold Your Hand *(Nolan & Hannah)*

Book 3: I Saw Her Standing There *(Colton & Lucy)*

Book 4: And I Love Her *(Hunter & Megan)*

Novella: You'll Be Mine *(Will & Cam's Wedding)*

Book 5: It's Only Love *(Gavin & Ella)*

Book 6: Ain't She Sweet *(Tyler & Charlotte)*

The Butler Vermont Series

(Continuation of the Green Mountain Series)

Book 1: Every Little Thing *(Grayson & Emma)*

Book 2: Can't Buy Me Love *(Mary & Patrick)*

Book 3: Here Comes the Sun *(Wade & Mia)*

Book 4: Till There Was You *(Lucas & Dani)*

The Treading Water Series

Book 1: Treading Water

Book 2: Marking Time

Book 3: Starting Over

Book 4: Coming Home

Historical Romances

The Gilded Series

Book 1: Duchess by Deception

Book 2: Deceived by Desire

Single Titles

Five Years Gone

One Year Home

Sex Machine

Sex God

Georgia on My Mind

True North

The Fall

Everyone Loves a Hero

Love at First Flight

Line of Scrimmage

Erotic Romance

The Erotic Quantum Series

Book 1: Virtuous *(Flynn & Natalie)*

Book 2: Valorous *(Flynn & Natalie)*

Book 3: Victorious *(Flynn & Natalie)*

Book 4: Rapturous *(Addie & Hayden)*

Book 5: Ravenous *(Jasper & Ellie)*

Book 6: Delirious *(Kristian & Aileen)*

Book 7: Outrageous *(Emmett & Leah)*

Book 8: Famous *(Marlowe)*

Romantic Suspense

The Fatal Series

One Night With You, *A Fatal Series Prequel Novella*

Book 1: Fatal Affair

Book 2: Fatal Justice

Book 3: Fatal Consequences

Book 3.5: Fatal Destiny, *the Wedding Novella*

Book 4: Fatal Flaw

Book 5: Fatal Deception

Book 6: Fatal Mistake

Book 7: Fatal Jeopardy

Book 8: Fatal Scandal

Book 9: Fatal Frenzy

Book 10: Fatal Identity

Book 11: Fatal Threat

Book 12: Fatal Chaos

Book 13: Fatal Invasion

Book 14: Fatal Reckoning

Book 15: Fatal Accusation

Single Title

The Wreck

ABOUT THE AUTHOR

Marie Force is the *New York Times* bestselling author of contemporary romance, romantic suspense, historical romance and erotic romance. Her series include the indie-published Gansett Island, Treading Water, Butler, Vermont and Quantum Series as well as the Fatal Series from Harlequin Books.

Her books have sold more than 9 million copies worldwide, have been translated into more than a dozen languages and have appeared on the *New York Times* bestseller list 30 times. She is also a *USA Today* and *Wall Street Journal* bestseller, a Speigel bestseller in Germany, a frequent speaker and publishing workshop presenter.

Her goals in life are simple—to finish raising two happy, healthy, productive young adults, to keep writing books for as long as she possibly can and to never be on a flight that makes the news.

Join Marie's mailing list on her website at marieforce.com for news about new books and upcoming appearances in your area. Follow her on Facebook at www.Facebook.com/MarieForceAuthor and on Instagram at www.instagram.com/marieforceauthor/. Contact Marie at marie@marieforce.com.